THE
GRIOT

By
VALARIE S. THOMAS

ISBN: 978-0-692-83951-5

Book design: Leslie Worell

Visit Valarie S Thomas at

ValarieSThomas.com

Facebook: Facebook.com/Valariesthomas

Twitter: Valarie S Thomas

Instagram: Valarie S Thomas

Email: Vsthomas@valariesthomas.com

To my husband, my babies, and my ancestors.

Griot – pronounced gree-o or gree-oat. A West African storyteller and oral historian. Often a musician.

Sometimes called Jali.

PROLOGUE

2004

"Where could you possibly relocate a group of disgruntled black people?" Naemah hunched her bare shoulders in defeat. "Africa?" Although it was late evening, her tormented face and chest were sweat-sheened. Repeatedly, she used her hand as a fan to no avail. The Atlanta humidity was thick, stagnant, and oppressive, and it wasn't even summer yet. The blue waters of my parent's seldom-used pool beckoned to us, but Naemah didn't do pools. She went out of her way to make that crystal clear. I suggested that we go in the house, but Naemah said she loved it out here in the expansive back lawn of my parent's estate. I understood. My homecoming (my brother's, too, I supposed) always sparked a small impromptu gathering of my parents, their equally free-spirited friends, and my old Academy friends. That meant loud, uproarious laughing and friendly, yet heated, debates about "the man" and the fucked up system in which we lived. Tonight was no different. Sitting in a circle were eleven eclectic individuals on the deck that abutted the 4,000 square foot home I'd grown up in; each person boisterous, educated, and jaded by a racist society. I pulled Naemah away from the noise and the curious questions about our relationship and we walked closer to the pool.

I bit my bottom lip and contemplated Naemah's question. Since I'd turned 12, my parents had taken me to various parts of the African continent, and my understanding of the world evolved and elevated every time. Each time my plane touched down on U.S. soil—the soil my ancestors had been forced to exist upon, I became more embittered with the horrid realities of what had been done to my ancestors. Africa was more than the acacia tree and the animals that made up the Big Five. The complexity of the Great Continent abounded. However, there was always one constant in the continent's vast diversity. His skin was alabaster and his greed ravenous. He was the White Man.

To answer her question, I shook my head and stroked my beard, then took a few steps toward the red-bricked edge of the pool. "Africa's largest lake is named after a white queen. Need I say more?" But as I spoke this, I knew that no place on this living earth was free from the spidery reach of the White Man. He had been a formidable foe to every being and resource on this planet, and his quest for riches and adventure was now turning Mother Nature against us. Why did those with brown skin also have to receive the White Man's karma? Was it because we had adopted his standards and dreams? In this mythical world that Naemah and I had created, I wanted everything European scrubbed from the minds of my people. Hell, if I could snatch the English language from our tongues and minds, I would.

"Then where would you go, and who would these people be? I mean, what black person would be foolish enough to leave the only home they've ever known to live in a new settlement?" Naemah argued. But blacks had uprooted during the Great Migration, and before that, blacks had uprooted to Liberia. Some of the Black Hebrew Israelites had moved too. The formula was quite simple: Give them something to run to and simultaneously give them something to run from.

I shook my head. Naemah's questions were dizzying, but I wanted to create answers for her, even though we were only fantasizing. It would never happen, but my father had taken on another case of an unarmed young black man who had been gunned down at the hands of…you know it…cops. That had sparked our conversation. Over a chilled beer, we had discussed everything, from black children not knowing or caring about their history, to blacks selling drugs to their own people, to global warming. Finally, Naemah exclaimed, "Fuck it!"

I raised my brow. I'd never heard her curse.

"Let's leave this goddamned country." That's how it all started, this intense and pointless brainstorming session about an all-black settlement that would never exist.

The fire in her voice and the passion in her eyes ignited a boldness in me, and I took her hand and pulled her body toward me. Naemah went with it. Her ass touched my groin, pulling at my desire. She didn't pull away, so I wrapped my arms around her. Perhaps it was the liquor that had emboldened me or the way her beauty and mind intoxicated me, but this wasn't us. We were friends. We never touched like this. We never even danced. We were quick hugs and back pats. I knew she could feel my heartbeat, but I prayed that was all she could feel.

"What would we call this place?" I whispered into her ear. She shuddered as she placed her soft hand on top of mine. Her perfume was seductive.

She was quiet as we swayed to Lauryn Hill's dark contralto. Her mini fro was soft and plush against the side of my face.

"Za!" she finally said, nearly shouting the revelation.

I laughed. "Za?"

"If it's going to be a kingdom, it has to have a formidable name. 'Za' is striking."

Who said anything about a kingdom? I was thinking a small settlement. I went with it, though. "Like 'we'll kick your ass if need be?'"

"Exactly."

Someone turned up the music, and I could've been wrong, but I felt Naemah grind her ass against me. I willed my body not to react.

I could hear my uncle pontificating with the intensity of Dick Gregory. My father guffawed at his brother.

"Religion?" she asked. "What will they believe?"

I cringed as I thought back to the time she convinced me to go to that Baptist church of hers. I embarrassed her, and I almost lost her as a friend. The preacher read from the Bible, and I scoffed at every promise. Hell, I even chuckled causing cross stares from women with ridiculous hats. These poor souls were still waiting for the Promise Land. The saints took off running, and I rolled my eyes at the spectacle. One woman caught the Holy Ghost and collapsed to the floor. I wondered if the people knew that being overtaken by spirit predated Christianity. When the pastor, who probably drove a Lexus while his people struggled, said, "Bow your heads." I sat erect, eyes glaring at him. He called souls to be saved by Jesus, and I told her, "I'll be in the car." Yes, I exited during the altar call. Nothing boiled my blood more than white supremacy committed by black people. Mention the religions of our ancestors and women clutched their pearls, and men called you blasphemous, but the religion the White Man brought us; now that was the truth.

My father's hysterical laughter brought me back to present. "You know how I feel about Jesus Christo," I said with a Spanish accent. That got under her flawless brown skin. We'd agreed she wouldn't try to save me, and I wouldn't try to convert her to the truth.

She grunted and was silent for a while. I feared that I had killed the mood, but she stayed in my arms. Finally, Naemah asked, "Have you seen the movie Love Jones?" There was dreaminess in her voice.

"You know damn well I've seen Love Jones." After the '90s, the black silver screen died a miserable death, and so did soundtracks.

She simpered. "Because of that movie, I've always imagined having conscious black friends who sat around politicking, beating drums, listening to records, and being…"

"Deep?" I offered.

"Yes. That's what your family reminds me of."

This was the only life I'd ever known. My whole life had been about building the black community. My mother and father were successful attorneys who had a knack for stocks and real estate investments. Before I was born, they chartered Dubois Academy, a private school for Atlanta's African-American children, and when I was an infant, my mother kept me swaddled to her chest as she interviewed and hired the most qualified teachers, taught law to the middle and high school students, disciplined wayward students, wrote grant proposals, and hosted fundraisers, not only ensuring that Dubois kept running but that it was the best private school in the South. All I understood was black pride; all I tolerated was black excellence. Hell, the people who brought me into this world unabashedly named me Malcolm X Dubois and dared a university not to accept me. Today, people flew their children in from all over America to attend the prestigious Dubois Academy. Each year, the Academy gave scholarships to students who could not afford to attend Dubois but had exceptional academic and behavioral records. The Academy also attracted the finest educators who poured

5

pride, history, and values into us. We studied science, engineering, mathematics, the arts, and all religions. We ate organic foods. The day began with yoga and ended with athletics, ballet, gardening, music lessons, or whatever filled one's soul. If you wanted to explore it, the board members would probably fund it. When my college friends cringed at the memory of standardized tests, I couldn't relate. From the Academy's doors sprung entrepreneurs, educators, attorneys, scientists, doctors, and even an astronaut.

I asked, "You mean weed-smoking Nubians who talk shit until the sun rises?" My mother and father and nearly all of their friends smoked weed. It shocked Naemah. Everything about my parents shocked her. She had expected a snooty millionaire couple who would look down their noses at her, but my mother, in her flowing red tunic, touched Naemah's smooth face and then embraced her like a long-lost child. Then my father, whose dreadlocks were like hundreds of ropes dangling down his back, approached her with a hearty laugh and a hug. I chuckled. "I'm glad you like my family." I felt a stabbing pain in my chest of nerves attacking as I asked her what I so desperately needed to know. "Do you like me?" She'd agreed to the four-hour drive from Charlotte to meet my family, but we were just close friends, friends who were self-proclaimed philosophers, friends who educated each other.

She pulled away from me and paced a few steps.

My heart sunk. Why had she pulled away? Had I misinterpreted her kindness toward me for way more than it was? "I mean, at first, you hated me," I explained, taking a tentative step in her direction.

"I didn't hate you," she sung, twisting her body to and fro like a nervous child.

"When Dr. Reeves paired us together for that project, I could feel the steam rising off your skin." I smiled.

That day I had walked over to her. She set her jaw, and

her nose flared as I sat down. "How are you?" I had asked.

She'd huffed and given an abrupt, "Okay." I had noticed her before, but her processed hair aggravated me; it turned me off. Well, I wanted it to turn me off, but her eyes, her focus, was attractive. Later, I would ask Naemah why she put The Chemical (I'm dramatic, I know) on her scalp—not even an inch from her mind—altering what her ancestors had gifted her and endangering her health. She laughed and said she had never in her life used a relaxer. She used heat to straighten her hair. Still, a few weeks later, when she arrived at my showcase, she blew my mind. Her hair was in a beautiful textured twist out, and she'd painted her lips a dark plum hue. That was four months ago, and I have been captivated ever since.

"I had a misperception of you." Naemah blushed over her shoulder. "You were always starting shit in every class, challenging every professor, pissing off the students. I thought you were arrogant. I now know you're only a little arrogant." She pinched her fingers together, and we laughed.

What Naemah said was true. I was raised to never accept bullshit, whitewashed miseducation. People squirmed in my wake. I liked to make people uncomfortable, especially my own blind people, and many of them hated me until they found out I was a damn good rapper and lyricist. In the Student Union, I snatched the crown from the rap battle champion at our university and the black student population went wild. I had always used my voice to invigorate and move the crowd. My voice, my energy, and the unique rhythm of my words made them dance and shout, but in reality, my message never went past the door. It never penetrated their frontal lobe. Not one word. Blind and deaf. Women licked their lips and gave me long hugs. The guys gave me head nods and high fives and asked to collaborate, but that wasn't my desire. I wanted them to really feel what I was saying about our community. That night, Naemah gave me that look. I'd fucked her mind with her words. And I still hadn't seen her uncloaked her body.

When I snapped out of my daydream, I released a long and drawn out, "And now?" My soul read her soul. Our vibes were in tune. Our frequencies matched. I knew how she felt about me, yet I wanted to hear it from those beautiful lips.

Her movements were loose and fluid now as she walked back to me. Contact high? Had Mother's reefer wafted over to this woman? Was it Lauryn? With a crooked grin, and her eyes peering at the mosaic slabs that we stood on, she said, "Maybe if every girl at school didn't want you, I would consider pursuing something more."

I scoffed. Those girls were infatuated with who they thought I was, but they weren't Naemah. They hadn't exposed me to a higher level of thought. She wasn't Afrocentric, but on that day our professor partnered us and she lowered her impenetrable persona, I asked her what she thought our project should be about. What problem in the world needed solving? I asked as a courtesy, but I was prepared to take over. Crime in the black community, senseless music ruining our consciousness, the disproportionate rate of African-American incarceration… Her eyes snapped to mine, and she flat out stated, "In thirty years, Manhattan will be under water." I thought she was crazy, but Naemah continued to speak, and I ingested every word. I later found out that she was a minimalist and only used a car when necessary. Using anything plastic was a sin to her. She and her mother lived in walking distance of the campus and grew their own produce. Naemah was a vegetarian. I started questioning how I could claim to be Afrocentric when I didn't know or care about saving the earth.

I stammered, "I haven't fucked with those gir—"

She touched her fingers to my lips, halting my words

before they tumbled from my mouth. With that simple embrace, she injected her energy into me. For the first time, Naemah kissed me. Then she looked at me with those large and enchanting Diana Ross eyes. She didn't have to say more.

That night, she gave herself to me after making me promise not to make her scream in my parents' house. I told her I couldn't promise that, especially when I tasted her. Now she stood naked and stared pensively at the Jacob Lawrence series that adorned my wall. "Who buys their child paintings by Jacob Lawrence?" she asked with amazement.

My eyes focused on where the curve of her back met her ass. Then my eyes lowered to her thick thighs. There was power in those thighs. Earlier, when she rode me, I had to fight the urge to cum. She might've prayed to Jesus, but Oshun possessed her as she rode me with the soles of her feet on the mattress. Otis Redding sang, "That's How Strong My Love Is" on vinyl. She loved the crackle of records. In that moment, I had no intention of ever letting her go. None. I didn't know, however, that I would have to go away for a long time. I didn't know the weight of not being able to awaken my people would crush me.

Ignoring her question, I asked, "If I found a place, would you join me?"

At first, she squinted at me. When she understood, she laughed. I didn't.

"Malcolm, you know Za will never happen."

But she had planted a relentless seed.

TWO HUNDRED HUNDRED YEARS LATER

CHAPTER 1

The sweat-drenched brown backs of the two African men baked in the blistering heat. They paced as they waited for the Outsiders to arrive. The younger of the two repeatedly asked, "Are we doing the right thing?"

"Can you taste the riches waiting for us?" the older man asked, closing his eyes in bliss. The younger man also closed his eyes and imagined finally having electricity, automobiles, phones, and so much more. His dark lips smiled, too, revealing a perfect set of white teeth.

Just then, faster than an impala or cheetah, two black trucks appeared on the horizon, leaving a trail of dust in their wakes. The two men rushed to the back of the covered wagon to retrieve the gift for their new friends. The girl bucked as they grabbed her tied arms and yanked her down from the wagon.

"Shut up," the older one barked to the gagged girl, but her muffled screams didn't subside.

The younger man stared into the girl's frightened, wet eyes. He quickly regretted it. He wanted to free her, but it was impossible. He'd told the 15-year-old girl to knock before entering his room, so many times. Now she knew the crippling secret, and although she promised not to tell, they couldn't chance it. The black cars sped along the savannah.

When the vehicles stopped, two male strangers with light skin and perpetually squinting eyes got out of each of the trucks. They smiled. It was the first time the younger man saw Asians before, and he tried not to stare.

"Hello," the stranger with graying hair called as he proffered his hand.

The older black man shook the stranger's hand but kept his other hand firmly around the girl's arm. The younger man suddenly became distracted as he looked out at the unending plains. How would these men change their world? He immediately felt that their vibrations were low and their intentions were wrong. He wanted to back out.

"How are things going?"

"The rebellion is growing every day," the older African man answered proudly. He was telling the truth. They needed the rebels to be strong in number and skill, because the people would never take this complete transition from the "old way" lightly. But as the older black man said, "The people won't know that they were tired of the old ways until we show them how much better things could be. Once they saw what life could be, it wouldn't take much more convincing."

"I don't understand why you won't let us supply you with weapons," one of the Asian men sung with his arms spread wide. The older man had told the younger one that they were Chinese and their wealth was astounding.

The younger man had asked the same thing, but the older black man had told him, "Although I'm working with them, I don't trust the bastards. We don't want to become indebted to them by letting them give us anything we didn't make an even trade for. Especially weapons. And, I believe the rumors about Za's hidden arsenal. We'll find it."

"What's this?" the gray-haired stranger asked, jutting his chin toward the girl. His eyes smiled.

The older black man grinned. "A gift."

The girl's eyes widened, and she gave a shrill cry that gripped the young man's heart like a vice.

All four of the light-skinned men smiled. One of the men opened his arms and laughed. "I accept."

The older black man added happily, "She's a virgin." He dragged her to the arms of the hungry men, who felt her up and whispered lascivious things in her ear as she cringed and pleaded to the young black man with her eyes. He was supposed to protect her. That's what men did.

A round Asian man said, "Even better. Do we bring her back?"

"No. Do whatever you want with her, just don't bring her back."

"Well, we have what we promised," the gray haired man said.

One of the other men handed over a bag. The older of the black men took it and looked into it, eagerly nodding his thanks. "In two full moons, the revolution will be complete. We'll come to you when it's done."

The four men nodded and got into their vehicles with the writhing girl. She would never see her family again. She would never see Za again. The men would probably kill her once they grew tired. To take his mind off of that, the younger man imagined himself driving one of those vehicles, but he quickly apologized to the ancestors who walked among them. Still, his soul sizzled with their fury. The kingdom of Za was about to be turned upside down, and it was all his fault.

13

Zul grabbed Sahel by the ears, and Sahel gnashed his teeth and grunted. I leaned forward to observe the two fighters. Damn it, I cursed Sahel. How did you let him get so close? Sahel yelped in pain as Zul mercilessly pulled at his earlobes. He was at the mercy of Zul, but with one quick sweep of his forearms, Sahel broke Zul's grip away. The smooth black skin of their bodies gleamed with sweat as they circled one another, crouched low as they crab walked. Their eyes scrutinized each other as each waited for the first sign of his opponent's weakness.

A breeze whipped my cottony kinks into my face as I watched from my seat on the ground. "Come on, Sahel," I whispered and tightened my fists.

"Auntie Zen." I looked toward the source of the high-pitched voice. Soweto, an adorable four-year-old girl with her hair cropped close to her scalp, stood trembling beside me. The fire from the nearby torches danced in her gorgeous eyes. "Why is Uncle Sahel fighting?" she whimpered. Neither Sahel nor I were truly her aunt or uncle, but it was how younger people showed deference to those older than them.

"Awww, come here." I reached for her pudgy brown hand and lowered her into my lap. "He and Zul are just showing off their skills. That's what young men do during the Yoni Fest. They attempt to impress the girls so that we'll want to make them our husbands."

"But Sahel will already be your husband."

The people gasped. I looked up and my breath caught in my throat. Zul and Sahel were entangled in each other's arms, baring their teeth and snarling. One would never guess that they were best friends. During this Laamb match, a traditional fighting style adopted from Senegal, friendship didn't matter.

I kept my eyes on Sahel, forcing myself to breathe, and said, "Yes, he will be my husband in just a few short months, but winning this is still important to him. The respect that

14

comes with winning this match will follow him even after he dies. His children's children will speak of his victory. And when he goes to warrior training next month, he'll be the leader of his age set. And maybe he could even be chief of Obsidian." The idea made my heart flutter. Sahel had already beaten four boys in his set. This was his final fight.

Sahel was the most gorgeous man in our small village, and my soul was wrapped up in everything that he was. I sat at the edge of the Harambe circle along with every other person in my village. Every eye focused on the two perspiring boys grappling in the center. Sahel was tall and slender like a Maasai warrior. His feet were swift just like the shifting sands of the Sahara Desert, and his mind was sharp. Zul, however, weighed more and was even taller. Zul struck Sahel at least three times, while Sahel hadn't even hit him once.

The crowd suddenly erupted as Sahel slammed Zul onto the ground. Dust powdered the air. I jumped up with Soweto in my arms and screamed.

"Keep him down! Keep him down!" I hollered. Sahel's brothers thrust their fists into the humid night sky as chief counted down. I squealed, praying that Zul wouldn't buck Sahel off him—he was trying with all of his might. Finally, the chief called it, and the crowd exploded with cheers. Sahel had won. The stern-faced chief held up his prodigy's arm. Sahel's white teeth shone brightly. I danced around as I held Soweto. She giggled.

After hugging his family and friends, Sahel walked over and held out his hand to me. I kissed Soweto, put her down, and ran over to him. Sahel hugged me with his sweaty body, and I pressed my lips against his.

"I knew you would win."

"Yeah right, Zen," he laughed. "I saw the fear in your eyes." Sahel looked around with exhaustion in his eyes. "I tell you what, I can't wait for this damned Yoni Fest to end so that I can have you to myself."

I looked at the others in my age set. They had begun following the elder women out to the bush to begin tonight's rituals.

I groaned. "I'll be all yours tomorrow." I touched his smooth hairless cheek. "Wow. I'm going to marry the head warrior." I gave him a quick kiss before turning to leave. He held on to my hand for a few moments before letting go.

CHAPTER 2

The sound of an elephant trumpeted in the distance. Or was it all in my delirious mind? It could've happened. It was nearly sunrise, which meant the big game, elephants, giraffes, zebras, and wildebeest, would be making their way to the salt-lick lake, about half a mile from my village, to imbibe its minerals. The gods led them there for zinc, phosphorus, calcium, and iron that would strengthen their bones and muscles. Not far behind them would be the stalking lionesses.

I opened my eyes, and they burned from exhaustion and the smoke of the fire in the middle of our circle. I closed them and prayed for this ritual to be over. With my palms facing the heavens, I pretended to "inhale the wisdom of my ancestors," as the elder woman who stood in front of us chanted. My head jerked back, startling me to alertness. Eyes wide, I looked from left to right. The fire illuminated our brown faces. We were beginning our 17th year together. The true year of becoming a Zaian woman.

It seemed no one had witnessed me drift off because they were all losing their own battle with the sleep spirits. There were several mouths wide open, and eyes were vacant and glazed. I stifled a giggle as my best friend's grandmother kicked her feet. Abebi startled awake. She didn't know where we were for a moment.

Eleven stern-faced elder women formed a larger circle around us seven girls. They didn't seem tired at all. In this ritual, the elder women pledged to keep and guide us in the proper ways of a Zaian woman.

The standing elder woman, a kind woman who taught us from the time we were four, repeated her mantra, "Inhale the wisdom of your ancestors." I felt like I could die from lack of sleep. For the past three nights, we were forced into seclusion after the sun went down. No men: fathers, brothers, uncles, or boyfriends. We were in the midst of the Yoni Fest. The annual festival honored the Zaian woman's beauty, ability to give life, and ability to nurture all in the village, including her man. This year's Yoni Fest was special to me because my set was being honored. We were the newest group of women eligible for marriage, and we were being trained in all the ways to honor our future husbands.

I watched embers escape the crackling blaze, float into the purple and orange heavens, and die. How serene, I thought as the repetition of the mantra lulled me back to sleep.

"Good morning, Zephyrs," a voice boomed, forcing me—and everyone else—back to the present. It was the voice of Subira, the blacksmith's wife—one of the most respected women in Za. She stood in a wide stance with her feet grounded and her shadow dancing on the rocky wall of the kopjes that hid us from the view of villagers. "Tonight we are here to celebrate our yonis. Yoni is Sanskrit, and in Za we embrace it fully. As women, we create from within our bodies, unlike men who form their creations with their hands." She limberly squatted her heavy frame into the birthing position. "Our wombs bring forth life. Our feminine energy is the life source of our kingdom, Za. There was once a time when women were ashamed of their yoni." She returned to her stance and nodded. "Men feared this power. They attempted to the deny women of their pleasure through shame and mutilation. Not in Za. Here, the woman embraces her pleasure points and praises her beauty." Subira smiled. "Use your yoni with pure intentions. Never, well almost never, weaken your husbands with your yoni." Her booming laughter filled the circle, and the elder women joined in. "Use your yoni to build him." With a proud smile and a crescendo in her vocals, she said, "Congratulations, Zephyrs, the men in Obsidian, Noire, and Ankara can now have the pleasure of courting you. Choose the best. Choose the one who will be a hero to your family. Choose the one who will excite your yoni." She winked at the elder women, who smirked back at her salaciously.

Most of the girls averted their eyes in embarrassment. Abebi pretended to stick her finger down her throat. I bit my lip and stifled a laugh. Subira pushed her hands together and bowed to us. We all jumped up with renewed energy as Subira shouted, "Don't forget to be at the feast, ready to dance! Just before sundown, ladies."

The elders and girls yipped and screamed. The torture was finally over. I could now marry the boy I'd loved since I was thirteen. I jumped to my feet with renewed energy. Vividly, I could see our babies and my father's smile when he held them. In a few short months, I would be the bride of a head warrior.

The girls in my set all embraced. They hugged each other with joy, but me they quickly hugged out of obligation. This didn't hurt me. It was just the way things were. For seventeen years, I spent nearly every day with these girls, and frankly, I couldn't wait to be free of them. It wasn't that I didn't love them; I did. But I never shared a sisterly connection with them. The more I tried to connect, the more awkward things became. Abebi was the only one I loved like a sister.

19

As the sun came into view over the horizon, I paced, watching the girl who was not only my best friend but also the crown jewel of the Zephyrs—and our village. Abebi soaked up the love of the girls, as well as the elders. Her gravitational pull was astounding.

I felt a cool breeze, and I stroked my bare arms. I looked in the direction from which the wind came. I froze. Near the gates of our village, I saw the griot, stone-faced, glaring back at us. Or was it just me? I shivered.

The griot—the village historian, storyteller, and advisor—was an enigma to everyone. She frightened the shit out of me every time I found myself in her presence. When I was a child, my father forced me to take music lessons from her. Although I loved playing the kora, I hated the way the griot used to frown at me when I made a mistake.

Haughtily, she turned around and headed back into the village gates. I shook my head, attempting to get her ominous energy off me. I shrieked as Abebi pounced on me and squeezed my body playfully. I placed my hand on my heart. "You scared me."

"Good. That was the point," she laughed. "We are officially women now." She pursed her lips and wound her rounded hips. "Let's go get married to a sexy warrior."

Although we'd been without sleep for three days, Abebi looked radiant. Her head was bald and smooth, her clear skin was as black as coal, her slanted brown eyes gorgeous, and her smile wide and infectious. I was pretty enough, but Abebi's beauty struck down all who saw her.

"You'll be the first to marry," I said as we walked arm-in-arm to the entrance.

"Yeah right. You already have your man waiting for you." There was sauciness in her vocals. "The poor boy is sick. You should just be with him. There's no question that you two will marry. Why make him wait for your yoni?" She

20

rolled her hips sensually.

I pinched her arm and giggled. Then, I groaned. "It's getting more and more difficult, but I have to wait for the night of our wedding." And my boyfriend, Sahel, wanted to wait until the elders circumcised him at the end of warrior training when the gods sanctioned marriage and, therefore, sex. I didn't want to share that intimate secret with Abebi, though.

From the corner of her eyes, she glanced at the other girls in our set trudging up to the village. She lifted her shoulder and coyly stated, "You better hope no other girl gets to him first."

She was joking, yet I felt a jolt of pain in my chest. Frantically, I whispered, "Has anyone tried to tempt him?"

"Daddy!" Abebi screamed as she let my arm go. She jogged to the chief, who stood waiting for his precious daughter at the gate of our village. And without so much as a "bye," she was gone.

Fury washed over me as I turned to eye the laughing girls. Just like hyenas.

The sun was showing its brassy orange face, and the air was warming. In a few hours, the Serengeti's sun would be relentless. I made my way home with my spirit stirred up. Obsidian was already busy with women in the fields and most men heading outside of the gates to tend to their livestock. Food came first. Those with special talents like the plumbers, builders, the blacksmith, artisans, glassmakers, and hair braiders would practice their trades once they finished planting or harvesting the maize, beans, wheat, sweet potatoes, and potatoes in the fields, or tending to the livestock in the kraal or cattle enclosure. Whatever one needed to supplement the food from the fields was augmented by what they grew in their gardens or traded for. Those without special skills remained in the fields until the sun beat them down and dried them out.

Everyone I passed either lifted their hand in salutation, called me by name, or gave a warm smile. The people in Obsidian all knew each other. Our village had no more than 400 people whose survival depended on each person carrying their weight and looking out for one another. We attended every wedding, funeral, festival, and ceremony. If one had a breakdown, the village was there to build them up. If a child was born, the whole village presented the child with gifts and necessities. If a young man needed a house for his new bride, every man took a hand in building it. If the crops were ruined in a drought or by the natural fires that threatened the plains, the village rationed whatever food was left to feed everyone. Every adult was responsible for the rearing of every child. In Obsidian, each person was taken care of spiritually and physically. If one was poor, we all were poor.

Obsidian was one of three provinces that made up the Kingdom of Za. Each province was separated by more than fifty miles of land owned by outside entities. Obsidian was at the southern tip of the kingdom, situated at the edge of Kenya's portion of the Serengeti, or Maasai Mara.

Fifty miles to the north of Obsidian was Za's capital, Noire. It was also the largest and most impressive of the provinces, boasting grand architecture and the greatest minds and artists of Za. Noire was also the first city our founders created and it became so large that Obsidian and Ankara had to be created to stave off starvation. Our great ruler, King Akonos, his wife Queen Finda, and son Prince Zaire resided there. From Obsidian, one could reach Noire in nearly twelve hours if you had healthy, rested horses and a professionally designed stagecoach. Most, however, could only afford meager carriages so it could take them 24 hours to make it to Noire. There were other factors that affected the speed of travel like the weather, whether or not the roads had been washed out in the short but torrential afternoon storms of the two rainy seasons, and if the animals were migrating over the roads. Runners, who transported messages between the provinces, could make the journey in 5 hours because they traveled light with no carriage and only the horse they rode.

Sixty miles to the northeast of Noire was the Ur Rainforest. Hidden in the dense forest was Ankara, the smallest province. Because of the winding roads and elevation, it took a day and a half to make it from Noire to Ankara. Runners could make it in twelve hours, however.

A chief who answered to King Akonos led each province. The three chiefs acted as both political leaders and military commanders. In all three provinces resided a Council of Elders who maintained and created laws and traditions and passed judgment on the people who fell short of the Zaian way.

Over the past two centuries, what had begun as one small city had grown into a respected kingdom, and our laws and traditions prevailed. I loved my kingdom and found comfort in its stability. In the back of my mind, however, was the nagging feeling that made me wonder if it could possibly last forever.

CHAPTER 3

The faint but relentless rhythm of the tumbadora drum pried and pried until I was prematurely snatched from a blissful slumber. I dragged myself to the bathroom, grumbling a few curses. The long nap did nothing; my energy was far from replenished. But it was feasting time, and I hated the feeling that I was missing something, so I rushed to prepare myself for the festivities.

Once I took a hot shower and brushed my teeth with a miswak stick, I unwrapped my scarf and considered how I would wear my hair. I thought of pulling my twists up, so when I danced they wouldn't slap against my face. Instead, I poured neem oil over my palms, rubbed it onto my hair, and separated my strands from each other with loving gentleness. I fluffed and fluffed my mane until I could put a lion to shame. My hair was my crown. My smile faded into a frown when I thought of the day that Abebi shaved her head. Everyone flocked to her. They cooed with adulation, and immediately I yearned to shave my hair too, but I knew better than to copy her overtly. Envy burned at my core. I just hated that she always grabbed the attention of people in ways that never crossed my mind.

The drummers beat with great intensity, and I itched to be out there. I tugged on the dress that the Zephyrs would wear as the elders presented us to our people. I tied the cowrie shell belt around my waist. Some of the women from our village strung the shells together, so that when we danced, the movement of our asses would be accented visually and audibly.

I slipped on my satchel, and for a moment, I considered my reflection in the mirror—my big brown eyes, soft and thick hair, full brown lips, too thin nose, and smooth skin. I supposed that although my beauty wasn't comparable to my best friend, I wasn't ugly. I shook my hips and smiled, thanking the gods that I had not cut away my hair to be like Abebi.

As soon as I exited the home I shared with my father, the scent of a delectable dinner accosted me. I was hungrier than I had realized. With my shells rattling behind me with every step, I jogged to the Harambe circle, the gathering place, where most of the village had already congregated. In seconds, sweat ran from beneath my breasts and over my stomach.

Chairs and tables from nearby houses had been grouped near the smoking fire pit where wild boars lay in the ground with hot coals roasting in their bellies. Since last night, the men manned the pit as the pork smoked slowly to perfection. Several tables held dishes of yams, beans, rice, pork, cabbage, and stews. A line formed, and proud women heaped food on the villager's plates. The babies on their backs were in a sweet slumber, only waking for their mother's breast.

I waited for little Soweto and her two friends, with twisted, braided, and coiled hair, and joy in their spirits, to bound past me. I found two chairs at a vacant table and settled down with a clay plate and glass of water.

A cheerful voice called, "Zen! Sit with us!"

I looked up from the medley of meat and vegetables on my plate, pretending to look for whoever called me, but I could never mistake Abebi's voice for another. I also never needed to look for her. I just looked for the swarm of humans surrounding her like flies buzzing around a decayed animal.

When I was with her and people came around, I would fade into the background. People couldn't see me. Why did Abebi draw people in, while I repelled them with my nervous energy?

I feigned a surprised grin and replied, "I have to wait for my father. I've barely seen him in the past three days."

Abebi pretended to pout but quickly looked back to five of the girls in our set. They continued their hilarious conversation. A scowl took over my face as I wondered which heifer wanted Sahel. Was it Jema? She was tall and lean like a Maasai woman. My eyes shifted and lowered to where Keeke's black and white printed fabric gripped her ass. Sahel liked a full ass. Every Zaian man did. My stomach churned.

I was halfway through my goat stew when I saw Maki leading my father over to me. Maki's husband died a few months ago, but if you asked me, her eyes had been all over Father for years. She always laughed a little too hard at his jokes and placed her hand on his forearm a little too frequently, causing great agitation within me. She was all right, I suppose, but not for my father. It had been just him and me for seventeen years. He didn't need another girl in his life. Maki brought my father to my table, smiling like she was his proud wife.

"Hey, Father." I stood and hugged his stocky frame tightly. Abebi was my best friend, but my father was my source, my truth teller, and my guide.

"There's my baby," he sang. He felt for his chair and sat, propping his walking stick against the table. "How was the fest?"

"Torture," I exaggerated, but I knew it was nothing like the rites that the warriors went through. "I hardly got any sleep."

He nodded his head vigorously as he stroked his long, black beard. "No sleep brings out the lioness in Zen."

I laughed. I rose to fix Father a plate, but I plopped back down and rolled my eyes. The widow had wasted no time retrieving him a plate with a mound of food. She sat the plate on the table before him.

"Bachwezi, you're going to love this goat stew," she purred before placing her ashy hand on his shoulder. I should leave some shea butter in front of her door tonight, I thought. But I would never waste my shea on her. Shea was imported and therefore expensive.

He smiled. Older women loved fighting over Father because he was charming, handsome, and blind. My mother died moments after giving birth to me, and my father never married. He had not been married to my mother, either, and for this reason, he would never be on the Council of Elders. Being an elder was one of the highest honors in our kingdom and one had to be married to enter. The only exception was the woman who was appointed to the Griothood. Once she retired, if she chose not to marry she would be removed from the Council. So because my father never chose to marry, he was denied entry into the Council. That always made my blood boil. Never to have been married was an unspoken disgrace in Za, but Father didn't give a damn about that or the eldership. Still, people respected Father's wisdom and looked to him with the same respect as those in the Council.

Maki's lip curled as Father tasted the goat and gave a satisfied smile.

"How is it, Bach?" she asked sweetly.

"Perfect. Thank you." He liked the attention.

27

"Of course. There's more where that came from. I've hidden some away just for you," she sang. As an afterthought, she looked at me. "Congratulations, Zen."

I ignored her and hoped she could see my contempt.

"Yes, congratulations," my father said. "My baby is a woman." Then Father leaned over to me and whispered, "They have too many damn festivals in Za. A festival for puberty, a festival for being able to marry, a festival for getting married, a festival for being a woman, blah blah blah." He held up a finger for each festival.

I giggled.

Wondering why the horny woman was still in Father's face, I gave a curt, "Thank you." She frowned, clucked her tongue, and switched her hips back to the serving tables.

"How was work? What are you carving now?"

He lifted the spoon to his lips and slurped. He nodded his approval. It was not every day we ate meat. In Obsidian, cattle were only slaughtered on special occasions. Pork was available when boars were caught, and having goats for milk, soap, and keeping the grass low was more important than eating them.

"I'm done." With a cloth, he wiped his mouth, beard, and worn hands. He reached into his pocket and pulled out a small black idol that fit into the palm of his hand. The idol was in the form of a nude woman made of Kenyan black wood and carved with the undeniable skill and style of my father. There was intricate detail in her hair. She had exaggerated nipples that protruded a half-inch from her breasts, paying homage to her fertility, and her nose was flat and broad. Father had polished the idol to perfection and made it into a necklace. "For you," he held her out to me.

I smiled. "She is gorgeous, Father." I took the wooden idol into my hands and stroked her nose and chiseled full lips.

"It's Ayeki, the goddess of feminine energy and beauty. I had the shaman bless her for you. She will give your strength when you are weak and guidance when the world is hazy. She is the keeper of your feminine intuition."

I hugged Father's neck.

He patted my back. "You're my favorite person to create for. You're my muse."

Grinning, I slipped the hemp cord over my fro and onto my neck. I always got my father's best carvings, and that meant a lot because Zaians from all three provinces sought his work. His skill was astounding, but the fact that he was blind made his carvings even more coveted. People wondered how he carved such intricate designs without sight. He told me once that when he was a young boy, he was an apprentice to a master carver. He practiced day and night until he was a master carver, too. At sixteen, his vision faded rapidly, but he never allowed himself to lose his precision. He learned to use his fingertips as his eyes, and before he went completely blind at eighteen, he could carve with his eyes closed. Every wood carver in Za could somehow trace his skill back to my father. If Father hadn't trained him, he had trained his teacher.

I took a deep breath to build up the nerve to ask Father if Sahel had asked him for permission to marry me, but something hard and small hit me on the back of my neck. I turned around quickly. Everyone was chatting and eating. No one was looking in my direction. Perhaps it was a bug. There were enough of those around, especially during a feast. I fixed my mouth to ask once more, but something hit me again. I whipped my head around, and I saw the culprit.

"Sahel!" I yelled. Saying nothing to Father and leaving the rest of my food for the flies, I grabbed my satchel and jumped to my feet. He took off. I chased after his long, lithe, black body. I knew I could never catch him, but I sprinted anyway. People glared as we sprinted past. Some had to jump out of the way, but I had no time to apologize. Chickens scattered, and children clapped and laughed at us.

The red kanga wrapped around his slender waist rippled behind him, as did the dreadlocks that reached his mid-back. I panted as he took me through a labyrinth of beautiful earthen homes and buildings. We ran past the blacksmith's shop, the salt house, the glass house, the candle maker, carriage maker, and other shops that kept Za going. My shells rattled noisily behind me. I took the same right he took, but I lost sight of him. I slowed my run to a walk. My chest heaved, and my heart thumped. I had been more suited for this when we were children.

"Sahel!" I yelled. "Sahel!" It was too hot for these games. I let out an exasperated breath, and after a few moments I turned around, giving up. In a flash, Sahel grabbed me with his long arms. I squealed and pounded his chest. At seventeen, Sahel was not muscular like some of the warriors, but he was strong, swift, and agile. Selfishly, I hoped his attributes would take him to the highest ranks in Za's military. When a man gained respect, so did his wife.

In part, his masculine beauty drew me to him—his deep-set eyes, broad nose, smooth skin, high cheekbones, his height—but it was also his compassion, his sense of humor, and his devotion to the ancestors. Our ancestors guided our lives and our gods controlled nature, sometimes wielding their wrath through natural fires, droughts, and floods. Sahel had a special relationship with both the deities and ancestors. Perhaps he was born with it, perhaps it was the countless hours he spent in prayer and meditation, or it was his dire need to please the gods no matter what they asked that granted him spiritual wisdom and peace in his young age. Sahel trusted that the gods would provide everything Za needed, and he believed he could manifest his every desire. What I admired most about him was that he feared nothing, except my father. I knew girls wondered why he had chosen such a boring and plain girl like me, but he had. Sahel's favorite thing to say was that the gods created our bond.

Sahel laughed, still not letting me go. "Oh, calm down, Zen," he said, grinning, his white teeth a sharp contrast to his deep brown skin.

"You are so annoying. Don't you know better than to ruin a feast?"

Ignoring me, he stole a kiss, and I let him.

My demeanor softened. "What are you doing here, anyway? Shouldn't you still be in the pasture?"

"Yes, but the goats can wait. My brothers will take care of them for me. I needed to see you."

A demure smile crossed my lips.

"Why can't I marry you now?" he sighed, looking down at me. He made it so hard for me to wait until my wedding night to make love to him.

I ran the pads of my fingers over his smooth bare chest. I recalled Abebi's words. "Have any of the Zephyrs tried anything inappropriate with you?" I avoided his eyes.

He scoffed, "What?"

I looked up but only for a second. "Abebi said that if I didn't hurry up and have sex with you, someone else would."

"You and Abebi are ridiculous. Why do you let her mess with your head?"

"She wasn't messing with me," I whined. "She was trying to warn me."

"No, Zen. None of your set sisters have tried to do anything inappropriate with me, as you say."

"Has anyone been overly flirtatious or come to your bachelor hut—"

"Stop," he said in a serious tone. "I love you. I want you and only you. In two months' time, you will be my wife. Just be patient."

I nodded, begrudgingly.

"Oh, I see," he said slyly. "You're questioning me, but some boy is giving you jewelry," he joked, taking the Ayeki idol into his fingers.

"You know better." I rolled my eyes. I swayed away from him, just a few steps. I turned back to him and asked, "Have you talked to my father?"

He rubbed the side of his long neck and made a hissing sound as he sucked in air through his teeth.

I dropped my shoulders. "Why not, Sahel?"

"Your father makes me nervous."

I sighed. "How can you be afraid of him when you spent the last week hunting the rogue lion that slaughtered your goats?"

"I think that even if my father gave your father every single one of our goats and our cows, your father would still never let me marry you. The man hates me."

"That's not true. He's waiting for you to approach him like a man."

Sahel groaned. "Okay. Before I go to training, I will ask him…no, I'll tell him, 'Bachwezi, I am marrying your daughter. She is the loveliest and smartest woman in Za, and I have to have her.'"

I laughed.

He sauntered over to me and pulled me back to him. I feigned reluctance, but that familiar feeling was brewing in me like Ankaran tea. He nuzzled my neck. "After the second rainy season, you will be my wife. I can hardly believe it."

"I can't wait." I lowered my hands to his muscular butt.

"See, and Abebi thinks I'm the horny one when it's really you."

"Whatever."

He inhaled and kissed me again. "I have to go." Sahel let

my body go and backed toward Obsidian's front gate. The animals were kept safely from any predators outside of the village walls. Beyond the livestock kraal were the great plains of the Serengeti, where the herders allowed their animals to graze. Even before Obsidian's start, Sahel's paternal lineage kept those who lived in Za nourished and for this, we honored his family. Everyone in Za owned goats, but Sahel's family owned a plethora of goats, cows, and horses. In fact, every Nubian goat in Za had come from the goats that Sahel's ancestors raised. His family was just as honorable as the blacksmith who made the spears, plows, chains, nails, horseshoes, pots, and countless other tools that made our lives easier. They were just as honorable as the architects who performed magic from the earth when they molded our homes. Their stature was nearly equal to that of Abebi's father, the greatest chief Za has ever known.

"Make sure you're back to watch me dance," I cooed, the longing overtaking me the same way it did every time we had to separate.

"Hey," he called back, "what did you do out there, anyway?"

"None of your business. That's why our rituals take place on the far side of the kopjes." But I knew one day I would tell him what we did when the women went into the bush during Yoni Fest. I shared everything with him, even my worst moments.

"I heard that women learn how to keep their yonis wet and how to make it taste like passion fruit." He paused thoughtfully before asking, "Were all of you naked?"

My mouth dropped open. "You are so nasty," I laughed. It was rare for Sahel to speak that way, but when he did it set my stomach ablaze.

He grinned naughtily. "No seductive dancing at Harambe. I don't want anyone else lusting for you."

"Go," I said, feigning annoyance.

I waved, and he took off running. I took in his perfect physique for as long as I could.

With a dance in my step, I walked in the opposite direction, toward the Harambe circle. I felt something cover my soul with the heaviness of a weighted quilt. I looked to my right, and I saw her again. The griot. Still lurking. Stalking…me? I cocked a brow but kept walking, gripping my satchel nervously.

"It isn't ladylike to frolic around in public." Her voice was deep, her words drawn out like she was putting a hex on me.

My steps faltered. I came to a stop, and I watched her move closer to me.

The scent of her spices and oils surrounded me as she moved slowly into my space. "Do you hear me speaking to you?" Her tone was terse, and she formed slits with her eyelids. The griot was my height, but I felt as if she were towering over me. She wasn't a large woman, but she always hid her shape behind loose dresses and wraps.

Anger and embarrassment caused my ears to grow hot. I lowered my gaze. "Yes, Griot."

"People are always watching you, Zen. Always." She then sighed. "Never look down for anyone," she advised, softening her tone.

I mustered up the courage to look her in the eyes, which were the hue of honey with green flecks. Her sand-colored locs were hoisted above her head, and a white wrap was intricately tied, with endless twists and knots, around the crown of her head. The griot was fully cloaked in white, the color of mourning, yet no one had died.

She rolled her eyes, shaking her head in disappointment, her several earrings and nose rings glinting in the sunlight. "Go on, Zen." She dismissed me with a flick of her hand.

I went quickly, but I could feel her eyes on me, raising tiny bumps on my arms.

CHAPTER 4

"Why are you so quiet?" My father intruded on my thoughts. I had returned to where I was sitting before I took off after Sahel. "What'd that boy do?"

"Sahel has never done anything to me, Father."

He huffed. "And it better stay that way."

I pursed my lips. I was in no mood for my father's quips. My mind was on the griot, who had just arrived at the feast. I never liked being admonished. I felt heavy, like she had put an ominous root on me.

I shook her out of my mind. "I suspect Sahel will propose to me soon," I said carefully.

Father's body tensed. He closed his eyes and took a deep breath. "I hate how the elders make women feel like they have to marry right away. Take the time to get to know yourself."

My blood pumped hot. I knew where this conversation was headed. He was going to attempt to discourage me from marrying Sahel yet again. I felt the strong urge to walk away

35

from him before I said something I'd regret. Suddenly, the talking drums sounded, loud and strong, halting any movement in the village, fields, and pasture. Father stiffened and trained his ears, his milky eyes pointed to the sky. He deciphered the code.

"What is it?" I asked, eyes wide.

He lifted his hand, quieting me. The rhythm repeated, echoing off the walls of the houses. Once the drumming stopped, Father translated, "The griot has called a meeting." His words were slow and soft. His usual blissful demeanor had soured.

I huffed. That sting from my encounter with the griot returned. Was she purposely trying to vex me? I squeezed my eyes shut and pulled my lips into my mouth and bit down slightly. I wanted to scream. Tonight's Harambe was supposed to honor the girls in my set. The men would watch the gyrating hips and look for the girl they were most attracted to. That could lead to courtship and ultimately marriage. But now that woman would ruin our special night.

"Father, I don't feel well." It wasn't completely a lie. My spirit had been wounded.

"You know when the griot calls, everyone shows up. It isn't optional." There was no leeway in his words. "Besides, how will it look if you don't dance with the Zephyrs?"

No one would notice, I thought. I also already had my man. No one needed to see me dance.

I moaned. "I've heard it all before." I knew every fable, song, and warning that the storytelling wench told. I did not want to hear anything from her tonight or ever again if possible. "Not only that, I've practically been awake for three whole days. I was barely able to—"

"Zen," Father warned with finality.

I sulked. It was rare for my father to be firm with me.

Obsidian's people—the one's who had not attended the

feast—sluggishly made their way to the Harambe circle like debris in Sudd Swamp. Usually, people were upbeat for Harambe, especially during Yoni Fest. Today, most people groaned and rolled their eyes. There were some nosey women, however, who couldn't wait for the next day's gossip. When the griot called an impromptu meeting, it usually was to reprimand someone or the village as a whole. What if she was going to say something about me touching and kissing Sahel even though he wasn't my husband? I felt nauseous.

I heard Maki, who sat close to Father, murmur to her sister, "Who messed up this time?"

"It was probably you," her sister joked. Maki nodded in agreement. They cackled, and I wondered if Father had slept with her. I shuddered at the thought.

I pulled off my Ayeki idol, careful not to let the beads get tangled in my tresses. I took Father's large hand and placed the idol in it. It would be annoying to dance with it slapping my face. "Father, you want to move closer to the circle?"

"No, I'm fine. Go on." Although people loved helping him, he could get anywhere in the village as long as he had his walking stick.

"Okay. See you back at the house." I stood.

"I love you, sweet girl."

I smiled, letting go of my anger. "Love you, too."

I removed my satchel and sat with my set, and we looked beautiful in our outfits. Yalee, the best drummer in Obsidian and probably all of Za, created a complicated beat on his Ngoma drum. The growing crowd yelled and sang out. His drumming was a spirit that leaped out of the taut cowhide and possessed the people.

Yalee pulled back and tapped softly in a staccato rhythm. Everyone sat or stood in silent anticipation. He was toying with us. The other drummers waited on Yalee to make his drum speak. The girls rocked, itching to dance. His beat grew fast, and the people shouted, some jumped up and down, women waved their hands as if to fan him, and he backed off to tease them. We groaned. Then the pads of his fingers patted the drum, building until rage was in the palm of his hands and tips of his long fingers. The other drummers joined in, then the women without babies on their backs ran to the middle of the circle and wound their hips and backsides.

I wasn't ready to dance just yet. I clapped and laughed. I was saving my energy for Sahel's arrival. I needed to dance for him. I channeled Yemi, the goddess of feminine beauty and seduction so that I could dance in a way that made me irresistible to Sahel. If one of the girls in my set were trying to gain his attention, he would forget her tonight.

I shook my head as I saw yet another woman leading Father to the bench on the other side of the circle, where his own age set gathered. Father looked bothered. There was some sort of heaviness on him. I could tell by the way his lips were turned down at the corners. Was he really that angry about me wanting to marry Sahel? Sahel was honest, strong, and came from a prestigious family, and like Father, Sahel was deeply spiritual. What was it that he did not like about Sahel? Was he just against marriage altogether? I closed my eyes and nodded. Just then it occurred to me why he wasn't happy about our union—why his mood was uncharacteristically bitter. Father did not want to be alone. He should've known he didn't have to worry. I would see him every day, and he would eat with us every night. I would never leave him alone. I could even have Sahel build us a house big enough for Father to live with us. Living with an extended family was common in Za.

I smiled as the set just a year younger than my own performed a dance that they had prepared for us. Some of the girls had hair shaved to the skin like Abebi, some wore braids, some wore locs down their backs, and some had manes rising up to the sky. They were all gorgeous, and the envy in their eyes was evident, as they couldn't wait to be in our place next year.

Abebi sat down beside me. We hugged, and without a word, we swayed to the beat of the drums. I knew we couldn't hold out much longer. My eyes wandered. Where was Sahel? He should have been here by now.

Soon Abebi moved to the center of the circle. This meant we would all perform the dance we had created during the Yoni Fest.

I rocked at the center of the circle, moving with my eyes closed. I could feel that all eyes were on us. We were the girls who would soon be married. We would soon birth the children of our village. I was uncharacteristically at ease. Dancing and playing my kora was the only time I didn't mind eyes on me. An overwhelming sensation was building within me. Some of the girls gave high-pitched yips. They were encouraging Yalee, and Yalee was edifying our souls and lowering our inhibitions. Then I saw him. Sahel sat on a log with his friends. He was gazing at me in a way that made my heart thrash. His upper lip curled. I suppressed a grin.

Abebi began to dance, and we jumped right in, dancing for our men. Our hips moved fluidly to Yalee's syncopated rhythm. I was possessed by the drum, but not so much so that I forgot to charm Sahel, not so much that I forgot the steps of the dance. Before long, sweat ran down my forehead and stung my eyes. Still, I danced with fierceness, as if I were imploring Yemi for rain or fertility.

He was watching. I could feel it. I caught brief glimpses of Sahel's face as the world passed in a blur. The people screamed and clapped. Our arms slashed through the air in sync, feet tapped feverishly and rapidly, while we turned and jumped with precision. Our audience shouted in complete delight as our hips and backsides twisted and jerked. An untamed spirit moved through everyone. The young men watched as they searched for their brides, but most already knew which girl they wanted.

Then the contest commenced. One by one, each of the girls showed how fast she could move her hips and behinds. My heart thumped when it was my turn. I closed my eyes, dancing like my life depended on it. Sahel stood and hollered. I twisted my lower body to the ground and back up, all the time keeping my upper body isolated and still. The cowrie shells accentuated my movements. The crowd shouted, "Go, Zen!" I laughed as I returned to my space among my set sisters.

Then without warning, before the next girl took her turn, Yalee and the other drummers began the cadence to end the dance. The girls and the crowd shouted, "What?" How unfair it was for the girls to not be able to dance for their future husband? I gave a little grin as we went to our seats.

Sahel's group was perhaps angrier than the girls because they couldn't display their strength. These were the little boys we used to play with, and at one point, many of us girls were taller than them, but now they were gods, heads reaching to heaven, the contour of their pectoral muscles outlined by the fire's glow. They would not dance tonight and it was the griot's fault.

The stone-faced griot now stood by the drummers. She was poised, sullen, and wore a severe frown. Her stern eyes threatened us as they swept across the crowd. Many eyes looked down, confessing guilt that they believed she knew. The hoops of her two gold nose rings glistened in the fire's light. Even in silence, she was captivating and intimidating, and no one dared to speak. The respect that she commanded intrigued me. How did she do it, get these people to look at her the way they did? She was never boastful, never pushy, but everyone was aware of her importance; everyone respected her.

Behind the griot was the Council of the Elders, a position afforded to those who had lived long, cared about Za's health before their own, and were the epitome of Zaian citizenship. They, too, wore white. I was confused, not by the presence of the elders, but their decorum and solemnity. This would be no ordinary storytelling. My interest piqued.

The griot deliberately made her way to the center of the circle, and the elders stayed behind her, watching. Her white gown grazed the dirt. The coppery sun had lowered to a point just above her head as if the gods planned it that way. The sky was a fiery burnt orange. "Tonight," she said in a monotone voice, looking into several rapt eyes, "I will name the next griot." Her voice reverberated.

At first, there were gasps, and then the whole village buzzed with confusion. She was far too young to be choosing a successor. Many griots served until they were in their sixties or older. The griot could be no more than forty, but by law two decades was all she had to give.

I looked around, wondering who the poor victim would be. Although being appointed to the Griothood was one of the biggest honors one could have in Za, no one wanted to make the sacrifices. The girl had to be unmarried and had to remain unmarried for as long as she was griot—a mandated twenty years. What man wanted to marry a woman that old, I thought. This meant that there would probably be no children for her, either. It was a sad and lonely life. My eyes widened. The chosen girl would probably be from my set or the set under us. Most everyone older would be married. Someone's life was going to be destroyed tonight. Abebi grabbed my hand and squeezed. She'd made the realization, too.

CHAPTER 5

"She must be ill," Abebi whispered in my ear, her voice was saturated with dread.

I took in the griot's perfect posture, her commanding words, and her fiery eyes. "She doesn't look ill," I replied. But that meant nothing. There were many illnesses that could consume a Zaian. A simple tsetse fly could cause blindness, and a mosquito bite could result in a slow, agonizing death.

I glanced around. Sahel, too, had his eyes stuck on the griot. Torches now lit the Harambe circle.

Abebi whispered, "She's been following me."

I looked at her. My mouth parted, and I started to say that she'd been following me too.

Abebi trembled. "Just this morning, after we went home from the ritual, the griot was in my kitchen whispering with my father... It's me," she croaked, the realization consuming her. I threw my arms around her.

I turned my attention to the griot, who raised her powerful voice. "A woman must be in touch with her life source to be griot." Her hands were pressed together as if she were praying. "She mustn't be petty or trivial." She shook her head. "She must be able to live a life of relative solitude, and at the same time know the quirks, weaknesses, and sins of every person in this village." She tapped her temple with her middle finger. "Her memory must be impeccable, and her imagination vivid. If she fails, Obsidian fails. If Obsidian fails, Za fails." Her eyes went vacant. She'd been transported to another place.

I hugged Abebi tighter. Poor thing. She shuddered. I tried to imagine her as griot. She already commanded the attention of every person in this village, and the people respected her. But I just couldn't picture it. Her life was meant for something much larger, like the position of Queen. Also, the chief would never allow his precious daughter to be subjected to such a miserable life.

The griot put her head down and her hands behind her back. She paced. Finally, she continued, "This decision did not come without the blessing of the ancestors, the king, the chief, and the elders."

The elders nodded somberly. When the griot's head rose, her eyes were glossy.

"My life is over," Abebi wailed. Some of the girls in our set turned to see what she was blubbering about.

"It's going to be okay," I said softly.

Then, as if I'd been struck down by the hands of Qwei, the mighty war god who could kill a whole army in the instant it takes lightning to strike, I heard the name loud and clear. "Zen Akke."

The crowd gasped. I stopped breathing, and my arms fell from Abebi. I had been hearing things, right? I felt like the world had become hazy, and suddenly I could only make out the crackle of the fire and nothing else. In a daze, I turned to look at my father. His head was down, and he rocked from side to side in mourning. For some reason, he didn't seem to be shocked. It was like he knew the blow was coming. I turned to Abebi. Her eyes were wide and her mouth ajar. My eyes flitted to the griot. Her eyes stared at the dirt. Then out of the sea of faces watching me for my reaction, my eyes rested on Sahel, the boy who would be my husband, my man, and the father of my babies. He looked as if he'd been stabbed.

"Come to me, Zen," the griot commanded.

I stood on weak legs as the eyes of everyone in Za watched my every step. I wanted them to stop staring at me. My ears pulsed. I stepped in her direction, and in a split second, I took off running. Sahel stood, and I nearly knocked him over as I wound my arms around him. The whole village inhaled at the same time. Sahel and I held each other tightly.

"Zen!" the witch yelled, her tone clipped. I couldn't see her, but I could tell her teeth were clenched.

I wailed, and Sahel repeatedly sobbed, "No."

People patted my shoulder and urged me to "Go on." Or they said, "It will be all right." But it wasn't them, so how the hell did they know how it would be?

"Come," the chief barked. But I wasn't letting Sahel go. I felt fingers on my shoulders and waist, prying us apart, digging into my flesh. I kicked and bucked. Sahel reached out for me as several of his friends held him back. I watched him fight them off as I was dragged to the middle of the circle and dropped at the griot's feet.

She scowled at me. I blubbered, snot falling from my nostrils as she commanded that I obey the gods and my ancestors. I wanted to scream, "Fuck you." But I couldn't get a word out.

I looked around. Every person was on their feet, watching in dismay. I would surely be the talk of the village. Ashamed, I swallowed and quieted my cries. I got on my feet and swayed like the village drunk. I'd lost all dignity in front of these people.

"You will serve this village as the next griot upon your initiation in a little over a month's time. Do you understand?"

"Yes, Griot," I whimpered. I cleared my throat and forced myself to stop shaking. "Yes, Griot," I said with feigned conviction. Not knowing what to do next, I bowed, and after a moment of hesitation, the people cheered. I rose with tears burning my eyes.

"Go rest. We will begin training in two days," she said softly to me. She gave me a weak smile. Perhaps the smile was apologetic or sympathetic. Or was she afraid I would embarrass her more? She raised her hands, and on cue, the drums sounded.

At once, my father was at my side. I didn't know who brought him to me, but I was grateful. He led me home. I hiccupped as we walked wordlessly until all eyes were off of me, then I collapsed in his arms

CHAPTER 6

I lay in my bed, eyes swollen and throat raw, waiting for the nightmare to end, but this was my reality. A few flicks of the griot's tongue snatched my future away from me. Father came into my room repeatedly to check on me.

He forced the Ayeki idol into my hand. "You need her now."

I threw her at the wall.

Father looked hurt, but I didn't care.

I replayed over and over the characteristics of a griot. I was none of the things that the griot described. As hard as I tried to be one with my source, to be in a state of Zen, I rarely was. Anxiety ruled my life. And there was the fact that no one in Obsidian would listen to me, not my own set and certainly not the elders. The witch had to be blinder than my father.

There was a rapid knock on the front door. I sat up. I feared it was the griot offering more torment. I listened to Father's shuffling, then to the door opening and the level discourse that followed. Even though the voices were muffled, my heart rate surged, and there was a pang in my stomach. Sahel.

After a short conversation, Father reluctantly called my name. My face was encrusted where my tears had fallen, but I didn't care. I parted my door, which opened to the common room. Sahel was standing outside our door holding the satchel I left at the Harambe circle. Father had not invited him in, as doing so was against custom. Although premarital sex was not forbidden, discretion was essential. A single man should never enter the home of a single woman. She had to go to his bachelor hut when there was no one to witness. I rushed to him, knocking him back a couple steps as he wrapped his arms around me. I sobbed as he kissed the top of my head. Father quietly walked to his bedroom, and though I could feel that he wasn't happy with Sahel's visit, I didn't care.

Sahel's palm rested on the back of my head, and the other was on my back. I quavered as each cry left me. I felt the tension in his body. He was trying hard to be strong. "Why did she do this to us?" I wailed.

"Zen. Shhh. Not out here," he cautioned. He put his arm around me and led me away from my home. I kept close to his body, my head on his shoulder, eyes looking at the dirt path. I was unaware of anyone we passed. When I lifted my head, Sahel was opening the door to the bachelor hut his family had secured for him once he turned seventeen. When he moved out, another young boy would inhabit it.

Sahel allowed me to enter before him. He closed the door behind us and stood there, hand still on the doorknob and eyes dead.

"I..." he started, then for the first time since we were kids, his dark eyes welled up. I went to him and held him.

"We have to go to her," he said, each syllable pointed. "We have to show her how much we love each other. She can't do this." His voice cracked. "She can't tear us apart."

My mind raced for a solution. I was too anxious to wait for one to come to me like my father had taught me. Father practiced Taoism, and in Taoism, patience was the way. I was too anxious for that.

"Going to her won't solve anything," I argued. The vile woman was heartless. "We have to take a different path."

"What, Zen?" he asked like my suggestion was ridiculous. "What can we do?"

In a low tone, I said, "We have to get out of Obsidian." It was the only way.

Appalled, Sahel pulled away from me. His watery eyes scrutinized me like he was waiting for me to recant or start laughing.

"We have to run."

His face contorted. "You're not thinking clearly."

"I am."

"How many times have you been so far away that you could not see the walls of this place?"

I deflated. He was right. I only truly left Obsidian once, and that was to go to Noire for a presentation celebrating my father's talents. I was seven.

I asked, "Do you love me?"

"Where would we go?" He paced.

"Do you love me?" I repeated with more force.

"You've lost your mind."

"Forget it. I guess you're willing to let me go without a fight."

"No, but I am being realistic." He huffed. "And, don't say that. Don't say I'm letting you go. I'm sick right now. My life just got turned upside down, too."

"But you can still have children." I paused as hurt flowed through me. "You can still marry. You will marry, while I rot, alone."

He exhaled a slow stream of air. "I can be very convincing. Let me try to get through to her."

I toned down my own voice. "The griot won't change her mind, not after she's announced it to the whole village."

He scratched the new growth on his scalp. Once we had this mess figured out, I would oil his scalp and retwist his locs for him. "Zen, we will be together. You will be my wife."

I threw my hands up. I was about to tell him that saying I would be his wife didn't make it so. But that was how Sahel's mind worked. He believed that if he put something out into the universe as if it were true, it would become true. I wasn't so sure.

He grounded himself in front of me. "Do you believe the ancestors want us together?"

After tonight, I didn't. But still, I said, "Yes."

"Then they will work this out."

Those words did nothing to soothe me. I did not know what the ancestors wanted. Apparently, they wanted me to be a lonely and bitter storyteller. Why the hell couldn't storytellers marry, anyway? Right now, I was having trouble trusting my ancestors. They had created the idiotic decree.

Without a word, I kicked off my sandals and crawled into his bed.

Sahel stopped pacing and raised his brow.

I shrugged. "I need you tonight."

"Your father will murder me." But he smirked slyly.

"No, he won't." I pulled his cover over me. I'd never been in his bed before. I felt grown. I felt sensual. Cautiously, as if fighting himself, Sahel slipped into the bed meant for one. His skin was warm and soft. His locs fell over my shoulder as he kissed my neck. I shivered. I tilted my face up to his, and his lips pushed against mine. His lips were soft and moist. This was dangerous. My yoni had awakened, and I felt I would lose control of her.

Our kissing became aggressive, and I felt him grow stiff as he gripped the flesh of my thighs. That scared me, but I wanted him.

He slipped his hand under my wrap, and my yoni responded in throbs and wetness. Then he stopped abruptly, his breathing heavy. Sahel cursed. "We should wait." He removed his hand from my flesh.

"Why?" I whined. I no longer wanted to wait. We would never marry, anyway.

"You know I am not circumcised. It goes against the gods—"

"Your friends have done it."

He looked away. "I won't, Zen. I'm sorry."

I turned away from him. Tears burned in my eyes. He was saving himself for his wife, and that would never be me. I buried my face into his pillow and ignored him when he tried to comfort me. Eventually, I fell asleep.

The next morning, the sun shined into Sahel's single window. He sat on the edge of the bed, his brown back to me. He'd pulled his locs up above his head.

I sat up.

Without looking at me, he said quietly, "My father has maps. We can go to Nairobi."

My heart surged.

CHAPTER 7

I didn't sleep the next night. We were running away, thrusting ourselves into permanent exile. If Sahel could get the maps from his father's home, we would leave the following night. He would also find a way to secretly get two horses and a carriage, and we would take enough water and food for the journey. I was exhilarated, but I was also afraid. I knew the Serengeti was vast, but for me, a girl who had only left once, the massiveness was unfathomable and the dangers overwhelming. The Serengeti was the gods' way of showing humans how insignificant they truly were.

Doubt crept into the marrow of my bones repeatedly. The maps that belonged to Sahel's father were a hundred years old. They'd been created just after Obsidian's creation. Things could have changed drastically. What was Nairobi like? Would they accept us? What would we do for food and money? We grew our food in Obsidian and bartered our skills, so money was of no use to us.

The more I thought of all that could go wrong in the bush, the tenser my body became. I felt sick. If Sahel and I ran, we would never be able to return to Za, and I would never see my father again. Was my love for Sahel enough for me to forsake my father and my home?

I thought of my alternative, staying in Obsidian,

becoming a griot, never marrying, or having children of my own. The fear of that prospect weighed heavily on me, but at least I would still have my father, Abebi, and my home. I loved Obsidian, its beauty, and the fact that it provided everything my people needed. We needed no assistance from anyone outside of our walls. Acquiring food, crafts, and furniture from Ankara and Noire were luxuries. It was rare that things were imported from outside of Za, and only a select few were allowed to venture to other cities for those goods.

The next morning, I was silent at breakfast. Father didn't talk much, either. I knew he was upset at the griot's decision. He was also probably hurt that I had spent the night with Sahel. I had disgraced my father, but it was nothing compared to what I would do to him tonight. As I ate, I studied his worn face, his mustache, and his void eyes. I had to remember him just like this. These would be one of our last moments together. A tear slipped down my cheek. For once, I was glad he could not see my face.

Father lifted his head up when he heard me sniffle. He reached out his massive hand, which had years of gardening and carving etched on it. I took his rough hand and squeezed it tightly.

"There's nothing I can say to make you feel better, I know. But know I am here for you," he said. "You will get through this."

"I know, Father," I lied. I wouldn't give myself a chance to get through this. I was about to commit a great act of betrayal. After tonight, my father would never know what became of me, or I of him. Soon, his heart would be ripped out. I was the only family he had, his only child.

After breakfast, I went to the sacred space. It was a place where nothing was to be built or grown. It lay next to the Elders' Mound. Groups meditated there and performed Zaige, which was similar to Kemetic yoga. I was there for another reason.

"Zen," Sahel whispered from the side of the mound.

I scurried over to him. "Did you find the maps?"

"Yes. I got them at breakfast. Once the sun goes down, I will be able to get the horses." His eyelids lowered, and he expelled a long breath. He shut his eyes, and intense ridges formed on his upper lids, then a small tear escaped.

My eyes welled up, and I put my hand on his shoulder.

He was quiet for a moment before opening his red eyes. "What have I become, stealing from my father?"

Guilt weighed my chest down. I was going to ruin his life, take him from his father, mother, brothers, and his beloved goats. Ever since he started courting me, I'd asked myself why, out of all of the beautiful and charismatic girls, he'd chosen me. I had doubted his love for me, waiting for his feelings to change course, waiting for him to realize that I wasn't worthy. Now here, Sahel was making this grand sacrifice for me, for us. I would never question his love for me again.

"Are you sure you want to do this?" I placed my cheek on his chest and felt him breathe deeply. Half of me hoped he still wanted this, and the other half hoped he'd back out.

With a seriousness that was so out of character for him, he said, "You were right. Leaving is our only choice." He paused for a few beats, and then he said, "Don't attend Harambe tonight. Once everyone is there, go to the back gate. Say you're going to meet with the griot, and find me at the kraal." His words were urgent and hushed.

"How will we find our way when it's dark?" I asked, my voice trembling.

"Very carefully. We won't be able to light our torches until we're far enough not to be seen by the lookout tower. Zul has hidden a carriage for us. He will have the horses there and prepared to go."

I removed my face from his skin and looked up to him. "Are we crazy?"

He kissed my forehead after looking around.

"Yes," he answered, and he headed away to tend to his goats for the last time.

All day, people stopped to talk to me about my appointment to the Griothood, and I feigned excitement, but every mention of it made me want to vomit. To get away, to hide the worry and guilt that wore me down, I went outside of the gates with my blanket and my kora. I played the instrument that had belonged to my mother as I watched the zebras and wildebeests take their places at the salt-lick lake. I looked for giraffes and their slow, majestic gait. There were five grazing from a lone acacia tree. I took in the distant escarpment and the Obsidian bush for the last time. In Nairobi, there would be tall buildings, cars, and people everywhere. I heard there was so much pollution in Nairobi that smog-tinged the air and poisoned the lungs. I felt the weight on my chest increase.

The breeze flowed past me, blowing up my hair across my face. It was a lovely day. The air was fresh and the sky a deep blue only interrupted by a few swiftly moving clouds. I played until my forefingers and thumbs ached from plucking the strings. I hugged my kora as I made my way back home. I would have to leave the instrument here. I gripped the long wooden handle, imagining I could feel my mother. I need you, Mother, I thought. Guide me.

The day dragged on. I went to the fields to help plant seeds before the first rains, then I slept the rest of the day away. I couldn't face my thoughts and fears. I couldn't face the reality that if I went against the ancestors, they would wreck my world.

When I could sleep no more, I visited with Abebi for a

short while. I needed the familiarity of my best friend.

"I cannot believe she chose you. You're so awkward and anxious. She's a madwoman." There was humor in her voice.

I sat on her floor (no one sat on Abebi's bed) and silently wondered if she knew or cared that she was insulting me.

"I embody all the things she said a griot was, thank the gods that she doesn't know that. Zen, confident? Zen, with impeccable memory? The Zephyrs think she's crazy." She cackled.

I swallowed uncomfortably. It hurt to think of my set sitting around talking about me, laughing behind my back. I shut my eyes, refusing to let the tears pass.

"What are you and Sahel going to do?" she asked obliviously.

"Huh?" I panicked. How did she know we were up to something?

"Now that you can't get married. I guess he has to find another girl." Her words fell on my heart like the blacksmith's mallet.

I swallowed my anger and didn't respond as she gave me a fake look of pity. Abebi crossed one leg over the other and straightened her back. She looked regal. She always did. She loved to talk about how she was descended from a long line of nobility and heroic ancestors. I, on the other hand, had no family outside of my father. Both sets of my grandparents, who died before I was born, only had one child survive infancy. Father didn't feel the need to discuss the dead. I always figured it was too heavy for him to bear. He never discussed any other relatives either.

I said nothing about Sahel. I brooded over the insensitive words that exited Abebi's mouth. Last night, I wanted to tell her what I had planned, but I decided against putting that burden on her. If the elders found out she knew I was running away, they would punish her. I wasn't just an everyday person leaving Obsidian. I was now a griot initiate. But now there were other reasons I could never tell her about the plan that Sahel and I had concocted. One being she didn't give a damn about me.

Abebi ran her fingers down the flawless black skin on her arm. "You'll be fine, girl." It was amazing how upbeat she was. Just the other night, she was beside herself with grief when she thought the griot had chosen her.

I gave her a fake smile as I rose. "I have to go," I told her, hiding the contempt I held for her. It was then that I realized I wouldn't miss her at all.

There would be no telling how long it would be before I had fresh, warm food again. I should have eaten as much as possible at dinner that night, but I couldn't. My nerves had me rattled. All Sahel and I packed was dried goat and pork and fruit.

"What would my mother have thought about me becoming griot?" I asked my father who sat across from. He wasn't eating the dinner I had prepared either.

Sadness crossed over his face. He sat back and stroked his beard. With honesty, he stated, "It would tear her apart, but she would come to terms with it because it was for the good of Za."

I didn't believe him. No mother would want this for her child. No mother would deny her child the chance to have children of her own.

He forced me to think, however. For the first time, I thought of all the individual people I was letting down by running. Would this kingdom crumble from me not taking my spot as griot? I didn't believe my actions would have repercussions that deep. I thought about how angry the griot would be, but that thought became sour. She hadn't thought about my future when she chose me. She deserved to hurt.

By leaving, I would make her look like a fool in front of her precious Griothood. The people would lose respect for her. Good.

"You ready for Harambe?" Father asked. The drummers had already begun, forcing my pulse into overdrive.

"Father, tomorrow is a big day. I just want to prepare my mind."

He nodded and rose. Before he could walk out the door, I walked over and hugged him tightly. This man had raised me alone and loved me unconditionally. He was my friend, and I was stabbing him in the back. He kissed my forehead.

"You are the greatest father." It was true.

He chuckled. "I love you, too, baby. Tomorrow, you will find that the griot isn't so bad."

I let him go, and I choked back tears as I laid eyes on my father for the last time.

I paced behind the door of my home with my satchel on my shoulder. It was filled to capacity with everything I could fit inside. When I emerged, I could hear the excitement of the people as the drums summoned them to dance. I headed for the back gate, trying to seem as normal as possible, knowing that if anyone called my name, I would jump out of my skin.

I approached two guards. Paranoia set in, and my stride became stiff as I looked around for the griot. I caressed the idol, praying for protection and that I lived to see Nairobi.

A guard smiled and took a few steps in my direction. "Good evening, Zen."

The other said, "Congratulations."

I waved. "Thank you. I have to see the griot," I said without being asked.

The one who spoke first eyed me with suspicion. "You sure you want to go out there after nightfall? The simba hasn't been found."

I'd forgot about the damned lion. My mind crowded with visions of the cheetahs, snakes, crocodiles, and elephants. Those were just a few of the formidable creatures that ruled the Great Rift Valley.

"I'll be fine," I answered impatiently.

"Let us get someone to walk with you. You don't even have a torch."

I barked, "No, thank you." Then calming myself, I continued, "I'm fine, honestly."

They gave each other wary glances, silently communicating with the proficiency of people who'd worked together for a while. I shifted from one leg to another. The nape of my neck perspired. Finally, they nodded.

I passed. My legs were feeble. I pretended to head to the griot's home, but when I was out of sight, I took a left and stuck close to the village walls. When I saw the kraal in the distance, I broke away from the path.

Seeing Sahel did not make me feel better. Realization hit me. We were about to do this. We were leaving the only home we knew. Silently, he grabbed my hand, kissed it, and we marched to a thin grove of trees. I wanted to ask him if he was sure about this, but he was walking with such haste and purpose, I figured I shouldn't bother him. My heart was beating to the rhythm of the drums.

I smelled the horseshit before I saw the horses. One of them gave a high-pitched neigh, warning us that we were stupid and therefore going to die a miserable death. Both horses were handsome and stout, veins raised beneath their thin skin. They would definitely be missed. It took so much to be able to acquire and keep horses in Obsidian. I swallowed my guilt. I had to focus.

"Zul," Sahel called quietly for his best friend. "Zul."

However, more than one person exited from behind the trees. I shrieked. My heart dropped to my stomach. None of them was Zul.

CHAPTER 8

Sahel's father, the griot, and the chief approached us with fury in their eyes. The blood drained from my face. My body quaked violently, but Sahel stood strong with his chin squared. He squeezed my hand, signaling that he would take care of me.

"Leaving, are we?" the griot asked with the corner of her lips curled. "I, at least, made it to my destination before I got caught." She laughed as she stroked one of the horse's necks. I sobbed. I was livid, embarrassed, and a little relieved.

"I can't believe you would steal from me!" Sahel's father shouted.

I looked down, embarrassed to hear Sahel being yelled at like a child. Please don't hit him, I thought. How shameful would that be?

"My horses." He seized Sahel's satchel, opened it, and snatched out the contents. "My maps. You know nothing of the world out there. Nothing at all."

"I know I love her."

"You would have gotten this girl killed. What type of love

60

is that? You're both selfish." He frowned at me. "Children."

The griot hummed in agreement. My nostrils flared.

"I see you are not yet man enough to be a warrior in this kingdom," the chief finally spoke. There was always anger in his eyes, except when it came to Abebi. The chief was outraged now, and he looked as if he could kill Sahel. All of the boys in this village belonged to him. He'd trained and molded them since the age of five. The chief continued, "But I am determined to make you a man. You leave for camp tonight. Trust that my training will be worse than the safari you were about to embark on tonight. Oh, and Zul will pay, too."

Sahel's head fell.

I crumpled to the ground weeping.

The griot stopped rubbing the horse and approached me. I looked up at her through my clouded eyes. She looked down her nose at me. Her arms were folded, and the crux ansata necklace fell at her breast. My father's creation. The griot had haughtiness in her eyes that made me want to claw her tight face. She'd been fucking with me for the past three days. She knew exactly what I would do, and she allowed me to fall on my face. "You will move in with me tonight," she said with a satisfied grin. "I will explain to your father what you tried to do." She shook her head again.

With one hand, the chief shoved Sahel in the direction of the village. It was a forceful thrust. Sahel pitched forward. Catching his fall with his palms and moving his feet quickly, he regained his balance. He growled as he whirled around and squared up to the chief, balling up his fists. They were face to face, and both men were prepared to strike.

I threw my hands over my mouth. Sahel was delirious. His wide eyes and lips curled into a snarl, and it jarred me. I had never witnessed this side of him. Qwei, the god of war, had possessed him.

"Sahel," his father bellowed.

"What?" the chief stood with clenched fists and his eyes searing. "Allow his skinny ass to try whatever is on his imbecilic mind." The chief's voice was frighteningly calm.

Sahel steeled his jaw. His chest heaved. He is going to do something stupid, I thought. But after an extended moment of tension, he finally turned and stormed away.

I said a silent prayer for Sahel. He was going to pay heavily for his insubordination, and it was my fault.

"Get up," the griot growled through clenched teeth. I refused to obey the witch. I would stay out in the bush all night, rather than go live with her. I remained on the ground, my rage brewing. She snatched up my wrists in her hands.

"Ow," I howled. I jumped to my feet to stop her from yanking my arms from the sockets.

She snarled, "Get up right now, and act like the woman you were summoned to be. Will you continue to disobey the ancestors? They don't care." She tightened her grip, cutting off my circulation. "You will be griot no matter how hard you fight it. Make things easy on yourself." She shoved my wrist away from her. I looked incredulously at my wrists, and by the light of the lantern, I could see the imprint of her fingernails. I was stunned. She'd never been this cruel as my music teacher. Tonight, she put her hands on me, and I knew I had better do as I was told.

My body trembled as I followed her through the darkness. I cried silently, drifting from thoughts of what was I thinking, to how did they know, to when will I see Sahel again, and how will I make the witch pay for grabbing me like that. I stole glances at her back. Her locs swayed, swishing against her ass. Her gait was worry-free as if she wasn't the bitch who just grabbed me and sentenced me to living with her. She even had the nerve to hum a little tune. Her arrogance made the blood run scolding hot in my veins. I was glad she hadn't said anything else to me because I would have come undone.

We headed through her little wooden and rickety gate, a gate that wouldn't stand a chance against a predator who wanted her chickens. Her hens put up a fuss and ran to her when the gate's springs slammed shut behind us.

"What are you doing out?" She tisked. "You're the leader of this foolishness, aren't you?" she asked a horrid and nearly featherless hen. She swooped down and with one arm, picked up the squawking, flailing thing. The other chickens followed her like loyal dogs.

I stood awkwardly at the gate waiting for her to return. The architects hadn't put much thought into her home. From the outside it looked plain and simply functional, with a circular frame and a thatched roof. I was sure the inside of her dwelling was just as bland though I'd never been inside. When she used to instruct me, she always came to my house, or we practiced outside.

I sensed the slightest movement, and I jumped, my breath catching in my throat. I didn't see the man at first. A man with unruly hair and an unkempt beard was waiting, stark still, in the shadows of the griot's house. I knew him. He was more of an enigma in our village than the griot. When children saw him, they ran away. It had become a game. He and the griot were two of the three people who lived outside of the village walls. The other person was the shaman.

The griot returned, brushing her hands off. "Zen, you know Mansi," she said, but he headed around the back of the house without any acknowledgment. Good. I wasn't in the mood for pleasantries.

"Mansi, can you bring Bachwezi to me, please? Not now, but a little later," she called after him. My body stiffened at the sound of my father's name. How would I face him after my botched escape? Now, just minutes later, the idea of fleeing seemed so stupid.

"Let's go," she said. The edge had gone from her voice.

She let us into her house, and the soothing smell of sage, lavender, and lemongrass greeted me. Her home had an orange glow. A few lanterns hung along the walls, their fires illuminating the common room and the hallway. Her home would have been serene, cozy, and inviting under other circumstances. Now, though, these walls caused my stomach to constrict.

"This will be your home until you're initiated, and then you will get a home of your own." Her tone was even.

A home of my own, I thought as my eyes took in the colorful furnishings. There were plenty of chairs as if the reclusive witch had friends. She walked, and I followed. "This is the kitchen." She stepped in. "You're welcome to anything in this house."

I held back any sign of interest, but I allowed my eyes to survey the kitchen. There was a porcelain sink, a wood counter with exposed shelves below, and a dining table that could seat six.

She led me to another room. "This is where I read, paint, or meditate. You can use this room also." I noticed her many candles, paintings, a colorful mat for meditation, and carvings made by my father's hand. I would make it so that he never created for her again. We moved down a hall. There were two rooms on the left, one on the right, and one directly at the end of the hall. From the outside of her home, I never would have guessed her house was this spacious, far more spacious than the homes inside of the gate. Why?

"We will share this bathroom." She waved in the direction of the doorway to our right.

I peeked in. There was a nice sized tub with a shower, sink, and toilet.

"I keep a pitcher of water by the sink, in case you want to brush your teeth or wash your face. They cut the water off here, too, unfortunately. I also keep mint water in the kitchen, in case I get thirsty at night."

The griot took me further down the hall. "This is your bedroom."

I was relieved that I had my own room. I looked inside. There was a lit oil lamp on a wardrobe. I was surprised to see a beautifully made bed and not a pallet.

She added, "Your father can bring you anything you want to make yourself at home. For now, there are nightgowns in the wardrobe." She was being kind and hospitable. This change in her demeanor didn't fool me. I wouldn't forget how she ruined my life. This would never be my home, but I murmured an obligatory, "Thanks."

The griot considered my face for a moment. "Well, I know you've had an exciting night." And just like that, her bitchiness had returned. Her words cut me as the horror returned of seeing her standing alongside the chief and Sahel's father. "I hope you can get some rest." She walked past me, toward the front of the house.

I turned. My eyes followed her down the hall. "Are you still going to tell my father what I've done?" I had the voice of a little girl. I hated the power she had over me.

"Of course," she cackled. "Goodnight, Zen."

As soon as I shut the door, I broke down. I prayed that the chief didn't hurt Sahel because of what I'd coaxed him into doing. Training was already brutal—scarification, circumcision, and beatings—but now he had a huge target on his back. He'd been weak and defiant. Worst of all, he'd bucked at the chief.

I woke up in a confused state. It was still night, and it took a few moments for me to realize where I was. Once it came to me, I felt weighed down. I couldn't believe I actually fell asleep in this strange place. I tried to fall back asleep, but I heard voices. I listened for a while, before recognizing the easy cadence and bass of my father's voice.

I eased out of the bed, padded to the door, and slowly pulled it ajar. The hall lanterns had been snuffed out. Praying that no one heard me, I eased the door open more so that my body could fit through and walked quietly on the clay floors toward the voices.

"I know you don't agree with my decision." That was the griot speaking defensively.

"But you did it anyway," Father snapped back with unusual frustration. "You acted as if you had changed your mind."

"No, I told you I would search for another answer, but there wasn't one."

"Please," he said with exasperation. "All those other girls in her set and you're telling me none of them would have worked as the griot? Zen has been through enough, now she can't have a family, either. That's fucked up, Queenie."

"Don't curse in my home."

"I don't give a damn about your home."

I brought my fingers to my parted lips. I had never heard my father speak with so much hostility. I peeked my head around the corner, but it was too dim to see into the common room.

My mind attempted to understand the full meaning of their words, and my heart quickened at the thought of Father knowing she was thinking of choosing me. I felt the painful stab of betrayal. He knew. He was talking to her as if he had some type of say in the matter, or as if he thought he did, and he had been fooled. I returned my head into the shadows, still listening.

"Bach, you know I would never do wrong by you or Zen."

What a weird thing to say. And Bach? Only Father's friends called him Bach. She wasn't his friend.

66

"Oh, really? Do you know how much she loves that boy?" He was speaking of Sahel. Had Father actually cared about my feelings for Sahel?

"I know, Bach. I did what I had to do." Her words were lilted.

I heard Father groan.

"She can handle it," my father acquiesced to my horror, "but she doesn't know that." He paused. "She slips into this fog sometimes."

My heart raced. No. I knew he wasn't going to tell her.

"A year ago, for no apparent reason, she tried to kill herself."

Blood rushed to my face, and my gut cinched.

"What?" she squawked. "The marks on her wrists? Why didn't you tell me?"

"I couldn't."

"I need to know things like that."

"Would you have made another choice?"

"I don't know. Deep in my soul, I know it had to be her," she cried out, and then they were both silent for a long time. What is happening, I wondered, but I didn't dare stick my head out again. I heard shuffling. Then I heard whimpering.

"Stop crying, Queenie," my father said compassionately. "Stop it."

"She hates me, and now you do, too. What if it's too much on her?" Was the witch actually torn up over choosing me, or was she simply gaining the sympathy of my father?

He laughed lightly. "Come here," he cooed. What was he doing? I couldn't help but stick my head out again, but again I could see nothing, just one dark mass. I could tell he was holding her. I grimaced. He was consoling the enemy.

I returned to the room the griot had given me. I had to navigate my way through the maze of confusion.

CHAPTER 9

The next morning, I arose to the delicious scent of fatback. My stomach growled.

I stretched and headed to the bathroom to relieve myself. I couldn't stop thinking about my father and the griot. The intimacy. The way he told my saddest secret with ease. I looked at the scars on my wrists and shook the vivid memory away.

I walked to the kitchen with reluctance. My mind wanted me to stay in my room, but my stomach refused. It felt strange navigating a place that I didn't belong in and asking the vile woman for food.

The griot looked up from the book in her hands and twisted her lips in contempt. This didn't bother me, but I would've been bothered if she would have looked at me with pity, now that she knew I was weak. "Good morning," she said dryly. Her locs were now in long, spiraling tendrils. She was seated at the table with a nearly empty plate in front of her. Natural light filtered into the kitchen, highlighting her undeniable beauty.

"Good morning," I said almost bitterly. I looked

everywhere but into her eyes.

After a few beats, she said, "Have a seat." She rose, went to the counter, and heaped food onto a plate for me. Over her shoulder, she said, "I tried to wait before I ate, but I guess you were quite tired."

I sat, eager to eat and eager for her to stop talking to me. She placed the plate with steaming fatback, hominy, and eggs in front of me.

"Thank you," I said. I really meant it. I stuffed food into my mouth. The griot put a cup of goat milk in front of me. She cleared her throat and stood with her hands on her hips.

I gave a drawn out and annoyed, "Yes?"

"You know better."

I set down my fork. I'd been so hungry I forgot to honor my ancestors. "Sorry." I rose to my feet. I picked up the milk, and I headed out the kitchen door. Outside, the fire that the griot used to cook was out, but the coals still smoked. Cooking outside was the best way to prevent house fires. When the weather didn't permit outdoor cooking, we cooked inside, mainly boiling food over the hearth.

I closed my eyes reverently. "Thank you to those who have gone before us. Thank you for your wisdom, nourishment, and protection. To the gods who have been merciful, thank you. Ase," I said out loud before pouring out a dribble of milk onto the earth. Even with the resentment in my heart, I knew that without our ancestors, my people wouldn't be able to survive the rough blows nature gave us, the droughts, the wildfires, the diseases, and high infant mortality.

"Ase," the griot repeated. I jumped. She'd followed me and listened to my prayer. Her omnipresence was both haunting and irritating. I squeezed my eyelids together, calmed myself, and followed her back into the house.

We both sat at the table, but I ate in silence. She noisily

flipped through the pages of the book. I stole quick glances at her. The griot seemed more human now, not some untouchable being who happened to live amongst us. As a child, I had always thought of her as being a goddess or a perhaps a witch walking among us. For the first time, I noticed that the griot didn't look as old as her spirit felt to me.

She looked up, catching me scrutinizing her. My eyes flitted away.

"Your father brought your things."

I thought about what he told her and my mood dimmed even more. A few seconds passed before I asked, "What did he say?"

"About your failed escape attempt?" she asked facetiously. The griot pursed her lips. "He wasn't surprised." She shrugged then stared at the nails she'd used to dig into my skin with the night before, her expression smug.

I glared at her. How did she know how to get under my skin with such little effort? My father had said much more than that, and she was keeping all of that from me purposely. The griot wanted me to think he was mad at me when he was pissed at her.

She got up and cleared her dishes from the table. "Once you wash the dishes and wipe the counters, get dressed and prepare for meditation. Make haste."

For a second, I was annoyed. The griot hadn't asked, she'd commanded. Then I remembered that she did cook a delicious breakfast for me, and she fixed my plate. "Yes, Griot," I answered.

"Call me Queenie." And with her shoulders thrown back, she walked out of the kitchen.

I found my way around her kitchen, washing plates, pots and pans, and putting them away. Afterward, I returned to the bedroom. While I'd been eating, the griot had placed my bags on top of my now made bed. Father had packed the things he knew I needed to get through this ordeal. He'd packed my miswak sticks for brushing, my three favorite hair scarfs, my most cherished book, and my two favorite wraps to make dresses from. But what meant the most to me was seeing the aging and bruised wood of my kora standing on the far side of the bed. I rubbed my hand down its large round calabash sound box. I plucked the taut strings a few times, and the sound brought a smile to my lips. Suddenly, I forgave my father for whatever role he played in my undoing.

I put on a black shirt and tied my dark indigo wrap around my waist. I touched my hair with a sigh. It was tangled and dry. In all of last night's events, I hadn't thought once to twist and tie my hair before lying down. I shuddered when I thought about what my hair would've looked like after we made it to Nairobi—if we had lived. Right now, I didn't have the energy or the time to deal with my hair. Instead, I grabbed one of the scarves that father had packed for me, and I tied it around my head, leaving the challenge of combing my hair for tonight.

The griot was in a Zaige pose, in the middle of her naturally lit meditation room. She stood on one foot with the other leg wrapped around the first. With her eyes closed, she stood as motionless as the trunk of a baobab tree. Incense smoke snaked up to the window. I sat down on a floor pillow and tried to act as if this woman wasn't more balanced than I was. She was so in tune with herself that she didn't seem to hear me enter her sanctuary.

Finally, she released her pose. I shut my eyes hurriedly. I felt her lower herself to the ground. Ignoring her presence, I began to breathe deeply and asked my ancestors to release me from this prison, from this hell. Zaians didn't believe in hell, but I'd studied religions that had. The Griothood had to be hell on earth. I was slipping into a blissful trance when someone knocked on the door. I hoped it was my father. I needed him right now.

"Oh good, the twins are here," she exclaimed. She had to be speaking of the root doctors, or root twins, Inkar and her albino sister, RoRo. There were only three sets of twins in Obsidian. The other two sets were two- and four-year-olds, so it couldn't have been them.

In Za, twins were always treated with the utmost respect. From the moment they were born, they were seen as charmed. They were perfectly balanced, representing good and evil. They possessed a magic that made people want to stay on their good side. In the past, some societies would murder twins in their infancy because of the ominous powers they possessed. Because Inkar and RoRo knew how to work roots, they had no enemies.

I watched, perplexed, as the griot danced out of the room, her wooden bangles clicking against one another. "Come on," she called to me.

I groaned and rolled my eyes as I got up to follow her to the door. She let them in, and she and Inkar embraced like long-lost sisters. RoRo wrung her hands and lingered by the door. I also hung back, wanting to fade into obscurity, but I knew never again in my life would that comfort be afforded to me.

"Hello, Young Griot," Inkar sang with vibrant energy.

I don't know why but the name Young Griot sent chills through my body. My head lifted a little higher. "Hello, Auntie," I said.

"Should we set up in the bedrooms?" RoRo asked dryly. RoRo didn't greet me or even look at me, but that was how she was—forever detached, the opposite of her sister.

"Yes," the griot said as she excitedly rubbed her hands together and grinned.

I moved closer to her. "What are they setting up?" I asked

quietly, noticing the leather satchels that both twins wore.

"I figured we needed to start this training with the toxins and built-up stress removed from our bodies," she said as we all walked down the hall.

RoRo and the griot went straight back to her room.

Inkar stopped and folded her arms. "Well, where's your room?"

Ten minutes later, I was naked, face down on the bed, and hollering as Inkar gave me an excruciating body massage.

"Shut up, girl," Inkar said as she squeezed a knot in the fleshy part of my shoulder until it dissolved. She moved another knot up my neck. "Tell me if pain resonates into your head," she instructed. "That would be dangerous." I was in so much pain that I didn't know how I would tell.

"You don't want to be griot, eh?" she asked.

"What?" Embarrassment crept over me. Did the whole village know about my failed escape?

"You heard me. I feel your stress and worry all around your spine, neck, and shoulders. Don't you know any anger or anxiety you feel will be transferred to your cells? You're holding all your resentment in your body. A very unsafe thing to do. And, your fifth chakra is blocked."

"What?"

"I know you know about chakras."

"I do."

"Your fifth chakra, your vishuddha, is blocked."

I gritted my teeth as she shook a knot out of my neck until it burst. I don't know if it was my imagination or not, but I could have sworn I heard that knot pop. I squeezed my fist, digging my nails into my palms. I prayed that she would stop soon.

"Can you clear my chakra?"

"I want you to clear it," she answered.

"How?"

"Talk. Speak your mind."

"That's it?"

"Is it easy for you to speak your mind?"

It wasn't easy. It was damn near impossible. Keeping my feelings within was easy. I lowered my face into the pillow.

Inkar continued to knead my flesh. "Your body aches when you are anxious. You'll reap that worry in disease, emotional imbalance, and pain."

That would explain my stomach spasms and headaches. "I always worry," I confessed.

"My hands can tell."

"How do I stop?" I felt silly for asking, but I yearned to know. I hated the way fear and depression gripped my life. My meditation and my Zaige stretches had not lessened the heaviness I carried.

"Let life happen and trust the ancestors."

Inkar spoke the words with ease, as if it were the simplest thing in the world to do. She had spoken the same words my father and Sahel had, the same words that were spoken in every religion that I had studied in school. Let life happen. Yet that was the most difficult thing to do.

"No matter how bad things become, say, 'things will always end up okay.'" Then she administered a relaxing massage that didn't make me grit my teeth. She moved energy through my hands, thighs, calves, and out of my body by way of my feet.

I wasn't sure if I believed things would always end up okay. Being a part of the Griothood would not be okay. Not marrying Sahel would never be okay. I wanted to tell Inkar and the griot that the ancestors had chosen the wrong successor. But no one gave a damn.

"Damn it. You even have knots in your feet." She clucked her tongue and laughed.

For the first time since I found out I would be griot, I laughed.

I felt light on my feet afterward. As advised, I drank mint water to flush out the toxins that had been released during the massage. Shockingly, my muscles were not the least bit sore, and my mood had lifted.

"You look refreshed," the griot said with a grin after the twins had gone. She looked rejuvenated too as we sipped water at her table.

A soft smile crossed my lips. "I guess I should thank you."

"No." Her face straightened. "Don't say thank you if you do not mean it," her words were clipped.

I looked down. The euphoric feeling had passed.

She said, "Go ahead. Get it off your chest." She pushed up the sleeves of her black djellaba. "You don't want to be here. You have no respect for the ancestors and for what they said is right."

"How do I know that it was the ancestors who chose me and not just you trying to ruin my life?"

"Your life!" she snapped. "You think I picked you out of a crowd and said let me mess up her life?"

"Yes!" I shouted. "I was going to marry Sahel in a couple months. Now, what? Do you even know anything about me? Do you even know that I am the farthest person from a griot in this village?" I pointed my finger at her. My temperature had risen, and my body quaked. Would Inkar be happy? I was speaking my truth.

She narrowed her eyes and took two steps closer to me. I shut my mouth and stepped back, eyes wide. Her eyes cut through me. I looked away, bending into myself.

"I will be respected. So will the ancestors." Her tone was low. "You won't know love, Young Griot, until you sacrifice everything for this kingdom. Now as far as me knowing you..." she looked me up and down with contempt, "you are the next griot of Obsidian. Once you see that you are worthy, no one will stop you."

Her words chilled me.

"Now grab a basket, we have to tend to the garden and the chickens. We have to make incense, too. Then, we must prepare for your big day."

CHAPTER 10

I stirred all night. Earlier that afternoon, the griot had given me a rundown of the colossal events that awaited me the next morning. As we picked ripened tomatoes and yams and cleaned the pulp from gourds, she told me that the formal naming of the griot was a big event. People were already traveling from the other cities in Za to meet me. Me. The idea made my stomach upset and my shoulders heavy with burden. Even the king, queen, and prince were coming from Noire to meet me. The royal family was coming all this way to be disappointed. The Griothood would be here, too, sizing me up, testing me. I knew nothing about storytelling, I couldn't articulate the history of my people, and I hadn't done one bit of griot training yet. Right now, I could barely remember my name. All I'd been was the griot's servant. For the first time, I wished she'd teach me something so I wouldn't fall flat on my face in front of all of these expectant people. But that was probably what she wanted. She had a streak of evil in her specially reserved for me.

When I awoke the next morning, the sunlight was soft, and the griot's house was alive with voices and movement.

My door was open and lying on the bed beside me was a bright orange fabric. I got out of bed and looked out into the hall. Someone I'd never met hurried past my room. The stunning woman with long braids ignored me. I stepped back into the room and placed my hand on my chest. What was happening?

"Oh, good morning," the griot said as she walked past my door, headed the same way the stranger went.

"What's going on?" I whispered, my eyes round.

She stopped and looked back at me with a smirk. "Didn't I tell you today was a huge day for you?"

"Who are the people out there?"

"The elder women, the griots," she said nonchalantly.

My breath caught in my throat.

"Are you okay?" Her eyes registered concern. "Zen?" She came closer.

My calves bumped into the bed, and I sat. I struggled to catch my breath. My chest tightened, making me even more afraid. I was breathing too fast. My heart raced.

"Zora, get me some water, fast!" the griot shouted. Her hand was on my shoulder. She looked as scared as I felt. "Calm down, Zen."

Soon, the griot was holding water to my lips. I shoved it away, and the gourd hit the ground.

"Tell Mansi to get Bachwezi." She wrapped her hands around my forearm. "Calm down, Zen." Her voice quivered.

The room shrank. My chest heaved, but no quality air came to me. There were now so many faces in my room, but I could not focus on them. I was dying.

It felt like forever before I heard my father's voice.

"Where is she?" He sounded frantic. I looked up and saw four faces staring at me. That did nothing to soothe me. Finally, my father's face emerged. The griot led him to me, and he fell to his knees in front of me. I threw my arms around him.

He pulled back and reached up and placed his fingers on my wet face. "Leave us be," he demanded and everyone left the room. "Zen, calm yourself."

I couldn't. My throat ached.

"Calm. Breathe like me. Slow." My father breathed with exaggeration. He put his hands on my shoulders. "Slow," he repeated. "That's right. Everything is fine. Everything is fine."

For a minute, I fought to control my breathing. He put his fingertips on my neck to check my pulse. When he was satisfied, he kissed my palms.

"I can't do this," I croaked. My face was wet with tears and snot.

He waved his hands. "Shhh. You are fine, Zen. Don't worry about anything. Bring some water," he called. I saw that in all of the commotion the previous gourd had cracked.

Just then, the griot came and placed a different gourd into his hands. Although he couldn't see her, she gave Father a look that I couldn't decipher. Then she left the room, closing the door behind her. I knew she saw that she had made an awful mistake. To my surprise, the idea of her being disappointed in me stabbed my heart. I didn't understand why I cared.

"For thousands of years," Father spoke evenly, "two people have always come together at the perfect moment, and from that union came a child. That child was nurtured, and he or she grew up and paired with another bringing forth a new life. And so it happened, perfected and ordained by the gods again and again. People were always placed in the perfect place at the perfect time. Many things could've killed these people or sent them in other directions, but everything happened just how the gods planned it. And now, here you are, Zen, divinely placed here in Za. The gods didn't make any mistakes. You being chosen as griot, you being in this room, those people waiting to put their eyes on your face and behold you is no mistake." My father shook as he spoke. "Your fear is a slap in the face to the gods and the ancestors who guide you on your journey."

I closed my eyes and tried to internalize his words, to make myself know these things spiritually. I knew what my father said was my truth, but knowing and walking in that truth were not the same. The gods made no mistakes.

"Now, who are you?" Father said with a hint of his teeth showing.

I exhaled. "I am Zen."

"And?" he beckoned.

"I am Zen, and I am a piece of the gods." It was what father used to make me say every night before bed when I was a little girl. It had been years since I'd uttered the phrase.

"And the peace of the gods is always within you if you calm yourself, breathe slowly, and listen." We hugged for a while before he slowly rose to his feet. He moved like he was much older than thirty-seven. Bush life aged you fast. Living to be sixty was rare, so he maybe had twenty years of life left. "Are you okay?"

"Yes," I said softly, but I was unsure.

"Good. Now do what the Divine sent you on this planet to do. Head up, smile. Make all the girls in your set envious."

"That's not nice, Father," I laughed, wiping my eyes.

"I am not perfect." He shrugged, grinning proudly.

I stood and hugged him again then led him to the door.

"Your initiate is ready," he announced proudly when we entered the common room.

CHAPTER 11

I took a warm shower and washed my hair with black soap. In the solitude of my bedroom, the griot put melaleuca oil on every part of my scalp, opening my pores; she then rubbed olive oil and shea butter on my damp strands. It felt wrong for her to touch me, but she had soothing hands. To my surprise, she was gentle enough to slip the comb through my tangled and densely packed kinks without snapping off my ends. She then pulled up my hair into a puff at the back of my head.

The griot exited, and Subira, the blacksmith's wife, entered. She kneaded shea butter over my naked body and face as she hummed. She rubbed rosemary over me, sweetening my scent. It felt awkward to be touched so intimately, but having such attentive care made me feel like royalty. Inkar entered and arched my brows with a razor. I held perfectly still, afraid that she would slice my skin. I'd never had my brows shaped, but she said it would change my life.

Once the women were finished grooming me, the griot returned and held up the garment that had been on my bed.

It was a piercing burnt orange like the setting sun. My mouth parted slightly. I slowly shook my head. Something so stunning, with dye so rich, and fabric so expensive would be worn on my body?

"Are you ready?" she asked. I could feel pride rising from her skin. Perhaps I'd been wrong about her wanting to sabotage me.

I inhaled and let out a shaky breath. I stood, lifting my arms as she wrapped the stunning material around me. "This cloth," she said as she worked, "is from Noire. Skilled artisans have been working on it for months."

I mouthed, "Wow," as I imagined their fingers weaving the soft material and dying it repeatedly until it was perfect. Months. I silently thanked them for their time, patience, and remarkable work.

My smooth back that shined with oil and shea butter remained bare as she tied the garment around my neck.

"Is it comfortable?" she asked, rustling the fabric so it fell just how she wanted it.

"Very," I answered, twisting so the flowing material could brush against my skin.

She went to the wardrobe and pulled out an intricate beaded headpiece. "This, too, is from Noire."

"Oh," I gasped. I had never seen such beautiful beadwork from Za, only the astounding skill of the Ndebele compared.

"Is it not the most amazing piece you have ever laid eyes on?" She shook her head. The beauty of the headpiece amazed her, too.

I nodded as tears clouded my eyes. I blinked until they dissolved. What the hell was wrong with me? I knelt so that she could place it on my head.

The makers had created combs to hold the headpiece into place. One long, beaded strand with a copper coin hung down between my brows.

"What is the coin?" I asked.

"A small part of our ancestors. They called it a penny, I believe," she said. I wanted to ask her more about the penny, like who was the man on it, but I doubted that she knew. She added more pins to my head. Queenie stepped back. "You are gorgeous." Her hand was over her mouth, and her eyes were glossy. I felt my chest swell. I felt gorgeous. She pointed to the mirror.

I couldn't believe what I saw when I walked over. The only time I felt as stunning as I looked right now was when Sahel looked at me. My eyes moistened again. I forced him out of my mind while gazing at my deep brown skin and its smoothness. My thick lips had a glossy sheen. I puckered them. I knew the name would feel peculiar leaving my mouth, but I said, "Thanks, Queenie."

Inkar was right. The shaping of my brows did enhance my features. My shaped brows revitalized my whole face and drew attention to my eyes. Sahel had once said my eyes were intense and could wear any man down. Today, I saw that intensity in my eyes, also. I twisted my head from side to side, scrutinizing my pointy nose. It wasn't so bad.

"One last thing," the griot said. From under the bed, she pulled out leather sandals. "Sit."

I sat on the bed. She placed the sandals beneath my feet and then slid them on. The leather ties were complex, and they went all the way to my mid calf. The shoes had been designed with care and passion. They were the perfect size, made with precision and especially for my long and narrow feet.

"You are now ready to meet your village as the griot initiate." Queenie's voice shook. She was working hard to contain her excitement.

The drums were beating in a voracious pattern as we approached the gates, and my heart beat with the same force. I was in a procession behind the griot and the eleven elder women flanked me as if they were protecting me. The closer I got to the meeting space, the more nervous I became as the importance of this moment settled in. Was Abebi seeing this? She had to be envious of me right now. That would be a first.

Those villagers who hadn't yet made it to the Harambe circle stopped and gawked at me. I wanted to disappear. They were wearing their very best garments for my big day. I could see in their eyes that they were proud. I did not deserve this attention. I was the same ignored girl I had been before I was named as the next griot. I saw Zul, and surprisingly he smiled at me. I figured he'd probably hated Sahel and I for involving him in our botched escape attempt but I guess I was wrong. I smiled back.

The scent of the food that had been cooking in every home made me sick. It was then that I realized I hadn't eaten. My heart was beating an off-kilter rhythm. Please don't let me have another attack in front of all these people. Do not panic.

As we approached the circle, everyone stood. The griot and the elders began to sing a call and response song that I had never heard before. The elders left my side, and having no clue what to do, I continued following Queenie. She stopped, and we stood for all to see. I was her shadow, her apprentice, but soon, I would eclipse her. The idea knotted my intestines.

Yalee gave his cadence for the drummers to cease, and suddenly, a high-pitched voice began to sing yet another song that I was unfamiliar with. I didn't know the singer, either. The woman in beautiful foreign silks stood next to the drummers as a man beside her accompanied her on the flute. No one dressed that fancy here.

I looked over Queenie's shoulder, and two women came forth slowly and deliberately. One was older, bald, and had a slight limp. The other was probably a few years older than me and had long thin braids, some of which fell over her shoulder. I remembered them being in the room when I had my attack. The one with the braids had walked passed my room this morning. Once the women made it to Queenie, all three connected their hands, forming a triangle. Queenie whispered into the older woman's ear. The older woman nodded and then whispered into the younger woman's ear. She nodded and said something back to Queenie. What was this? I stood back, not knowing what to do as I watched.

Their triangle broke, and Queenie turned to me. The singing halted at once.

"Griothood," she said to the women beside her, yet she was loud enough for the crowd to hear. "I present to you our newest griot initiate, Zen Akke."

I stopped breathing, my stomach contracted as the crowd cheered. This was the Griothood, the griots of Ankara and Noire. I curtsied, and they gave a subtle nod, their faces stony and unwavering. Intimidation swept over me. Damn. They saw me have a breakdown. I felt quite pathetic.

Quietly, Queenie put her hand on the shoulder of the older woman with the weather beaten face. "This is Nok, Griot of Ankara." Then she touched the shoulder of the younger woman. "This is Zora, Griot of Noire."

Should I shake their hands? Should I say something? Why didn't know the proper protocol? I simply bowed; then the two women walked over to me and embraced me.

From the other side of the large circle, a man with a large drum attached to his body with a leather strap began a slow beat. Everyone looked at him. There were excited whispers in the crowd. The energy caught and spread like fire in the bush. I heard repeated shouts saying, "The king!"

I let out an audible breath. I looked at my hands and

willed them to stop trembling. The energy of the crowd heightened even more. The king, Akonos, our beloved ruler, was in Obsidian.

Then I saw a woman sweeping the ground with what looked like the tail of a horse. She had on an emerald green silk gown. Behind her was a man walking tall and proud in his regalia. His massive frame showed that he had not missed a meal, but his weight was all solidified. This man looked like he could go head to head with an ox and be triumphant. He was our king, mighty, and confident. A deity walking on earth. A long procession followed him around the inner circle. The Obsidians were in awe of him. They jumped and clapped hysterically and reached out for his hand.

The robe draped over his shoulder and bare chest was sky blue with a golden geometric pattern. His waist was swathed in a matching kanga. King Akonos' head swiveled from side to side, flicking his flywhisk as he nodding with paternal pride to his people. On each of his fingers sat a large gold ring. He graciously shook several hands. The chief rushed to him and bowed reverently, then shook his hand.

Once I came to my senses, it struck me once again that the king had come all the way from Noire to see me. Zen. In my lifetime, he may have set foot in Obsidian five times. It was the chief's job to run Obsidian and keep the king abreast of all that was happening, either through visits or letters sent by runners. How do I live up to what I had been called to do? What the hell had I been called to do? Why was telling stories so important? Everyone told stories; that's how we entertained each other. What made a griot so damn important?

The sweeping woman made her way to me and stopped when the drumming ceased. She stood tall. I hoped I looked as strong as she did. Her jet-black skin was smooth, and her smile radiant. She looked me in the eyes. "Good morning, Young Griot." She curtsied. "I would like to present to you—" Her projected voice echoed off the buildings, "the third King of Za...the third King of the Diganda Dynasty...King Akonos."

I stopped breathing as the beaming king approached me. I curtsied low and was slow to rise. When I rose, the king bowed to me. My eyes widened. He bowed...to me.

King Akonos took my hand. My hands were swallowed in both of his calloused hands. "I am so glad to meet you." His eyes said he actually meant it. "I hope to speak with you after the ceremony."

"Yes, Sire," I said; my voice was surprisingly strong.

He turned and then held out his arm. "My illustrious wife, Queen Finda."

The stunning woman stepped forward with a brilliantly white smile and waved to the people in the crowd. She was the most beautiful creature I'd ever seen. She didn't even seem to be of this world. The way she swayed her body with every step and smiled with fake demure let me know that she had no doubt of her own beauty. But as captivating as she was, I couldn't focus on her. I had caught a glimpse of the striking young man standing behind her, and he captured my attention.

All of Obsidian cheered loud enough to burst eardrums. The queen was from right here in Obsidian. Of course, it was something that was spoken of frequently and with great pride, but with all of the chaos, it hadn't occurred to me that she was coming home. This was probably her first time back since becoming queen almost two decades ago. What a dream, to leave this small village and rule the entire kingdom.

The queen approached me, smiling. I forced my attention back to her. She, too, took my hand and cuffed it.

"Beautiful to meet you, Young Griot."

"Thank you," I said breathlessly.

When the queen let my hand go, the king stuck his chest

out. "I would love for you to meet the one next in line for the throne, the one who will be the fourth king in the Diganda Dynasty, my son who is stronger than ten simbas, the one who will make this kingdom even greater than I have, Prince Zaire." Obsidian went crazy yet again. I felt faint as the man who had held my gaze just moments before was introduced. The tall, muscular young man came forth, and I beheld the most striking man I had ever laid eyes on. Thank the gods, I thought.

Once I realized that my mouth was ajar, I closed it and smiled bashfully at him.

The crowd continued to roar, but he paid them no attention. It was as if I held him rapt, also. The way he looked at me made my temperature rise dangerously. Prince Zaire's brown eyes pierced through me and burrowed through to my soul. I couldn't help but look away. He stood almost a foot taller than me. The frankincense aroma rising from his brown skin was just as seductive as his beauty. He wore no covering on the top of his body, and his chest bulged. His stomach was tight and rippled. My eyes traced a vein that ran over his left breast. I felt feverish.

The prince took my hand and lifted it to his soft lips. His complexion was clear and perfect, only hidden by a perfectly trimmed beard and mustache. I stared at the crown of his head; his hair was cut low and precise. Unlike his father's, the prince's hands were soft and smooth. It was embarrassing to have him caress my rough hands that had known labor every day of my life. His well-groomed beard rubbed the back of my hand. I forced myself to look him in the eye, and my yoni awoke.

He stood straight, and with a thoughtful gaze, he slowly said, "Congratulations, Young Griot." The bass in his voice was inebriating and alluring.

I could only nod as I watched his broad muscular back and defined shoulder blades move away from me.

CHAPTER 12

The ceremony held in my honor was spectacular. The children in Soweto's set sang to me with their shrill voices. They were so adorable with their shiny faces. The little ones brought tears to my eyes for many reasons, one being that I would never hear my own child sing. I felt uncomfortable when my set danced for me, but I plastered on a smile. It felt wrong that they should dance for me like I was royalty. They barely even liked me. What was worse, there was something off in Abebi's spirit. She didn't smile as she danced; she just went through the motions. Afterward, she looked bored every time I glanced at her. She'd rather be anywhere but at my naming ceremony. I couldn't blame her. I wasn't worthy to be called a griot. I hadn't spoken to her since the night I tried to run away. I wondered if she'd heard. I imagined Abebi laughing at what had transpired on that night. I swallowed my shame and returned my eyes to my best friend and wondered if someone had proposed to her yet. It occurred to me that today she could meet a man from Noire or Ankara, though I knew how much she loved Noire and loathed Ankara's primitiveness. She would never move to Ankara, no matter who her suitor was. A strange realization came over me. I wanted her to move away. There was heavy resentment in my soul when it came to her. Guilt rushed over me, but I was sick of being in Abebi's shadow.

When the warriors performed, my pride for Obsidian swelled. Again we gathered around the Harambe circle. This time, however, I sat amongst the elders. I beamed, knowing the king would never forget the performance by the tough and stalwart men who protected Obsidian and Za. The warriors did the infamous Heathen Dance that terrified children and adults alike.

The Heathen Dance began with two male actors in war regalia. They wrestled with intensity as if they were in warrior training. The musicians slapped their drums for added effect. Ever so slowly, the dreaded heathen monster appeared and roused the audience. In reality, every child and adult feared the monsters that lived in the forbidden White Mountains. It was believed that if any of the Zaian cities strayed from the carefully laid rules that the ancestors set, the heathens would return to Za and ravish each city, taking all of our lives. The rules that our ancestors set forth were simple enough to obey: no outsiders, all rapists would be exiled, all homosexuals would be exiled, everyone worked for the good of the kingdom, all lazy people would be exiled, all murderers would be murdered, and all had to stay away from the White Mountains. The crowd shouted for the warriors to watch out, but true to their art, they could not hear the warnings.

The warrior who portrayed the heathen monster wore a white wooden mask, created by my father, with gnashing teeth and bulging eyes. The beast was formidable with its long white fur (painted savanna grass), three horns on the top of its head, and long claws that nearly grazed the ground. Yalee drummed slowly, and the monster moved one step per beat, and with every step, the beast's head snapped to a gruesome angle. Every time the heathen came near the audience, people shrieked and backed away. Little ones clung to their mothers, screaming in terror, yet no one allowed their child to look away. This dance was a tale woven by the first griots, and it was the highest warning. Follow the law, or else.

The skin around my knuckles stretched as I gripped the handles of my chair. No matter how many times I witnessed it, I always detested this part. I saw that tension in the king's face, as well. Even Prince Zaire, who I hadn't stop peeking at, was gripped with expectancy. His muscular thighs were gapped, and his hand rested on his knee as he leaned forward and looked on, pensively. The heathen stepped closer to the wrestling men. There was a net in his hands, and the drummers hit their drums with deafening bangs. The heathen cast his net over the unsuspecting warriors, and they tried desperately to fight their way out. The heathen unhooked his whip from his belt and whipped the warriors. Crack. The sound of the whip jolted the crowd. It was a horrid noise. The warriors screamed in agony. A woman, an actress, stumbled into the middle of the circle with a basket of vegetables balanced on her head. She squealed when she saw the white monster and attempted to run away, dropping basket, but the beast grabbed her with his arms and laid on top of her as she screamed once more. From beneath the net that trapped them, the warriors reached for her hopelessly. They had failed to protect the woman. That was the ultimate job of a man. The audience watched open-mouthed and their heads shook in distaste. The adults knew that the woman had been raped, and the children would figure it out as they grew older.

Five warriors with long spears and leather shields snuck up on the beast. The crowd grew agitated again. The men moved closer and without being detected, they pierced the monster several times until he rolled off of the woman. But it was too late. She had perished. The men wept, and the performance was over. Immediately, all of the warriors joined together and performed the Terror Dance. They moved their feet rapidly. Everyone, including the royal family, danced with gratitude, for our ancestors had slain the heathen. In our minds, however, was the constant threat that the beasts would return. That's why we always had to please the gods.

Once the ceremony concluded, everyone feasted and fellowshipped. I tried to eat, but the interruptions wouldn't allow it. Every person came over and congratulated me...except Abebi.

At the large circular table, the griots sat to my right and my father sat to my left. I had never seen him smile so hard. I was sure that his face was aching. Facing me was the royal family. I had to fight not to stare at the prince, but it was impossible. He was amazing to observe, his stature perfect, and his grin seductive. Why would the gods give so much beauty and power to one man? There wasn't a woman who wouldn't be weakened in his presence. The prince was the same age as Sahel, but Sahel was still a boy to me, and the prince was a man. I wanted to know what made him so different.

Soweto ran up to me with a wide smile. I told her how well she sang as I hugged her little body. When she ran away, I saw the prince laughing at something Abebi said. Where the hell had she come from? She'd changed from her usual dance garb to a patterned dress that accentuated her curvy hips. This morning, I'd felt like the loveliest girl in Za. Now I was a distant second. Her shaved head shined, and all of her white teeth showed when she giggled. I felt as if my heart had been gripped with a metal fist. She spoke to him with such ease. Abebi never questioned her importance. It was nothing for her to walk up to Prince Zaire and charm him, while I could barely look him in the eyes.

I closed my eyes and inhaled. What are you feeling, Zen? I asked myself. You don't even know him. Of course, he would fall for Abebi. Who wouldn't? Abebi touched his shoulder and snickered dramatically, and the prince looked as if he'd been seduced by her cat eyes. I frowned. What if she became the princess? Fury and envy consumed me.

Just as I tore my eyes from the prince and Abebi, Queenie leaned over to me and whispered that the king was ready to speak to me.

My eyes widened as I looked where the king had been sitting. I'd been so consumed with jealousy that I didn't see him leave. "What do I say?" I cried.

"Just listen and answer any questions he has." She acted as if it was all so simple, but this man was our ruler. He spent his days talking to the most important people in our village, and I was just a simple village girl.

I glanced back at the prince and Abebi. Her eyes met mine, and her lips curled in delight. It was as if she was saying, "I saw how you looked at him, but let me show you what he really likes." Feeling dejected, I stood, and Queenie led me to the Elders' Mound.

I entered the sanctum for the first time in my life. I used to always speculate about what the sacred mound looked like and what mystical rituals went on inside. Now, I would find out.

An idol for each of Za's deities—Qwei, Sibo, Yemi, Ayeki, and Khan—hung on the inner walls of the mound. The king was already seated on a high-backed chair in the center of the room that glowed with light from the oil lamps and candles.

I approached him with apprehension.

King Akonos rose and held out his hands. "Zen," he said cheerily.

Nervously, I gave him my hands, and he gently squeezed. He motioned me to sit in a chair that faced his.

"How did you like the ceremony?" he asked as he sat.

"It was perfect," I said touching my chest. "I hope it was to your liking?"

He shook his head in agreement. "Obsidian's warriors perform the Heathen Dance the best."

I felt his sincerity.

King Akonos took a deep breath and asked, "Do you know the meaning of the Heathen Dance?"

"It shows the prowess of our warriors, how they can protect us from any earthly being. It also shows that our ancestors overcame the heathen monster, which is why we're here today." The smoothness of my words surprised me. Something about the king made me feel so comfortable in his presence.

He nodded in approval. "Yes, but there is more to that dance."

My brows furrowed. "Yes. It is a warning to our people to continue to please the gods."

He took a deep breath before saying, "Yes. But there is more. The safari you will take with the Griothood will transform your entire life."

What safari?

"Your understanding of Za will evolve. The safari is the first part and perhaps the most important piece of your initiation."

I wondered where I was going and for how long—and when the hell was Queenie going to mention this safari to me?

"I know I do not have to express to you that you should take this journey seriously. You must keep every word a secret. In the coming week, you will learn things that even I do not know."

I squinted. How could the king not know everything about his kingdom?

King Akonos read my expression, perhaps. "It is the way Father Malcolm planned it in 2014, and it will remain that way forever.

How Father Malcolm planned it? Father Malcolm had brought clean running water to Za. It was an important development, but what did he have to do with this safari, and why did he want things kept from the kings of Za? When Father Malcolm was alive, there was only Noire. Therefore, there was no need for a king. I didn't understand what King Akonos was trying to convey.

"Work hard, Zen, use your mind well, and protect our kingdom."

"Yes, Sire," I replied although I didn't know what my task was. I only knew that I couldn't do it.

"There's one more thing." Suddenly, his expression grew troubled. In an instant, he seemed to age. The energy in the room had been peaceful and calm. Now, it turned grave and heavy. In a somber voice, he said, "There is a quiet rebellion underway."

I stopped breathing.

"Zen, this rebellion will not remain quiet." His voice wavered. He scooted forward in his chair, leaning closer to me. The fear radiating from his body was unsettling.

I stiffened. "Our people?" I gasped.

"Unfortunately."

I couldn't believe it. In Za, every person had everything they needed. What could anyone be unhappy about? Everyone ate. No one was oppressed, or were they? It was then that I realized that I or the griots not being able to marry was oppression. Not being able to choose what I wanted to be in life was oppression. I wasn't happy and perhaps others weren't either. My soul became agitated.

The king broke into my thoughts. "When your griot told me that she was stepping down at the end of the next rainy season, I was saddened, frightened even. However, I also saw your appointment as an opportunity. Your youth will be beneficial to us. I think you can help me fight these rebels."

I shook my head incredulously. More pressure from people who had no clue how weak I was. "How?" I scoffed.

"Well, I am assuming this rebellion is with the younger Zaians. You are young, only seventeen. I need you to become one with the young people and find out what they are saying. Why are they unhappy, and who is in this rebel group? Most importantly, I need the leader." His sadness had transformed into bitterness.

I swallowed at the thought of the rebellion's leader being executed. Would the king do that? I wondered if the rebels wanted to completely overthrow King Akonos. I wanted to tell him that he had the wrong person. I barely spoke to my peers. They never told me secrets, and they definitely wouldn't now that I was in line to be the griot. I would never be able to infiltrate a group of rebels. All I could say, though, was "Yes, Sire." I prayed that the rebellion would die down before he needed me.

The king sighed before reaching out for my hands again. I placed my hands in his. "May the gods continue to bestow blessings on you, Zen." He stood. "I have had a long journey, and I should rest."

I stood and bowed my head as he exited. I saw the toll the rebellion was having on him, and my anxiety peaked. What if the rebels succeeded in whatever they wanted? What if our kingdom fell? The charge was now on me to protect us?

I did the only thing I knew to do in such a heavy situation. I sat on the floor and centered myself with meditation. It took a while for me to reach that space of nothingness, but finally, I was there and felt nothing. The sacred mound had a cool and calming effect.

When I opened my eyes, I screamed. Three bored faces

were before me. One was my griot, Queenie, and the other faces belonged to Nok and Zora.

"My goodness, you meditate like a monk," Zora stated with a snort. "She didn't even hear us enter," she said to the others. I didn't like her condescending tone.

My eyes moved back and forth between each griot. Zora and Queenie sat on the floor with ease. Nok pulled over the chair I had sat in earlier and took a seat. We formed a small circle.

"How does it feel to have the whole kingdom dying to be in your presence?" Zora asked dryly. She really didn't care. I understood her attitude. I was taking her place as the youngest griot.

"Okay," I said.

"Just okay!" Zora exclaimed. "I was floating all day."

"Not everyone lives for attention," Nok said in a raspy voice.

"Oh, shut up," Zora said, playfully slapping Nok's led. Nok laughed with her abrasively dry vocal cords.

"You're not the baby anymore," Queenie said to her.

"Good," Zora said, playing with the tips of her long braids. "Now maybe everyone can stay out of my damn business."

"Fat chance," Nok laughed.

They all snapped their eyes to me. I jumped. They were witches speaking a silent language. I could tell they enjoyed frightening me. The three were sinister together, and I wanted out of the dimly lit mound.

Nok asked, "Are you ready to take the position of Griot?" Her words were direct.

I inhaled. No, would have been the truth. But regretfully, I had no choice but to be ready. How could I disappoint the king after what he confided in me? For some reason, he believed in me. I'd always been loyal to him, but now even more. I swallowed and said, "Yes. I am."

Queenie tried to suppress a smirk before she said, "Tonight, at dusk, you will embark on the griot's safari."

All I could think was, Oh God, no sleep. I was already functioning on a few hours of sleep as it was.

Seamlessly, Zora added, "You will embark on a journey of truth. You will learn—in just six days if we're fortunate—a truth that will knock your world off its axis. You'll find out some secrets about our people that will destroy all you thought you knew."

I took a deep breath. What were these secrets?

Nok said, "The secrets that you learn will go to your grave with your flesh and bones." She was silent for a beat. "Do you understand?" she asked, glowering at me.

"Yes, I understand." My words spewed from my mouth. Why were they so aggressive? My arms were wrapped around my body as if I was cold.

Queenie said, "Now, eat and hydrate yourself. The journey is long and treacherous. There is a strong possibility that we won't return. Hug your father and your friends."

My heart stopped.

Then Nok and Zora guffawed, clapping their hands in delight. I loosened up and gave a relieved laugh, too.

"No, she's serious," Zora snapped, tossing a braid behind her. The smile might as well have been smacked off of my face. My cheeks grew hot with embarrassment as I watched them rise. I rose, too, with a scowl on my face. Full of dread, I followed them out of the mound and into the blinding sun. I despised these women.

CHAPTER 13

The griots wouldn't allow me to sleep at all during the journey. Mansi, the strange man that had been lurking in the shadows of Queenie's home on the night I went to live with her, navigated the carriage along the dirt road that ran through the pitch black Serengeti. The ride was frightening, but not enough to keep me from falling asleep. Every time I nodded off, one of the women would kick or nudge me. Queenie said I must remember the way. The way to where? It looked like we were going nowhere at a very slow pace. And, it was pitch black. All I could tell was that we were headed south into Maasai Mara. Interesting. How could I possibly remember the way? I would've given anything to be in my own warm bed.

After two hours, Mansi stopped the carriage. He lifted his lantern and climbed down. Without a word, he opened the back of the carriage and helped us out.

I pulled the strap of my satchel over my head. It contained the two changes of clothing that I had been instructed to pack. I stretched my body and yawned as I watched my surroundings carefully for lions and cheetahs, but that was pointless. If I laid eyes on one of the big cats, it would already be too late.

"Here," Queenie said. She thrust a large sloshing clay jug of water and a bundle of blankets at me. I groaned. Carrying water was something I wasn't accustomed to. "Don't drop it. Our clean water is limited."

Zora carried two bags and a cage with two plump chickens. Queenie placed a folded cloth on her head and a bundle of bush wood on top of it. When Nok grabbed her cloth bag, I heard the clinking of tin pots. With her other hand, she reached in the wagon and pulled out a leather quiver full of sharp arrows and a wooden bow. If I didn't fear for my life, the image would've been comical. What was the old woman going to do with a bow?

Queenie said a few words to Mansi, and he nodded, but I detected a hint of worry in his eyes. She hugged him affectionately. Once she pulled back, she gave him a sad look and said to us, "Let's go."

I balanced the jug of water on my head. Already, my neck protested at its weight. I held the blankets close to my body.

We walked away from the carriage. I looked back at Mansi, and he just stood there watching us, or watching Queenie, with trepidation in his eyes. This unnerved me. I couldn't see far in the night, but I felt like there was nothing nearby. That probably meant we would be walking for some time. The more we distanced ourselves from Mansi, the more afraid I became.

Everyone froze when we heard the howling scream of hyenas. We waited in stiff stances. Nok dropped her bag and calmly pulled out an arrow. Her motions were smooth and her face at ease. She put the arrow on the bow and anchored the bow against her face. I knew right then that she knew what she was doing. The fact that she believed she needed it right now scared the shit out of me. Hyenas could and did kill humans, especially if they were starving. It was no doubt that they already knew we were there. Our fate depended on the hyenas caring that we were there, and if they were hungry. My biggest worry was whether there was a group of lionesses trailing them? I felt the urge to cry.

After pivoting around and listening carefully, Nok lowered the bow from her cheek. She placed her arrow back into her quiver. "It's fine. We have to move. I smell rain and my joints are starting to ache." We all let out a breath of relief and resumed our trek.

"Should Mansi have come with us?" I said, speaking for the first time. My voice was more high-pitched than normal.

"No," Zora whispered. "He can't know the way to the Grotto."

"The Grotto?" I asked.

"Yes. Grotto means cave," Zora replied.

We approached the foot of a mountain, and I froze.

"What's wrong?" Queenie asked.

I swallowed as the realization became clearer. "Are these the White Mountains?" My words quivered as they left my mouth.

The griots looked at each other.

"Very good, Zen. Yes," Queenie replied.

I stepped back, shaking violently.

"Zen." Queenie moved closer to me, the bush wood on her head perfectly balanced and her voice reassuring. "The White Mountains aren't what you believe. There are no monsters here."

I shook my head. Queenie was lying to me. This was some sort of initiation test.

"It's true," Nok chimed in. "There never were any monsters."

My eyes coated with tears. "That's not true," I said, my voice deep and throaty. "All my life I've known that the heathens lurked here, and they could come back to Za at any time."

"It was a lie," Queenie said in a soothing voice. "The ancestors made the legend up to keep the people from coming here."

"Why? Zaians don't travel to Maasai Mara."

"That's precisely why Father Malcolm put the Grotto here. There are secrets here that need to remain hidden. If someone comes up here and discovers these secrets, Za will collapse." Queenie shook as she spoke.

The waning moon highlighted the mountain range's silhouette. I'd never known fear like this in my life.

"Look, you can stay down here, or you can hike up with us," Zora said impatiently. "What's down here in the valley is far worse than anything up there." She marched to the trail, the chickens squawking as she handled their cage recklessly. Nok followed. Queenie looked back at me apologetically, then walked behind them, her hand on her bundle of wood.

I released a desperate sob, but there was no one here to rescue me. I gripped my idol and prayed to the gods that what these women were saying was true, that the thing the elders held over our heads was a lie to keep us in line. I hugged the blankets to my chest with one hand and put the other hand on the water jug, and I hurried after them.

We moved with care, especially as the ascent became steep and the gravel loose. The temperature in the highlands was much colder than I was used to and the higher we climbed, the stronger the wind gusted. Here and there were sprinkles of rain, so we pushed faster. After what felt like an hour into the hike, I doubled over in pain. There was a spasm in the side of my abdomen, and my feet were blistered. The water jug that had been on my head tumbled to the ground, but mercifully it didn't break. I was going to die of thirst and exhaustion, and the sandals I wore for the ceremony were not for long treks. I hadn't hydrated myself as well as I thought. My mouth was scorched, and my tongue stuck to the roof of my mouth.

"Come on," Nok said grabbing my forearm, attempting to pull me to my feet. "I am three times your age and in way worse shape." I refused to stand, hoping that the incredibly durable griots would call for a break.

"Hold on," Queenie told Nok. She walked over to me, taking her load from her head. She removed a corked drinking gourd from her bag and lowered herself. Queenie placed the gourd to my lips, and it partially wet my arid pallet.

"Not too much now," she said in a maternal tone. Her lips were ashen. She needed water, too. After I drank, so did she and the others.

"How much farther?" I asked, breathing hard as the rain fell steadily.

"Please," Zora quipped. "We walked it when it was our time, too. No more complaining," she commanded. "I hope you remember the way. We can never draw a map to the Grotto."

Her coldness cut deep. I took a deep breath, and I stood and resettled the jug on my head. No, I did not remember the way. I trailed behind Nok and Queenie, and Zora followed.

As we hiked, my mind jumped to the heathens, to the predators that loved high places, and to Nok. In Obsidian, only a few skilled men carried bows and arrows. Outside of books of great women warriors of the past, I'd never seen a woman with a bow. I thought about her perpetual limp and how it hadn't slowed her down on this hike.

Earlier, when I first heard about this safari, part of me had been excited. Now, I saw that this was a suicide mission. Perhaps it wasn't meant to kill me, but it was meant to injure me physically and break me mentally. With every step, I prayed that the gods would keep their creatures sleeping or at bay. Every foreign sound and animal cry made me stiffen as I imagined being stalked by a four-legged creature. At any moment, a venomous Puff Adler could insert its deadly fangs into our uncovered feet. There was no coming back from the snake's bite, especially without the root twins.

Abruptly, Nok stopped and observed our surroundings. Her body tensed, and everyone watched her with wide eyes, preparing to run if need be. Had she heard something?

"Are we lost?" Zora whispered.

I narrowed my eyes. She'd just said I had better remember the way. She didn't know the way, either.

"No," Nok snapped, but her deep breathing and rapid head turning said otherwise. Queenie looked around, too. She didn't know the way, either. What if we'd come all this way for nothing? What if we never found our way back to Mansi? My frustration and my fear mounted. I wondered how many times these women had been here?

Finally, Nok's coarse voice stated, "We're here." A smile slowly spread across her dry lips.

The other two women chuckled in relief. A grateful tear sprang from my eye.

Two minutes later, the Griothood stood before me, their eyes on me. We'd dropped our bags and bundles on the barely-there trail, breathing laboriously and shivering from the cold wind. Thank the gods it was not raining hard. The ladies and I stood at the mouth of a pitch-black cave.

"Are you ready to enter the Griot's Grotto?" Zora's voice echoed. There was a proud smile on her face. Now it was her chance to make the revelation that was made to her a few years before.

Hell yes, I wanted to say. Instead, I gave a casual, "Yes."

From her satchel, Queenie pulled out something wrapped

carefully with a black cloth. Nok held up her lantern, allowing light to pour over the object. With care, Queenie removed the cloth, revealing a brown book bounded with cracked leather. I didn't know what the book was, but the way the griots stared at it reverently told me it was significant.

"This," Queenie said bombastically, "is Father Malcolm's tome." With a hint of fear in her eyes, she handed the book to me.

I took it, feeling as if the whole world was in my hands. There was his name again. Father Malcolm was our most well known ancestor along with his wife, the mother of all the griots, Naemah. When my people broke away from the great Maasai clans due to near starvation brought on by the government's efforts to assimilate us, Father Malcolm brought fresh running water to Noire. Over two hundred years ago, he saved countless lives from disease, famine, and thirst. The life of the Zaian woman was transformed, as well. She no longer had to roam the dangerous bush for hours searching for clean water every day. I was grateful for him, but I didn't see why reading a book about him was so damn important at this moment.

"What do you know about Father Malcolm?" Nok asked.

"That he brought fresh water to Za."

She nodded with a sly grin. "Well, he did so much more. He brought our people to Za. Zen, our whole history is a lie."

CHAPTER 14

I shook my head. "What?" That made no sense. First, the heathens were a lie, and now all of our beliefs about our existence were lies.

Nok turned around and shone the lantern inside the cave. She seemed to be checking that there were no creatures using it as their home. She turned back to me.

"Come inside." She pointed her head toward the cave.

As we entered, our lanterns exaggerated our shadows on the cave's walls. Other than a few sleepy bats hanging by their feet and droplets of water dripping from ancient stalactites, there was nothing there except a few boulders. No proof that a human had ever set foot in this cave. The cave was underwhelming and quite disappointing. They risked my life to bring me here? The griots could've given me this book in Queenie's common room.

With the bush wood, Zora lit a fire near the mouth of the cave. Queenie took some of the damp blankets I had been carrying and spread them over the four large boulders situated around the fire. We sat, happy to be off our feet. My body was sore all over. I needed Inkar's hands.

The griots talked amongst themselves for a few moments. I simply stared at the book, overwhelmingly afraid to open it. When there was a lull in the conversation, I asked, "What did you mean when you said Father Malcolm brought us here?"

Nok looked at Queenie, who nodded.

"Our people differ from most other Africans on this continent." Nok seemed to be thinking of the right words, which was surprising since she'd been telling tales the longest. "Our ancestors have a complicated saga. While our roots are here in Africa, our ancestors were stolen from all over this great and vast continent."

"Stolen?" I whispered.

She nodded. "Kidnapped. Snatched from their villages."

"By whom?"

Nok held up her aged hands. "By the English, Portuguese, Arabs, other Africans, and many others, but hold on. We will discuss all of that." She put her hands on her knees and continued. "After centuries of living in a world where we did not belong, Father Malcolm, a descendant of these stolen Africans decided to bring his people back to Africa. He created Noire with the hopes that it would grow into a great kingdom. He handpicked 200 African-American people to begin this great legacy."

I looked at all three women. They watched me as they warmed their hands in front of the fire. My lip twitched as I waited for the women to begin laughing...they didn't. "That's not true. We are derived from clans of the Maasai and the Samburu people. Our people have been in around the Serengeti for at least four hundred years.

"You are a scholar, Zen, and you know we are nothing like the Maasai or the Samburu," Queenie said, leveling with me.

I stared into the fire in disbelief. I went over all I knew about the people of the Serengeti—their rituals, their

107

customs, their clothing, their facial features, body statures, and their diets. Their one god Ngai was not our god. We were polytheistic. She was right. If we were of those people, why were the similarities so few? It had only been two centuries of separation, yet we'd developed into a completely different people. I could speak some words from the Maa language, but in our language, barely any Maa words existed. I massaged my temples and fought the urge to cry. How could I be so damn stupid? We spoke some Swahili. We borrowed some Sanskrit words, but mostly, we spoke English. I'd always wondered why. When I would ask, my teacher would just shrug and say the missionaries forced English on our people. How could I be so stupid? Tears filled my eyes, but I quickly wiped them away.

Queenie nodded. "Our ancestors come from all over this continent. We are a mixture of so many different people. That is why Za is so beau—"

"Why?" I cut her off. "If you're telling me the truth, why are Zaians being told lies?" My speech was rushed, and my voice rose in agitation.

"Calm yourself," Queenie warned, lifting her hand. "By the end of this safari, you will know the whole truth."

I gave her a sidelong glance as I stroked the book with my thumb.

"Father Malcolm began writing that journal shortly after he created Noire. The story ends on his deathbed," Nok offered as she poked at the fire with a stick. "At first, he probably started writing this for all to see where they'd come from, but as you will read, Father Malcolm realized he had to keep the past from the people. Now the griots are the only ones who can read his words."

Queenie added, "In that book and in this cave lie the secrets of our people, secrets that you must never set free, secrets that not even the king can know."

Looking around, I said, "There's nothing here."

Nok nodded to the others before grabbing her lantern, and without a word they helped her rise. After assisting her, all three silently walked to the back of the cave. Bewildered, I stood, too, and followed with the book in my hand.

We kept walking, and the cave's ceiling grew higher. Nok paused. Together, the three griots placed their palms on the cave wall and slid it aside. I stood there with my mouth parted. Then I looked down and saw the metal tracks that allowed the camouflaged wall to glide.

Where the false wall once stood was now a metal door with four keyholes positioned laterally. A long metal handle was to the left of the keyholes. I watched, wide-eyed as each griot pulled, from between her breast, a hemp cord necklace with a large metal key. First, Nok inserted her key, then Queenie, and finally Zora. They turned their keys in unison. Then Nok pushed up the handle, making a large thunk sound. Queenie and Zora dragged the heavy door open while Nok and I watched.

I strained to see what was on the other side of the door, but there was only darkness.

Queenie turned to me. Her shoulders heaved as she drew an exaggerated breath. "That tome," she pointed to the book in my hands "belongs in your safe-keeping until the next griot is to be initiated. When that time comes, you will rewrite it word for word and then burn this copy."

Nok lifted her lantern to a pad on the wall with numbers on it, and she pushed several buttons, which made beeping sounds. This stunned me. There was electricity in the cave— the only electricity in Za.

"Why burn the book?"

"The original book would have long ago fallen apart. That is why each new griot rewrites it. I rewrote it for you, and you will rewrite it for another. Can you be trusted?" she asked with hope burning in her eyes.

It was as if she truly needed me. My head was dizzy with confusion and wonder. My voice shook as I answered, "Yes, Griot, but why burn the book?"

Nok spoke up. "We don't want too many copies out there waiting for the wrong person to get their hands on it. We rewrite it because, over time, books fade and tear especially with how much we reference the tome. We can't afford to lose one word of this book.

I rewrapped the book in the black cloth and hid it inside of my satchel with care. Now that I understood the importance of this book, I was deathly afraid I would damage or lose it somehow. If I did, there would be no physical link to my people's hidden past.

"You first." Queenie motioned.

I took a deep breath, gathering my courage. I entered into this world of the past. Just hours ago, I was hyperventilating as I prepared to meet the king. Now, my knowledge would surpass his.

CHAPTER 15

My mouth hung agape as my eyes flitted around the room. At first, I couldn't see much with just my lantern, but when the others entered with their torches, I beheld something I'd never imagined. The room was a magnificent time capsule. Though far more advanced than anything in Za, the relics were all from almost two hundred years before. Placed on metal shelves were machines, some small enough to fit in the palm of my hand while others looked as if they weighed more than me. I yearned to know what these devices were used for. Did they still work? There was electricity here. After two hundred years, I doubted the machines worked. Why had Father Malcolm kept this equipment hidden here? Was there a reason the griots had access to them, or was this space simply storage or a museum of sorts? He had purposely denied us this technology in Za. Why? He thought simplicity was better. Why?

What intrigued me more were the numerous books, binders, and papers. I yearned to rifle through pages and take in everything I could about our ancestors.

"I know it's exciting, but we must rest ourselves," Queenie said with a proud grin. "The journey was long. We eat first and rest, then we conquer the task of unraveling your miseducation." It was as if I'd been starving and she let me lick a spoonful of food just to pull out of my reach.

"I'm ready now." My eyes had yet to leave the back bindings of the books. *Souls of Black Folk, The Klan, Their Eyes Were Watching God, Race Riots, The Peculiar Institution, From the Big House to the Ghetto.* What were these books?

The women chuckled.

Queenie said, "Trust me, we have plenty of time to take in everything you wish, but you must be of sound body and mind first."

I tore my eyes from the relics, and reached into my bag and stroked the cloth that wrapped Father Malcolm's tome again, as if making sure it was still there.

As we exited the reliquary, something bothered me. There were four keyholes, but the door opened with only three keys. "Is there a fourth key?"

"Presumably, there's a master key, but, if there is, we don't know what became of it," Nok said.

Nok sautéed dried goat meat, onions, and yams in a pan. My stomach grumbled when the scents hit me.

Nok's food became the best I'd ever tasted.

"What will Mansi eat?" I asked before stuffing my mouth.

Queenie laughed. "Don't worry about him. Nothing tastes better to him than wild game. In fact, we will be going down to see what he has caught us tomorrow."

I nodded, noting the admiration for him in her eyes. "Where will he sleep?" I didn't like asking about him, but I couldn't help wondering.

Queenie chewed then said, "He has a tent. Mansi loves being alone with Mother Earth."

I considered him out there alone, with nothing but a thin tent. I couldn't fathom being out there alone and unprotected. "If this place is a secret, how come he's allowed to bring us as far as he did? I mean, he could figure out where we are if he wanted."

Queenie shot me a deadly look as if I'd slapped her. "I trust Mansi with my life." She looked to the other griots. "We all do. Even if he were tortured, he would never reveal where the Grotto is."

"Also, he's mute, so that helps, too," Zora said, smiling until Queenie threw her a look of disapproval. I guess no one disrespected Queenie's lover, if he was in fact her lover. I'd learned something new. I thought Mansi chose to not talk. I didn't know that he couldn't talk.

The sun had begun to make its morning ascent by the time we finished eating our meal and drinking sweet wine from lambskin and water from the gourd.

The sleeping mats we brought up were thin, and our blankets were damp, yet no one complained. Sleep came swiftly and lasted for hours. I didn't even worry whether or not a cheetah would maul us. I was too exhausted to care.

I was the first to awaken and though I wasn't quite prepared to embrace my calling, I wanted to—no, I needed to—find out what was in those books. I longed for the secrets they were about to hand down to me. If we had been lied to all this time, I needed to know why.

The first thing I did was reach into my bag and pull out Father Malcolm's tome. I rose and went closer to the natural light at the mouth of the cave.

I opened the book. Father Malcolm's first words were biting, yet simple.

May 5, 2014-How much pain will it take for black people to

113

realize we don't belong in America? How long can one stay in an abusive relationship? My own people laugh at me and call me crazy for starting a settlement in Africa. "We are not African-American, we're just American," the fools shout with ultimate conviction. Our ancestors are weeping. "This place is as much mine as anyone else's." Yeah. Okay. You've been telling yourselves that for centuries.

Those were his first words. I thumbed through the tome and stopped on a random page.

July 3, 2014-I cannot sleep. She comes tomorrow. What will she think of this place? Will she laugh at Noire like so many others have? Will she call us a cult? Or will she embrace Noire? If it weren't for Naemah, the idea of a settlement in the Great Rift Valley for African-Americans would have never come to be. There are two-hundred people already here, farming, creating traditions, and living out from under the thumb, influence, and the threats of the White Man. We have used our hands to build each and every home. The community is ours.

A year ago, I went to see her at the very same university we attended together twelve years ago. Naemah could not believe that I had created Noire, the first village in what would become a part of the kingdom of Za, if God allowed. I saw the fear in her eyes when I first came to her. She thought I had gone mad...again. But I hadn't. Noire was a reality. A month ago, I wrote her and begged her to see it for herself, and finally, she agreed. I pray that Naemah will stay. We need her expertise, and frankly, I know she will not believe me, but I need her love. However, I know living in a place like this, out in the wild, one with nature, no electricity, and no stores will be a drastic change for any American woman.

July 4, 2014-Everyone ran out of Noire's gates when we heard the whooping of the helicopter blades. My heart raced. I stood there with my legs weak. I wondered what she thought as she beheld Noire from the air.

My mother and father stood beside me. My father patted my shoulder in reassurance. My mother beamed. After all these years,

Mother still asked me about Naemah. She had only met her the one time she stayed at our house when we were in college.

It took a few moments for the door of the helicopter to open and for her to exit.

Naemah had tears in her eyes, and her mouth hung slightly ajar as she took in my creation, our creation, and the hard work and will of the people. I rushed to the beautiful woman, and we embraced.

"You did it, Malcolm. You did it," she cried. And, that was the highest moment for me. That was my confirmation that I wasn't some crazy person in the middle of nowhere, risking the lives of so many for no reason. I had done something real and meaningful.

We have musicians, poets, a painter, teachers, farmers, a scientist, plumbers, a carpenter, a midwife, and so many other pieces of the puzzle. But still we needed her—a historian to help us cultivate a culture with rituals, spiritual practices, rites of passage, and organizations that will help our people thrive mentally and draw them closer to the Africans that lived before Europeans ever stole our ancestors from Africa. We needed traditions that would be passed on from generation to generation. Naemah could do this.

Will she stay, though? To ask a modern American middle-class woman to live in the African bush, with no electricity, the internet, cars, stores, fast food, and so on, is insane. Yet there are over one hundred and ten women and girls in Noire already sewing their own clothes, eating the food they grew with their own hands, fixing each other's hair with products they grew and blended, sewing their own feminine products, dancing and telling stories to entertain themselves, and already two healthy babies have been born to two healthy women. Noire is all Naemah truly needs. Will she see that?

"Is Noire sovereign?" She asked.

I sighed. "It's complex. No one bothers us, but I hope to one day have sovereignty."

"Did you sleep well?" Zora asked.

I jumped. When I caught my breath, I replied, "I did."

"Mountain air and a good meal will do that for you." She rose and yawned audibly. I'd noticed that everything Zora did was like a sensual dance, even the way her lashes fluttered. The sunlight that managed to enter the cave highlighted Zora's curves and her slender waist. She stood, and without shame she undressed, tied a bright pink wrap around her waist and put on a tight blue shirt that stopped at her midriff, leaving her flat stomach out for all to see. The bold color was lovely on her. I guessed that she looked phenomenal with any color against her skin. It was rare to see such a vibrant color in Obsidian, but in Noire, male weavers specialized in making the most potent and colorful dyes.

"You can go in." She motioned to the secret room. "I know you're eager. The Grotto is now just as much yours as it is ours." I could tell she had to swallow her pride to say that.

I put the book away, and I took my time rising as if I didn't want to tear through the room like a storm and put my hands on everything.

In the room, the mildew smell of history overtook me. I gave Father Malcolm thanks for having the hindsight to create this space and charging the Griothood to care for it. Zora followed me into the room. She busied herself, lighting the six torches that hung on the cavern walls. The room came alive even brighter than before. It was then that I noticed another metal door at the back of the secret room with only one keyhole.

I pointed. "What is in there?"

"No one knows," she replied. "Whatever key opens it is long gone, just like the master key. I wish I knew, though. It drives me crazy." She shook her head and went back out into the outer cave. She returned with a pewter cup. "Here," Zora said. "Rinse your hands. Our fingertips contain oils that can ruin these ancient books. They're all the proof we have of our past." She sprinkled water onto my hands, and it splattered on the floor. She pointed to the numerical pad that Nok messed with earlier. "That controls the temperature and moisture in here. It was Father Malcolm's attempt to keep the books safe for as long as possible. I'd say for being two centuries old, they're still in okay condition."

I worried about the tome. I'd already handled it, but then I remembered it was not the original.

Zora went on. "Once a year, you will journey here with us to ensure the Grotto is safe, secure, and free of dust."

I looked around, thinking that someone forgot to dust last time.

"As we told you earlier, we must all be together to open the Grotto." She held up her brass key.

"Good afternoon," Queenie sang upon entering the room. Nok was behind her, not looking quite as cheery. She walked like all her joints ached. I wondered when Nok was going to retire from the Griothood. She could've done so decades ago.

All three women rinsed their hands, leaving a small puddle on the stone floor.

"Sit, Zen," Queenie instructed kindly. She placed her hand on the back of an old and cracked leather seat that was in front of a dusty desk. There was a blissful calm on her face.

My heart raced in anticipation as I did as I was told. The chair creaked and cracked as I sat, and I feared that the old thing would collapse. I wondered if Father Malcolm had sat here. Exhilaration surged through my body. Queenie took a cloth and wiped the desk, and Nok placed an old leather book upon it.

Queenie parted her lips to speak then closed them. She centered herself and began again. "This book contains just a short portion of our peoples' true identity." She pointed to

117

Nok and Zora. "We are the only Zaians who know that an unfathomable number of black people were stolen from this continent. The Zaians descended from a small sect of those stolen people. Our ancestors left the Americas and chose to return to the motherland.

"This book," she pushed the pads of her fingers down on it, "will tell you things our people don't know about. There are a million other stories that would never fit into this room, but by the end of your safari, you will get the gist of it."

I swallowed.

Queenie nodded at me, indicating that I could open the book. When I did, I saw that the first pages contained names. Malcolm X Dubois being the first.

Queenie pointed to the names. "These are the names of the first people who moved here. The first ritual they had was the burning of their names. Most African-American's last names tied them to the institution of slavery, which we will tell you about soon. So in the first column you see their slave names and in the second column, you see their altered last names. There were a few who chose to do away with their English first names as well."

I took in the names and considered their replacements. I looked for my last name, but strangely it wasn't there. I turned the page. There were pictures of people with various shades of brown skin. They looked no different than the people in Obsidian. The women carried their wares effortlessly on their heads and their babies on their backs. The men stood tall and strong. There were different groups, Afar, Dinka, Yoruba, Sans, Ibo, Senufo, Pygmy, Fulani, Ashanti, and others. This visual was nothing new to me. I had been learning about the people of my continent since I could speak. I knew their histories, and I knew their gods. Then came a page of typed writing. In 1619, the first nineteen or so enslaved Africans arrived in the American colonies.

"Enslaved Africans?" I asked.

"Turn the page," Queenie instructed gently.

I saw a drawing of naked black women lying closely on the floor with chains, agony etched on their faces. My eyes snapped up at Queenie.

Receiving no emotion from her, I read a passage beneath it.

They lay in their own fecal matter, vomit, blood, and urine. They wailed ceaselessly because they had been torn from their villages, parents, friends, husbands, and children. They spent months in captivity and in the humid, rancid hull of a ship. They wailed because of sickness, open sores, fleas, flies, lice, rats, disease, and the cowhide whip lacerating their tender skin. Where were they going now? They had already been snatched from their homes. They had been marched for days upon days. They had been held for weeks in a crowded prison. Death would be merciful.

"What is this?!" I shouted, my stomach threatening to let go of its contents.

Zora answered, "White men began stealing Africans from their villages by the millions. They took them mostly to South America, North America, and to the Caribbean Islands. This was called the Middle Passage. Many of our ancestors didn't make it through the horrid journey. The ocean is their graveyard."

Shuddering, I turned the page, and I saw what they called white men. My nose flared. I had never heard of one, let alone seen one. However, they didn't look like the monsters I expected. They were just...men. Their skin was alabaster, somewhat like RoRo's albino skin. Their hair didn't have kinks. It was very straight, stringy, and varied in hues.

"Why would they take our ancestors?" I asked her forcefully.

"They desired the labor on their plantations or farms.

They were greedy, lazy, heartless bastards, and they called our ancestors their slaves, their property."

I turned to see images of black people picking cotton with black and white men watching over them. White people owned them like the Zaians owned cattle.

"Why didn't they fight?" I sputtered in disbelief. I thought of our warriors. I thought of the chief. They would never allow this to happen.

Nok said, "The White Man's weapons were superior, and sometimes African clans betrayed others for survival and for greed."

That revelation heated my bloodstream. I thought about being snatched away in the middle of the night, never to see my world again. I thought of how I tried to run from my village. I had been so foolish and ungrateful. My heart ached for those millions of souls.

I flipped through the horrifying images of what Queenie called American Slavery: people with slashed and sliced skin on their melanated backs and a man being ripped apart by four horses. That picture was captioned as "quartering."

I turned away as my stomach shifted.

"No," Queenie said sharply. "You are a griot initiate, and you must know the history, the whole bloody, filthy, putrid, inhumane truth of it. You must see every laceration, mutilation—all of the brutal things the White Man did to our people. Their blood runs in your veins. If you don't feel the truth in your soul, you'll never be able to weave stories that will keep this from happening again. Our stories protect the people from losing themselves again."

"Again?" My pulse raced as I thought about the white men returning.

"Sure," she said. "This time, they may not be white men." There was a look of fear behind Queenie's eyes, and I knew she was talking about the rebels.

I rubbed my temples and forced myself to view the pictures.

There was a beautiful woman with coal-hued skin. There was a white baby suckling on her breast. I squinted one eye.

"They thought we were disgusting, subhuman," Zora spoke forcefully. "They made us cover our hair. They said we were stupid. Black men were beasts, and black women were promiscuous. Our ancestors were not even allowed to look them in the eyes, but they had no problem with us breastfeeding their offspring."

"Or raping black women. Then they had the nerve to fear that black men would rape their precious white women." Nok grunted.

"Rape," I croaked, turning to face Nok. Rape was nearly unheard of in Za. Rape was punishable by immediate exile into the bush, on foot, with no water and no weapons. It was a death sentence—a slow death sentence. If the exile didn't die from starvation or exposure, the predators would surely attack the exile in their weakened state.

Young boys learned before the time they could walk to respect their mothers, sisters, and any woman. Their rites of passage were laced with parables and missions that strengthened these values. Each girl was taught that her yoni was priceless and her own, and that she should only give her yoni to a man who was worthy of loving her and capable of raising their children.

Nok stood and began to pace. "Imagine a husband, the defender of his wife, knowing that the woman he loved was being brutalized by the white demon that owned them. Owned them." Nok's voice and her wiry body quivered with rage.

"Did the husbands kill the rapists?" I asked, riled up.

Nok answered, "Only if he wanted to die a horrific death, and maybe his wife and children would face the same fate."

121

I imagined the helplessness and emasculation a man must've felt knowing his wife was being violated and there wasn't a damn thing he could do about it. I clenched my hair and fluttered my lashes until my tears receded behind the dam.

Queenie quickly turned through the pages, searching. "Have you ever noticed our various complexions in Obsidian?"

Queenie herself was the color of sweet potato skin, my skin was the earth being rained on, and Abebi was the color of a starless, moonless night. That was the beauty of being Zaian, so many skin tones and hair textures—or was our many shades just the White Man's stain, his DNA in our veins? We were walking vestiges of rape.

She pointed to a picture of a woman whose skin was almost as pale as a white man's, but her hair had the texture of loose cotton. A black woman.

"Nearly every one of us has the White Man's blood in our veins. They are just as much our ancestors as the Africans."

I shook my head in disgust. I had descended from a man who'd raped a woman in my bloodline.

"Yes," she stated sharply. "The White Man is in our veins, and there is nothing that can be done about it."

I examined my outstretched hands and shuddered. How could my ancestors allow this to happen? Why didn't the ones left behind copy the White Man's weapons and ships and rescue those who had been taken? In the book, there was a man with crisscrossed lashes across his back. A gut-wrenching sickness consumed me.

"They ruled them with the whip and the threat that they would separate their families," Zora sighed. "It was ingenious, really. Evilly ingenious." I stared at her beautiful face and wondered how she took it when she heard these terrible stories. The pictures were making me physically ill.

Every horrific image was engraved in my mind and would surely haunt me forever.

The more I read, the more I understood how these people stole almost everything from my ancestors. They strategically drowned out their languages, their names, their rituals, their foods, and their religions. In Za, we worshiped our skin tones and our hair textures. The women in Za coveted their hair just as much as the Maasai man. There were ceremonies just to commemorate our beauty and our darkness. Here, darkness meant peace. In America, darkness was synonymous with evil. Now more than ever, I understood why there was so much emphasis on our blackness in this kingdom. Father Malcolm and Za's founders had attempted to reverse the hatred that had been instilled in our predecessors. It had been ingrained in them that the pale skin, thin lips, and straight hair were the epitome of beauty. It was beaten into them. After a few generations, the Africans in America lost sight of black brilliance. They forgot about Imhotep, the physician and architect. They forgot about Timbuktu, where people came from far and wide to study the arts and sciences. The people lost recipes for natural medicines and cures. They lost the notion of spiritual balance. They forgot about the riches traded by the kingdoms of Kush, Mali, and Songhai.

Za's founders were somehow able to ensure that this wouldn't be the case in their settlement. How had they done it? How had the founders erased centuries from our history?

CHAPTER 16

July 5, 2014-We made love on her second night here. I hadn't touched this woman in a decade. We had changed so much. We were both obviously more experienced and calmer than we had been in college. It made the night sensual and emotional.

After we indulged in each other, we laid upon my bed in silence. Our locs intertwined, and a lantern burning, with the exotic sounds of the grasslands in the background like a relaxation soundtrack. I wondered how no man had married her yet.

Finally, Naemah said, "I fell apart when you left me." There was a trace of bitterness in her tone.

I cringed. Like a coward, I had hoped she'd never bring it up, that we would go on as if nothing painful had ever transpired between us. "I apologize for that." It was an insubstantial statement.

"You could've told me you were leaving. You just left school mid-semester, and I didn't hear from you for over a decade. If your parents hadn't told me you were going through something, I would still be confused." Her words rushed from her mouth so fast and with so much resentment that I feared I had lost her.

I took a deep breath. "I have always suffered from anxiety and depression," I confessed. "When I was in the throes of depression, I wouldn't reach out to anyone, even though I felt so lonely."

"What depressed you?" Her words were slightly softer now. She turned her face toward me.

"I was different. I had a big mouth and a strong opposition to the oppression of my people." But she knew this.

"That's what I loved about you. You didn't care what people thought. That was amazing for a twenty-year-old."

"It was a farce. Every word people said about me, especially my own people, was another stab through the heart. When the University tried to expel me, I fell apart."

Her face contorted. *"Expel? But you were exercising your freedom of speech. The University is liberal."*

I scoffed. She was now a professor there. She should've known better. *"I was accused of 'inciting the students, which could lead to a riot.' The Board of Regents wanted me to beg for their forgiveness. They wanted me to stop writing controversial papers. My first paper as a freshman was entitled, 'Amerikkka.' That put me on their radar, and I never bit my tongue when it came to the racial injustices. When I organized a walkout protesting the lack of an African-American Studies major at our school, I felt like Malcolm X after he said the chickens had come home to roost, after Kennedy's assassination. They were seething after that. But after the campus police beat Ron Johnson down because he wouldn't lie face down in front of his white girlfriend, I said some things that some believed called for retaliation. Perhaps it did. I'd always thought marching was a foolish waste of time. I wanted a more direct approach. That's when they called me to come in front of the Regents. The worst thing was none of the black professors would back me up— except one."* Dr. Reeves now lives here in Noire and was in charge of recruiting villagers. *"On the day of my hearing, only Dr. Reeves and my parents showed up. I was ready, dressed in the White Man's garb, prepared to tell them that their interpretation of my words was incorrect. I was there to plead my case. I was there to beg 'massa' to let me stay. I would promise to be a good nigger. But my pride wouldn't let me grovel. Out of nowhere, I looked at my parents and said, 'I won't do it. I won't beg these bastards to keep me here and keep me quiet.'"*

I laughed. Naemah's mouth was ajar.

"My mother smiled the biggest smile ever, and my father hugged me. We left, and until I came back to see you, I never set foot on that fuckin' campus again."

Naemah looked at the ceiling. She was quiet for a while. I watched her chest rise and fall. "I was right there, and you didn't say a word." Her voice quaked with each word. "I wasn't your girlfriend, but I loved you. I would've been there."

"If I could do it over again, I would." I turned and put my arms around her. She didn't move from me, so I kissed her neck, and she accepted.

I continued, "I had a nervous breakdown after that. I wouldn't leave my room. I wouldn't eat. My parents told me you called, but I couldn't speak to you or anyone else. I could only sleep.

"My parents brought a spiritualist to me, and at first, I didn't speak to her. It was about four sessions before I looked forward to her coming to see me. She would give me these anxiety exercises, herbs, roots, crystals, and oils. She taught me about meditation, and she weaned me off of the Zoloft the university clinic prescribed me months before my dismissal. Eventually, I emerged out of that hole. I studied Buddhism, Taoism, and different indigenous spiritual practices. The ideas lifted me and brought me into my purpose. I sought out what God wanted of me. I visited monasteries and villages, and I soaked in all the natives would allow me to. I backpacked around this continent and my life transformed. I knew I belonged here. The ancestors had been calling me. Not in Johannesburg or Nairobi, but in a fairly unexploited Africa, sans the tourists, and I discovered what it would take for me to live here, out in the bush.

"I heard about this woman from Atlanta who lived in a way that I admired. She and her husband had been here for a decade and virtually lived alone. I learned so much from them, and several times, I wanted to go back to America in tears. I stuck it out, though. I learned to be fairly self-sufficient, and I learned to thrive. However, I missed my parents, I missed friendship, and I missed you."

She tensed. She thought I was lying.

"I thought about Za. The kingdom we made up that weekend you came with me to meet my family."

She finally spoke. "You never told me you lived in a mansion or that your family had founded a black private school," she said nostalgically.

"But I showed you," I said softly. "No one at the University ever knew that part of me."

"I still can't figure out why you didn't go to Harvard or Princeton. You had the intelligence and the money."

"God was leading me to you." I imagined her rolling her eyes. I believed that was true. "God led me to every soul in this village. It will grow into a great black nation. Noire is just the beginning. More people want to join us. There was a time when I knew no one would move to this place and live like the ancestors. If a camera crew arrived, they would say we were in poverty. But we are so rich. We have every single thing we need and nothing we don't. Souls are craving this—not sneakers, not unchecked consumption, and not stuntin' for the next man to envy. Once the ego is out of the way, people see that. I think all the progress and development will drive everyone back to a simpler lifestyle, anyway. Humans are wrecking Mother Earth, but she won't die. We will." I laughed a little. "There I go."

"You're starting to sound like me." Naemah turned back to her side and looked at me with those gorgeous big eyes. She put her hand on my chest.

I outlined her full lips with the pad of my index finger. "Stay," I whispered. But I deserved for her to hurt me like I had hurt her.

"I don't know, Malcolm. I have a career and this place..."

"I know." I kissed her. "I know."

127

CHAPTER 17

Septembe 19, 2014- *Every person in Noire sat around the fire yesterday. That is when I told them that Naemah was coming to Noire for good. My people were happy for themselves and for me. The women had embraced her and actually cried when she left. When Naemah first got here, she wanted to know who these people were. Who was crazy enough to undergo this drastic lifestyle change? Most were Gullah people from South Carolina's Low Country. They'd been forced off of the land that had been in their families since the emancipation of slaves, all in the name of condos and hotels. The audacity of the White Man. The world was his playground. He moved the Native Americans, and he moved us.*

I knew if Dr. Reeves could convince the displaced Gullah people to move to Noire, they would be the perfect people for the new community. They were the people tied closest to our African ancestors. The name Gullah had been derived from the word Angola, the land from which the Gullah people had been stolen. Many of them knew how to work the land. We needed that, as well as their natural remedies and their spiritual attachment to the ancestors of the motherland. It took years of courting, as they rightfully mistrusted so many, but eventually Dr. Reeves had convinced enough to move here. The other people who populated Noire were disenchanted young people. Some were friends of my family. There were others who loved the idea of a new nation for African-Americans in Africa, but couldn't stomach it. We asked them to support the cause financially. Unlike Liberia, Noire had no white financiers who wanted Negroes out of their America. It was our board members and my parents who provided the plumbing and running water, the Nubian goats, the cattle, building supplies, seeds, and the tickets to get people to Kenya.

The crops were growing well, and life was good. I should've known that things would go wrong at some point. It was a month ago that I'd noticed that my mother was sleeping more and eating less. Even with the diet change we all underwent when we got here, she looked too frail. I told her to level with me. I stopped breathing as she and my father looked at each other with fear in their eyes.

"Before we left the U.S., I found a lump in my breast, and the doctors confirmed it was cancer." Her eyes moistened.

My face contorted in horror. I threw my arms around my mother and wept like a child. "Why didn't you tell me?"

"You needed to focus on your purpose, and I needed to see your dream realized."

I pulled away. "We have to get you to Johannesburg. They have great doctors there."

She shook her head. "No! Sending me there will undermine all you're trying to do here. The people will panic. When I die, I want to die here in Noire. I'm at peace with that, Malcolm."

My brother will be here to see mother before the inevitable. That makes me anxious. We've never got along, but maybe for our mother we can.

The griots tore me from my studies early on that second night. We went down to eat with Mansi. He had caught and smoked fish for us. Then we drew water from the river and washed with red soap from Nok's village in the rainforest. When we returned to the cave, we laughed, drank wine, and smoked weed. The griots shared their best tales, their scariest tales, and finally their most sensual tales, the stories that they kept for themselves and their male friends. I smiled, laughed, and even got aroused while listening to Zora's story, but there was something heavy in me that would not go away: my ancestors in America. I still wasn't done receiving their stories. Nok brought out a wooden flute. She played a lovely melody, and we danced. It was then that it occurred to me how little I had thought of Sahel since being here.

I fell asleep with ease that night, but my dreams were unsettling.

CHAPTER 18

I saw Jesus Christ. Blood from the crown of thorns dripped down his white hollowed cheeks. The blood stopped dripping and began to pour, and at his feet, a pool of blood grew deeper and deeper. Then, black charred bodies bobbed in the pool of blood. Christ faded, and there was a humongous tree with wispy moss. As the tree came more into focus, I saw that there were bodies hanging from the tree. Women's bodies, hundreds of bodies, swayed with the wind. Their babies had been cut from their stomachs. I stared at the tree of swaying bodies. Two joyous white children appeared and ran in circles around me. Impossibly fast and dizzying circles. They disappeared, and suddenly, I was naked, and there were two white babies suckling from my nipples, their jagged teeth cutting into my tender brown skin. Sahel appeared, and I reached out. He took my hand, even though I was feeding the babies. Suddenly, I was being torn from Sahel, by forces unseen, while his grandfather watched in sadness. The babies had faded away.

I swayed. I was at the bottom of a slave ship now, lying on a plank, chains cutting into my skin. I heard the melancholy moans of men. Weak men. I was ashamed of them. They couldn't save me. I screamed for them to stop moaning.

"Zen."

Who summoned me? I looked down, and my keloids from where I'd slashed my wrists were discharging blood.

"Zen, wake up."

I was snatched out of my slumber. My teeth chattered. My body ached at every joint, and my head throbbed. It was too cold in the highlands.

"Her skin is searing," Zora cried. Her cool hand felt good against my forehead.

I saw Queenie come close. Zora removed her hand, and Queenie put her palm on my forehead. "This is bad," she remarked.

"What?" I groaned.

Queenie asked, "How do you feel?"

"I'm so cold," I tried to sit up but gave up. "My body aches."

"You have a high fever. You've probably been sweating all night." Queenie turned to the others. "We have to get Mansi up here. He'll carry her down the mountain."

Zora said, "But he can't see the way to the Grotto."

"Blindfold him, then," Queenie snapped.

Zora threw up her hands. She was mad at me.

"I'll bring him back," Nok said.

Zora added, "You can't go out there by yourself." She paused and finally and woefully conceded. "I'll go, too."

Queenie looked at me and said, "Thank—"

"No," I moaned.

They looked to me.

I closed my eyes as a violent chill passed through me. "I

132

haven't finished learning the truth. I want to know everything about—" I shot upright and vomited on the floor.

The griots raced to clean it up.

I cried, "I'm sorry I ruined the safari. I'm sorry I got sick."

"Stop it, sweetheart," Queenie said. "Our bodies all need rest and special care from time to time."

"Please don't make me leave just yet."

Queenie stared at me long and hard. Then she rose and motioned the griots to go to the dark mouth of the cave.

I closed my eyes. My weakness was winning as I tried to make out what was being said.

Queenie's voice had a grave tone. "I'll never let anything happen to her."

"She wants to stay," Zora argued.

Queenie's sounded muffled for a moment, and then I heard, "Just teach her back home. She could die without the proper medicine. The rain and change in temperature made her ill."

Nok grumbled something that I couldn't decipher. The next thing I knew, Queenie settled down beside me. The cave was quiet, and I realized I had slipped into sleep.

"Nok and Zora are going to search for the justicia flava root. It should lower your fever. The problem is whether or not they will be able to find it in the highlands." She placed a cool, wet cloth on my head. "In the meantime, Nok always travels with olive leaves. I'm heating the water to make your tea. It should provide some relief. If you aren't better by midday, we're gone. I can't believe I'm allowing this."

I squeezed my eyes shut. I needed to get better. She held a gourd to my lips and I gratefully drank the cool water.

I could feel Queenie's eyes on me. She was terrified.

I thought about my nightmare. "Why did our ancestors believe in the god of their captors?"

133

"Well," she said, making herself comfortable, "they had nothing else. Our ancestors came from many different parts of this continent. They were as different as the Zaians are from the Pygmies. Indeed, some were Christian already, some Muslim. However, most had traditional religions. Some were Yoruba. They worshiped Elgguá, Ogún, Oshosi, Obatalà, Oyá, Oshún, Yemayá, Shangó, and Orunmila. Other worshiped Nyame, Ngai, or Mawu. Some practiced Vodun. The commonality was the reverence of the ancestors. But in America, the Africans were forced together, and their religions were snuffed out and beaten out of them. Meeting was forbidden. Drumming was forbidden. Over time, our ancestors lost all knowledge of their gods, and they had nothing else to cling to. They were given Jesus. Forced even."

Drowsily, I thought about our gods. Our founders had created them, I realized with anger. Or was Yemi derived from Yemayá? Was she simply made up out of thin air? The deception was too heavy. I felt alone in the universe. Qwei, the god of war, warrior protection, and iron; Sibo the god of the gods; Yemi, the goddess of rain, water, seduction, and feminine beauty; Ayeki, the harvest and fertility goddess; and Khan, the cattle god. Made up. I felt like I was floating. Nothing grounded me to the earth. Nothing was true. Queenie's voice faded as I drifted into a deep slumber.

CHAPTER 19

November 17, 2014-*Hard times have fallen on us swiftly. Yes, we have food, thank God. Yes, we have each other—but Mother is gone. We buried her near the stillborn baby. How many will populate this cemetery by this time next year? The people asked if they could pass the village children over her grave. They said it is the way of the Gullah people. They said it keeps the dead spirits off of the children. I allow it.*

The novelty of the African bush has worn off, and people are bored and depressed, especially Naemah. I knew adjustment wouldn't be easy for her, but she lies in bed all day. She has no purpose. I've been there before. She hasn't asked, but I'm thinking of telling her to go back to the U.S. I know my soul will die, and it will further damage the morale of the people. But I love her too much to let her feel this way.

My brother sent my father a letter. After visiting during mother's sickness and again for mother's funeral, he wants to join us permanently. There's always been a rivalry between us that never let up, even though we're men. But I wouldn't deny him the right to live with us. I know things are becoming uglier in the U.S., especially for a black man. It's not 1850 ugly, 1930 ugly, or 1965 ugly, but my generation isn't used to it, and there are so many cameras now, documenting the murders of unarmed black men for all to see. I told my people it was coming, especially with President Obama in office. It girded my soul to hear the ugly things they said about the man and his beautiful queen. God bless his soul. God bless African Americans because the racists would soon get their redemption.

Dr. Reeves is in the U.S. interviewing people who want to come to us. This time, they sought us out. The Awakening is happening. Ase. Yet I fear that this isn't the time to bring more people here. My queen is broken. If she's broken, I'm broken. If I'm broken, Noire is broken.

The next morning, my fever subsided. I still felt weak, and I ached, but I could walk. That satisfied Queenie, and she reluctantly said I could finish my studies.

I read about a man by the name of Marcus Garvey. I knew right away that Garvey was Father Malcolm's inspiration. He created a back to Africa movement, but due to corruption and him being sent back to his country, his mission failed. Although the White Man said he didn't want blacks there, he wouldn't allow a black man to be in control of their exodus.

On the fourth day, I drowned in horrific readings about Jim Crow and Civil Rights. Bodies in muddy river banks, bombings, and children dying. I read a speech by our founder's namesake, Malcolm X, later el-Hajj Malik el-Shabazz. It wound Malcolm X up that other black leaders were begging the White Man for a piece of his pie, begging him to be nice, play fair, integrate, give jobs, give equal compensation for equal work, and to stop murdering them. He argued that black people needed to cultivate their own businesses, communities, and schools, like the other people who had come to America. If only he could've seen Za, I thought. If only Father Malcolm could've seen Za now.

I read about a black Christian preacher by the name of Martin Luther King, Jr. He and Malcolm were at odds in the same way that W.E.B. Dubois and Booker T. Washington had been. I liked both men, however. They were more fearless than I would ever be. What intrigued me about King were the pictures of him marching with white men. White men and women also risked their lives. They had been battered and murdered, too. This baffled me.

My shoulders lurched when I turned to a page plastered with the disturbing headlines announcing that they had been slain. I was even more devastated when I read that blacks assassinated Malcolm X. I saw the picture of him being rushed away after being shot. The griots did not comfort me. They watched silently as I sobbed.

CHAPTER 20

On the fifth and final day, the griots taught me about the Black Panthers, the Black Pride movement, and integration. The hairstyles of the 1960's and 1970's had begun to look familiar to me. Not replicas of white women's hair. Queenie told me that people put harsh chemicals on their scalps to decimate their original texture. The thought of it made me shudder. Some bleached their skin, also. It churned my stomach that many of these people didn't know how ravishing they naturally were. Then I realized that I was no different. I was always looking outside of myself for beauty and never within.

I saw pictures of many successful black people in the early 2000's. Many had incredibly large homes. Their hair was straight again, but they looked happy. Then I learned of a president, a black leader who was elected by the people. Blacks and whites elected a man named Barack Obama. He was from this land. I felt warm inside. This mystified me, after all the hatred I saw toward my ancestors, but it made my chest swell. He, his wife, and their daughters were stunning.

Then the griots stood before me. "In 2004, Father Malcolm dropped out of his place of higher learning," Zora said. "He had struggled with much of what was happening in America. Yes, some blacks were seemingly successful, but some white people only saw black men as beasts that needed to be controlled. And for every successful black person, there were so many who had been left behind in the ghettos of America. Many of our ancestors frequented white businesses, we worked for whites, and we made them richer. Many of our ancestors did not support other blacks."

"But there was a black leader," I chimed in.

Nok tisked. "Don't be stupid, child."

I winced, remembering why I didn't like the old woman.

"That's when the hatred grew like an inferno in the White Man's belly," Nok said with a frown. "It was nothing for a law keeper to murder a black man or black boy who had no weapon and get away with it. Everything about the black man was a threat, from the way he wore his clothes to the way he wore his hair. For many, Africans in America were trash, the stepchild, the White Man's burden. The ghettos were still full with our ancestors and so were the prisons. Yes, some blacks achieved the American dream, but the White Man ruled America and still yearned to hold blacks down.

"Father Malcolm was just as disgusted with blacks as he was with whites. No one hated our ancestors as much as they hated themselves. He said the blacks were bigger white supremacists that the white people. No one destroyed them as much as they destroyed themselves," Queenie handed me a sheet of paper.

I read the fiery words. Bitch, get over here and suck my dick. The filthy words gripped my gut and knotted my intestines. "What is this?" I yelped.

"Do you know what a bitch is?"

139

"Yes. A female dog."

Queenie shook her head, the pain in her eyes profound. "This is a song in which black men were addressing black women." She handed me other equally disgusting lyrics in which black men showed their utter hatred for black women. It seemed he reviled black women more than white men hated him.

"A dick is a penis, by the way," Nok added.

I knew what a dick was.

"What's wrong with sucking—" Zora's words faded out as the older griots looked at her with bulging eyes. She giggled. I tried to hide my smile, but then Nok guffawed, and we all laughed hysterically.

After a while, Queenie continued, "Those are lyrics from a popular song. The singer was cherished, worshiped, and made wealthy for saying these vile things, and worse, to and about black women." Her eyes became distant. "Little girls danced to this, boys sung this. Little girls learned that they were to be disrespected in the most disgusting ways. As griots, we know the power of words. They go right to the soul. When you sing, the universe listens, and the message proliferates. Many of our ancestors didn't know that."

Nok said, "You know people who hate their women are doomed."

I exhaled. Men are supposed to lead the people. They have to care for each woman like she was his mother or sister, or the world becomes broken. The familial ties deteriorate. I understood why Father Malcolm broke down.

Zora spoke. "Father Malcolm was livid that black people were yet again begging whites to see us as human beings, so he left the country. He went to live with as many indigenous people as possible, not all African. The state of Africa had saddened him, too. Much of the 'developed' Motherland had become a mirror of Europe with European values and greed.

Black people were so proud of the 'civilized' Africa and turned a blind eye to people like the Dogon and the San, the people Father Malcolm looked to for guidance. To him, they were the civilized ones."

Queenie rose and paced, hands behind her back, bangles glinting from the light of the lanterns. "He knew he wanted to bring his people back home, but how, if whites still controlled the Motherland, even if remotely? The Chinese were also playing puppets with African leaders. Africans were seen as poor when they had riches all along, and not only diamonds, oil, and minerals. They had the ability to be self-sufficient. They had their own gods, laws, and images of beauty. Over and over, Africa was being raped. How would he bring his people home?"

CHAPTER 21

December 25-I believe Naemah has finally found her purpose here. I asked her to use her knowledge of our ancestors to build up our people, give them purpose besides growing food and tending to the animals. She rose to the occasion. The Gullah people also have a wealth of information and rituals that we failed to tap into. We have appointed our most promising people to the Council of Elders. They guide the people and set the laws. Naemah has also created several festivals and feasts that keep the people busy and entertained. Some of the festivals coincide with the rainy seasons and harvests. There will be a festival of fertility. Naemah suggested that we give the young men warrior roles. She has placed the villagers in age sets. Many of our ancestors used age sets. Some Africans still have them and even generational sets. The groups will have a distinct identity, name, and bond. The people are embracing the changes.

Dr. Reeves has found more than fifty new candidates for Noire. The elders voted that they should join us, so the villagers have begun building new homes for them. Naemah and I have prayed over the names. Again, there are more women than men. We have considered polygamy as an option. She balked, but I told her not to look at polygamy through the lens of Christianity, but out of necessity. We need to grow the next generation.

My brother is on the way, too…with his husband.

The next morning, the Grotto was locked and hidden, as was any evidence that we had been there. Carefully, we descended the mountain using the same trail we'd come by.

Twenty minutes into our walk, Nok placed her hand in front of my torso, stopping our progress. She pointed downward with her bony arthritic finger. There was a long line of men snaking through the valley, wearing piercing red and deep blue swaths. I didn't need to see the long braids that extended down the length of their backs. I knew they were Maasai warriors.

Smiles extended across all of our faces. Where we Zaians were aspiring Africans, the Maasai were real, and they ruled—and had named—the Serengeti.

"Where are they going?" Zora asked.

"On their Odyssey, Eunoto," Nok answered. "It happens once every seven years. Once Eunoto is complete, they will no longer be warriors. It is a rather sad time for them. They'll return home as elders." She put down her bag to admire them. We put our loads down, too. "When the White Man attempted to assimilate them and took away their right to hunt game, Eunoto was mostly carried out by the Maasai below the Tanzanian border. Once the government lost funding to protect the reserves and enforce their foreign rules on the Maasai, some of the Maasai returned to a semi-nomadic life of their ancestors." She pointed to the six men who wore lion manes on their heads. "It is interesting that now that the White Man is mostly gone from the Great Rift

Valley, the wildlife is thriving, even though the Maasai have returned to their ancient ways of hunting."

"Should we be worried?" I asked, admiring and fearing the beautiful men. I knew the history of these great people. They had fighting skills that myths were made of. Griot told countless stories of their great raids, and although they never bothered our village, we feared that a day would come when the Maasai wanted complete control of the plains.

Nok laughed. "They saw us far before we noticed them. It is because of them that Father Malcolm was allowed to create a settlement here. See, even though the government granted Father Malcolm permission to move just above Maasai Mara, he wanted the blessing of the Maasai. So much had been taken from them, and he wanted to respect them. Reluctantly, their chiefs granted him permission to build a settlement."

I gave a silent prayer of gratitude.

"Look." Nok giggled. "They're flirting."

Several of the men shook their long hair in perfect rhythm while their brothers sang. One whipped his long hair extensions in a perfect circular motion. Some of them playfully swatted their hair at each other. They all wore brilliant white beadwork created by their mothers or girlfriends for Eunoto.

"That one right there—" Zora pointed. "I'd drink blood and milk for him." Cow blood and milk was a special drink for the Maasai people. The children loved it.

"Something is truly wrong with you," Queenie laughed.

"She's just long-eyed," Nok said. "She wants every man she sees."

"Just the beautiful ones," Zora retorted playfully.

We danced to their rhythm and clapped when they were done showing off. Then the Maasai continued their trek. Nok took out her flute and played for them for as long as they could hear. When they were far out of sight, I felt warm until Queenie said, "It's too bad they will return with no hair."

CHAPTER 22

With a heavy heart, I thought of all the information I had learned about my ancestors. Several times, I asked myself why the ancestors kept our history from us. It was ours. We learned from birth about the great African kingdoms, but they neglected to tell us about the raiding of the villages. We were lied to so thoroughly; we hadn't even realized that a large mass of our history—the Trans-Atlantic Slave Trade—was missing. And here we were, the descendants of liars.

Before we reached Mansi, the griots stopped and looked at me with stern eyes. "Do you understand that your mouth must never utter any of what you have heard on this safari?" Nok asked with firmness in her voice.

"No. I don't understand. I disagree with the way the griots have lied to our people," I said, expecting to be yelled at or even struck.

"How do you feel?" Zora asked with an ironic smile on her lips. "Do you feel proud? Do you feel joyous knowing that your ancestors were enslaved? How would a child feel when he finds out that his people were beaten and sold like cows? Tell the babies that everything about them was once considered ugly. Let's tell that to our warriors. Let's tell them that if the White Man comes back, they don't stand a chance of protecting us. How is that for morale?"

My eyes fell to the ground. I understood, and I realized the White Man was who the ancestors were warning us about with the Heathen Dance.

"Mother Naemah believed that the burden was the griots' and the griots' alone. We could never devastate our people with this information. No soul can ever know outside of the Griothood," Zora reiterated. "This is why griots can never fall in love and marry until they complete their twenty years."

"That makes no sense," I said, shaking my head. There was no reason to keep me from Sahel or to keep me from having children.

"Every night after lying next to your husband, after he begs you for your secrets, secrets not even King Akonos knows, you will divulge all to him."

"I wouldn't."

Zora came closer to me, squinting her eyes. "Have you ever made love? Have you ever been fucked so good that you will do anything for a man?"

"No!" I cried, shaking my head incredulously.

With her mesmerizing eyes digging into me, she said, "Then you don't know what you would do when a dick strokes you the right way." She turned around, and we walked on. "Anyway, it's the way Mother Naemah wanted it."

It was as if her husky voice had stirred my yoni to life. I cleared my throat. "Why twenty years? Why not make a woman griot for life? She's no longer bound, she could tell."

"She is always bound, and you will find how much you love this sisterhood and will do anything to keep the secrets in the dark." With stern eyes, Zora added. "If ever a griot or former griot decides to reveal any secret, she will be executed.

I shuttered.

It wasn't long before I knew what they meant about telling a man the secrets of the Griothood. More than once on the journey back to Obsidian, I felt the strong urge to discuss all I had learned with Sahel, and I'd never even had sex with him. I could see his eyes growing large and his head shaking in amazement. Slavery, lynching, rape... But then I'd remembered that I was not allowed to say a word. But Sahel... I knew he could keep a secret.

My mind fell on the rebels. Out of ashes, the founders had constructed this self-sufficient, pride-filled land of the descendants of African-Americans. None of us had ever seen a white face, none of us had to beg them for equality, none of us shopped at white businesses, or cooked or cleaned for whites. We were thriving, we were strong, and if necessary, we were formidable. Yet the rebels wanted to dismantle everything. I didn't know their desires, but I knew we, over anything else, had to remain banded together. I couldn't help feeling in my veins that somewhere in the shadows were white men waiting for a fissure in Za's foundation.

CHAPTER 23

*F*ebruary 12, 2015-Naemah is pregnant. Thank God! Nothing *can fully represent the joy that I feel. I have created a life with the woman I love, in Noire. I ask her what our ancestors might've done when his child was born 600 years ago. She tells me I would introduce my child to the ancestors. Ancestors, I can't wait for my child to meet you.*

My brother is here, and we are getting along well. Let's see how long that shit lasts. His husband is okay, but I don't want that type of relationship in my village. Am I homophobic? I guess. We're trying to repair the black family and give our young men role models. What does my brother kissing his husband or holding hands in the streets say to our boys? What does it say to our girls?

On another note, I purchased more land. This space is smaller than Noire and farther South. In a few weeks I will send contractors to lay the infrastructure for plumbing and sewage. I don't expect the land to be inhabited for decades to come, but when it's time, the space will be ready. I only hope, however, that when the people have to move to this new place, which will be called Obsidian, it's not because something horrible has severed Noire. Naemah and I have also realized that to keep these far spread provinces united there will need to be a king.

Hours later, a smile crept across my face as I saw the walls of Obsidian on the horizon. We all clapped and sang. The talking drum sounded, announcing the return of the griots.

While we drew closer, I asked, "What do we do about the rebellion?"

Nok, Queenie, and Zora stopped their chatting. Their heads bobbed back and forth with the motion of the carriage. Their grins faded and fright registered in their eyes.

"How do you know about the rebellion?" Queenie asked.

"King Akonos told me," I said proudly.

"Frankly, Young Griot," Nok said after a moment, "we don't know."

Well, that's comforting, I thought as doom crept over me.

Then I saw him. My heart raced, and I cried out. He stood like a beautiful shepherd on his left leg; his right leg bent high, and his right foot planted on the inner-curve of his knee. Sahel was alone, far from the guards at the gate. I could see from the carriage that there was sorrow in his eyes.

"Stop!" I hollered at Mansi. He brought the horses to a stop, and I quickly climbed down.

Even though I had not fully recovered from my sickness, I ran to Sahel.

Queenie barked, "Zen, no."

But I didn't care if I wasn't supposed to show my love for him. Sahel was back, and I needed him.

CHAPTER 24

"Sahel," I cried.

Slowly, his long leg lowered to the ground, and he turned his gaze to me. His locs had been lifted to the crown of his head and twirled into a ball, making the brown skin that covered his high cheekbones even tauter.

He forced a weak smile. He should have been running to me, too, but he was as still as the acacia trees.

I broke down when I wrapped my arms around him. He held me tightly. My eyes closed, and I inhaled his herbal scent. I felt disgusting because I'd only bathed with water from the river, but I quickly let that go. The hardness of his chest and the softness of his skin felt like perfection. I could feel, however, that there was something weighing heavily on him.

"What's wrong?"

"My father found my grandfather's body cold last night," he said quietly, his voice wavering.

Stunned, all I could say was, "Sahel, I'm so sorry." I rested my nose and lips against his chest.

Sahel said nothing. He rocked with me in his arms. I felt wetness drop on my bare shoulders. The men in Sahel's life were very close. Each male in his family—from the time they could walk—was taken out to the pasture and was taught to care for and protect the cattle from the dangers of the bush. Sahel and his grandfather, Habtamu, were particularly close. Sahel did everything for him—read to him, brought him food, and kept him company in his old age.

"I spent his last days training. I should've been here," he said in a barely audible voice.

I was afraid to look up and see him crying. Guilt stabbed my heart. His set had yet to leave for training. If I hadn't convinced him to run, he could have been around for his grandfather's last days.

"You should go," Sahel said and then unwound his long arms from around me. His body had become rigid.

"No." I shook my head. I looked up, and I noticed his eyes weren't on me. I turned around and noticed that Queenie was standing at the gate: part of the evil triumvirate. Her arms were crossed, and her eyes were burning. My chest expanded until it felt like it would burst. Breathe. Breathe.

The safari nearly made me forget about Sahel. While I'd been gone, he barely crossed my mind, and when he did, I didn't get that stabbing pain in my chest. The witchcraft of the griots was more dangerous than I knew. Their tales had seduced me. The exclusivity of knowing secrets had made me forget what truly mattered.

My lips pursed, and tears spilled from my eyes. I turned back to him, and again I embraced the boy that would have been my husband had the Griothood not called me.

"I'm so sorry, Sahel," I whispered again and put my palm to his cheek, and then I trudged to the gate.

Queenie waited with her arms crossed and her lips in a

tight straight line. "Are you going to walk with us?" The drums had already told the village that we had arrived, and the people would be waiting to greet us.

I waved her off and marched past her, through the gates, and straight to my father's home with my arms folded and my eyes downcast. I ignored the village women who had brought us bread after our long journey. Eyes were on me, taking in my sulkiness. They only made me more cross. I heard people murmuring, but I didn't care. They hadn't been sacrificed, yet they would still call me selfish and ungrateful for my childish display.

The sight of the home I had grown up in lightened my irritation just a bit. The familiarity had a soothing effect. I'd never been away from this loving place for so long. The fire was not smoking in front of the house. That meant Father hadn't cooked tonight. Then, I remembered that tonight would be Habtamu's funeral, so the village would all eat together. I knocked, always taking care not to startle Father. I opened the front door, and the scent of sage hanging by the door to ward off bad spirits greeted me.

"Father," I called out. But there was no answer.

I went into my room and fell back on my soft mattress. I coveted the comfort and luxury after lying on the hard, bat shit-covered floor of the cave. I thought about Abebi. She could've never slept in that condition.

I wanted to rest, but I decided I'd better go find my father. I found him in his beloved shed working alongside his apprentice, Mali. Father's forehead sweated as he polished a fertility idol. There was no finer wood than that of the Mpingo tree. The blackness shone magnificently when polished by my father's hand. The tree's inner black bark, from which the idol was carved, was once desired so much by Africa's tourists, the tree had nearly become extinct two hundred years ago. What were once vessels for the gods had become mass-produced meaningless trinkets for tourists.

153

"Father," I called softly.

His face lit up as he dropped the polishing rag and stood. I hugged him tightly, and I thanked the gods that he was still here. It could've been him the ancestors had taken.

"Zen!" he said.

"You didn't come when the drums sounded."

He laughed. "I figured the griots would be whisking you off somewhere to do something in secret."

"You always come first. How many times do I have to tell you that?"

I looked at Mali. He looked exasperated as he held an unidentifiable carving in his hand. My fathered didn't mind teaching people the craft of carving, but he complained that Mali lacked passion and that his parents had forced him to into carving because it was a prestigious trade. "Hello, Mali."

"Hello, Zen." He gave me a doleful look. Mali was in Sahel's set, so this would probably be his last week with Father before the whole set went to training. He returned his attention to the horrendous carving in his hands. I took in Mali's sharply angled cheekbones, sunken in cheeks, and discouraged eyes. I felt bad for him. Like me, he'd been forced to do something he didn't want to do.

"Father, who is the idol for?" I looked closely at the detail in the fertility idol.

"A girl in Ankara is being prepared for marriage."

I nodded, ignoring the twinge of envy, but I couldn't help to think about what that girl was going through. To be prepared for marriage, she would go off with the women in her family and her husband's family, and they would teach her to be a wife for three days and three nights. No men would lay eyes on her until her wedding day. Before she and her husband consummated their marriage, she'd get the idol and place it in their room until a baby was born. When she wanted more children, she would return the idol to the bedroom.

"Have you heard about Habtamu?" Father asked.

"It's so sad. At least the chief let Sahel come back."

He nodded in agreement.

I changed the subject, not wanting to remember the pain in Sahel's eyes. "Have you been eating well?"

"Maki's been cooking for me."

I rolled my eyes at the sound of her name. "You two seem to be getting close," I meddled.

He scoffed. "Never."

I returned begrudgingly to the Griot's Lair. I could hear the women inside fussing like hens. I swallowed. I had disrespected the griots. When I stepped into the house, the common room went cold and silent. Queenie's lips were pursed, but she said nothing. None of the griots spoke, nor did they look at me. They ignored me, and that made me feel uneasy like they would punish me when I least expected it. It was like I had destroyed all of the bonding we had experienced in the highlands.

The griots had already donned white for the wake. They had been impatiently waiting to see if I would arrive. If they had to walk to the wake without me, I would have brought further embarrassment to the Griothood, so I decided to stop sulking.

I took a long, hot shower—partially to piss the griots off even more, but I also desperately needed it. It felt so good for hot water to fall over my skin and wash away what river water could not. I dressed in white for Habtamu's wake, where the villagers would visit the home of the bereaved and view the body, ensuring that he didn't wake. After, when the sun fell, Habtamu's funeral would take place.

The wake took place in the common room of the dead.

He had been an important elder. Habtamu's daughter, who had been married to a man from Noire, had made the long journey to Obsidian. She sat with Sahel's father. She slumped, her head on his shoulder. Her eyes were distant. I gave everyone in the family a solemn nod while Queenie expressed our condolences.

I tried hard not to look at the body, but I couldn't stop my morbid curiosity. Habtamu looked stiff and angry. It was then I remembered Habtamu had been in my hallucination when I was ill. Was it just a coincidence? I shook the thought of the dream away and noticed Sahel had not made it to the wake. I wondered if he'd even set foot in this house since his grandfather died. I imagined he was still outside the village walls in deep meditation, yearning to connect with his grandfather's spirit.

CHAPTER 25

*M*arch 10, 2015-Two days ago, Naemah lost our child. I keep asking God why. I crave death, and Naemah is flirting with it. I look into her sorrowful eyes, and I know she blames me. I know she blames this place.

I forced her to go to the nearest town. She had to see a doctor. I trust the midwife, but I don't trust the midwife. Yes, I'm still in the clutches of western medicine. The villagers say they understand and that we should go, but like my mother said before she died, they will lose faith. I don't care.

I paid to get a truck out here. When we arrived at the hospital, the doctor said my soul mate had an irregular-shaped uterus, and there is a high probability that she will never be able to carry to term. My soul ruptured, and that is just a fraction of what happened to her. Fuck that doctor.

The funeral began at nightfall. Six of Habtamu's grandsons, including a dazed Sahel, carried the prepared body in a stark white burial sheet. Earlier, before the wake began, the elder women washed and oiled the body, then wrapped it with a black cloth. The shaman was called to ensure the spirit was truly free of regrets. No one knew how he did this because he was left alone with the body for nearly thirty minutes.

The drummers drummed slowly as each person in Obsidian walked in procession to the graveyard with their burning torches. The night air was hot and humid, and the mosquitoes were ruthless.

I switched from a mourner to a student. Queenie sang a beautiful song about souls flying away, joining the realm of our ancestors to watch over us and walk among us. With simplicity, she recited the list of the people Habtamu descended from since the start of Za and all of his children, grandchildren, and great-grandchildren. How would I ever do this?

Once Queenie stepped aside, every family member and elder drank from one lambskin containing wine then some was poured over Habtamu. Several men shoveled dirt into the grave and over the body. It was the part of a funeral that I hated the most. Sahel fell to the ground. His wails floated across the grasslands. My heart broke as his brothers and Zul carried him away. I looked away, ashamed to feel embarrassment for his emotional display.

After the grave had been filled, the elders passed the children who had not yet reached puberty over the grave. This was done to ensure that the spirit of the dead didn't attach itself to a child. Although a spirit could jump onto anyone, the spirits found it easier to jump onto youth.

Following the funeral, everyone gathered at the Harambe circle to eat and comfort the family. Every household cooked something to bless the family. I ate, but all the while I looked for Sahel. My soul ached for him. He was somewhere right now, feeling a deep hurt. I wondered if he wanted my presence or if I should let him be alone.

I waited until the griots were busy with people who wanted to meet them and ask advice to leave. I should've been using this time as a learning opportunity, but instead, I slipped away to Sahel's bachelor home with a covered plate in my hands. I knocked on his door.

"Mother, I said I wasn't hungry," his gruff voice said through the door.

"It's Zen," I said with compassion, but I heard nothing. Feeling rejected, I turned away, but then the door parted slightly.

I pushed the door open more. Sahel was back in his bed. I closed the door behind me. His clothes were everywhere, so were his books. His birth idol had been knocked off of the wall. I had never known him to have a violent temper, but I understood his loss had shattered his world.

"I brought you something to eat." I sat the plate on the counter next to a shattered glass jar.

Sahel didn't speak, nor did he look at me. He just lay there on his back with his forearm covering his eyes. I cleaned up the mess he made, and then I made myself comfortable on the edge of his bed. I hoped he didn't ask me to leave. Although I could feel that his vibrations were low, I felt good being in his presence.

After several awkward minutes, he said in an even tone, "Did they beat you?"

My brows crinkled. "What?"

"The griots," he clarified. "I imagined them beating their initiates. Their presence is intimidating. All they do is scowl."

I chuckled, "No, they didn't beat me." I became less rigid. My shoulders relaxed, and I leaned back on his thin mattress, propping my body up with my forearms. He still had his sense of humor, and a warm familiarity flushed over me.

"That's because I prayed. I said 'Ancestors, please don't let those wretched women beat my Zen. She's far too skinny.'"

I laughed and punched his leg. He laughed a little, too.

"In fact, you take the food and eat more."

I pinched him, and he jumped up to wrestle me. We tussled on his bed until he pinned me down. We both had smiles as we breathed heavily. His long hair fell like a curtain around my head. I stared into those dark eyes. Damn, he is beautiful, I thought. His body was warm.

"I missed you," I whispered.

"I missed you, too," he said. He kissed my lips. Blood rushed to my yoni, awakening her. "Have they..." I looked down, indicating his penis.

He rose up disappointedly. "Not yet."

I figured they would save circumcision for last, but it would've been nice. The Maasai boys were circumcised at puberty. It was torture to make our boys wait until they were seventeen.

I thought about what Zora asked me. "Have you ever made love?" I hadn't. And even though he would surely marry another girl, I wanted to make love to him. I wanted to experience what Zora talked about. The type of sex that would make you do anything. I let it go, though. I knew better than to force the issue. I wasn't here for myself. I was here to comfort him. "How long are you here?" I asked, straightening my white dress and fluffing my hair.

"A few days. Turns out the chief isn't as awful as I believed."

"Really?" I asked in disbelief.

"Yeah. Most of the time, it's just the two of us out there in the savanna. I've gotten to know him pretty well. He's still going to make me the head of the warrior initiates, even though I messed up."

"That's wonderful, Sahel." With my thumb I caressed his upper lip, pretending he was still mine.

We sat holding each other until I left his home with what I hoped was discretion. The griots were still out when I got in. For this, I was thankful.

CHAPTER 26

*M*ay 1, 2015-Naemah is a part of our world again, but since losing our child, she isn't the same. But she is the reason I'm working so hard to carry on with this venture. I created Noire so that our people can live free of the White Man, but we're still so tied to them that every other word from the people in Noire is a complaint about what whites have done to us. I think that it will die down, especially with the next generation, but the rage that my people harness when it comes to racism is crippling. So, of course, I ask Naemah what she thinks about it. She says I should stop them from dwelling in the past. I ask her how, and she says we'll figure it out.

Two weeks later, she says "I know how to bring the people to the present. I know how to free them of their hurt." Naemah peers at me, her brown eyes smiling. "Erase everything from their minds."

I raise a brow.

She says, "Not literally, but if you want to stop reliving something, stop talking about it."

I get it. I wonder if that is why she never speaks of our child.

"There will be no more talk of the White Man. No talk of slavery. Hell, let's completely leave America behind."

I balk. "Why?"

"We don't need that negative energy in this space. No more lynching or they stole our land." She was talking about the Gullah villagers. "Nothing to do with them."

I pace a few steps and ingest her words. "So…you're saying that we erase our complete history?"

She shrugs. "Just the part about America and white people having ever made contact with our people." The corner of her lips curl.

"What about Martin Luther King? What about Harriet Tubman? Ida B. Wells. Malcolm X." My face contorted. "What about President Obama?"

"No America." Her straight lips and expressionless face told me she was serious.

I laugh incredulously. "How will we get people to agree to that? Why would they agree to such a thing?"

"It's like you said, people are being weighed down by the past. We're creating our own truth in Noire. We don't need to keep sending that pain out into the Universe. Malcolm, you made them part with their surnames. You can do this, too."

I like it, but I say, "They'll never go for it."

"Let the elders vote."

I inhale. This is big.

"You humiliated me!" I screamed. I slammed the door to the room, which, to my consternation, was starting to feel like my own. It was two days after the funeral, and we'd just left the mound. I was supposed to share my first oral story with the elders, but I'd lost my nerve.

"It was only your first time." I could tell by the closeness of Queenie's voice that she was directly outside my door.

"You knew I'd fall on my face," I accused.

"You needed to experience the pressures of storytelling in front of the people." Her tone was comforting, but it did not help cool the heat in my cheeks.

Well, now I was completely traumatized. "They weren't the people; they were the elders. They're judgmental. They don't believe in me, and neither do you."

"You are the only person who doesn't have faith. We have to get your anxiety under control, Zen. Practicing is the only way."

"I hope you see now. I can't do this!" I hollered.

There was no sound on the other side of the door. She had walked away as I brooded. I imagined how stupid I looked as I stood there hyperventilating. Every word of the short story I had prepared had vanished from my mind. All the frightened eyes of the elders stared back at me like I'd grown two heads. My father had to be called again. I felt like an idiot.

"The griots are leaving tomorrow." She hadn't gone.

Surprisingly, I felt a sting of sadness. I didn't want them to leave.

She continued, "Zora requested that we travel to meet her in Noire and stay a few nights. I told her there are things we have to do before we could go. I also told her I'd ask you. Maybe we would join her in a week's time. What do you think?"

I smiled. "I suppose that's okay," I said, downplaying my excitement.

"Then we can go to Ankara. I think it would be good for you to see the whole kingdom." I could tell she was smiling as she spoke. "If you're going to tell stories of Za, you should know it firsthand. What do you think?"

I calmed myself, pushed my humiliation to the side, and answered, "I think that would be good," but truthfully, my heart was racing. I don't know if I had ever been so excited. I was going to see the rest of Za. I thought of Abebi. Now I would go someplace she wasn't familiar with: Ankara. While

Noire had over a thousand people, busy streets, and lively markets and festivals, Ankara was situated in a dense jungle, north of the Noire, with slightly over two hundred people.

Because of East Africa's natural dangers—dangers that hadn't been diminished by Man in the name of development—it was rare for women to travel. Only during funerals, weddings, and naming ceremonies did most women leave their cities. Men traveled more because they were warriors, and it was vital for the regiments to train together. Griots, however, traveled whenever they deemed necessary. I thanked my ancestors for the privilege to be able to embark on such a journey.

I imbibed on the lineages of every person in Obsidian, intending to make it a part of my flesh and bone until I could spew it from my lips backward and forward. The monumental task often made me scream out in agony. I could feel my brain splitting at the seams and my nerves fraying. I cried often and slept seldom. My world was gray, and my chest was being crushed under the weight of the Griothood. It was in those times that I became frightened of myself, and I'd slide my fingertips over the keloids on my wrists. Noticing my struggle, Queenie devised a way to make learning the ancestry of every person in Obsidian more attainable. She didn't just feed the names to me. Every time I sat with the ancestors and beseeched them to increase my knowledge about them, I drank frankincense tea from the root twins. With her words, Queenie painted a picture so vivid that I could envision the person's quirks, mannerisms, accomplishments, and demons. I sang the names of the ancestors as I played my kora. I played, again and again, giving each family line its own melody until the names imprinted into my mind.

I don't know when Queenie bewitched me, but in our weeks together, I developed affection toward her. Almost like a girl with her aunt. She'd lost her hard exterior along the way, and although I blamed her for allowing me to go before the elders prematurely, I knew she truly believed in me. Her trust, the trust of the other two griots, and the brewing rebellion kept me going, at least what I'd been told about the rebellion. I had yet to see any evidence of insurrection. I guessed that was a blessing. We spent every waking moment together, sometimes breaking to fellowship with the root twins. It made me smile to see how effervescent Queenie was in their presence. She and Inkar laughed with their whole bodies, while RoRo was always busy in her own world. Besides the griots, the root twins were the only close friends Queenie had. People came to her for advice at times, but other than official business, they were leery of her. Perhaps they were afraid she'd use them in a story and divulge their secrets. It was a transformation I was now beginning to feel, too, although people were never really drawn to me. There was an untouchableness and veneration when it came to us griots. The people feared and respected griots because they believed we could read everyone's dirty thoughts. We couldn't. People simply gossiped too much.

Since I'd returned from the Grotto, I noticed even Abebi had been avoiding me. That made this time for me more challenging. Before I'd been chosen as griot, we spoke every day. Now I barely saw her, though that could've been because of my studies.

Finally, I went to her home. My spirit craved sisterhood. I hadn't been able to speak to her since a brief exchange at Habtamu's funeral. I needed her, and I needed familiarity to get through my depression.

I held up my hand to knock. In that split second, I almost turned away as fear gripped my gut. Why? She was my best friend. I knocked.

She rushed to the door like a whirlwind. "Hey," Abebi said upon opening the door. I could she in her eyes that she was surprised to see me.

We hugged, and after an awkward moment of stasis, she motioned me to enter her home. She didn't want me there. I shrugged that feeling off. It was ridiculous.

"You're growing your hair out?" I asked, staring at the tiny black coils sprouting from her scalp as she led me to her room.

"You know my hair changes like the wind," she sung.

She sat on top of the colorful spread on her bed. As always, I sat on the floor. Perhaps it was my new position, but for the first time, sitting on her floor irked me. I tried to understand the present tension between us, wondering if it was all in my unstable mind. My father told me that although I had a sensitive spirit and could detect people's vibes, sometimes I projected my negative feelings about myself onto others, and I had to stop.

"So, I see you survived your trip with the griots." She grinned, looking down at me.

"It went well."

"What?" she scoffed.

I nodded with ease.

"So the witch is not a witch, after all?" A throaty guffaw escaped her throat, and she shook with mirth.

I averted my eyes as an uncomfortable twinge of pain struck me, even though I used to call Queenie a witch all the time. "Not most of the time, anyway," I remarked, betraying my mentor.

"So training is going well?" she said with a brow raised and in a tone laced with suspicion.

I forced a smile and nodded. "It's the hardest thing I've done, but it's coming along."

"I'm just shocked." Abebi nearly cut off my sentence. "It was only days ago I was wondering how long it would be before you had a mental breakdown," she chortled. It was not a happy chortle, but one meant to debase me and slap away any joy I felt.

My stomach constricted just as it had when I knocked on the door. My temperature shot up. I looked up at her with reproach as visions of me clawing her face materialized.

She reached down and nudged me playfully. "You know how you are—nervous and fretful." All of her white teeth showed as she laughed. "There's not an ounce of self-esteem in your body, Zen. But maybe you're evolving." Her cruelty had advanced to a new level as she threw one devastating blow after another, and I sat there and took it. My weakness angered me.

My eyes flitted down to my thighs. I gave a self-deprecating chuckle. Her words stabbed me. Did Abebi know about my performance, or lack thereof, in front of the elders? I thumbed the keloid on my left wrist. I'd never told her about my suicide attempt. It had been on the edge of my tongue so many times, but my spirit wouldn't allow it. Only Queenie, my father, and Sahel knew about the night I tried to end my life. I thought back to how Sahel found me in the bush bleeding. I had used one of my father's carving knives to slit my wrists. That night, my father nearly tore Sahel's door down looking for me. He had thought we'd been together. Once Sahel assured my father he hadn't seen me, he ran throughout the whole village searching for me. Finally, he went out into the bush, near the kopjes where he found me and stopped my bleeding. He was somehow able to get me to my father without raising the suspicions of the villagers. He and Father cared for me without the assistance of the root twins. Suicides didn't happen in Za.

She said, "I told Daddy about how overwrought you were about being a griot, and he said—"

As she spoke, I took a deep breath and held it for a few beats. "You told your father about our conversation?" The depth of my voice sounded unfamiliar to my ears.

"You were so sad. I was worried." She waved her hand dismissively. "He said he doesn't know what the griot was thinking by choosing you, and if you can't do the job, he has the authority to make her appoint someone else." She beamed as if she'd saved my life, and I should throw myself at her feet.

"He does?" Through my shame, my mind raced.

"Of course. My daddy can do almost anything in Obsidian. He's the chief," she said unnecessarily. She crossed her smooth black legs and propped up her head with her fist. Her eyes drilled into me. "So?" She batted her long lashes and grinned conspiratorially.

If I were, in fact, able to step down, it would mean I could be with Sahel. I could have a family of my own right now. But it would also mean humiliation for both the griot and me. I inhaled. What about what the king charged me to do? He sat before me and asked me to help stop the rebellion that could end his reign and the world as I knew it. I thought of the prince never being able to take his rightful place as king. The thought of letting everyone down made me sick. I also knew the secret now—the secret of our people. There was no unknowing. How would that be handled? I knew. I would be executed if I tried to step down. The reality made me tear up. Quickly, I wiped my eyes. I couldn't let her see my weakness.

I looked back at my friend, who was waiting with a slight curl of her luscious lips. I couldn't help feeling that it would bring her so much joy if I gave up. Could it be that Abebi hated the attention I was getting, just as much as I always hated the attention she got?

I drew the conclusion that Abebi and I were toxic for each other. Friends shouldn't wish for each other's undoing. If a friend found success, it shouldn't gnarl your intestines every time you laid eyes on them. My soul was screaming for me to separate myself from her. It always had. Now I was going to listen. Feeling that this was the last time I'd ever allow her to get close to me, I answered confidently, "No, I will be the griot." I told her I had to go and prepare for my trip to Noire and Ankara. The look she gave me when I told her where I was going dripped with undeniable jealousy. Only she went on trips for the heck of it, not Zen.

I allowed the brief moment of delight to warm me before I pushed the memory of visiting Abebi from my mind. Even with my heart full of rage, my learning progressed. I had to succeed. I had to prove Abebi, her father, my set, and all who doubted me wrong. By the end of the day, I had more than half of the lineage of Obsidian memorized. The griot determined that this was sufficient. It was time to lay eyes on the rest of my kingdom.

CHAPTER 27

A few hours into our uncomfortable and bumpy ride, Mansi slowed for a herd of elephants crossing the dirt road. A mother elephant stopped in the middle of the road, protecting her cute baby as it crossed in front of our carriage. It was the first time I saw Mansi smile.

Shortly after, Queenie asked, "Have you decided if you want to live inside or outside the gates of the village?"

I looked at her puzzled. "I always assumed that I would take your home, and you would move back into the village. Is it not the Griot's Lair?"

"Lair? What am I, a monster?"

I backpedaled until she started laughing hysterically. I rolled my eyes, annoyed. I hated when she toyed with me.

"No, my home is my home, and I plan to live there until I cross into the realm of the ancestors. You get to choose your own place to live. As soon as you let me know, I'll have a runner inform the builders."

"So, you chose to live alone outside the gates?" I asked incredulously. I always thought that griots had to live

171

separate from the people.

She nodded. "I need my space from people." She flexed her fingers. "I'm an empath, and I can't have everyone's pain and thoughts around me at all times. I need space to breathe and feel my own feelings. I'm still close enough to join in when I want to or when I am needed. If I choose, I can scurry away after I feed the people wisdom. It is my choice."

"Don't you like people?" I asked.

She chuckled. "Of course. If there were no people, I would die out here alone. We need people."

"No. I mean do you enjoy their company?"

Queenie shrugged. "Sometimes. Sometimes they make me tired, annoyed, and they down right piss me off at times. They always expect griots to have something to say. Most times I just want to sit back and listen." She looked into the distance. "Since I was a little girl, I've always been more mature than others. There aren't many people who operated on the same frequency as me. It makes it difficult to fit in. I had to learn to be comfortable with just me."

"I feel like people don't like me." Immediately, I cursed myself after saying it. Why would I tell her something so personal and painful?

Her face puckered. "Why do you say that?" she asked like it was hard for her to believe.

I thought about instances throughout my life where people were uncomfortable in my presence. I could feel those instances pricking the surface of my skin. They'd rather be elsewhere. I inhaled and looked onto the splendor of the savanna. There were hundreds of zebras and wildebeest grazing. "I look at the other girls. People are drawn to them, and they have tons of friends who flock to them. They hug and laugh and have secrets they giggle about. No one does that with me."

"You have Abebi," she offered.

I stiffened. "Abebi is not my friend," I said with bitterness.

Queenie's eyes saddened. "Although I'm sorry to hear that, I knew that day would come."

My eyes widened in surprise.

"She was never kind to you even when you were little, and you always treated her like she was a damn goddess. That girl ain't no more important or beautiful than you. I couldn't wait for you to know your worth. This separation will be good for you." She smiled to herself. I hadn't realized she'd observed me back when I was younger. She continued. "Don't worry. The gods wouldn't put you on this earth alone. They gave you a father who is a good friend, isn't he?"

I smiled softly, but a father's friendship was not the same.

"I have a few great friends—the root twins, the griots, and Mansi. Your friends needn't look like anyone else's friends. They just need to make your heart swell when you see them and make you laugh 'til it hurts." She smiled. "They should tell you the truth, but in a gentle way."

A few moments passed. I tilted my head toward Mansi, who was navigating the carriage across the rough terrain. "Will I get someone like Mansi to help me if I choose to live outside the gates?" I asked, lowering my voice. Our driver had always been a mystery to me. Where had he come from? Why did he live outside of the gates? Most men were forced to marry upon completion of warrior initiation. Not him, though. I'd always figured he was mentally unstable.

Queenie smirked. "I'm afraid not. Mansi is a special case. He's my brother and my very best friend."

My face broke into the widest smile I could manage as surprise consumed me. I quietly pondered Mansi, who had his back to us as he drove the horses. Now that she spoke it, I didn't know how I couldn't see it before. They had the same skin tone and opalescent eyes. Although he was mute, they communicated fluidly. I let out a joyous laugh.

My joy increased when the grand walls of Noire came into view. The walls were earthen, but built high, protecting the massive city. A willowy guard with a spear in hand ran to our carriage well before we approached the gate. Mansi stopped, and the griot spoke, telling the guard our business. The guard bowed deeply because of who she was before letting us proceed to the gate, but even before that, I could hear the buzz of a bustling city.

Only the royal horses were allowed into the gates, and a young boy was sent to tend to Mansi's horses. I noticed Mansi's agitation. He made guttural sounds to Queenie. I looked between them and the guards. I could tell the guards were embarrassed and confused by Mansi's odd behavior. Calmly, Queenie advocated for her brother. She told them that he stayed with the horses and only he took care of them. The guards stepped back as Mansi unloaded our bundles from the back of the carriage. Two young men picked up our bags and headed to Zora's house ahead of us.

We entered the gates, and the city stole my heart. I stared with wonderment. The plethora of sounds was glorious. It never let up. Children ran through muddy puddles, and people meandered down the dirt paths. Each person waved to one another. Some people walked briskly, some moved lazily down the narrow roads. Although I'd been here as a child, Noire seemed so much larger and grander than I remembered.

Even though brightly dressed people were everywhere, everyone moved without obtrusion. The city smelled of spices, delectable food, and sweaty humans. Even with all the people, I noticed the roads were pristine.

I couldn't get enough of the homes that were just as flamboyant as the dresses the women wore. I took in the majestic patterns that wrapped around each house. Some homes had huge and intricate mandalas carved into the walls.

174

"The designs are the crests of the families. The more ornate, the wealthier or nobler the family," Queenie informed me as we walked. She moved slowly so I could gawk at the unfamiliar surroundings.

Musicians dotted the streets, providing music for the pedestrians and expecting a piece of fruit or something small and handcrafted in return. There were also hair braiders outside of homes making their clients look gorgeous. There were so many houses and so many people, I quickly felt overwhelmed and severely out of place. But then I saw something that jarred me. A man held a long chain that was tied around a muzzled hyena's neck. Children laughed and gawked at the animal. Even adults looked on. Somehow, Queenie saw my outrage mounting. She placed her hand on my back and said, "Let's head to Zora's."

I nodded. I followed behind her but kept my eyes on the miserable and ugly hyena. I knew the ancestors were not happy with such foolishness. Beasts were not meant to be exploited. Domesticating them for our survival was one thing, but what was the purpose of this?

After awhile I said, "There are so many people here."

"Yes, indeed. The population swelled nearly a hundred years ago. Then suddenly, there was a terrible food shortage. To survive, many people sought another place to live."

"That's why Obsidian was formed," I jumped in.

"And later, Ankara."

Obsidian seemed so old and meager compared to this colossal place, but Noire was a century older.

We headed through a maze of homes. How did Queenie remember the way to Zora's?

"This place is huge," I exclaimed.

"Size it is not what's important. It is important that every mouth is fed, and the people are at ease." Then she shook her head. "Only, the people are not at ease, are they?" She drew in a deep breath. The rebels always pulled us into the reality that Za might not always be safe.

We continued to walk. Each home had its own spirit, and each person seemed larger than life. I wondered what their lives were like in such a city. Then I thought, how in the world did Zora remember all of these peoples' histories?

It wasn't long before Zora opened her door. Immediately, her face filled with elation. She squealed as she embraced Queenie as if they hadn't just spent a whole week together. She hugged me with the same enthusiasm before we went inside her home.

Unlike Queenie, Zora resided in the heart of the city. The inside her home was just as energetic as the world outside her door, with vibrant paintings on every wall and plants covering nearly every space. Each chair, and there were many, had a colorful blanket thrown over it. Dozens of non-ceremonial masks looked down on us ominously from their perches around her dining room.

"Rest yourselves sisters," she sang. "Someone just brought your other bags by." Zora danced as she led us to the kitchen. She wore her braids in a regal bun at the top of her head. Her gold and red silk gown swept the floor. Openings at her waist revealed her tight, dark skin. There were several earrings in her ears and bangles all up her forearms, each one unique. She was only two years older than me but seemed so much more mature and confident.

I took in the aroma. Whatever she was cooking smelled spicy and divine. We sat at her table. I was starving.

"So, what do you think of Noire?" she asked me, turning from her stove. Her smile was wide.

"It's very beautiful. There are so many people. Does it ever become too much?" I asked.

"No. Every sound is music to my ears. The buzz of the city lulls me to sleep and wakes me in the morning. I crave the action, the excitement." Her bangles clinked together as she stirred.

I thought about Obsidian. Did I love it as much as Zora adored her city?

"What is that wondrous smell?" Queenie asked, cutting to the chase.

"Githeri," Zora said, "and it is ready."

We washed our hands, and I poured libations outside of the back door while Zora prayed. In her backyard, we ate two bowls of the bean and potato stew. The spices were unmatched, and the goat meat was the perfect texture.

After cleaning, Zora showed me to the room I would be staying in—her room. I objected, but she insisted I stay there. She and Queenie would share the guest room. I realized Zora had become a lot nicer to me than when we first met. Had her jealousy had worn off?

The walls of her bedroom were painted a dark purple hue, and I was glad she put me in the gorgeous space. The room was more Zen than I was.

"I hope you're not like Queenie and too tired for Harambe?" Zora asked with a knowing grin.

Exhaustion wouldn't win tonight. I couldn't imagine Harambe in a city so large. Since I had entered the walls of Noire, I wanted to experience every bit of it.

I ran a warm bath in the porcelain tub that was inside of Zora's bedroom, a few feet from the foot of the bed. There was no separation or privacy for someone bathing. I imagined a man watching Zora from the bed as she washed her glorious body, putting on a sensual show for him, or a man in the tub with her as she did carnal things to him. As the tub filled, I allowed myself to roam her intimate spaces. I picked up and sniffed her bottles of oils. There were so many. Mint, frankincense, orange, lavender, and myrrh. I poured a few drops of orange and mint oil into the water.

Eclectic jewelry hung from her wall. There were stunning oversized medallions, some with big amethyst crystals, copper, or wood. Her wardrobe had no doors, and bright garments were either rigidly folded or hanging freely. The array of colors was stunning, many of the hues I had never laid eyes on. Her flowing dresses hung to the ground. Each one was a statement. Her jewelry and clothing were a part of the room's decor.

A rolled up canvas, stuffed behind Zora's dresser, caught my attention. I knew that I should not pry, but the canvas had been shoved back there with haste or fury. I quickly unwound the crinkled canvas and revealed the face of a handsome man drawn exquisitely with a granite pencil. His features were lifelike. His eyes were despondent and made me want to know more about him. Was he real? Why was he hidden?

CHAPTER 28

The drums echoed off the buildings. Fire-lit light posts led the way. There were people everywhere, but they were not the rowdy crowd I imagined. They laughed, embraced, and made their way to the city's core. Noire's Harambe circle was huge, larger than I had imagined. People stood shoulder to shoulder to see brave people dance. Some people danced in small groups, some danced in pairs, and some danced alone. Hips jerked and rolled, and butts bounced. Feet moved fancily to the drummers' beat.

"You know everyone here?" I asked Zora, moving subtly to the beat.

She nodded. "Yes, I can't always recall their names right off, but I know everyone."

I shook my head in awe. "And their ancestors and families?"

"Yes," she smiled widely. Then she squeezed my arm. "Don't worry. It'll come to you. Now, come dance with me."

I objected, but she pulled me into the circle in front of all of those eyes. Zora moved like the people forming the circle weren't there or like she knew they thought she was

179

stunning, and she agreed. She danced like she fluttered her lashes, like she walked, and like she talked. Everything about Zora was flirtatious and seductive. I wanted her to inject her ability to allure into my veins.

I knew if I just stood there, I would look like a fool so I danced, subtly, at first, looking around to see who was watching. Everyone. Zora moved more energetically, and I learned to ignore the observers. I fed off her energy and her sensuality, hoping to look half as beautiful as she did.

Soon, people danced over to us to say hello, and they stayed. Zora drew people to her, and she loved it. She was like her own flame. At first, I hated it. I just wanted it to be Zora and me. Strangers made me uncomfortable and self-conscious. That night, however, I forced myself to smile and continue dancing. I became who I pretended to be. Her friends asked me questions as we danced, like: "What's it like in Obsidian?" "What do you do to your hair?" "Do you think I can do it, too?" We laughed and sweated and laughed some more. Zora's hair had fallen completely out of her bun. I had never had so much fun in my life. The only thing missing was Sahel. I danced his memory away. In quick instances, the void threatened to swallow me. I had to get over Sahel.

"Come," Zora called, putting her arm around my neck. "There are some people I'd like you to meet."

I said goodbye to my new acquaintances and moved through the crowd, dodging some people who were high on their wine and cannabis. Zora took me to where the elders had gathered and segregated themselves. They embraced her warmly, and she introduced me. I hated speaking to important people, and I hated adulation, but I survived. Then she led me to an elderly, bald man who was standing with the aid of a younger man. The old man had a beard that rivaled Father's. Zora hugged the frail man, who smiled a nearly toothless and genuine grin.

"Zen, this is your father's uncle, Jo Akke," Zora told me

180

with a great smile on her face.

I looked from her to him a couple of times. I'd never seen anyone else from my family besides Father. I never knew anyone else existed. No cousins, no living great aunts or uncles. Father had omitted them like they'd never existed. I couldn't remember meeting Jo when I came to Noire before. It was always just my father and I, alone in the world. Shaking off the revelation, I reached out my hand to greet the old man, who was a bit shorter than me, but he insisted on a hug, which I welcomed. It was like I was embracing a skeleton, and I worried that I would hurt him.

When Uncle Jo pulled back, I noticed there was wetness in his jaundiced eyes, more than the watery eyes of some people his age. "Do you know you're named after my mother?"

"Aunt Zen," I smiled. "My father has told me stories about her."

"Good. Good. How is Bachwezi, anyway?"

"He is blessed, Uncle."

He nodded with gratitude. "Good. This here is one of your many cousins, my grandson, Kwame," he said, indicating the man acting as his crutch.

The young man, my cousin, had the same deep-set eyes of my father and Uncle Jo.

"Great to meet you, Cousin Zen." Kwame smiled. He was missing one tooth at the bottom, but it didn't detract from his handsomeness. He reached out an arm to hug me while still holding his grandfather steady.

"How many cousins do I have?" I beamed. Noire was like a treasure trove.

"Oh my," Uncle Jo said, his eyes looking upward.

"He has 14 children, 29 grandchildren, and 7 great-grandchildren so far," Zora said. The words just rolled off her tongue.

"My word," I laughed as I clasped my hands together. My family was thriving. I released the fact that I knew nothing about them.

"I know you're a busy woman, but I sure hope you can meet the rest of your family soon," Kwame said.

I nodded. "I can't wait." I felt peace in knowing that my father and I weren't alone in the world, yet I felt unsettled at the core. Why had my father kept my family from me?

I spoke for a short while with my uncle. He told me about my father as a child, before he went blind. When Father was a boy he would sometimes visit Noire. Jo said Father was a mischievous kid, and I wasn't surprised.

"Uncle, did you ever meet my mother?"

Just then, my uncle broke into a wet cough. My cousin looked at me. "I am sorry. The smoke from the fire is too much."

"It's fine." I frowned as his cough grew worse. "Take care of yourself, Uncle." I patted his back.

"Please. Don't forget to visit us," Kwame reminded me as he led Jo away.

"Of course."

The drums recalled everyone's attention. We turned toward the center of the circle. Several dancers in their ornate regalia were in place at the circle's core.

"That was wonderful. Thank you for letting me meet Uncle Jo and Kwame. I wonder why my father never mentioned them."

I noticed the younger griot's face grow rigid. "I don't know," she said absently.

Something in her demeanor told me she knew why. As much as my father loved people, it was strange for him to never mention his close cousins. They never visited him, and he never visited them. Was there something to hide or protect me from? Deep in thought, I watched the masked men dance in their cowry shell-covered costumes. I'd never seen feet move so fast, but my mind was a maze of paranoia, and I couldn't enjoy the show.

Zora shouted an unfamiliar chant with the crowd, which made the dancers move faster. Impossible, I thought, returning my focus to the show.

Abruptly, Zora went rigid. It was like the air around us was in stasis. I looked at her. Her face was etched with sorrow. I followed her troubled gaze. Her eyes were captive to where the circle arched to the right of us. Then I saw him, the man from the rolled up canvas. I had no doubt. Those eyes were unmistakable. With his austere handsomeness and gloomy expression, it had to be him.

I looked back at Zora, and her eyes were now lowered to the ground. She was the type of woman who never looked to the ground. I wondered if it was shame or pain that sucked her energy away. She had wrapped her left hand over her right elbow. She was lost inside herself. I looked back to the man. A woman had come and lovingly wrapped her arms around his. She was far shorter, and her head rested on his arm. The woman was jovial, and a cute, firm pregnant belly stuck out from her skinny frame.

I understood. "I'm afraid I am more tired than I thought," I said, feigning a yawn.

Zora left her world of hurt and returned to the present. Relief passed over her face as she wordlessly led me away from the circle. I found comfort in the fact that she, too, was in love with someone she could not have.

CHAPTER 29

The next morning, after eating a hearty breakfast prepared by all three of us, Queenie and I headed to the market to trade her wares. I hadn't known it before going to stay at Queenie's house, but she was a brilliant painter. She created gourds for holding water and wine, but on the smooth surface of her gourds were beautiful landscape scenes of the Serengeti and the Ankaran rainforest. In my opinion, the gourds were too beautiful to drink from.

Many people stopped to examine Queenie's gourds. They were curious about us, too. We were strangers from a place many of them had never been. Queenie drove a hard bargain for those who wanted her drinking gourds. She even convinced someone to part with a plump hen in exchange for two gourds. Queenie knew the worth of her hard work and refused anything less.

I loved Noire's market, mainly eyeing the people passing, each one seeming to lead a life of excitement and complexity. I wanted to know these people and to have Noire running through my veins like they did. I wanted to not feel flustered in the bustle of the city.

To the right of our setup was a group of women who sold gorgeous, grass-woven head baskets that they assured people were light and sturdy. Woman after woman walked over to them and tried them out on their heads. To our left was a family selling pottery, from small plates to huge vases I could climb inside of. The talent in Noire was endless.

"You should go look around," Queenie said after we'd been baking in the sun for a couple of hours. I was glad I had tucked my hair away under a scarf because it would have surely dried out and become brittle under the sun rays.

"Are you sure?" I said, feigning nonchalance.

Queenie fanned a fly away from her face before she handed me a gourd with a picture of the sun setting over the ocean. I had never been to the ocean outside of a book, and I was sure she hadn't either, but I knew she had captured its beauty. Painfully, I remembered my ancestors' bodies at the ocean floor.

"Go, girl. Get something nice for yourself with it," she said pretending to be exasperated.

I jumped to my feet. "Thank you," I said reverently. She put her soul into these gourds, and she'd just given me one to trade with.

I zigzagged down the market's main aisle. The sound of passionate bartering was loud and unyielding. I moved with the flow of women carrying vegetables on their heads and babies on their backs. Children ran playfully as they dodged people, some being slapped on their behinds. All adults had authority to straighten wayward children out. Men talked with one another and rushed away. I was in no rush. I wanted to remember every color and every new word I heard. I sniffed soaps of so many different scents. Foreign oils and spices were offered at every other stand. Handmade candles hung for people to purchase. Men dyed fabric in compelling hues.

A stand with brightly colored wraps captivated me. Some wraps were folded neatly on a large table, and some flowed in the meager breeze. These wraps would make marvelous dresses and skirts. There were smaller head wraps that would draw every eye back home to me.

A young girl approached me in a manner far beyond her years. With vacant eyes, she asked, "What color do you like?" She swung her hand over her wraps. She wore two wraps herself, one white and one blue, to form one flowing dress. Spectacular. I wouldn't know how to begin wrapping like that.

I inhaled. There were so many astonishing colors that I couldn't choose. Eventually, I pointed to a dark pink color with a gold pattern.

"Please sit." Her words were coarse. Did Noire do that to a person: make them hard and detached? "This is imported Egyptian cotton. The finest." I was ashamed when she removed my sweat soaked, dingy beige head wrap. The girl busied her hands wrapping, tying, and twisting until she stood in front of me and gave an approving nod. "You made a fine choice. Perfect for your skin." I noticed people had stopped and watched. I perspired more.

The girl took out a mirror, and in all my years of wearing head wraps, I had never tied mine with such skill and detail.

I swiveled my head from side to side. "Wow," was all I could say to the girl. Pink looked good on me.

"You want?" she asked dryly like she couldn't care one way or the other.

I nodded. "I also want the wraps to make a dress exactly like yours and another headwrap to match." I pulled out the gourd.

She took it in her little hands and examined it. Her face hardened. "No. No, Auntie. This is imported cotton, dyed for days on end for the truest color. It won't fade with washing. What else can you trade?"

I turned down my lips and stuffed the gourd back into my satchel. "Thank you for showing me your wraps." I turned and took a few steps before she called after me.

"Auntie, hold on. Let's talk. Please." There was a melody to her words now.

"No talking. I want all I asked for." I turned back and made the gourd resurface. I looked down at her with the same take it or leave it attitude that she displayed a moment ago.

She sighed. The child was a great actress. "Okay, Auntie. My momma will be so angry." Her little hand plucked the blue and white wraps from the counter, then a blue scarf. We made the trade, and I went away happy with my bartering skills.

My victory had me on a high until I saw the perfect carving knife for my father a few stands away. It turned out that the man selling it wanted a blue wrap for his wife. Another victory.

"Zen?" A deep voice called from behind me.

My face crinkled. Who could know me here? I imagined my new cousin Kwame running up to me, but I whirled around, and I forgot how to breathe. Prince Zaire was in the midst of the market's chaos, staring at me.

CHAPTER 30

The prince walked closer, still looking unsure. Then an easy smile spread over his lips upon confirmation. "Hello, Young Griot," he said, his mesmerizing eyes taking me in. He stopped in front of me and proffered his hand. I reached out for a handshake, but he took my hand and lifted it to his lips, just as he had in Obsidian. The whole market faded around us. I could see nothing and no one else.

When he released my hand, I said, "Hello." My voice was airy and trembling. I took in Prince Zaire's shirtless brown chest. My eyes moved to his full lips that the gods had flawlessly etched. A perfectly groomed beard and mustache framed his lips. Each of his jet-black strands laid perfectly against his scalp. I wondered how many attendees fussed over him each morning.

"I heard you and the griot were here." With the same intensity that the moon's glow pierced through Earth's atmosphere, his brown eyes pierced through me.

I nodded and reached for my hair, as I did when I was nervous, only to feel my new scarf. There was fluttering in my lower abdomen.

"How do you like our market?" Prince Zaire pointed to the cloth I had draped over my arm and the knife in my hand.

"It's incredible," I said, finding my voice.

"I am so glad you like it. Your wrap is lovely. Did you purchase it here?" he asked pointing to the pink and gold wrap the young girl tied for me.

"Of course. We have nothing quite this beautiful at home."

The prince gave a low laugh, and then motioned in the direction I had been walking, I tried to calm my nerves as we strolled together. He said, "I love my city, but Obsidian has a splendor of its own. Artisans in Obsidian, like your father, make things that could never be duplicated here. I have imagined myself living in Obsidian many times."

I scoffed. "Why?"

He simpered. "I love the quiet and the feel of a small village. The people in Obsidian are connected in a way that is impossible here because of Noire's size."

I smiled softly. I noted the people pretending to shop, but they were really just watching us out of the corner of their eyes, just as Obsidians would have had they seen the prince walking down our street. I felt unfit to be at his side. I'd been working and sweating all morning, and my lips were dry. Relax, Zen. Prince Zaire was only being friendly. He didn't care what I looked like.

I asked, "They let you walk alone?" I'd imagined a protective entourage with him at every moment.

He laughed freely, showing all his gleaming teeth. He stopped walking and faced me. With a voice laced in grit, he said, "Of course, Zen. I am a grown man."

Indeed, he was. I didn't know if he had done it on purpose or if it were involuntary, but his right breast muscle flexed. I pretended it hadn't made me weak, lowering my eyes to the thin trail of curled hair below his stomach. I swallowed.

"Besides," he continued, "I cannot stay locked up in the palace all day. Nor do I need a babysitter. My father, however, would be ecstatic if I stayed under the watchful eye of my attendees." We continued to move through the crowd.

A pretty girl standing with her friends called out the prince's name. I felt the sting of jealousy and looked down at my worn sandals, yearning to fade away.

Prince Zaire lifted his finger in greeting, but quickly returned his gaze to me. The girl looked hurt. I wondered if they had a relationship. He didn't seem to notice. He asked me questions about home and regarded me with genuine curiosity. His attentiveness gave me confidence, and my discomfort slowly waned as I began to enjoy our conversation. I felt light, and even though I didn't look my best, I felt lovely with his eyes on me.

Just then, there was a shrill scream. We whirled in the direction of the cry and saw a beautiful little girl. She screamed again. "Awww," I said, poking out my lip as the little girl cried after having her ears pierced.

The prince walked over to the stand. I watched his broad back move away.

"Rahj, what are you doing to this poor child?" he asked in a teasing tone.

The middle-aged man, with gray hair shooting up from every angle of his scalp, placed the needles into boiling water. "Blame her mother," the man said, throwing up his hands.

Her mother wrinkled her nose and held the girl tighter.

The prince lowered himself to one knee in front of the girl. "Did Uncle Rahj hurt you?"

"Yes," she blubbered, giving the man the most formidable glare a three-year-old could.

"As the prince of Za, I will punish him. Would you like that?"

"Yes." Suddenly, the little girl turned giddy. She jumped down from her mother's lap and wrapped her arms around his neck. He patted her back.

I walked closer to him with a sentimental smile on my face.

The girl's mother mouthed "thank you" to Prince Zaire, took the girl's hand, and led her away. The sassy child squinted and wrinkled her nose at Rahj.

The prince and I laughed.

"Thanks," Rahj said. "She'll hate me forever," he joked. "I keep telling mothers to let me pierce the children when they're babies. But no."

"She'll forget all about it when she looks in the mirror," Prince Zaire assured him.

"Who is this?" Rahj asked with a flirtatious smile.

"Where are my manners? This is Zen. She is Obsidian's griot initiate."

Rahj bowed his head respectfully. His eyes lit up. "Well, I think something that important deserves a piercing. Feeling whimsical, Zen?"

I bit my lip. Noire did make me feel whimsical. I considered going home with Noire's mark on me. Since I was thirteen, I had admired the women with their noses pierced. I loved the embellishment. Even Queenie had two holes in her nostril.

"Do you pierce noses?" I asked.

"Of course."

The prince raised his brow. "You want your nose pierced?"

I rubbed my neck. "I don't know."

Prince Zaire smirked. "Oh, you know, Young Griot. Do

not fret. Rahj is the best piercer in Za. In ten minutes, you will be pain-free."

I wanted to think it through, so I shook my head. "Perhaps later."

Prince Zaire looked back at Rahj and nodded a goodbye.

We walked a few steps, and I exclaimed, "I want it! I want to pierce my nose."

The prince grinned. We headed back. "Can you pierce her now?" he asked Rahj.

"I can." Rahj held out his hand led me to a battered chair.

Zaire moved close to Rahj and whispered something to him that I couldn't make out. Louder, he said, "Take good care of her."

I took deep breaths as Rahj brandished a long sharp needle.

"Left or right?"

"Uh. Right."

Prince Zaire moved closer and whispered, "Ready?"

I nodded my head, but my stomach churned.

The prince took my hand. "Calm yourself," he whispered soothingly.

"Close your eyes." Rahj stood on the other side of me, and I screeched as he stabbed a needle through my cartilage. I placed my left cheek onto Prince Zaire's hard stomach. A sweet scent rose from his warm skin. He placed his hand on my shoulder.

I cursed and pounded my thigh with my fist. The prince still held on to me. "It's over. It's over," he assured me, but Rahj swiftly pulled out the needle from my nose and stuck in the nose ring. I yelped again. My tear ducts overflowed. I hated myself.

"Okay. Okay," the prince said calmingly. He let me go, and with a small cloth, he wiped my eyes.

192

Rahj placed a small piece of cotton in my nostril until the bleeding stopped. He lifted the mirror to my face as he told me how to care for the piercing.

I was enamored with what I saw. I gave myself a pained smile, my wet-eyed reflection looking back at me.

The prince placed his hand under my chin and lifted my face so he could get a clear look. For a second, I allowed myself to get lost in his eyes. "I did not think that you could get any lovelier," he said. His touch was deadly. My heart thumped, and it took me a moment to regain my senses. The prince gave me a coy smile as he removed his finger from my chin.

I stood. "Thank you, Rahj." My voice was laced with fake contempt.

He grinned and held up his hands in defense. "I guess all the ladies hate me today."

I lifted my brow and held the mirror closer. "This stone almost looks like a diamond."

"Almost?" Rahj joked as he organized and sanitized his tools. "Well, it's the real thing."

Embarrassment washed over me. I stammered, "Oh, I can't afford..."

"Don't worry. It's taken care of." Rahj's eyes flitted to the prince.

I looked at the prince, and my mouth dropped. "Prince Zaire," I cried.

"Zaire. Please, just Zaire. I think me buying you a diamond makes us friends."

I placed my hand on my chest. "I thank you, but I can't accept a diamond."

"No refunds," Rahj joked.

Again, I looked at the dazzling diamond and the way it collected the sun's light. It was the first diamond I'd ever owned. It felt wrong for it to be just jewelry for my nose. I felt bad for accepting it, but I said, "Thank you, Zaire." I handed the mirror back to Rahj.

"You are welcome, Zen. Unfortunately, I have to go." He paused a moment. "I would love to show you the palace. My mother would love to see you, too. She's been talking about how beautiful you are. Do you think you have time to come by tomorrow?"

I swallowed. The idea of being in the palace intimidated me. But the way the prince stared at me—a crooked smile on his lips and his right brow lifted slightly—was endearing. Zaire was afraid I would reject him.

"Okay." I wondered what it was about him that made me feel so comfortable.

"Breakfast?"

I nodded.

He smiled, proud of himself. "I'll send someone to escort you. I should be off. I would hate for your griot to see me talking to you."

"Why?" I snickered.

"I do not think she likes me very much. You may not want to tell her that you are coming to see me, either," Zaire winked, and before walking away, he kissed my hand again.

I felt exhilarated. I couldn't believe I just spent time with the prince, nor could I believe the searing pain in my nose. I stared at him for a while before I walked back to Queenie. Even in his kanga wrap, I could see the definition of his thigh and butt muscles. His back was wide and strong. Don't do it, Zen. Don't become infatuated with him. I returned to Queenie hotter than before, and not from the sun.

"What did you do?" Her mouth hung open.

I was so busy imagining Zaire touching me inappropriate ways, I forgot about my piercing. I touched it and winced.

"I found a man piercing ears, and I asked him to pierce my nose." I conveniently left Zaire out of the story. I proudly produced all that I manifested at the market.

She nodded. "I love it. Almost looks like a diamond." She eyed it closely. I swallowed but said nothing. "My gourd bought you all that?" she said suspiciously.

"I had more wraps, and I traded them," I lied partially.

She grinned and nodded in approval. "A true business woman."

There were only two small gourds left in her possession. She'd started with over twenty. Queenie had done well, I thought as visions of Zaire's smile, the veins in his arms and chest, and the intensity of his eyes replayed in my mind.

CHAPTER 31

That night, we didn't attend Harambe. A small gathering formed between Zora's and her neighbors' homes. I met her two sisters and mother, who were just as alluring as she was. There was a drummer who was quite talented; a man created music by clanking two metal spoons together, a warm fire, wine flowing freely, and hemp passing between fingers. I drank wine as I laughed with the griots and Zora's family and friends. Everyone's vibrations were high. Every once in a while, I thought about how at ease I was and how I was never like this back home. Noire had done something to me.

All three of us danced drunkenly. It wasn't long before a tipsy Queenie wandered off to bed. I stayed and enjoyed the warm night, wishing Zaire would show up, but I knew better. I sat back and debated whether another drink would keep me from breakfast with him. Then I saw that man again. The guy from Zora's painting. He was with his pregnant wife, standing amongst the group that had gathered. She was pulling him away—or trying to. His interest, however, was unabashedly on Zora, who was still dancing with a small circle of women. What amazed me was that he wasn't trying to hide his attraction to her. How disrespectful, yet intriguing. I sat up in my seat and continued to observe him. The man turned to his wife. He was holding out his upturned hands and speaking firmly. His wife, who was defeated and bruised, walked away, probably to bawl. I felt for sorry for her, and I disliked him. Who would treat the mother of their child that way? I thought about the lyrics I saw in the Grotto. The artist gloated about how great of a father he would be once he got his bitch pregnant. Was this man's wife just a bitch to him? There was a pang in my heart.

Zora continued to dance, her copper bangles glinting from the light posts and her eyes closed. She was blissfully oblivious to the drama that had just taken place. She swayed her hips as the wine coursed through her veins and lifted her braids and let them fall.

Eventually, Zora danced over to me, sweat shining on her chest, stomach, arms, and face. Even covered in perspiration, she was gorgeous. "Why aren't you dancing?" she whined.

"I'm all danced out."

Zora sucked her teeth. "Ol' lady," she slurred. "You need to come dance," she insisted, taking my hands. I stood, ready for more. Zora pulled me, but just as before, she froze, this time just for a few beats. She pretended that she hadn't seen him and that he hadn't changed her chemistry. She continued pulling me toward the musicians, yelling for them to play on and play louder. Zora clapped her hands and gave the drummer a beat, and he reciprocated, his eyes trained on her hips.

We danced, but Zora moved differently than before. She was more fluid, glancing over in the man's direction, pushing back her braids, swaying her hips, poking out her ass, and biting her lower lip. I noticed he didn't look so severe now. A cool grin passed over his lips as he watched her, his hands behind his back. He looked at her as if he could taste her, and she was delicious. I could feel that he wanted to join in, but he knew better. He was bold, but not insane. After only a few minutes, Zora cooed drunkenly, "I'll be back."

I hadn't noticed when the man left, but he was no longer there. I waited until she rounded the corner, then I followed. I don't know why I did it. I kept my distance, attempting to keep to the shadows. Wherever she passed, the scent of her frankincense lingered. It took a while, but he appeared again. He'd been waiting. They looked at one another for a while, fighting a primal urge. Then they slipped into an alley that didn't contain torchlights. I tiptoed to the corner.

I heard her ask, "What were you thinking?" She wasn't mad but flirtatious.

"I can't stay away," he said with yearning.

"You have to. You know how I get when I see you," she moaned.

"How?" His voice was teasing her.

They were quiet. I imagined them kissing passionately, and it was not long before I heard the tale-tell moaning that came with lovemaking. Stimulated, I retraced my steps back to Zora's home. I declined another dance with a young man who I had danced with earlier and took my tired body to bed. Today had been the most wonderful day of my life.

CHAPTER 32

The next morning, I jumped out of bed, happy that my prior night's drinking hadn't impeded my ability to rise before the sun. No headache. No nausea. I was ready to spend more time with Zaire. I was thankful the water had already been turned on, and I prayed that the griots didn't hear me bathing because they would want to know where I was going with such enthusiasm.

After donning my dress I had fashioned out of the wraps purchased the day before, then taking a moment to tease my hair, I managed to slip out of the door before anyone else in the house woke.

When I stepped out of Zora's house and positioned my satchel around my neck, I noticed a man leaning against the house adjacent to Zora's. I recognized him as one of Zaire's attendees who had accompanied him to my village.

"Morning," he said dryly as I tentatively approached him. "I am here to deliver you to the palace."

I started to thank him, but he walked with such rapidity that I kept my mouth shut. I could tell guiding me to the palace was the last thing he wanted to do with his life. I followed him down the street, turning the same way Zora and her married friend had the night before. People were headed to the fields. We turned down so many streets and side roads, I would've gotten lost for sure. I was glad for Zaire's foresight. We turned on a wide road, and I instantly saw the walls of the palace. Its architecture was grand, with white walls raised two stories. I took a shuddering breath. I hadn't imagined a building so imposing. Father Malcolm wrote that he lived in a mansion as a child; I wondered if it was like this.

"What is the palace made out of?" I asked in awe.

"Marble," the attendee said with minor annoyance in his voice.

I made a mental note not to speak to him again.

Two uniformed guards stood at the ironed entrance. With precision, they parted the gates. Our steps were loud as we walked over a marble bridge. Beneath us flowed a man-made stream, where large healthy orange and white fish swam aimlessly through tall stalks of decorous grass.

I wanted to stop and take in the beauty, but the attendee gave off an impatient air. He opened one of the wooden double doors that were twice our height. They seemed thick and solid, but slid open with ease. I held my breath as we entered. I was struck by the massive openness of the breathtaking rotunda. The glass ceiling was two stories high and brought in the blue sky.

After closing the door behind us, the stone-faced attendee told me to wait, and he disappeared up one side of the grand two-sided staircase.

My mouth hung open as I took in the fortress. Lush green trees in massive pottery planters lined the walls, giving the majestic entryway the ambiance of a calming forest. Wooden masks depicting the four gods stood against the walls. Straight ahead was an enormous corridor that opened to the outdoors, making the palace bright and cool with the morning breeze.

"Zen."

My pulse surged as Zaire appeared at the top of the staircase. "Good morning," I greeted him, attempting to hide my astonishment. It was only fitting for someone so attractive to live in a magnificent home. I bowed.

"Good morning to you," he replied as he hurried down the stairs. He wore a gold-trimmed vest that exposed his bare chest. "Welcome to my home." He kissed my cheek, making my stomach contract. The effect Zaire had on me scared me.

"It's lovely," I said.

"Thank you."

A young woman in a simple dress appeared. Her hair was wrapped, but not in a fashionable way.

"I will take your bag, Young Griot," she said politely. I looked from her to Zaire. I thought about the tome hidden within.

"It's okay. Pema is one of our housekeepers. She will put your bag in a safe place," his eyes looked down to my tight grip on the handle, "or you can keep it on you if you like."

"I'll hold on to it," I answered quickly. "Thank you." I attempted to look into her eyes, but she scurried off. Her servitude made me think of my enslaved ancestors. No one should be a servant.

"Are you hungry?" Zaire asked.

"Starving."

He held out his hand, indicating that we should walk through the corridor. There were doors on each side of the wide hall. I wondered what took place behind those doors. I imagined grand balls, feasts, and meetings. Between each door hung a large tapestry with village scenes and landscapes woven into them. They reminded me of Queenie's gourds.

"Mother wanted to say hello," he informed me. "I hope you don't mind."

My heart pounded, but I shook my head. I felt so unworthy of her time. I hoped I was poised and calm enough to dine with her.

The house opened up to splendid grounds that had to be large enough to fit a quarter of Obsidian in. The grass was dark green and lush and, therefore, unnatural to this part of Za. The thought of the amount of water it took to maintain the grounds weighed on me. I wondered what Father Malcolm would think—conserving water was important to him.

"Mother," Zaire called.

The lovely queen made apologetic noises as she wiped her mouth and chewed quickly. She rose, swallowing the remnants of food. Her emerald tunic looked casual but expensively made.

"Good morning," she sang as she glided around the large table with a huge smile. She opened her arms to me and hugged me tightly. "How is Noire treating you?" she asked.

"It's wonderful. This city is quite amazing."

"It beats Obsidian, huh?" Her tone was biting like she hated the place from which she came.

I felt a minute sting. Obsidian was in my soul, although I lusted for Noire's magic.

"Mother. That is not kind," Zaire warned. I wondered if he had read my expression.

"What? I can say that. I am Obsidian, anyway."

This was true. I let the feeling fade.

"Have a seat, Zen. I hope you can enjoy what we had prepared for you this morning." As if Zaire had said magic words, three women appeared from inside the house, carrying covered plates. There were green and red mangoes, purple grapes, yellow pears, and passion fruit sliced open to reveal its gooey yellow inner fruit already arranged beautifully at the center of the table. In front of each of our settings were tongs for us to place the fruit on the plates. The array of fruit alone was enough to fill me. I sat, and Pema placed a napkin on my lap. This was unfamiliar to me. I hoped I had enough etiquette to not embarrass myself in front of my hosts.

The three housekeepers removed the lids from the plates and steam rose, as did the delightful smell. Bacon, sausage, eggs, grits, and lentils overflowed my plate.

"Passion fruit juice?" Pema asked me as the other women attended to the queen and prince. She'd been assigned to take care of me.

"Yes, please."

"How does it look?" Zaire asked with a sly grin. He was enjoying my unfamiliarity to this sort of treatment.

"Wonderful."

Smiling, the queen held out her hands. We joined hands, and she gave thanks to our ancestors for their guidance and the gods for our food. We poured libations into the grass, and we ate. The food tasted as delicious as it smelled.

"Mother, notice anything different about Zen?"

The queen squinted, and then she beamed. "Your nose was not pierced when I last saw you." She shook her finger.

I giggled.

"Did my son get you into trouble?"

"No, Queen Finda." My eyes moved to his and then quickly away. "I've wanted to get my nose pierced for a long time."

"Well, it enhances your beauty." She smiled.

I blushed. "Thank you."

"Zen, did Queenie ever tell you we were in the same age

set?" She inquired before spooning grits into her mouth.

My face twisted. "No, she didn't." That means they spent much of their early lives together. How could that be so inconsequential to Queenie that she never mentioned it to me?

The queen twisted her lips and rolled her eyes. "Of course."

What was this attitude toward Queenie? Queenie angered me often, but a protective feeling fell over me when the queen showed distaste for my mentor.

Zaire cleared his throat.

The queen seamlessly changed the subject, stretching her lips into a fake smile. "How is griot training going?"

"It requires a lot, but I'm determined to be a wonderful griot." I feigned confidence and hoped my hosts couldn't tell.

She grinned, lifting her glass to my declaration. "I have no doubt that you will be a magnificent griot." She winked before taking a sip of juice. She ate a few more bites and said, "Well, since you are Zaire's guest, I will intrude no longer." She rose, as did Zaire. I jumped to my feet also.

Again, my nerves went crazy at the thought of being left alone with Zaire. I wanted her to stay so that all of his attention wouldn't be on me. The comfort I felt with Zaire in the market seemed so foreign. My heart drummed in my ears.

"Enjoy your morning, Mother."

Shakily, I added, "Thank you for having me."

"Anytime." The queen reached over the center of the table and grasped my hand for a moment, before she sashayed away, leaving a steaming plate of food behind. A servant quickly whisked the plate away.

A cool breeze blew, and I wrapped my scarf around my shoulders.

"Would you like to eat inside?" Zaire asked with concern

in his eyes.

"No, please. I am enjoying the view."

We ate in awkward silence. I fished for something cunning and cute to say, but nothing emerged.

I was relieved when he said, "What did you like to do before you were called to the Griothood?" He had stopped eating and had been staring at the side of my face for a while, making it hard for me to focus on eating.

I thought back to the time before I was an initiate. It felt like such a long time ago. Still looking forward and avoiding his eyes, I replied, "I loved meditating every morning. I still do. I loved spending time with my father and my best friend." My stomach knotted when I thought of Abebi. I left out Sahel. "I loved dancing and playing my kora."

There was a glint of surprise in his eyes. "Hopefully, one day you can play for me."

"That would be nice."

"You did not mention your mother," he observed. "She wasn't at your ceremony either."

I felt a sudden stab in my chest. Everyone in Obsidian knew not to ask about my mother. I hadn't asked people to not ask. They just assumed that it was the polite thing to do. For this reason, Zaire's words caught me off guard.

I looked to him, but then I dropped my eyes immediately. His intensity was too much. "My mother died just after I was born." I'd never had to explain this before. Everyone just knew. It felt so strange to form the words and even stranger hearing them leave my mouth.

Zaire sat up straight and stammered an apology.

"No, don't be sorry. You didn't know."

"It is my job to know about my guests." His eyes went vacant. He was punishing himself.

I was sure the queen knew. Why hadn't she told him?

Perhaps she left Obsidian before my mother died and didn't know. For a second I found it curious that he knew that my father was an artist but didn't know my mother was dead. I gave him a soft smile. "It's okay, Prince Zaire. Really."

He said sweetly, "I told you to call me Zaire."

I scoffed.

"I am serious. I now consider you a friend."

I gave him an easy smile. "What do you like to do?" I asked.

He sat back, one leg crossed over the other in confidence. "I like to be with friends, laughing and learning. I love practicing the ancient art of Laamb."

"Are you fearful of becoming the king?" We were in similar situations. Waiting to take over an important position. Being griot was nowhere near as important or difficult as being king, but I yearned to hear about his journey and struggle. I craved inspiration.

He shook his head with a hint of arrogance in his eyes. "I have been groomed for this my whole life. I am prepared. My father does not think so, but I am ready for my throne. Za needs me."

Just when I thought this man couldn't be any sexier, he was. Damn. Zaire had the perfect amount of confidence.

"What about you, Young Griot? Are you ready?"

I felt compelled to be honest with him. I shook my head. "I don't know what Queenie was thinking when she chose me. She says she sees that I am the one, but I don't believe her."

"You should, Zen. I have not spent much time with your griot, but I know she is wise." He wiped his mouth unnecessarily with his napkin. "Are you finished eating?"

"Yes."

"Please, take a walk with me."

206

I smiled and rose with him. Like a gentleman, he held out his arm. I let out a rush of air and willed myself to not tremble. I placed my hands around the crook of his arm, and we ambled toward the gardens. I tried to visualize Zaire as a boy playing in these gardens, being spoiled to no end. "I can't imagine living in a place this grand."

"I have found it best to never want what another has," he said. "I try to find delight in my own blessings." He chuckled, "Now, of course, that doesn't always work."

That was easy for him to say. I nodded. "I agree. This is just beyond words."

"You are welcome to visit anytime, just as my mother said."

A guard standing in the garden saluted crisply to Zaire, who gave a subtle nod and kept his attention on me. "You seem nervous."

"I'm not," I lied, but he saying so made me more nervous.

He laughed a little, and said, "You make me nervous, Zen."

Like a cheetah that spotted a maimed gazelle, my insecurities jumped out. I pulled my arm away and stopped walking, lowering my eyes to the ground.

Zaire stopped too. He looked at me with raised brows. "What's wrong?"

"I don't like being toyed with." I pulled my wrap tighter around my arms.

"What?" he asked, screwing up his handsome face in confusion.

My cheeks grew warm. Why had I had such an outburst? I took a deep breath. "There's not a nervous bone in your body, yet here you are pretending that I make you nervous." I scratched the back of my neck. "Just because I'm from little old Obsidian doesn't mean I'm naive." I thought about the girl in the market that he ignored. I didn't want to be her after he played with my heart.

"You think I am playing games? What motive do I have to lie?" He lifted his hand.

"You tell me. All these beautiful girls in Noire and *I* make you nervous." I pushed my fro back.

"Do you not think that you are beautiful enough to make me weak every time I see you?"

He might as well have grabbed my stomach and squeezed.

Sweat appeared on his forehead. Perhaps I was making him nervous. He smiled. "You think I'm just trying to get you into bed. Well, even I like to court a lady first, Zen."

I blushed. He stopped talking for a moment, and my mind raced. Did I just make a fool of myself? Was I projecting again? Should I leave the palace now? I prepared to tell him good day and thank you for breakfast, when he said, "Walk with me, please. I have something that will soften even you, Lioness."

I pursed my lips and gave him a distrustful look. My whole body told me to run. I couldn't decipher whether it was fear or intuition. Reluctant but intrigued, I took hold of his arm again.

His face contorted, and I could tell he wanted to say more. Finally, he confessed, "I lied to you back there, in front of the servants."

I raised my brow.

"I am afraid of what is before me," he said, glancing down at me.

I looked at him with compassion.

"I am even more concerned that there may be no Za for me to rule."

My eyes widened. His words shook me, as did the way he stared into my eyes. "The rebellion?" I asked.

He nodded gravely. "Father isn't proactive enough. We have to get to the bottom of this." He pounded his fist into his palm. "The rebellion is expanding like cancer."

I looked into the horizon. I shook my head. "What exactly have they done? I keep hearing about these rebels, but how are they making themselves known?" My eyes went back to him.

He was in deep thought. Then he said, "They slashed the throats of two elders."

CHAPTER 33

My hand flew to my lips, and my eyes moistened. His eyes widened. "No one can know that, Zen."

I wondered if the griots knew. "I won't say a word." I tilted my head and squinted. "The people don't know?"

"No, we have sworn the families to secrecy with the threat of exile." It was the horrid way things had always been done here. It was the way Father Malcolm handled things. Secrecy with the threat of exile. But the people knew. There was no way two elders died so close together and no one thought it was strange.

I exhaled a shuddering breath.

Zaire gave a low groan. He regretted revealing that to me. "Let us abandon that for a moment. I want to show you something." We walked over to some large, well-maintained shrubbery. Zaire smiled and held out his hand. "Look."

"Oh my goodness. A lion cub." The furry thing tried to break free from a large cage.

I looked back at Zaire. He was pleased with himself, but I was uneasy. I thought of the captured hyena. "Why have you captured him?" I said, revealing more outrage than I intended.

Zaire's eyes grew large at my reaction. "He was rescued. Poachers killed most of his pride. He would have starved or been killed by other lions or predators."

My heart broke. Poachers had always been a problem in the Serengeti.

Although I was taught to respect wild animals and not treat them as pets, I cooed, "He is adorable. How long has he been here?" I knelt down to get a better look.

"Only a few days. Would you like to hold him?"

"I shouldn't."

"Come on." Zaire opened the gate. "When else can you say, you have held a simba?" He gently picked up the cub and stroked his chin. The cub tried to gnaw his finger.

Not wanting to seem even more uptight, I took the cub into my arms. He was so soft and restless, just like an overgrown puppy. I smiled, although it was wrong. Getting the cub used to humans would make him more likely to approach villagers, and that would end fatally. Still, I couldn't resist nuzzling the cub's head. I squeezed him and gave him back to Zaire, who returned him to the cage.

"What's his name?"

"Kongo."

Without a word, we continued to walk, but my mind was on the cub.

"I thought showing you the simba would bring you joy, but it didn't. You are upset, aren't you?"

I closed my eyes.

"Tell the truth, Zen."

"It isn't right for him to be here." I walked up to an exotic

211

pink flower and sniffed. "How long will you keep him before he isn't cute anymore?"

"But he would have died," he repeated.

"That would have been the will of the gods."

"No. It would have been the will of man. The poachers decimated his family."

I sighed. This was true. The fate of the simba was a dilemma. I thought of the lion that killed some of Sahel's father's goats and how the warriors were hunting him. It was unfair. The animal just wanted to eat.

"Any other girl would have been giddy to see him," Zaire said, breaking into my thoughts.

I mentally kicked myself. I had never been one to rock the boat, yet here I was browbeating the future king, again. I fixed my mouth to apologize, when he stated, "You see me." His eyes brightened as if he had a revelation.

"Excuse me?" Zaire had lost me.

"You did not just blindly go with what I was doing merely because I'm the heir to the throne."

I looked at the prince incredulously. Confrontation pleased him?

"I knew when I saw you, the griot had chosen the right person to succeed her."

I looked down.

"I am serious," he said. "And that is what I meant when I said that you made me nervous. It is more than just your beauty, Zen." The bulge in his throat bobbed. "Perhaps this is insensitive to say, but the other girls, they want the throne. I am like you, always wondering who is playing games and why. I know I can trust you."

"Because I can never have the throne since I can't marry." It burned.

"I am sorry. I am usually eloquent, but I keep saying the

212

wrong things around you."

"Don't be sorry, Zaire. It's a truth that I have to live with." I was ready to vacate the palace and never return.

In awkward silence, we made our way back toward the palace. I could sense that he was beating himself up.

Finally, he spoke. "Do something for me?" He stopped walking and looked to me.

My eyes went to his, which sent a shock through my body.

"Say, 'I deserve this.'"

I rolled my eyes.

"Please, Zen. Say it." He reached for my hands. He moved close. I felt faint, and my pulse sped up.

"I deserve this." My voice wavered. The words flowed through my veins.

"Say, 'I am worthy.'" He beckoned me with his dark eyes. His lips curved into a slight smile.

"I am worthy."

"Say, 'I am the griot.'"

I smiled, but he remained serious. This was truly important to him. I straightened up. Feeling ridiculous and like a liar, I said, "I am the griot." I felt it, unlike when I said the words to Abebi. The proclamation prickled my skin.

"Now every morning, noon, and night say those things to yourself until you know it to be true. Right now, I am speaking as your prince."

I felt the blood rise to my cheeks. I nodded. "You say those things, too, until you have no doubts about being king."

Zaire laughed. He rubbed his thumb over my knuckles. I watched his pink tongue peek out and slide over his bottom lip and disappear back into his mouth. There was something carnal about the simple action. "Do you mind if I attend your initiation?"

The question shocked me. "No. That would be nice," I said shyly.

He moved even closer and peered down at me, the ever-present eroticism in his eyes more intense than ever. Tension built up between us as his lips drew closer to mine.

Just then, his rude attendee raced toward us, his steps falling hard, stealing our attention.

"What is it, Adesewa?" Zaire cried, pissed that he'd interrupted. Adesewa went to Zaire's side and whispered something in his ear.

Zaire tensed as he nodded. Adesewa jogged back the way he came.

Zaire turned to me with a sliver of fright behind his eyes. "The griots have come calling for you."

CHAPTER 34

The blood drained from my face. Shit. I wasn't hiding exactly, but I wanted to know how the griots found me so quickly. I hadn't been here more than an hour. I realized that, although this city is several times bigger than Obsidian, news here traveled just as fast. Irritation overtook me. I liked my privacy, and I liked going wherever I pleased. I also recalled Zaire's remark about Queenie not liking him. I calmed myself. There was nothing to fear. Who cared if I was eating breakfast with the royal family?

Adesewa and the two griots stormed the palace grounds. Queenie looked vexed as she locked eyes on me. I'd never seen her face so taut and her locs in such disarray. My fear returned.

"Good morning, Griots," Zaire said in an official tone.

"Good morning," Zora replied in an overly friendly tone. Queenie said nothing; she was busy glaring at me. She didn't acknowledge the prince's presence. A flash of heat passed over me.

"What are you doing here?" she asked.

"I was invited to breakfast."

Her nose flared as her venomous eyes moved to Zaire's. "I wonder why…"

"I have to go," I stammered, mortified. Now I looked like a child to him.

I walked back toward the palace, my whole body quaking. As I passed Queenie, I frowned, but she didn't notice. Her eyes were searing a hole into Zaire, and my blood pumped hotter. Who did she think she was, storming into the palace like she owned it? Why was she treating him so cruelly? I came here of my own accord. Zaire didn't force me.

I stopped walking and looked apologetically back at him, ashamed of her behavior. Instead of anger, I noticed a trace of a satisfied grin on his lips. There was a deeper transaction taking place before me that I didn't understand.

"Take care of yourself, Young Griot," he cooed, snubbing Queenie.

Queenie stared a few more seconds before turning back to me. Tears built up in my eyes as I marched to the door. Queenie and Zora were on my heels.

We made our way to the front of the palace. To my horror, the queen was ascending the grand staircase. I slowed to a stop.

"Hi, there," she called with bewilderment in her voice.

I glanced back at Queenie. She rolled her eyes and took a deep, exasperated breath before facing the queen. My eyes moved between the two proud women. I didn't like the way Queenie's eyelids were lowered. I could tell at breakfast the queen resented Queenie, but if Queenie felt the same, things could explode.

"Hello, Queen Finda," Zora jumped in, her eyes round with worry. She gave a quick bow. Again, Queenie said nothing, her steeled jaw refused to unclench.

I wiped my tears. Trying to have some dignity in front of the queen.

216

"Is something wrong? Zen just arrived," the queen asked with worry etched on her face.

Queenie let out a puff of air and plastered on a fake smile. "Finda—"

"Queen Finda," the queen corrected Queenie with her shoulders back and her long neck straight. She glowered at Queenie for her mistake.

I looked back and forth between the two women. My fury had dissipated, and now I was scared. What was this?

Queenie pulled her lips into her mouth and bit down. Her eyelids were pressed closed. Finally, she surrendered, her fake smile returned. "Queen Finda," her words were drawn out like it pained her to call the other woman queen, "I would prefer that Zen stay under my care in her time of training."

Queen Finda gave a superficial laugh. "We are not going to hurt her, Queenie. We were just trying to show her something besides that mud pit you call a village." She paused. "After all these years, you still don't trust me," she put on as if she was disappointed, casting down her eyes dramatically.

In an instant, Queenie's smile vanished. "We must be going." Her words left her mouth in a growl.

"Zen," the queen said, ignoring Queenie. "As I said, you are welcome here anytime. Zaire adores you. I've never seen him take to a girl the way he has to you." Her chin was lifted in defiance.

Infuriated, Queenie nudged my shoulder, indicating that I had better exit the building.

I marched over the bridge and through the gate, turning right. The griots murmured. Queenie's voice was inflected with rage. She talked about me with distaste, as usual. I stopped, whirling around to face her with my fist clenched. I was livid—and I also didn't know the way back to Zora's.

"How dare you humiliate me like that?" I shouted. My

eyes were brimming with tears that I didn't want to spill. As soon as the aggressive words left my mouth, I shrunk back. A few weeks ago, I feared this woman. I could barely look her in the eyes. Now I had yelled at her in front of all the people walking in front of the palace.

Queenie's eyes moved left to right taking in the people who had slowed their steps to take in the drama unfolding on their streets. Zora smiled with her teeth clenched, waving at everyone as if nothing was taking place.

"Little girl, I am saving you from a lifetime of humiliation," Queenie said in a low tone. She hadn't raised her voice like I had, but she had a stare so piercing, I averted my eyes.

"We should go," Zora remarked uncomfortably.

I stood there, holding my left arm until both griots passed, leading the way.

Upon entering Zora's house, I threw myself on the bed and cried. Sahel was on my mind, my future or lack thereof was on my mind, the prince and how we almost kissed was on my mind. I was sorry for how I'd talked to Queenie. My life had become so complicated in a very short amount of time.

There was a soft knock on my door. It lifted me out of a shallow sleep I had not planned on falling into.

Before I responded, the door opened, and Zora stuck her head in.

"Are you okay?" she asked sweetly.

I considered her. I tried to assess her sincerity. Finally, I nodded.

She walked in and sat alongside me, and I sat up. I wiped my hand across my face, feeling the dry crust my tears left behind. My head ached.

"She wants the best for you," Zora said.

I folded my arms. "If she wanted the best for me, she wouldn't have chosen me as griot."

"I know that resentment well. Sometimes, I still resent the griot who chose me, and I am sure Queenie resents the griot who chose her, as well. The sacrifice we make not to love, to probably never bear children, goes against everything a woman is." She had a remote look. I knew she had her mind on the man from the canvas.

"Why doesn't she like him?"

"Who?" Zora snapped back into the present.

"Prince Zaire?"

She chuckled. "Have you seen him?"

"What?"

"A man that pretty is no good."

I groaned in agreement. "That is not fair."

She sighed. "You're right." Her eyes rolled up. She sat in contemplation for a few seconds. "The prince is a bit of a rebel who loves to undermine his father often. He is known to have his way with many women." My pulse quickened. "They lose their minds in the presence of a man with such power. Power is intoxicating. Queenie thinks—"

"She thinks I am naive."

Zora bit her lip and crinkled her eyelids. "Zaire is sneaky, arrogant, and immature, Zen. I think that's why the rebellion is occurring. People are afraid of what Za will become when he becomes the king."

"What does that have to do with me? I was just having breakfast."

"I don't know. Perhaps he's up to something. Queenie doesn't think his intentions are pure."

Her words ached. It hurt me to think Zaire's kindness was insincere. But then, why would he like me? There were many girls more beautiful than me, who led more interesting lives

219

than me, a small village girl. I was plain. I wasn't even a good conversationalist. There was no reason for Zaire to look at me with such passion.

"I'm sorry. I'm not trying to hurt your feelings." She squeezed my shoulder. "I know you'll do whatever you want, but I agree with Queenie. Stay away from him, Zen." She rose, squeezing my shoulder again before she walked to the door.

"Who is he?" I asked her on a whim. Immediately, I wanted to snatch back the words.

She froze. "Who?" But her rigidness told me she knew very well who I was speaking of.

"The guy that changed your spirit at Harambe? He was also here last night." My heart raced. Was she going to curse me for delving into her personal life?

"Queenie told me you love a young man back home." She said still facing the door, still rigid.

I inhaled deeply. "Sahel." It had been so long since I said his name.

"The man I love is Olwethu. Most of my soul is wrapped up in him, and I can't let him go." There was agony in her words.

I was surprised Zora was confiding in me.

"I suppose I could leave him be if he would just leave me be, but he won't. I would die if he said 'we have to stop. I have to fully devote myself to my wife.'" She sniffled and turned to me, her eyes red. "Soon, he and his wife will have their first child. A child I will have to hold at its birth and naming ceremony," Zora's face contorted. She sobbed and shuddered.

I jumped to my feet, and with apprehension, I put my arm around her. It felt so unnatural, but she embraced me tightly. She wept for a while.

"His wife thinks I am bewitching her husband." She laughed a little. "I suppose I am." She let me go and swiped the tears from her face. "I pray you have an easier way than I am having when it comes to love." Zora finally looked at me. "I suppose if there was ever a man to cut your teeth on it would be Zaire."

"What?" My mouth hung open.

Zora gave a wilted smile and shook her head. Then she exited the room with her ever-present grace.

CHAPTER 35

May 8, 2015-The elders have spoken. I can't believe it, but they agree with Naemah and me. The ugliness of America is still weighing us down and determining our course. The people will no longer speak of the U.S., the slave trade, or the White Man... ever. The people are not to tell their children or grandchildren about what went on there. They will believe that our people descended from the Samburu and Maasai and decided to break apart because of the restrictions placed on us by the government. Because of those restrictions, we faced starvation and illness. Tomorrow, the people will part with all artifacts of the U.S., and we will hide them in the mountains.

Naemah has come up with a brilliant idea of a secret society that will be charged with keeping the secrets long after we have gone, and long after everyone forgets. She says they should be women, and they should be called griots like in some West African traditions. By knowing the true history of our ancestors, they will keep the people from falling off track, from repeating the mistakes of our ancestors, but they may never reveal those secrets. For this reason, they should never marry. She says marriage will make them weak. They will tell their lovers everything. She also says that they should have no children. She says they'll want their children to know. This I don't agree with. First of all, that's cruel. Second, who would want to be a griot with such harsh stipulations? Naemah wants to tie them to the Griothood for life. I've convinced her that they should serve a term of twenty years. Twenty years is enough. In my mind, they can perhaps marry and have children once their term is complete. After twenty years why would they reveal their secrets? If they do, they die. As for anyone stepping up to the responsibility and making the sacrifice of twenty years without love, she says the chosen ones will have no choice. However, Naemah says she'll make the sacrifice first. I ask her if that means we will never marry. She doesn't answer.

I hugged Zora for a long time. My sorrow was heavy as we left her home. We were outside the gate, and for the first time in four days, I saw Mansi. He was holding the reigns of his horses. It was two mornings after the incident at the palace.

"I will see you soon, sister," she said to me. "Next time, you'll be a griot."

Zora then hugged Queenie. Their foreheads touched as they exchanged quiet, loving words.

Zora waved for a long while as we drove away. The heavy urge to cry came over me. I'd clung to her in our short while together. I sat back and closed my eyes thinking of how she accompanied me to my cousin's Kwame's home, and I met all of my relatives. She was now my sister.

"How long to Ankara?" I asked, attempting to redirect my thoughts.

Queenie and I had spoken very little since our middle of the road tiff.

"If it's the will of the gods, we will be there before nightfall."

I took a deep breath. There was magic in visiting new worlds, but the journey itself aggravated me. It was boring, uncomfortable, and lengthy. My only companion was a woman who worked my nerves and her brother, the mute.

I awoke when the carriage slowed considerably. I was startled by the dense, lush forest and thick fog that surrounded us. I'd never seen so much green. The wonderful scent of Mother Earth entered my nostrils. I could hardly tell if it was almost dark out or if it was dim because of the thick canopy above. It was the most spectacular place I'd ever seen.

"Where are we?" I asked, pulling my cape closer around me. The temperature had dropped at least twenty degrees since I had fallen asleep.

"The Ur rainforest," Queenie said. The foggy beauty entranced her, too, even though she'd been here before. The ancient trees had massive trunks and far-reaching roots that traveled above ground for a while before burying themselves in the rich black soil. The birds flitting from branch to branch were a bright array of colors, and their songs majestic and never ending. Several species of monkeys I'd never encountered bounded above us. They were curious. I was, too. Gigantic and unusual fruits hung from the foliage.

Mansi slowed the carriage to a stop, and I looked around. There was no village.

"The road becomes impassible here. We have to walk."

My mind flashed back to the griot's safari and the blisters that formed on my feet.

Taking in my angst, Queenie said, "Don't worry, it's not far."

We walked slowly, negotiating the roots and thick mud. This time, Mansi was with us, and he helped us carry our belongings. Suddenly, Queenie touched my arm. She nodded in the direction of the trees to our right.

I looked, but I only saw trees.

"Look closely," she whispered. "The Dembi Warriors are among us."

I stiffened and tried to focus. Finally, I saw a warrior blended perfectly next to a tree. The woman was stock still and formidable with a long spear in her grasp. A chill shot down my spine. Then I saw another. And another. The women stood motionless on a cliff. As if my blindness was stripped away, I noticed there were at least ten women on both sides of the path. I'd ignorantly walked past most of them. They were spread out, scrutinizing us as we passed. Some stood straight, some were crouched low, but they all possessed the same menacing look. White paint across their faces added to the terror they induced. They wore short wraps that revealed slender and muscular legs, and their breasts were bare.

I had heard many stories about the fearsome women who protected their village. They were deadly when need be. Their men could fight just as well, but it was the men who went away to hunt. The women guarded the village perimeters. They were impeccable with their arrows, spears, knives, and hand-to-hand combat.

"Will they attack us?" I asked in a shaky whisper. I knew they could kill us in seconds.

"No." Her voice shook, however. "They have open communication with our brothers and sisters in Ankara, so they know who we are. If they didn't, we'd already be dead."

I swallowed. "Do they just wait out here all the time?"

"They rotate shifts with the others who are taking care of cooking and the children. If someone enters their forest, they silently signal the others. Frightening, isn't it?"

We kept moving. I nodded as we passed more motionless warriors. "They let our people move here?" It was the wish of our founders for us to leave native people as unengaged as possible. In no way were we to study them, impose our ways on them, or impact their way of living more than we already had by settling into the three provinces.

"Before the Ankarans moved away from Noire, scouts went out to find the perfect place," she spoke in her deep storytelling voice. "When they entered the Ur Forest, the Dembi women nearly slew them on the spot. Then Nok threw up her hands and begged the women to spare them. They said they would allow them to live, as long as Nok became their prisoner."

My mouth dropped.

Queenie nodded proudly in response to my surprise.

"Did the scouts leave her?"

"They had no choice. There were thirty livid Dembi women surrounding them with sharp blades aimed at their throats. So many people have come into these forests, so much has been depleted that they will do anything to protect what's left."

I waited for her to continue.

"The Dembi women kept Nok captive for about a month before they walked her back to Noire."

"What did they do to her?" I whispered frantically.

"Nok never told. All I know is that she can shoot her bow better than any person I know, and our people now live in Ankara. After that, there was no doubt who would be the Griot of Ankara."

"Griot? She should have been queen."

Queenie snickered, "Indeed."

Finally, the fearsome faces tapered off. We approached an enormous stone wall, with doors as high as the palace's doors. The grand wall was an amazing masonry feat. Carved into the stone were the symbols of all four Zaian gods. The guards parted the doors without asking any questions.

That's where Mansi stayed behind. We gathered our belongings, carrying some things on our backs, arms, and head. We climbed stairs that had been created with tree trunks and packed dirt. The people smiled genuinely and welcomed us. Men crowded us and took our loads.

We gave them thanks.

I gasped. There, just beneath the canopies of the heaven-reaching trees, were wooden homes. Between the homes ran a maze of roped bridges. Children waved down at us.

"Oh, my." Father Malcolm wouldn't have liked this at all. In one of his rants, he wrote about people not knowing anything about Africa. It pissed him off that they thought Africans lived in trees. And here we were.

"Is it not divine how they live in Ankara?" Queenie walked on. We moved up a wooden ramp with rope handles.

"Why do they live so high off the ground?" I asked as we rose higher and higher, navigating the ramp's switchbacks. I wasn't afraid of heights, but this was unnerving.

"There are many flash floods here. It is safer. Less destruction."

We reached a horizontal bridge. Nok and a tall man who looked so much like her greeted us. Nok's bald head was shiny and her smile serene. She wore a bright red tunic that stopped mid-calf. Her rough feet were bare. I looked at Nok with newfound respect. She was the savior of her people.

"Griots," she announced with her scratchy voice. She gave Queenie and me a quick tight hug. "My sisters," she sang. "Thank the gods you made it here safely." She turned to the man beside her. "I would like you to meet my brother, Jih."

"Hello," Queenie and I said in unison.

"So wonderful to meet you. Before you leave, my wife would love to cook a meal for Obsidian's griots," he told us.

"Oh that would be marvelous," Queenie cooed as she smiled flirtatiously. Jih's eyes lingered too long. Queenie stared back, unflinchingly.

"Excellent. Well, enjoy your stay. I must be off." He gave

his sister a hug before he headed back the way Queenie and I came.

"You didn't tell me how handsome your brother was."

"He is taken," Nok joked.

We followed Nok across the surprisingly sturdy and nearly unwavering wooden catwalks, which crisscrossed between the homes. The layout was a labyrinth to me, but not to those who lived here. Nok introduced us to every person she passed. They all hugged us warmly. I noticed the Ankarans dressed with ease, their colors neutral. Like the Dembi warriors, many of the women's breasts were exposed, and they had the most intricate scarifications across their stomachs. I winced at the thought of being repeatedly sliced.

I was enamored with the architecture of the homes. A few were even two stories, and some rose above the trees. In the center of the homes was a small gathering deck. Nok told us it was used for school in the mornings and other small gatherings throughout the day. Right now, an elderly man with loose, wrinkled skin around his eyes and mouth slept comfortably with a wooden headrest beneath his head.

Unlike Noire, none of the homes had any distinct paintings. Here, people decorated their homes by hanging painted gourds above and around their doors.

The village in the trees was more simplistic than Obsidian, yet it possessed more magic than Noire. Ankara did not have running water. To relieve oneself, one had to go into the woods and into the outhouses. Since rain was ample here, the water was gathered and stored for washing and cooking.

We headed to a particularly luminous part of the village. The sun was lowering, but it was still bright there. The mountains beyond were covered with dense green forest. Slivers of white, misting waterfalls cascaded to unseen pools in the distance. The relentless music that rainforest provided made me long for my kora. I was in awe of the striking natural beauty of this world. There was green and rich brown everywhere. I rubbed my idol. Yemi and Ayeki's presence here was overwhelming. If only they were real. Did the names of the Divine matter? Did it matter if we had one god or if we split them into many? Since I was a child, I read about people being murdered because they didn't believe what another human wanted them to believe. Beliefs felt so superficial now.

Four trees reached high above the canopy. Situated on one tree was Nok's home, a small one-story dwelling with dark wood on the exterior and many windows allowing in the natural light. We crossed the walk, passing over many trees. I can't wait to tell Abebi about this majestic place, I thought. Then, I bitterly remembered I was through with her.

Nok opened the glass door. The warmth rushed out into the cool outdoor air. A fire burned in a metal fireplace that was perched off the ground to the left of the room, but what stole my breath was the massive and ancient tree that reached through the floor and jutted through Nok's roof. I walked over and placed my palm on the tree's bark and laughed as its spirit moved through me. A gorgeous, large bed with bright red bedding hung from the ceiling with four chains. It was enshrouded with mosquito netting. Her kitchen was meager. Gourds hung from the wall, a shelf held four plates, four bowls, and several pots and kettles. The smell of burning wood was accented with the delightful smell of food.

After eating, I retreated to my bed, which was a hammock. Because Nok was older, she kept her bed and shared with Queenie. I needed real sleep, not sleep punctuated by bumps in the road. This was my first time sleeping in a hammock, and it was surprisingly comfortable. In no time, I drifted off.

"Zen, look at this," Queenie called, jostling me from a deep sleep. Disoriented, I exited Nok's home, and my soul fluttered. The sun had set, but the stunning glow of hundreds of fiery orange torches dotted the tree houses, walkways, and the ground below. It was absolutely stunning. In the dark, the torches seemed to float in mid-air.

Voices sang in unison from all around the village. A song echoed eerily through the trees. The Ankarans were singing, chanting to the ancestors and the villagers, asking them to gather.

"I will watch from up here," Nok said pointing to her knee.

"Me, too," Queenie said, waving her hand, indicating that I could go. I was weak with tiredness, but I let my feet lead me. I wrapped a quilt around my body and walked across the zigzagging rope bridges and down to join the circle of serene people. The air was frigid, like the weather at the Grotto, and vapors left my lips. I hoped I didn't get ill again.

The energy in Ankara's Harambe was different from Noire's. I smiled as the little children danced with agility and perfect rhythm. People grinned at me, but no one bothered me, and I was thankful for the peace.

Ankara's masked warriors performed their supernatural dance on stilts. The stories their bodies told were magical and transformative. I looked above to the menacing wooden mask, with slits for eyes, high bony cheekbones, long ostrich feathers for hair, and metal earrings and nose rings. I hated to admit it, but the craftsmanship rivaled my father's. The stilts were secured by being wrapped up the leg with strips of cloth. Long and wide leaves were wrapped around the warriors' waists. I don't know why, but at that moment, I wept for my ancestors who had been enslaved, and the ones who would've thought something as beautiful as this dance was wicked. I was ashamed of my ancestors, and what they allowed to happen. I begged the gods to carry that shame away.

The warriors on stilts balanced, jumped, and shimmied

with ease. They danced for the gods, thanking them for ample food, fertility, life, health, and wisdom. I wiped my tears and cheered with the crowd, and a warrior brought me a beaded necklace of cowry shells. My eyes misted as I beamed at him. I laughed like a child, placing the necklace around my neck along with my idol. I nodded thanks, and the villagers clapped and congratulated me on my new position. I realized I would also be serving them, as well. Many of the women and little girls came over to hug me. They were my sisters and their feminine energy lifted my vibrations.

That night, I fell into a sleep filled with many dreams, frightening and horrific dreams, but none as frightening as my Grotto hallucination.

Later, frantic movements in the tree house awakened me. I lost the memories of the dreams, but not the traces of inner chaos and the threat of future disturbances.

Nok closed her front door, where she had been speaking in a hushed and frantic tone to someone. She brushed her teeth with a miswak stick and rinsed her mouth with sage water.

I threw my legs over the hammock. "Is everything okay?" I asked groggily.

"An ancestor is returning," Nok said with delight.

Queenie rose. "Well, the ancestors planned it this way," she slurred and staggered, wiping her eyes. "Zen, have you ever seen a child born?"

My energy spiked. "No, I haven't."

"Do you mind if we attend the birth?" Queenie asked Nok.

"I'm sure the family will delight in having three griots at the birth of their child. Eat first. This could take hours or even days."

But by the time we made it, the child's head, full of silky

and slick curly hair, had already crowned. The mother screamed in horrific agony as her mother, mother-in-law, grandmother, aunts, sisters, a midwife, and three griots gathered around in prayer and assistance. As instructed, I covered all of the mirrors in the room to keep spirits from entering the space. With a match, I lit a dried bundle of white sage and let the flame burn wild for a few seconds before blowing it out, leaving white smoke and the pungent scent of sage behind. I "washed" the smoke over my fingers and body before going to the mother and allowing the smoke to flow over the crown of her head and then all over her sweating body. I smudged all of the women who had come to the space to help her bring forth this child, and I cleaned the doors and windows to the cabin to keep evil ancestors from crossing the threshold and attempting to possess the child. As I smudged every part of the room, Nok played her soothing wood flute for calm energy, but I don't think the perspiring and screaming woman drew any relief from the melody.

The mother crouched in the center of the room. The fire made her sweaty, sepia skin shimmer. She squatted as she bore down, her teeth clenching together, the cords in her neck strained. The muscular pressure was amazing. Tinged fluids leaked from her yoni onto a towel beneath her. I felt queasy and faint. The midwife held out her weathered hands and the baby boy fell limply into them. The women sang praises to the ancestors as the baby wailed mightily as his arms and legs quaked. His smiling grandmother wiped the slimy blood from his little body as the midwife used a string to cut the umbilical cord.

The mother cried as she held her naked baby against her bare breast, calming him. I felt ashamed after jealousy shot through me. This was life. An ancestor had returned. This was not about what I couldn't have. With a tired grin, she asked, "Do you want to hold him, Young Griot?"

I looked around. She wanted me to hold him next, not her mother. Frantically, I nodded my head. The midwife placed the small and beautiful baby boy into my arms, and immediately my vibes lifted. I simply melted, and tears flowed down my face.

The mother seemed to be giving birth again, but the midwife removed something bloody from her that was not a baby.

Nausea swept through me again, and I passed the baby to Nok. After holding him, she passed him to Queenie. Finally, his paternal grandmother wrapped him in a blanket and took him to his father, who stood outside of the door. He burst into tears upon seeing his child and looking in on his smiling, sweating wife. The father would take the child out to Ankara's sacred spot and present him to the ancestors. He would give thanks and pray for their protection and guidance in the child's life. And if it were Ayeki's will for the child to live, if the spirit who inhabited the child's body needed to stay longer, the father and the infant would return to that spot in a few months for the naming ceremony. The ceremony would be huge, and family from all over Za would come to celebrate the life.

I thought of Sahel. He would do this for his child, the child he created with another woman. I swallowed the dread and heartache.

CHAPTER 36

The next morning, I rose, cleaned myself, and dressed with vigor. Seeing life being brought into the world had revived my spirit. I was ready to explore this amazing village. The griots were still sleeping soundly when I left Nok's warm hut. My goal was to go down to the gathering deck and meditate amongst the trees as the sun rose. As I made my way to the confusing pathways, the dark sky gave way to blue dawn. I had to pause and take in the horizon and listen to the breeze move through the leaves. Africa was so diverse, so perfect, and yet deadly. Its power was immense, but my ancestors navigated this world perfectly. They didn't abuse our Mother Africa, our Mother Earth. They seldom took what they didn't need or what couldn't be quickly replenished. We sought to honor them by doing the same.

I placed my forearms on the wood railing and became rapt with the splendor of the mountains.

An elderly man, short and stooped over, shuffled past and paused. "Good morning," he said, turning back to me like he didn't see me at first.

"Hello." I looked at him and smiled softly.

"You are blessed to rise so early. That is Mount Qwei." He pointed to the tallest mountain with his head. "Its peak can best be seen on a clear morning just before sunrise. After that, the fog tends to be thick."

"Amazing."

"Enjoy," he said, whistling as he went about his business.

Instead of heading to the ground, I returned to Nok's home. I walked around the back where the view of Mount Qwei was unobstructed. In several pots, Nok grew onions, herbs, spices, and radiant flowers. I sat on the floor, folded my legs, and took in the mountain's apex.

I sat that way, meditating, aligning my outer body with my core. I had lost myself in the last month, and it was wearing on my body and spirit. I needed Inkar badly. I stretched out my body. Was I still balanced enough to do a headstand? I attempted, but gravity brought my body to the wood floor. I was out of practice in every way.

An hour later, the back door creaked opened.

"Oh," Nok said, and she moved to close the door.

"Oh, no. I'm just sitting here looking at Mount Qwei."

She stepped out and smiled at the mountain named after our war god. There was an ornate teapot in her hands. "Would you like some of Africa's finest tea?"

"Yes." I joined her at the small table for two.

"Tea is only one of our many specialties," she bragged, pouring me a cup. She went back into her home and brought out a steaming bowl of rice and vegetables. "Ankara also grows the best rice and bananas, and the pineapples are to die for."

We ate quietly. Queenie hadn't yet emerged.

"It won't be long now until you are the griot," Nok said, peering over a still steaming cup of tea.

235

I exhaled slowly. "I feel ill-prepared. I've only memorized half of Obsidian's families."

"That's only part of your training, a small part. You'll pick it up." She waved a hand dismissively. Everyone was so confident of this except me. "You've learned more on this safari than you have realized." She poured herself more tea, then leaned forward. "Queenie says your initiation will happen very soon. She thinks you're ready."

I nearly choked. I figured it would be at least another month or two.

Nok smiled and put her twig-like finger to her dark lips conspiratorially. Changing the subject, she stated. "Once Queenie wakes, we must meet with Ankara's chief."

"What for?" I said, creasing my brows.

Nok sighed. "The pending problem of the rebels."

I grunted. This shit again. After a few beats, I said, "What can we do? I keep hearing that they need our help, but what the hell can we do?"

She considered me for a moment. "I know what you mean."

I crossed my arms and shook my head.

Nok said, "The chief knows firsthand what is taking place. Let's hear from him."

I already knew about the two murdered elders, but I got the feeling she didn't.

Just then, a small gray and black monkey with bulging brown eyes jumped up on the railing in front of us. I shrieked and recoiled. With its penetrating eyes, it beseeched us for food.

I calmed and saw how cute he was. "Can I?" I said with glee, lifting a piece of pineapple from my plate.

"No. The creatures are deviant, waiting to bound into anyone's home at any moment and wreak havoc. The children refuse to stop feeding the vile things." Nok eased a sling shot out from somewhere under the fabric of her clothes. The knowing monkey bounded away. I laughed, and Nok shook her head.

Once Queenie rose, we made our way to see what the chief had to say concerning the rebels. The Ankaran chief lived in a tree hut that was undistinguished from the other huts on the outside. On the inside, however, he had long and sharp spears that served as both decor and protection.

The chief was handsome, tall, and muscular. Unlike Abebi's father, he didn't mind laughing or letting go of his rigid demeanor.

"Thank you, ladies, for joining me," he said with a smile as he motioned us to sit around his large dining table. His wife graciously served us mint tea before she headed out with their three well-behaved children.

We all sat in wooden chairs facing him. I could feel the angst in the room.

"It's a blessing that you are here today." His smile transformed into a frown, and his brows slanted upward. He inhaled slowly. "A few days ago, the king received a letter that was quite disturbing. Indeed, it wasn't the first, but…" He paused and looked hopeless. A chief shouldn't look hopeless.

My pulse quickened. I looked at the other women. All three of our energies changed.

"What was in the letter?" Queenie asked.

He huffed. "The rebels say the king hasn't met their needs, and they'll now attack and keep attacking until they have what they want."

"Which is?" Queenie asked, impatience creeping into her voice.

"They want the king to modernize Za by bringing electricity, automobiles, and currency."

I looked at the women. They both shook their heads angrily. To me, this did not seem like such a bad thing. If it meant keeping Za intact, why not give them what they want? What was wrong with modernization, anyway? I remembered my father once telling me that technology existed that could help him see. He said it had existed for centuries. I kept my mouth closed, though. I knew better than to side with the rebels.

"They also want us to export Za's resources to the world, our teas, rice—and legend has it that there is plenty of oil underground."

Queenie threw up her hands and slumped back in her chair. "Rape Africa some more, why don't you? There is barely anything left as it is. Thank the gods King Akonos will never go for it."

"Greed. The very greed..." Nok caught herself before saying things that a griot couldn't say outside of the Griothood. I knew what she wanted to say. The very greed that had our ancestors stolen from this continent. The very greed that turned some of our ancestors into murderers of their own people. The very greed that led Father Malcolm to leave America.

Queenie stood. Her words spewed like she was boiling from within. "Do they not know what oil companies did to Nigerian villagers where oil was found? And when leaders tried to protest the toxins that were being ingested by the people, they had them assassinated. Do they not know of Patrice Lumumba?"

The chief lowered his gaze. "I also have to tell you that three weeks ago, an elder was murdered."

The women gasped. I looked at my hands, feeling guilty for keeping the secret from them.

He said, "A week ago, another elder was killed."

Queenie froze, her eyes and mouth wide open. "Oh no,"

Queenie wailed. "Za is crumbling right in front of us."

I shook when she said that.

"What do we do?" Nok demanded.

"First, use your tales to bring the people back on common ground. Let them know how blessed they are. Frighten the shit out of them if you have to."

"I beg your pardon, Chief," I said boldly, "but storytelling won't do a damn thing to stop people who are willing to murder the elders."

I waited, but the women did not admonish me. Instead, their eyes looked back at the chief with the same regard.

He shook his head helplessly. "All I can say is, listen to the people. If you hear anyone expressing distaste with King Akonos, report it."

"That could turn into a witch hunt," Nok said, shaking her head. She stretched out her arthritic fingers, making the cords in her hands freakishly pronounced.

Queenie said, "Chief, we'll do all we can to stop this, as I am sure you will, too."

He stood and bowed to us. "May the ancestors continue to keep us."

"Ase," we all said.

CHAPTER 37

All afternoon, Nok, Queenie, and I pondered the rebel problem. We were frustrated, and frankly, we didn't know what we could possibly do to stop an impending rebellion.

"Zen, bring me Father Malcolm's tome," Queenie instructed.

I fished it from high up on a shelf where I'd hidden it. I handed it to her, and she flipped rapidly through the pages. Finally, she gave a satisfied look and read as her fingers slid across the page.

"The Griot's Charge," she said, looking up. Then she looked into my eyes. "Who was the first griot?"

"Naemah, of course," I was frustrated. Now was not the time to test me.

"Good. Why even have griots?" She asked, glancing up as she continued to rifle through pages.

I sighed. "When Noire was first created, there were no griots, but our founders found merit in the West African tradition. The Griothood was created long before people left

240

Noire and created Obsidian and Ankara. The Griothood was created long before a king was needed to keep the spread out cities unified.

"The founders created the Griothood to end any knowledge of our true heritage. Griots were to be lineage keepers, storytellers, and a moral compass. The griots also kept the Truth secure."

"How eloquent," Nok said, nodding in approval.

Queenie pushed her shoulders back with pride. She stopped turning the pages. "You also know that the Griot's Truth must never be revealed to someone outside of our realm. It was the founders' wish that our people not know about the ugly stain in our history. Children change when they know their people were the lynched and enslaved. There is bitterness that steeps like tea and sends negative karma into the universe that relentlessly hits those people time after time." She paused for a beat and said, "Although Za's first settlers didn't tell their children about the White Man, they didn't want that history lost forever. So the griots carried that burden, so that if outsiders approached, we would know how to advise the leaders."

I already know all this, I thought with irritation.

"In our laws, we are commanded to be weary of outsiders, people just passing through, people who want to study us and take pictures, and most of all, missionaries, the people who want to spread their religion to 'backward' people and help people in villages like ours live their way, the 'better way.' They arrive with their noses in the air and convince you that what you believe is pure evil."

Queenie grunted. "They believe their way is the only way, yet they want to display our primitiveness. They say we worship demons. This is how the Native Americans, Asians, Africans, and every non-white society were demolished. It's our job to protect our people and make them fear outsiders. That's why we tell many of our stories. I think, however, someone has been conversing with outsiders." Queenie had a far off look in her eyes.

Her words clenched my gut. Outsiders.

Dismay crossed Nok's face. "What if they learn the Truth?" I felt what she was feeling. If our whole kingdom found out they were lied to their whole lives, they'd join the rebels no doubt. Had our kingdom reached its end? That sent a violent chill through me. "What do we do?"

"We create a more frightening story," Queenie suggested.

Nok nodded, but I remained neutral. I knew what we had to do. We had to betray our ancestors and tell the people the Truth, the whole Truth. Nothing would make them more terrified than our bloody reality. If they heard what outsiders did before—pit tribes against other tribes, conquered whole continents, destroyed whole groups of people, and enslaved our ancestors—they'd get their shit together. I dare not say this to the griots, though, but what if my tongue slipped at a meeting once I was griot? Nothing could be done then. No one could unhear the Truth, but would I be executed?

"How far have you read?" Queenie asked.

"I have a bit more to go."

"You need to finish soon."

A piercing scream made the blood in my veins ice over. Nok jumped up and quickly moved both hands to her knee. "What was that?" she cried, eyes rounded.

Queenie ran to the door and eased it open. I rose as more screams, cries, and hollers sounded. Then there was the loud rumbling of a human stampede on the wooden planks. The house shook. Queenie closed the door and locked it. She shoved the tome inside her shirt while simultaneously saying, "It seems we are under attack." Her voice was freakishly calm. "Fire arrows. They're going to burn Ankara to the ground."

CHAPTER 38

Tears clouded my vision. Suddenly, Nok could move without hindrance. My heart was throwing itself against my ribcage, and the floor vibrated as people continued to run for their lives.

"We have to get out of here. If we can make it to the ground, I have a hiding place," Nok said panting.

"But the ramp will lead us straight to the middle of the village. We'll be out in the open," I cried.

But Nok opened the back door. Queenie and I looked at each other and followed the old woman out. Smoke had begun to permeate the air, along with more screams and cries. How many had been murdered? What would happen to the new mother and the baby? Surely, she couldn't move as briskly as everyone else.

Nok pointed to the thick tree that rose into the sky far higher than her home. The tree was an arm's length from her deck. She pointed downward. "Those wood planks are ladders. I haven't used them in years." She swallowed. "I hope they're still sturdy. You two go first."

"No, you first," Queenie said to her.

"Listen, there is no sense in three griots dying because of my slow ass. So go." Nok's words were final.

Queenie motioned me to go first. I did so without argument. The fire roared and wood splintered. I had to quiet my anxious sobs as I descended the ladder.

"Let's go, Nok!" Queenie shouted from above me as we cautiously made our way down the large tree.

"Is Nok with us?" I called just loud enough for Queenie to hear.

She said nothing for a while. Finally, she answered, "Yes."

I breathed a sigh of relief. "We're almost there," I said after a while, praying that no one saw us as we descended into the thick greenery.

I heard a crash above us. A cadenced thudding ensued until someone broke through Nok's door.

"Move, ladies. The lock didn't hold!" Nok cried. We all managed to move faster.

There was an irate shout above us. "Stop or I'll kill you." It was a man's voice. A rebel, I guessed. My body quaked. He threw his spear down at us but missed.

I finally reached the ground and attempted to help Queenie down, but she landed on her ankle and let out a shrill scream.

"Oh, no," I whined as Queenie went down. She rocked with her hands around her ankle.

Nok lowered herself. "Help her up," she ordered. I put Queenie's arm around my neck and heaved her up.

Nok now had her bow and quiver. I moved Queenie away from the ladder and watched the man with a cloth-covered face hurry down the ladder. Nok plucked an arrow from the quiver and placed the arrow against the bow. She pulled the string tautly and touched it to her face. Without hesitation, she shot the man in the back. He hollered in agony but managed to hold on. Then she took out a match and held it to the tree until it caught on fire. He yelped. He was doomed.

"Let's go." Nok ignored the pain in her knees and took Queenie's other arm. We moved as fast as we could, keeping concealed in the densely wooded area beyond the village. I could hear my pulse in my ears. They were going to catch us. My heart was threatening to burst out of my chest. How were we going to do this? Nok could barely walk herself, let alone help me carry Queenie to safety.

Somehow, we made it to the base of a tall and rocky hill, and Nok stopped. She pointed upward. "There's a small hidden cave. The teens use it for fucking. It's not far, but..." She looked helplessly at Queenie.

"Go on," Queenie said. She reached into her dress and pulled out the tome and held it out to me.

I sobbed, but I refused to grab the book. Queenie gave me a soft smile, beckoning me to take it.

"No, sister. If you stay, I stay." Nok said.

"You must protect her," Queenie said, nodding toward me. "She already knows all she needs to." That was a lie.

"Where is it, exactly?" I asked.

Nok looked up at the rocky hill. "Just above our heads, behind that dense patch of shrubbery." She pointed upward.

I climbed upward, negotiating the rocks with careful footing. I made it to the cave in about thirty seconds. It wasn't high at all. I parted the thick vines and I crawled in, leaned over the cliff, and reached out my hand. "Push her up so that she can reach my hands." I could hear men shouting. Were they friends or enemies? All I knew was that they were close, and we needed to move. Now.

"It will take too long," Queenie protested. She handed the tome to Nok. "You two go. Protect the book."

"Put the book back in your shirt and get up before you

get us all killed," I demanded. I had never been so frightened in my life, but I had to try to save us.

Queenie looked at me with trepidation, but she obeyed. Nok helped Queenie move closer to the mountain. Nok knelt down, forming a step with her hands. Queenie stepped into her hands that were locked at the arthritic fingers with her good leg, and Nok forced her up. I clasped her hands, and Nok grunted as she pushed her farther. With her good foot, Queenie was able to push herself closer to me. I grabbed under her arms and heaved her into the cave. I don't know where any of us got the strength, but we'd succeeded.

Once Queenie caught her breath, she wept, "Thank you."

I nodded.

I could hear the men shouting as they searched for us. Queenie lay beside me. "Okay, Nok. You have to climb up some of the ways, and then we'll lift you."

Nok looked toward the voices. "If I stay here, and you hide, I can kill some of them."

"Some, but not all, sister," Queenie pleaded. "Get your ass up here."

Nok took a deep breath before moving to the wall and finding a place for her hands. Then her feet found purchase and she lifted herself.

Come on. Come on. Come on.

Finally, Queenie and I grabbed her hands. My arms quaked as we both pulled Nok up and into the cave. She collapsed on her back as I repositioned the curtain of vines and shrubbery to conceal our hiding place. Then we heard the voices clearly.

CHAPTER 39

The men were now directly below us. We stopped breathing. Were there footprints? Did they see us climbing? I prayed to Sibo that he would hide this place and any trace of us. I strained to listen. What if they were climbing up right this second? I prayed Nok had her bow ready.

I heard one say, "If we don't find the griots, he'll kill us."

My breath hitched in my throat. They were looking specifically for us. They burned a whole village to capture us. Why? And, who was the man that would kill them?

We all sat and pressed our backs against the stone wall, squeezing each other's hands, and attempting to breathe calmly. I prayed for the villagers. Did they have a hiding spot? What about the children? Would they slaughter them too?

Soon their voices faded. Once we were sure they had moved on, Nok helped Queenie elevate her ankle on a boulder.

"What do we do?" I whispered once the voices were gone. "All of those helpless people."

One of the griots sniffled in the dark cave.

"Nothing. We have no clue how many there are. We'll be nothing against an army. No use," Nok said. "Who would've thought that today would be the attack? And in Ankara."

"What if they attacked Noire and Obsidian, too? What if they hurt Mansi? I know him. He definitely tried to stop them." Queenie sobbed.

I swallowed. I thought about my father. If they attacked Obsidian, what could a blind man do? I had left him alone. I hoped there weren't enough rebels to also attack Noire and Obsidian on the same day.

"Listen," I said after some time had passed.

They were silent as I trained my ears. There was a child crying, and the whimpers were moving closer.

"Oh no," Nok whispered. "Poor child."

I crawled to the entrance of the cave.

"Zen, no," Queenie protested. I heard her move and then grunt.

"We have been cowering in here while the villagers are being slaughtered. I refuse to let a child be murdered when I could possibly help." I parted the vines. The protests from the griots were frantic as I carefully peeked out beyond the foliage.

"It could be a trap to capture us all," Nok warned.

I saw a little boy, about five, his face in distress. He was walking in useless circles, and his thumb was in his mouth for comfort. This could've been a trap, but I had to try. I waited. I saw no one else.

"I'll be back." They protested more, but I quickly made my way down the cliff, using different muscles than I had used to climb. I stepped closer to him with my palms up and a slight smile. "Hello," I called in a gentle voice. "What is your name?" His big eyes peered up at me. He scrutinized me. "Osun," he finally whimpered. A raspy cough left his little mouth. The smoke was heavy, but the fire hadn't spread to this part of the forest.

"Osun, I am a griot. Do you know what that is?"

He nodded.

"I came here to help you."

"I want my mother," he said and began blubbering again.

I looked around, frightened that the men who were after us would hear him. "If you come with me, I will take you to a safe place with Auntie Nok." I smiled wider, hoping to gain his trust quickly. "Then we can find your mother. Is that all right?"

Osun thought for a moment. I swallowed and looked around for movement. He then nodded and calmed himself.

I brought him to the side of the mountain. Nok poked her head out.

"Auntie Nok," he cried with relief.

She reached down, and I lifted his light body to her. She pulled him in, and I followed.

"Now we must be very quiet," I whispered to him. "We are going to wait here for a little while." I placed him on my lap. He hiccupped for a while. It wasn't long before his trauma put him to sleep.

"That was foolish, but it was the bravest thing I've ever seen," Queenie whispered then she hugged me. I stiffened, then relaxed.

CHAPTER 40

Hours had passed before Nok decided to take her bow and arrow and see what had become of Ankara. Queenie and I hugged her before we helped her down. The boy, now awakened, clung to me. Nok promised him she would look for his mother.

Nok called up from the forest floor, "If I'm not back in twenty minutes, go into the woods and run away from here. Find Mansi and get to the Dembi warriors. They will help you." Then she disappeared from view.

Queenie was trying hard not to cry. "If they hurt Mansi, I will die. I brought him here, and I left him outside the gates. I always leave him as if he's an animal." She broke down.

"Don't worry about Mansi," I said. "The ancestors have protected him." I hoped this was true. There was something so perceptive about Mansi. I felt he would have found a way to hide before they even saw him.

"Oh. How could I be so selfish?" Queenie said. "I didn't once think of Nok's brother."

"Don't worry, Griot. They'll be fine," I assured her.

Silently, I prayed that the rebels were long gone and not awaiting our return.

We sat, holding hands. Osun's chest rose and fell against my rib cage.

In the cave, I had no sense of time, but it felt much longer than twenty minutes. The longer time went on, the more pain I felt in my chest.

"Queenie. Zen. It's safe," Nok called to us.

I exhaled a trembling breath of relief. Queenie and I hugged each other. I looked out cautiously and saw that Nok was alone. Queenie went down first. I held her arms as she descended the cliff. Nok helped her from the base of the hill.

"Send him down," Nok said.

Queenie sat on the ground. Her ankle was puffy.

I held the boy over the ledge and Nok told him to drop into her arms. After some coaxing, he fell into her arms, and she grunted. I climbed down.

"How is Jih?" I asked softly.

"He and all of his children are fine. Thank the gods." Nok went over to a tree where two thick crutches lay. "Here. I managed to get crutches from the root doctor. They may be too short." Nok and I lifted Queenie from the ground. "Luckily, the root doctor's home was one of the buildings still intact. We will need him more than ever today." Nok handed Queenie the crutches.

"My home is gone." She gave a brave smile, but it faltered. Queenie and I put our arms around her. Nok protested, "Oh, stop. Things can be replaced."

After a few moments, we let her go.

"How bad is it in there?" Queenie asked, working her way into the village. The boy held my hand.

Nok said, "It's not pretty, but we didn't lose as many people and homes as I guessed."

I looked pointedly at Osun.

Nok shrugged her shoulders hopelessly. I prayed that his family had run into the trees, but why would they leave him?

I looked at the homes still smoldering and the disintegrated rope walkways. Warm tears ran down my face. There were people working hard to put the fires out. People cried, but they moved intentionally, dousing the flames, helping the injured, and taking away the covered bodies of the dead to prepare them for the grave.

I gave Nok Osun's hand, then I squeezed Queenie's arm. "I'll go see about Mansi."

Tears formed in her eyes. "Thank you."

I jogged to the gates. The guards stopped me. "Ma'am. You can't go out there."

"How did this happen?" I asked furiously.

The shorter of the men swallowed. "The two men on the gate let the warriors in. Why wouldn't they? They were our men. The warriors attacked immediately."

I angled my body away from him, eyes wide. My trembling hands rose to my chest. What if they were rebels? Anyone could be a rebel. I gave them a look of reproach. "Where are the guards who let them in?"

The short man's eyes clouded. "They were the first to die."

I looked away. The trauma of the attack weighed heavy on my body. "Have you seen Mansi? He came here with Obsidian's griot and me. He's a mute."

The guards eyed one another with worried glances. A sharp pain shot through my stomach. No. I waited for them to tell me that he'd been killed.

The other guard said, "He is in the jail."

"Why?" I was shocked but relieved.

"He nearly beat a rebel to death."

252

I spoke to the guards for a few moments and hurried back to Queenie. She had taken a seat again. Her ankle looked worse, but it was her last concern. She looked distant and fragile. "He's fine," I exclaimed.

She nearly screamed, "Thank the gods!"

"They put him in the jail because he wouldn't stop pummeling a rebel." I wondered why they didn't let Mansi finish killing him.

She rocked herself forward, and with the help of her crutches she stood. "So the rebel is still alive?"

"Yes. Actually, two are alive. The one Mansi injured and the one Nok shot in the back. The one Mansi beat is unconscious at the moment." We slowly made our way to the jail. "Where's Nok?"

"She took Osun to find his parents or a relative. I pray his parents are alive. They are still counting and recovering bodies."

The man who guarded the jail moved out of our way before we even said a word.

We went to the iron bars, where a seething and agitated Mansi paced wildly, pulling at his matted hair. Then he saw his sister and strode to the bars. They hugged as best they could. Tears spilled from both of their eyes. My eyes were wet, too.

"Release him," I said to the guard. He did so without hesitation. Queenie and Mansi embraced again. Queenie sobbed, and tears slid down Mansi's face and got lost in his unkempt beard. There was a deranged look in his eyes as he patted his sister's locs.

I took in the destruction of the once perfect village. I looked at the blood, the destroyed homes, the smoke, and the singed trees. Nothing was more painful than the look of sheer terror and shock in the eyes of the villagers. They were in the dark. Before today, they hadn't even known that there were rebels. We could've prepared them.

My heart ached. Who would do this to their own people?

Just then, Nok hobbled over to us. She still had her bow in her hand.

"Thank the gods," she said, laying eyes on Mansi.

"Did you find Osun's parents?"

"Only his mother," she said sadly. "Osun ran and hid in the commotion, and his mother lost him. She wants to give you all of her thanks. I knew his father, and his father wouldn't run off and leave his family," she said woefully.

Tears burned my eyes.

"Unfortunately," her eyes flooded also, "the child born last night and his mother were killed."

I cried out. My legs got weak. Nok hugged me.

"Halt," the shorter guard over near the gate bellowed. The other guard lifted his spear, over his shoulder. He was ready to send the spear flying. Other guards and male villagers rushed to the gate.

I stood stark still. Fear froze my body. Nok let me go. They were back. The first attack was only to rattle us and draw us out.

"Nok," I called after her as she hobbled to the gate, as well, bow at the ready.

I looked at Queenie, but her eyes were on the gate, and so were Mansi's.

Nok yelled in a language unknown to me. Voices returned with the same fervor. Female voices.

Nok lowered her weapon and raised her hand toward the guards.

"They have four rebels," she interpreted. "They killed four more. They want to bring them to us. They knew something wasn't right with their spirits," she explained. "When the rebels tried to flee the scene, the Dembi women

254

attacked them."

Nok spoke again to the female voice. She then turned to the guards. "Let them in."

The guards looked to one another fearfully.

"Do as she says!" the chief shouted. He looked exhausted and disheveled as he trudged to the gate with Nok's brother, Jih, by his side. The chief was fuming, and his clothing was covered in dried blood. I wondered about his family.

Nok said more, and I saw the people she addressed move closer to the gate. There were four Dembi women in front, each with their knives to the neck of a trembling man. Others dragged the dead bodies into the gates. More of the women warriors stood side by side behind them, their spears vertical and at rest.

I feared this was an elaborate trap and that they were in on this with the rebels. I wasn't the only one. Every Ankaran person with a weapon had it trained on the warriors. The women who had watched us enter this forest the day before, dropped the bleeding and bruised men to the ground. The rebels' hands were secured behind their backs. The women shoved the men down to their knees. The cowards tried to look stoic, but one sobbed.

The women said a few words to Nok after taking a heartfelt look around. I didn't understand the words exchanged between the women, but I know there was both sympathy and gratitude. One of the women with copious breasts kicked one of the rebels in the ass. He landed on his stomach with an "oomph." Then the women parted, and the village drew around the men. They thirsted for blood. The sobbing man cried harder.

Queenie turned to Mansi. "You should stay with us."

He pulled at her arm. His eyes were round with fear.

"I can't leave now. I have to find out what happened here."

He grunted his disapproval.

She hugged him. "Go prepare the horses for tomorrow. I will see you first thing in the morning. Be safe, Mansi."

He held her tight. He didn't want to leave her, but he wanted to leave this awful space. With his eyes burning through the rebels and his upper lip pulled back, showing his teeth, he exited the village.

"Are any of them from here?" I asked Nok. The frown on her face was severe.

"Hell, no. But someone from here assisted them. They knew the exact location of my home."

Several men jerked up the arms of the rebels and dragged them to iron posts used to tie up goats that were going to be slaughtered. The two rebels the villagers caught were already there. They forced the new men into a sitting position and tied their arms to the posts behind them. The chief, Jih, and another older man held spears in their hands and paced back and forth snarling and spitting on the rebels. I could see their restraint was waning. The rebels wouldn't make it through the night.

One of the men's head hung limp. His shirt and pants were singed, and the flesh on his legs and arms had visible burns. I believed he was the one Nok shot. Another injured man let out a moan, and Jih raced to him, giving him a hard kick in the ribs. He hollered in agony. That made Jih kick him again and again until Nok called for him to stop. The moaning man had been the rebel that Mansi beat.

The elders all gathered with Queenie and Nok. They were discussing how to proceed. I ignored them. I paced and trembled as I stalked each of the soulless bastards. I looked deep into their eyes. I thanked the gods that none of them had been from Obsidian. They knew they were going die a slow and painful death, but most of them remained brave.

The elders bickered. I thought about the new mother and

the precious baby who had been murdered, and my heart broke again. I thought about Osun's father and the fact that I didn't know if my father was okay. I could no longer control my rage.

"Who are you?" I asked the young one who showed remorse and fear, in an even tone.

He continued to wail and didn't answer.

I looked to Jih, and he stomped the boy's ankle.

He hollered. It was then that I could see that the boy was my age or perhaps a little younger.

The elders stopped talking and turned their attention to me.

Jih had no problem brutalizing the coward, and I was going to use that to my advantage. I waited for the crying bastard to calm a bit. "Tell me who you are."

He shook his head, pitifully trying to keep his secret.

Nok grunted. She took out a match from her pocket. "Hold his leg," she said to her brother. He pressed down his foot on the boy's right shin, and she lit the match and moved it under the muddy sole of his barefoot. It seared the skin, and his screams pierced the air. "Tell us," she growled.

I shifted my weight from one foot to another. I thought about the charred bodies of my ancestors.

"Nome," he shrieked. "I'm Nome from Noire."

"Who is your leader?" I asked.

He went tightlipped again.

Nok struck another match.

Before she could put the flame to his feet, Nome spat out, "I'm not certain."

Nok twisted her lips in doubt. She shook her head and moved the flame back to his foot. His skin burned. She and her brother were a lot alike.

His body writhed. "Okay!" he screeched.

Nok pulled the match away and let it burn down until it was dangerously close to her fingers.

"Okeygwo of Noire trained our men. We would meet late at night and prepare. He brought us to the forest last night, and we waited."

I leaned over to Nok. "The Dembi allowed this?"

"They probably thought they were warriors training. It is common for our men to camp in the forest."

"Shut up," one of the captives said through gritted teeth. Jih ran over to the man and kicked him in the jaw, knocking him out. I winced.

"Who is supporting the rebels?" Queenie probed.

"I don't know. Very important people in Za," Nome stammered.

"Are their warriors from Obsidian, too?" I asked.

Nome nodded, and my eyes clouded.

"Why were you looking for the griots?" Nok asked.

"We were told to take you to Noire."

"Why?" Nok barked.

"Okeygwo never told us. He only said we'd be punished if we did not take you to him."

"Give us every name of every man you know that is a part of the rebellion," I commanded.

The names rolled easily off of Nome's tongue. Everyone listened, holding their breath, praying that no one they knew was a part of this egregious treachery. He named twelve of his traitorous partners. Most of them had been from Noire. Four of them were Ankarans, and they had escaped. He didn't name anyone from Obsidian. He said he wasn't sure of their names.

I leaned forward. I snatched up the boy's hair. He yelped

and gnashed his teeth. "Are you sure you don't want to reveal your leader?"

"I promise," he cried. I yanked his hair harder, "I have no idea who it is." He swallowed.

Queenie said, "Nok, would you kill for someone you don't know?"

"Hell no. Nor would I risk my life while this anonymous person goes free."

I jerked his hair once more. "Are you sure you're telling us everything?"

"I promise," he blubbered. A snot bubble popped in his nostril. "Spare me please, griots. Please, Chief. Imprison them or kill them, and I will infiltrate. I'll find out all you need to know," he wailed pathetically.

I shoved his head down. For a moment I considered his offer. "How could you do this to your own kin? Your kingdom? Your people?" I asked. I shook with rage. "You killed a baby!"

He sobbed again. "I believed so much of what they said. They told us we could be wealthy and live an easier life. Cars, phones, all of the things the big cities have."

"Wealth?" I sneered. Tears streamed down my face. Visions of slavery played in my mind. Visions of black men degrading black women for gold chains and shoes accosted me. "Having food to eat, family, and a kingdom where your beauty is celebrated is wealth. You and your greedy friends want to ruin Za!" I screamed, my vocal cords straining. I looked each rebel in the eyes. "A baby born just last night was slaughtered and burned. I fell to my knees, sobbing as the fear gripped me as if the terror was taking place again. Even though her knees ached, Nok lowered herself to the ground and held me close to her.

The chief stepped forward, no longer the joyous man I met earlier. His face was stone, his eyes searing. "We can't

259

allow this to happen again. We can't allow you to crush our kingdom. You have to die."

Nome wept like a child.

Tears fell from the eyes of the other men. The brave façades had fallen away.

The chief continued, his voice leveled. "We'll kill each of you. We'll find the others and kill them also."

I looked to Jih. Something foreign and vicious resided in his eyes when he pulled out his knife from his band. The chief and several others pulled out their knives and machetes, too. I stopped crying. I wanted to watch. I desired blood.

The chief and the others hungrily moved in on the men.

Nok let me go. She stood and moved over to help Queenie move away from the torture. I watched Jih stab a knife into the chest of Nome. I stayed for a while, until I had to purge the contents of my stomach.

CHAPTER 41

*A*ugust 4, 2015-*Last night was the first naming ceremony for the Griothood. It was hard to deal with. The weeping girl cried as she was pulled from her parents. She was sentenced to twenty years in which she wouldn't marry or have children. That was tough for me to watch.*

Naemah believes, "If you want to bend a woman to your will, you take her family, take her ability to have babies."

There's something in Naemah that I fear but need.

Often I tell her, "Don't believe the shit that doctor said."

"Then why'd you take me to him? Anyway, this has nothing to do with that." She looked me squarely in the eye. "If you want Noire to grow into the kingdom you imagined, you have to do some shit you don't like." With those beautiful eyes ablaze, she says, "No one can leave."

"What?"

"Malcolm, aren't we trying to keep a secret from future generations?"

"Yes."

"It won't impact this generation of people in Noire, but we don't need the future generations going to other villages or cities. They can

easily learn the truth. It's no secret that we're here or where we come from. It will be all too easy for someone to say 'aren't you that settlement of people from the U.S.?' Then what?"

"But even though we're self-sufficient, there are still things we get from the nearest towns."

"We have to stop...or we appoint a group of people to go out."

"But how do we guarantee their silence?"

She smirked. "I'll find a way."

Naemah is the first griot, and she will train this poor girl in the way that she sees fit. If Noire had a queen, she would be it, even if it's her grief driving her. Should I let her grief drive us? Will she destroy us like the hurricanes formed off the coast of Africa destroy the U.S.?

The journey back home was long and quiet. We were in mourning and in shock. I wrapped myself in a quilt that Nok gave me and cried angry and confused tears. I called to my ancestors to guide me. What was I to do as griot? How could I stop this? I needed a sign.

For two and a half days, Mansi drove us home, his map perfectly etched in his mind. My heart rejoiced when the rainforest dwindled, and we began to see scatters of acacia trees and endless grasslands. I was getting closer to my father. Please let him be okay. Let Obsidian be okay. We frequently stopped to eat, drink, and rest the horses. Twice, Mansi had to replace the wheels due to the treacherous roads.

"Do we tell the people?" I asked Queenie as we neared home.

"Not yet. I think we should tell the guards and the elders first and then we decide how to tell the people. It must be delivered as delicately as possible. I also want to observe people first and see if anything incriminating slips from someone's mouth."

"The runners haven't been to Obsidian with the news yet?"

"They've been instructed not to pass on what happened in Ankara. We have to control the flow of information between the provinces."

"What if the runners are apart of the rebellion?"

Queenie groaned and stopped talking. I welcomed the silence.

Once we saw Obsidian's walls, my eyes welled with tears. When I got a better look, blood drained from my face. It was midday, and the drums were beating. A procession of people in white ambled toward the graveyard. I looked over to Queenie who had her quivering hand on her stomach. I couldn't see past the gates to see whether Obsidian had been attacked. No smoke plumed into the air as it had after Ankara's attack.

I cried out when I saw my father being guided at the end of the procession, with the elderly and sick people. Mansi stopped, and I climbed down. I left my things, the things that hadn't been burned at Nok's house, and ran to my father, who'd stopped. The processional snaked around him.

"Father," I called softly, trying to respect whoever was being carried on the white sheets.

His lips parted with a smile. The men let him go and joined back in with the people marching to the grave.

We hugged, and I wept.

"What's wrong, Zen?"

"I've been so scared that something happened to you."

"Why?"

"Rebels attacked Ankara, and I thought—"

His milky eyes grew large. "What? What rebels?" he croaked.

I had forgotten that the people didn't know and that I was supposed to keep my mouth shut, but there was no way I could keep the most traumatic experience of my life from my father. "There is a group of people who aren't happy with King Akonos. Queenie hurt her ankle, but we're blessed to have gotten away. Not everyone survived."

He embraced me again. Angry tears slid down his face. We stayed that way for a long while.

"Who died?" My voice shook as I prepared for the worse.

Father waved his hand dismissively. "The lion was killed. So they're burying him."

I had no energy to care about how ridiculous such a ceremony was. They purposely murdered the lion, and now they were burying him out of respect.

"Let's get you home, sweet girl." He sniffled and smiled, his face still slick from the tears.

I looked back at the carriage. Several people had gone up to the carriage to relay the message about the lion to Queenie.

"Tell me everything," Father said.

As we walked into the empty village, I told him how the attack happened, but that we hid until the rebels fled. I told him about the dead mother and baby, how we caught several rebels with the help of the Dembi warriors, and what the rebels admitted.

Tremors took over his body. "In all my days, I've never heard such a thing in Za." It would've have been comforting to hear him say not to worry, this happens from time to time. Or that discord in Za always fades.

"What are we going to do? It's only a matter of time before they come to Obsidian."

He shook his head slowly, his eyes filling with tears again. "It burns my soul. The gods have been so amazing to us; why would these so-called rebels destroy what we have?"

"We have to find out who their leader is, and we have to deal with the rebels, each one. The prisoner said there were some from each city." Ankara's chief had pieced together a trusted group of men, including Jih, and sent them to Noire to round up the men on the captured rebel's list. They speculated that the rebels from Ankara were probably hiding out.

"There are rebels from here, too?" Father's brows wrinkled.

"Yes."

"I don't believe that." He shook his head again, but the look on his face told me he was allowing himself to consider the possibility. "If someone from here trained with the rebels, we would have noticed that they had been gone for days."

I shrugged. "Maybe they are warriors, shepherds, runners, or others who leave frequently. No one would've noticed that they were gone." They always left for days or weeks at a time, and knew the way to the other cities. I thought of Sahel. What if he were a rebel? But he was in training camp, and I knew his heart. He would never betray the king or Za. I pushed the thought away and asked, "Have you heard people speak ill of the king or Za?"

Father didn't have to think. "No."

I huffed. "How can they be so tight that no one knows they're living amongst us? The king wants the griots to help end the rebellion. How?"

"You'll figure it out," he said with all certainty. "Right now, you need to rest."

Father was beyond right. I slept soundly until noon the next day.

I woke up with ease, feeling refreshed. I spoke to Father, grabbed some fruit, and prepared for an earful from Queenie. When I arrived at the lair, Queenie was quiet but not in a resentful way.

"How is your ankle?" I asked.

She had it propped up on a chair. The puffiness had gone down considerably. "Oh, it still hurts. I keep forgetting not to use it. RoRo gave me some roots for the pain and swelling."

That day she fed me the remainder of the families' information. I worked until sundown to remember them. Then we ate, speaking nothing of the horrors at Ankara.

"They'll begin building your home tomorrow," she said. I detected a little sadness in her voice. The griot is starting to love me, I thought. I guess I liked her, too. "I need to tell them where you want to live."

I hadn't thought much about it. It had felt like that the time to choose a place to live was far away. For the first time in my life, I would live alone. That made me nervous. I let out a puff of air. "I want to be outside of the village."

Her eyes betrayed her surprise, but coolly, she nodded.

Changing the subject, I said, "Father says he believes that no one from Obsidian is in the rebellion. Do you believe this?"

She shrugged. "You told him about the rebellion?"

"Yes. The people need to know. Perhaps the Ankarans would've been better prepared had they known they had an enemy."

Queenie nodded. "I have always valued Bach's opinion. I sure hope he's right. However, there are some people I'm leery of, but you must know people will not drop their guard around you and me."

I nodded knowingly.

"They're targeting the elders and griots, and we must be very careful. The twins offered for us to stay with them inside the gate."

"Closer to the people who may want to kill us?" I scoffed.

She sighed. "Under the watchful eyes of our nosey neighbors." With her crutches, she stood and began to pace as much as a woman with a sprained ankle could. Her face was twisted in angst. "Rebels infiltrated the warriors, and that terrifies me. Tomorrow, we meet with the elders and discuss the situation."

I was tired of discussions. I wanted action. "I don't want to move in with the twins. It will scare people if we do."

She nodded in agreement. "Okay. Mansi will keep an eye out for us."

That gave me more comfort than being protected by all the guards in all of Za.

That night, I meditated for two hours, vaguely aware of Queenie quietly entering the room to light new incense sticks. I emerged drowsily, but with purpose.

I was preparing myself for sleep when there was a loud knock on the front door.

Queenie's eyes peered out from her door. She said, "I'll get it." Her face was shrewd. I stood in the hall as she passed, her crutches clacking against the hard earthen floor. "Get me a knife." I slipped into the kitchen and returned with a large knife used for separating the leg of a chicken from the thigh with one swift motion. She had gotten rid of one of the crutches.

My heart quickened as she asked, "Who is it?"

"Elder Kinteke," a muffled voice answered.

Her grip on the knife did not ease.

I moved closer to her.

She put the knife in the hand that held the crutch. Leaning on the crutch, Queenie parted the door. "Yes?" she called, her voice drawn out.

The elder spoke. "The Mugabe boy is ill. He's been talking out of his head and destroying his house. His parents can barely restrain him."

Queenie opened the door more. That's when I saw that Mansi was so uncomfortably close to Elder Kinteke that I'm sure the elder could feel Mansi's breath on his neck. The elder's eyes were wide with fear. My lip twitched.

"Come in. Thanks, Mansi," Queenie said, dismissing her brother.

"Good evening, griots. I'm sorry to disturb you at this time of night." The graying Kinteke wrung his ashy hands. "Everyone agrees you're the ones who would know if the boy is truly possessed."

"Possessed?" I gasped.

He nodded with gloom and fear in his eyes.

"Thank you, Kinteke. We'll see about him right away." Queenie pivoted and grabbed her other crutch. She went to her room, giving me a look that told me to move.

Kinteke walked to the door. "Be careful, griots." As an afterthought, he asked, "Can I walk with you?"

"We will be fine!" she shouted.

I heard the door close behind him. I could tell he didn't want to walk anywhere near the house of the child in question. I didn't want to either, but I had no choice.

We donned our capes and boots and went out into the windy night. Queenie had her crutches, and I carried a lantern. It smelled like rain was on the way.

As if we manifested him, Mansi appeared out of nowhere, looking haggard as usual. His sudden and quiet appearance startled me, but it was as if the griot expected her brother to appear. She stopped to speak to him, attempting to ease the worry he wore on his face. "There is a sick boy at the Mugabe home. Please watch us get into the gate."

He pointed to her ankle. He didn't like the idea.

"I'm fine." She nodded her thanks and turned around, and we moved in haste.

"Why us?" I asked.

"Hmmm?"

"Why did they call on us and not the root twins?"

"We're the story keepers, Zen. No one in this village has seen a possession. I only know what to look for and what to ask because of the many stories I possess, stories that the people will never know. Tonight, you may learn what true possession looks like. Hopefully not, though."

"And then what? What if he is possessed? What do we do?"

"Get the shaman."

Many had gathered around the front of the house. They murmured to each other and clutched their capes as the gales increased. Then there was the first flicker of lightning that illuminated the clouds but didn't penetrate through them. A few seconds later thunder rolled across the sky.

"Gossiping fools. None of them will come near to help," she complained, her voice full of disdain. "I suppose it is for the best. If he is indeed possessed, which I doubt, we don't need this spirit to jump."

"Jump?" I questioned, swallowing. I thought about the Gullah people and their belief that spirits could jump into children. That fear had been handed down to us.

"Yes," she sighed. "There's a lot we need to cover—unfortunately, you may get a life lesson tonight."

Queenie banged on the door. She seemed to be annoyed and impatient. I heard a mass movement behind us. I turned around to see that many people had moved farther away. In the light that the lamppost created, I could see that their eyes were round. My heart rushed. I wished I could skip this lesson, but I was so thankful Queenie was here to guide me. If this had happened a few weeks from now, I would have been alone. The door to the Mugabe hut was snatched open.

It was the boy's father. Mr. Mugabe looked broken. The skin below short man's eyes was wet and swollen. I could hear growling from deep within the house. I heard gasps behind me. That's when even the bravest villagers dispersed into their homes. My lips moved in prayer as thunder roared perpetually in the skies.

"Please, come in," he said with a hint of gratitude and desperation in his voice.

Queenie and I looked at one another. It didn't help that she, too, had fear in her eyes.

The home was dim, with only a few candles lit. There was something oppressive and foreign in the air.

As if she were reading my mind, Queenie whispered, "You feel that energy?"

My stomach bubbled, but I said nothing, I just let my eyes fall to the boy's mother. She sat, despondent, in a chair with her mother's arm around her.

"What's going on with your boy?" I asked shakily. I wanted to know more before entering, and Queenie seemed too petrified to ask.

"Two days ago, Thabo had a bad fever. Inkar gave him tea made from tulsi leaves, and his temperature returned to normal. Then he started having these horrific night terrors. They were fierce and frightening, and there was no waking him."

"Did you mark an 'x' with a match on Thabo's head?" I asked. I had suffered from terrors as a little girl and father used that remedy to break the fits.

"Many times."

I shook my head.

He continued with desperation in his tone. "Now all he does is sleep and have terrible dreams. The rare times he wakes, he speaks as if he is someone else. He is a child, but he can speak with the baritone of a grown man. He curses us and breaks things. He has bitten me, my wife, and anyone else who comes close."

Queenie's body tensed, and she took a deep breath. "Show me."

No. No. No.

Mr. Mugabe looked to his mother-in-law fearfully. She averted her eyes. He took us to the boy's door. My heart lurched when his father slid a lock from the outside of the boy's door. The child had been locked in. That spoke volumes.

I shot out my arm and grabbed Queenie's shoulder. I pleaded again. "Can't we just call the shaman now?" My voice shook as I shuddered.

"I have to be sure." She gently reached for my hand and lowered it. She placed one of her crutches against the wall. Our fingers interlocked as we stepped into the pitch-black room.

CHAPTER 42

The growling ceased when the boy heard his father opening the door. The griot shone her light into the darkness. Reflexively, I slapped my hands over my nostrils, and she gave me an admonishing look. I lowered my hand and fought the urge to gag.

"Sorry about the stench. We can't get in to change his sheets. He refuses to use a toilet or to let us clean him."

The boy cowered in a far corner of his room, his knobby knees and elbows accented as if he hadn't eaten in days. The depraved soul glowered at us.

"Thabo," Queenie called with a wavering voice.

He didn't answer. His beady eyes studied her.

"Thabo."

"I am not Thabo," he barked, the voice far deeper, like the voice of a man as his father said. "Thabo is in the land of the ancestors."

His father went rigid. I swallowed and shifted from one leg to another. I was prepared to run if the little demon attacked.

"If you aren't Thabo, who are you?" Queenie's voice was steady, but her hand tightened around mine.

"Habtamu."

The air was sucked out of the room. The boy's father and I gasped at the sound of Sahel's grandfather's name.

"Just what I feared," she whispered to me. She raised her voice. "Habtamu, how many children do you have?"

"Woman, don't ask me silly questions."

"Humor me, Habtamu."

The boy's eyes rolled. "Seven boys, six girls. Two boys died. I have twenty-one grandchildren. And you... How many children do you have?" The words eased from the large smirk he wore.

"I don't have children. I'm a griot, we can't have children."

He laughed manically.

Queenie dropped my hand suddenly. She stopped breathing. With a quivering voice, she said, "Let's go. He is definitely possessed."

His raspy laughing fit grew stronger.

Queenie staggered back. She hissed after having put too much weight on her ankle. Then she threw her head to the side, indicating that we should get out of there, fast.

Once we exited, Mr. Mugabe placed the lock back in place, and immediately there was a loud thump, and everyone jumped. Then there was a violent turning of the doorknob, and when Thabo couldn't get out, he roared and clawed at the door.

Queenie grabbed her crutch and stepped to Mr. Mugabe. Frantically she whispered, "Was he passed over the grave of Habtamu?"

Mr. Mugabe looked down in shame. He cried, "He stayed home that day with his mother. She hates funerals."

Queenie threw up her hands. "You know better," she

hissed, her eyes narrowed. "We will return shortly with the shaman."

He nodded, but he looked hopeless. What would happen to the boy if he couldn't be cured? Anxiety gripped me as Queenie and I rushed out of the house. Big drops of rain now pelted the earth. The second rainy season had begun.

I put my hand on Queenie's shoulder. She stopped. "What?"

"I have to go alone." Regret weighed my words down.

"What?" she asked, crinkling her brow.

I looked down and shook my head. The rain attacked my eyes. "I can't have you go out there with your ankle injured. Besides, it would take you forever, especially in this weather. We need the shaman now." I looked back at the troubled house.

"Zen, are you sure?"

I swallowed. I wasn't sure. Going to the shaman's hut alone was the last thing I wanted to do, but I had to do it. "The child could be lost forever."

She conceded with a slight nod.

I wanted to cry, but I knew I had to do it. I jogged. The rain stung my face. It was raining steadily, and the wind howled with the wrath of the gods. I pulled the cowl of my cape around my face.

I wished to have someone, anyone at my side, but I knew better. Only a few were allowed on the Shaman's sacred ground. Griots were in that few. I pushed on. I remembered, in one of our fleeting lessons, Queenie had told me, "On the rare instances we have to disturb Shaman Amadi, it had better be for a good reason. The shaman doesn't take kindly to being called into town for trivial things. He put a root on a man once that made his bile black for weeks. The man nearly died. I saw it with my own eyes." What if we were wrong? What if the boy was somehow pretending? But that voice, I thought.

"Zen, is everything all right?" one of the guards asked, stepping in my path as I ran to the back gate.

"Yes, fine. Let me pass. I'll be back shortly."

They looked at each other; their wraps were soaked, and they shivered. I'd expected them to let me pass with no question, but they stood their ground. The older more robust guard said, "We can't do that, Zen. Not with what happened in Ankara."

I wiped the rain from my face and groaned as anger flashed through my core. "I have to see the shaman, now!"

"One of us has to go with you." He nodded his head toward me, indicating to the younger guard that he'd better go with me. I wondered if they wanted to protect me or if they feared I was apart of the rebellion and perhaps sneaking away to begin an insurrection.

"Well, let's go then," I snapped to the young one. The willowy guard reluctantly moved forth, and we rushed out of the village.

It had been years since I journeyed to where the shaman dwelled. He lived about a five-minute walk from Obsidian, past the Griot's Lair, in a particularly rare cluster of acacia trees that hid away his small cottage. He didn't have running water and, as he preferred, had little communication with people.

Amadi, the shaman, walked among the dead. It was his gift, his magic. In some tongues, Amadi meant destined to die at birth. Queenie's stories said he did die at birth, but the midwife was able to breathe life into him. This is how he became one with the dead. Amadi spoke to spirits, and they answered. He was highly sensitive to energies and vibrations. Therefore people—living people—exhausted him.

Being on his sacred land was strongly forbidden for most, but for children, it was almost a rite of passage to venture into the grove and take something from the grounds on which his home stood and run back to the safety of the village gate. When I was seven, Abebi and I had done so on a stupid dare from the boys. When we came back with a stone, no one believed we had actually gone up to his house, but we refused to ever return. For months, I feared I would wake up and see his ominous figure standing over my bed, and once, I thought I did.

The rain now came down in sheets. The guard and I had to stop several times to gain our bearings. The light from the meager lantern was nearly useless. I shivered, not only because of the cold dampness of my clothes, but now, on top of a boy being possessed by a dead man, the threat of rebels lingered as I wandered through the dark woods as the jackals barked. The scavengers had found a dead animal of some sort. When we came to the first acacia trees I stopped and abruptly turned my eyes to the young guard.

"What?" he asked, his eyes wide with fright.

"You know you can't pass."

Confusion passed over his face as he slicked water away from his eyes. I stared back at him impatiently, waiting for him to arrive at the same conclusion.

"I'll give you only five minutes and then I must follow you," he conceded. There was relief in his eyes.

I turned away from him and ventured into the trees. I kissed my idol before crossing the four wooden stakes with four unique wooden idols mounted on them. My father had carved each of the menacing idols far before I was born, but it was the shaman who gave them life, just as he gave life to my Ayeki idol. I hoped he would be kind to me because my father was one person he shared a bond with. The simple hut appeared in the little light that the lantern cast. Thunder crashed and resounded.

"What do you want?" a voice boomed with the fierceness

of the storm.

I screeched and whipped around, my breath loud and rapid. My eyes searched frantically. There was no one in the direction from where I heard the voice. The lantern's metal rattled in my hand as I lifted it. No one. Just scrawny trees yielding from the temperamental wind and flecks of raindrops blowing diagonally.

"Shaman. It is Zen, the griot initiate," I called into the dark, eyes searching.

"I know that," he said impatiently. "I said, what do you want?"

I jumped. The voice was again behind me. I whirled around, and there the stood the man who was one with the dead. I shrieked. The face was caked with ashes that was beginning to wash off in the rain. His beady eyes, much like Thabo's, were venomous as he stared down at me with vexation. The shaman's pierced ears had been purposely stretched nearly to his shoulders, and the wind blew his earrings. Lightning struck nearby, and I jumped.

I backed away. "There is a boy," I gasped, "his parents reported to the elders that he was acting peculiar." The loud wind forced me to raise my voice. "We went to visit him, and I strongly believe that Habtamu has possessed him. The boy, Thabo, knew things that a child wouldn't know. He spoke in a grown man's voice. It's quite frightening."

The shaman closed his eyes as if he'd fallen asleep standing up. Was he listening? His lips moved quickly, and wisps of air passed through like he was whispering to someone. I looked around, praying that the dead stay hidden. The ever-worsening rain made the ashes on his face run even more. He wore a Gegegi amulet around his long neck. The sacred amethyst crystal was used to ward off evil spirits in Za. I backed away again. I was in a nightmare. I swallowed, "Shaman, he was not passed over the grave."

The shaman's eyes snapped open, and they were on mine. He was seething. I ceased breathing.

He growled, "Come again."

I quivered. "He was not—"

He waved his hand for me to shut up. His cowrie shell bracelets clicked and clacked. "As griot, it is your responsibility to warn the people about what happens when they don't pass children over the graves of those who pass away."

I bowed my head apologetically, even though I wasn't even a griot yet.

The shaman grunted. He walked around me to one of the posts, and he then plucked off an idol that looked as if had been soaked in blood. If it was blood, I wondered what type of animal had been sacrificed. A chicken. A goat. Had he stuck his bare fingers into the wound of the animal to paint the idol? The idol's teeth were long and jagged, and the beady and mad eyes bored into the soul of any person who looked at it. But it was the undeniable kinky hair that sprouted from the idol's head that unsettled my stomach. Without a word or a lantern, the shaman strode to the village. I scurried behind him and we shot out of the grove so fast that the guard shouted. Upon gaining his composure, he ran behind us.

CHAPTER 43

We stood in front of the boy's door. The shaman cradled the ebony idol. He held it to his forehead, his lips moving frantically yet again. We waited with our heads bowed and hands clasped, and I prayed that the shaman was successful. What if Habtamu's spirit jumped again?

Then the shaman nodded to the child's father, who exhaled as he opened the boy's door. The shaman walked into the room fearlessly, then looked at us impatiently. Queenie nudged me. I held up my hand, my eyes questioning her. She made her eyes exaggeratedly big. I huffed, then I walked into the room, and she followed, closing the door behind her. Why did we have to go in with him? I was sure he didn't need our support.

My cold and wet body shuddered in the rancid, stale atmosphere. My lantern shined on Thabo. He was now standing. He looked depleted, skinny, exhausted, and his eyelids were dark and swollen. The boy stared at the ground, but he rocked back and forth, perhaps agitated at the shaman's presence.

"Thabo," the shaman called. The boy's head snapped in the shaman's direction. I snatched up Queenie's hand, gripping it. I knew I was hurting her, but I couldn't help it. Thabo's eyes penetrated the shaman.

With the idol in his hands, the shaman took a tentative step closer. "How are you, Thabo?"

"You know I am not him," the boy spoke in a quiet, raspy voice that sent a shiver through me.

"Who are you then?"

"Habtamu, but you know this, Amadi." The boy's tone was even.

"Why are you here?"

"Because I am not ready to go. Why are you here? To get rid of me?" The boy took a step closer to the shaman. Queenie and I stepped back. The shaman stood his ground.

"I just want to talk to you," the shaman said, holding out his left hand, his palm facing upward as he moved closer. The shaman was insane. I wished I had a weapon. The image of Nok holding her bow flashed in my mind.

Thabo's eyes were still locked on the shaman's. His lips contorted into a snarl.

The shaman knelt down, watching the boy carefully. Stupid. Stupid. Stupid. "I'm just going to sit right here." He lowered himself to a sitting position at the boy's feet.

"As you wish," the possessed boy said with a grin on his deranged face. Thabo looked down on the shaman, amused at his foolishness. He had put himself in a vulnerable state. Thabo watched the shaman nimbly fold his legs in the manner Zaians meditated in.

I could tell the very moment the shaman slipped into another world. This scared me. How would he protect himself now? How would he protect us?

I looked over to Queenie, and I could see the

280

apprehension on her tight face. We were sharing a lot of firsts together—our first time being under siege and now our first time being in the presence of a demon.

A low, eerie humming sounded in the shaman's throat. He made the noise again and again, like an African bullfrog. The haunting sound grew louder and stronger, reverberating through the static air. I moved closer to Queenie, my grip tightening around her hand.

The little boy collapsed to one leg and threw his hands over his ears. He shrieked, "Stop it. I don't like it. Stop it." For the first time that night, Thabo sounded his age.

Still, the shaman continued with a gradual crescendo. His eyes were still closed, and his body pitched back and forth.

The boy was now on both knees with his eyes tightly closed. He screeched and cursed.

I imagined his family outside of the door, hands over their mouths, listening to their baby being tortured.

"I want to see my children. I want to see Sahel, my grandson," the boy roared. The deep voice had returned. Sahel's name pierced my chest.

Abruptly, the shaman stopped rocking. Slowly and fluidly, he rose like an apparition from the grave. The idol sat where he had been. He moved to the boy and grabbed both his boney arms violently, all the while still chanting. The shaman forced the boy all the way down to his bed and pressed him into the mattress. I feared the child's tiny bones would crack.

"Remove yourself, Habtamu. Leave the child. Go home."

Queenie joined in, and she motioned me to do so, as well. "Leave the child. Go home." We went on like that for a whole minute, until finally the boy's body stopped fighting back and went slack. Had the shaman killed him? Had the child suffocated under his weight?

The room went silent like a tomb. The shaman kept his grip on the boy. He said nothing but breathed heavily.

Eventually, he let Thabo go and picked up the idol. The shaman returned to Thabo's limp body, opened the child's mouth, and held the idol close to the boy's lips like the idol could pull the spirit from the boy's body.

After a few confusing seconds, the shaman lowered the idol from the boy's mouth and motioned for me to come and grab the idol from his hands. I looked at Queenie, and she gave a curt nod. I rushed to the shaman and took the unnaturally frigid idol into my hands. Silently, I prayed that Habtamu and any other spirit didn't jump out of the idol and onto me.

"Wake up," he commanded. "Wake up."

The little boy's eyes fluttered open. His little body jumped when he saw us standing in his room. "Who are you?" he gasped hoarsely.

"I am the shaman, and I'm here to help you. What is the last thing you remember?"

The boy thought to himself. "I remember walking home from school with my set."

The shaman scrutinized the child before asking, "What's your name?"

The boy's face contorted incredulously. "Thabo."

The shaman kept his eyes on the boy, studying him for a few moments more. He heaved a labored breath and rose. He took the idol back into his hands and uttered, "To the ancestors, never allow another unfriendly spirit to enter Thabo's body. Thank you for giving me the power to cleanse this soul. May I never take that power for granted. Ase."

"Ase," Queenie said. I quickly repeated.

After we had spoken to his parents, letting them know their boy had returned, and Habtamu was gone forever, we exited into the stormy night.

The shaman turned to us. The white ash had almost

completely washed away. He wiped his eyes with a cloth. He looked into the distance, perhaps to the dead, as he spoke. "Griots, the next time you are in front of the village, you must stress to the people, under no circumstances should they refuse to pass children over the grave of the deceased. Put the fear of the deities in them." He wiped at his eyes again. "They must do so within the first hour of burial. No child can be forgotten. Although Habtamu was old, his spirit wasn't ready to go. Some spirits are smarter. Some are wicked. They hide until it is far too late for a shaman to remove them."

"I will," I spoke for Queenie and me.

Suddenly, the shaman went still. His eyes glazed. Queenie and I glanced at each other. She started to ask him if he was okay, but then his eyes focused again. He stepped to me and whispered, where Queenie couldn't hear, "Darkness is coming your way."

I froze.

"Someone is not who they say."

My body chilled to the marrow. The shaman stepped back.

Queenie eyed both of us curiously. Then she said to him, "Would you like some yam stew? We have some tea from Ankara."

"I appreciate the offer," he lowered his shifty eyes and turned his body away from us, "but I have to decline. Some other time." I knew he was lying and I registered his discomfort because I often felt the same when asked to join social settings. The shaman never dined with anyone. My eyes stayed on his skeletal frame as he scurried away from us with his head down, ducking into the shadows, as if he couldn't wait to be out of the village gates. The shaman's warning had agitated my soul.

CHAPTER 44

*A*ugust 7, 2017-I always wondered why the Jews didn't leave Germany when the Nazis were spreading their hate propaganda and especially when the Nazis gained good political footing. Perhaps they never imagined the atrocities that would be committed, and, once they did, Nazis trapped them. Some argue that they should never have to leave their homes because others hate them. I agree with that. However, when those bigots start calling for genocide and carrying it out, I think an immediate exodus is necessary. Most disagree with me. Noire is not for them. I pray for the millions I left behind. I feel history repeating itself.

The U.S. has entered its second Great Depression. Every time I got the paper, which was once a month, it seemed that the country was on the brink of war. War within itself and war with other countries. The media is stirring the pot, increasing tensions between races and religions. I wonder about America's future.

I still pray for America, but I see no hope for my people there. Every paper is speaking of riots and unarmed black men and women being gunned down by the police. I know, however, that I was not sent to here to save every African American. It is not for me to wake up every African American. I am not claiming that independence is the only way *for the Black Man, but as for the people who put their trust in me, I will lead to the best of my ability. I still feel the rage of my brothers and sisters burning within, and I know that by taking our bitter history from our future generations, we have done the right thing.*

Noire is growing, and the people are doing well. Our traditions are being cemented. I am proud. Still more want to come, but I don't welcome everyone with open arms.

The next few rainy days, I split my time between speaking the lineages of Obsidian's families with fluidity and memorizing the stories that had been passed down from the time of the founders. I also worked on creating my own story that was both entertaining and meaningful. I had to connect my people to the African Americans without them knowing. My head ached most of the time. I had no idea what my message should be. I kept thinking of the time I stood before the elders and choked, and I prayed that I didn't make a fool of myself in front of the whole village, especially Abebi.

"What's wrong, sweet girl? You're so quiet, I almost forgot my favorite person has come to visit me."

I looked to my father, my only solace.

"I feel like I don't even recognize my life anymore." I thought about the rebels I watched Jih and the others to slaughter. Their screams echoed in my mind. It would break Father's heart if he knew I had enjoyed watching people be slaughtered.

"Life as a griot will become normal to you soon," he assured me.

I hoped he was right. But there was something else on my mind. Sahel. The Warrior Festival was in honor of him and the other boys who would now be our protectors. "I'll be telling a story at the Warriors' Festival." I paused a few beats. "I don't want to see him." I shook my head. "I can't."

He reached for my hand. "I know that pain, Zen."

I felt selfish complaining about Sahel when the love of my father's life died. At least, Sahel would still be in this world and of this flesh, even if he weren't mine. "I'm sorry. I should be over this."

Father shook his head. "You'll never get over it." He sighed. "I'm afraid—" his body trembled. "I have something to tell you."

My pulse quickened at those awful words—a prelude to something dreadful, something shocking. All I could think was, Sahel was dead.

"Queenie told me that when Habtamu possessed the child, he said something. Something that probably confused you."

The boy said a lot of shit that confused me. I looked at Father, baffled. Tears flowed from his eyes as he wrung his calloused hands. This was the second time in a week I'd seen him cry. "What is it?" I cried.

"He asked Queenie how many children she had."

"So? He was out of his mind." Why had he and Queenie been talking about the possession?

Father shook his head again and began blubbering.

I rose to comfort him. "Father?"

"She has a child."

I stopped in my tracks. "She does? But that isn't allowed."

He steepled his hands in front of his face and attempted to control his crying. "I'm so sorry, baby girl. We only did what we could."

"We?" My brows knitted and my face contorted. "What are you saying?"

The words spewed from his mouth. "Queenie is your mother."

It was like someone had knocked the air from my lungs. I

deflated, collapsing into the nearest chair. "What? My mother died when I was born."

He shook his head. "She is alive and well."

Was this a weird and twisted dream? Was this a sick joke that was part of my initiation?

"Queenie and I were like you and Sahel. We were young, and we knew we were going to marry. There was no doubt in our minds or in our hearts. I had given her the most beautiful comb, and I worked so hard to have something I could trade to get her a beautiful new kora from Noire. I mean, who would fall in love with a man who was going blind? She did, and I wanted to give her everything she desired.

"One day, the previous griot summoned everyone. She said she was retiring and that her dreams had told her the name of her new replacement. This ceremony meant nothing to us. I mean, we were curious, but we never thought..." He took a centering breath. "That night, Queenie was called to the Griothood. She screamed and howled and caused an awful scene."

I clutched my chest. I thought my heart would burst. I remembered the night I was called.

"The ancestors, however, had other plans for us. You were their plan."

My mouth quivered.

Father continued. "Queenie trained with the griot, but we saw each other every night. We were foolish. The griot did nothing to stop us at first; then Queenie realized she was pregnant. We were so happy. How could she be griot now? She told the griot, and the griot backhanded her for being so stupid. She said all griots had sex, but none were stupid enough to get pregnant. Queenie told me she had to continue her training in hiding, and once the baby was born, they would take the child to either Ankara or Noire. We were to never ask about the child, nor tell anyone she'd been pregnant.

"I realized I'd hurt Queenie by defying the ancestors and putting my seed into her. I was a man. My mission was to lead and guide, and I failed her and my community. For the next six months, I didn't see her, and I didn't want to. I was a disappointment to her and to our child. I wanted to die. Then a dream came to me, vivid and realistic. The next day, I went to Mansi, and I asked him if he could take us beyond the borders of Za."

They were going to run? In the midst of my pain and disbelief, there was a sliver of intrigue.

"Mansi knew the way, as he was the only one trusted to journey past the borders for certain supplies because he couldn't speak to tell people about us or us about them.

"He was able to communicate my plan to Queenie. He prepared the horses, and I brought him dried food and other things we needed to pack. Late one moonless night, we were ready to leave Za forever. When I saw Queenie, she was so stunning, she had her own glow. The life in her was mesmerizing to me." He smiled. "Her hair was wild—she didn't have locs yet. It was the same way you like to wear your hair," he laughed to himself. "As we rode, I kept my hand on you, and you kicked and kicked. I knew I was doing the right thing."

His bright smile was replaced with a frown. "Then she went into labor." Father got up and paced. I could see the torment on his face as if Queenie were going into labor right that moment. "Perhaps it was the rough road. Perhaps it was the ancestors. All I knew was that if she delivered you in that carriage, you both would die. I had no idea how to deliver a child. Once again, I had gone against the ancestors, and I was going to pay the ultimate price. I had never been so frightened.

"Thanks to the gods, you held on until we reached a village. It was foreign, but not the city we were seeking. With my blurry vision I saw cars and people talking into phones, and most of all white faces for the first time, but that I didn't care about. In Swahili, I shouted 'please, I need help. She is in labor.' The strangers called for help, and a big car with flashing lights came to pick us up. They had all types of things that they hooked up to her. They put medicines into her veins. I was frightened that they were performing witchcraft. Soon after, you were born perfectly healthy and impossibly beautiful. It was the most incredible moment of my life. If I held you real close, I could see your eyes and your fingers. It was one of the last glimpses I got of you."

I tried to wrap my mind around the fact that I hadn't been born in Za. I'd been born in a modernized city. How did I get back here?

"I didn't know how I was going to take care of you in that new world where I had no experience—not to mention sight—but I would do everything it took." Displeasure crossed his face. "Then they arrived—all three griots, like a sandstorm in Kemet. How they found us, I didn't know. Nok was one of them. They looked like they could spit fire as they fussed at us."

Nok! The conniving bitch. All along, she knew that I was Queenie's child. What about Zora?

"I told them we weren't going back to Za, and they weren't taking my child. They said the Griothood was bigger than Queenie or our child. They said Queenie already knew too much, and if people found out she'd left, it would undermine the power of the Griothood, and they said if she did not return, they would kill Mansi."

My breath caught in my chest. Could the Griothood be so diabolical?

"They were that bent on keeping Za's secrets and keeping the Griothood intact. With their threat on Mansi's life, I knew we had to go back. 'Please don't take our child,' we begged. They told me there was no way Queenie could have a child. 'I'll keep the child,' I told them. The griots laughed, but Nok didn't."

"'How will we explain it to the villagers?' they asked Nok when she begged them to consider me keeping you."

"'Don't tell them anything. Let them speculate and let them talk,' Nok said. 'Our kingdom has many secrets.'"

"Nok spoke to the griots privately. After deliberating, they agreed to allow me to keep you. So we returned to Obsidian. They said if I ever told you or anyone else who your mother was, they would take you away. They wanted me to get married as soon as possible to have a mother for you, but I refused. I still loved Queenie and I promised I'd wait the twenty years."

I sat back. I stuck my nails into my palm just to see if I was dreaming. I wasn't.

"So just like that," I said, "She wasn't my mother?"

"Queenie is your mother. She nursed you until you were one. I would stop my work and take you to her whenever you were hungry."

"Motherhood is more than nursing!" I shouted bitterly. I banged the table with my fist.

He jumped. "I know you are shocked and angry, but you have to understand, it was the only way we could keep you near. Queenie has always been a part of me raising you. She gives me guidance on every issue. Before you moved in with her, she knew almost everything about you. Her coming to the school to tell stories and to peek in on the children was not for them. It was to be close to you. Queenie got as close as she possibly could without alerting you. Remember your kora lessons."

I didn't give a damn. "For seventeen years, I've been the laughing stock of Obsidian. Everyone knew except me." My voice thundered.

"Don't feel that way, Zen," he begged. "No one knew

besides the griots, Mansi, and me."

"You think they're stupid? You think they believed you all of a sudden had a baby out of nowhere? You think they don't wonder why Queenie was in hiding for months? As an infant, where did they think I got my milk? I was the town fool." My voice was brittle. "Did our family in Noire know? Is that why you kept me from Uncle Jo and the rest of your family?"

He nodded. "Seeing them just made the secret harder to keep."

I got up, pushing my chair back, and stormed through the front door. I couldn't breathe. Father called after me, and something crashed to the floor. I should've gone back to help him, but I ran until I reached Sahel's bachelor hut. I let myself in and fell into his empty bed. I inhaled his scent as I ruminated.

CHAPTER 45

The next morning, my feet took me back to the lair. I despised Queenie, and I was going to let her know it.

Queenie was in the kitchen cutting the soap we had made from coconut oil, shea butter, palm, almond, and castor oil, goat milk, and lye. In three weeks, it would cure, and she would trade the soap with the villagers.

Queenie looked up at me and swallowed. Her eyes were sad and red. I had to see her to see for myself. My mother. I didn't have her eyes, her skin tone, or her nose. I couldn't believe that this woman manifested me. I'd been nurtured in the witch's womb.

Cautiously, she said, "Bach told me that he revealed the truth to you."

Tears burned my eyes. Queenie dropped the knife and walked over to me with her hands out, her long black dress sweeping the floor.

"Do not touch me," I snarled, but she wrapped her arms around me tightly. I tried to fight her off, but she didn't let go. I broke down, and we wept together.

"I'm never letting you go again. Zen, I waited so long to hold you as your mother. Not as the griot, but as your mother. I'm so sorry I couldn't be there." She sniffled.

"How could you keep this from me? How could you stay away from your own child?"

"They would've taken you. There was no way some stranger was going to take you from us. I'd die before that happened. I'd murder before that happened," she said forcefully. "I had to see you grow and become a woman, even if it was from afar." She pushed her lips into my hair. Then she let me go. "The only person I trusted with you was Bach. I had no doubt he would be a wonderful father to you."

I stared at the wall as she went back to cutting her soap. Her sniffling ensued, but I felt no mercy.

"Did you choose me because I was your daughter?"

She looked up. "What?"

"Did you choose me to be griot because I was your daughter?"

"Hell no." Queenie dropped the knife. "I fought my intuition. I fought with the ancestors. I didn't want to put you through the torment I have gone through."

I grew hot.

She walked back to me and took my fist into her hands. "Zen, I chose you because you are the one, just as I said. You are the griot in every way. Making you the next griot, subjecting you to the life of loneliness I live—was the last thing I wanted to do. However, watching you grow up, I knew that it was you. I tried to find another. I needed to find another... But if I denied you of your calling, the ancestors would have sabotaged you at every turn."

I interrupted. "If you loved me, you wouldn't have made me do this. My life is nothing more than your bad decisions."

"One day, you will understand."

"No. I won't."

Queenie nodded forlornly. She let my fists go and left the kitchen.

My whole life had been a lie, but my future...that was mine. I was going to go against my vow to the Griothood and bare my soul to Obsidian. They would find out they weren't from a long line of great warriors, but from people who'd been enslaved. Queenie smudged me, painted my face, and sung a lengthy prayer that I ignored.

How would I shred their spirits and tear away my people's deception? I wanted them to hurt like I hurt. When the truth spilled from my mouth, they would squint as if they were seeing the sun for the first time, only they'd be seeing reality for the first time. I thought of my words to my people. I wasn't going to allow them to live a lie anymore, even though they let me live a lie. They knew very well who my mother was, and they left me under a cloak of lies. I was going to shatter their visions of grandeur. You aren't a great people. You aren't kin to the great Maasai and Samburu. You are the descendants of men who called women bitches and shamed them for entertainment—entertainment that their daughters danced to. Your ancestors were conquered by those with superior weapons and enslaved. Your ancestors thought love was calling each other the very name that their captors used to degrade them. Niggas. That's who you are. Father Malcolm deceived you in his own social experiment.

Amina, the hair braider, wrapped my strands with orange thread in Queenie's living room. Her curly haired baby was asleep on her back as she prepped me for the Warrior Festival.

I sat there stone-faced. The walls of Za were going to come crashing down.

CHAPTER 46

*O*ctober 28, 2017-Two months ago, a car delivered my last paper. World War Three had erupted, the paper said. This time, it wasn't mostly between greedy European nations that dragged the U.S. into its affairs. This time, it was between the U.S. and Middle Eastern and Asian countries. Of course, the U.S. allies had joined in. I wondered if the war would take us out of the 2nd Great Depression. Had it been started purposely for this reason?

I told the deliverer, no more papers. A month later, planes stopped flying overhead. I feel totally isolated. I have no idea what's happening out there, and I'm glad.

November 18, 2017-Noire is not and never will be a democracy.

I've tried so hard to keep my distance from my brother Kevin because I know how we rub each other the wrong way, but last night, I almost took his life. I'd heard that he'd been saying foul things about me and causing dissension amongst my people. I didn't approach him…yet, but last night, at our gathering time, he stood before the elders and me and spoke his truth.

Kevin stood beneath the orange dusk and professed, "My brother has done the same thing to us that the White Man has done. He's limiting our information. He's even telling us what to teach our children. He won't even let us have a church." That asshole didn't even like church.

I sat there and smirked at him. I couldn't believe the motherfucker's audacity. *He never came to me personally, but here he was, addressing me in front of all of these nervous people, people who had put their trust in a man who was barely thirty, people who'd been burnt before. I knew there was a reason he wanted to be here. It had been his whole life's mission to ruin everything I touched. My successes ripped him up. He was trying to overthrow me.*

"Malcolm expects to hold us here like prisoners. We can't leave? Why? Because he wants to keep the truth from our descendants? Can you contact your family back home?" He eyed some of my people. They looked away, but they were pondering his words. *"In a hundred years, there will be no one in this settlement who knows anything about our history. Also, we barely even get any imports. What if the crops fail?"*

The murmuring and worried fidgeting began in the crowd. I stood but suppressed my rage.

"What if we have an outbreak of disease?" he continued. *"We don't even vaccinate our babies. Speaking of the babies, yes, we've had 14 babies, but three have died. That just isn't right. We need access to modern medicine."* He turned to me. *"Brother, you know I'm right. Your own child died."*

I reached behind me to the waistband of my pants and touched the metal of my gun. He'd gone too far. Some people were nodding. Some were whispering. The insurrection was beginning.

"My mother could've lived if Noire had access to modern medicine. We're all a part of Malcolm's cult, his disillusioned world."

Before he could tell them about my previous breakdown, I tugged at the gun, but I felt a gentle hand on my arm.

"Don't." It was Naemah. *"Not now. Not in front of the people."* She saved him.

I swallowed and tried to raise my vibrations. "Kevin. The elders have spoken. We don't speak against the elders, and we don't go against the elders." I spoke evenly. He watched me with amusement. "What we're trying to do here is reverse the pain that has been done to us. I'm trying to do a little bit to heal the earth. I believe that our ancestors provided the best medicine. I believe we have all we need." I looked to the people. "Because I love Noire so much, I am willing to send my brother into exile. You need to see how much I'm willing to risk so that this will work." There was a buzz. "Anyone who does not agree with what we're doing here can go as well. We'll take you to the nearest town."

My brother looked at me with a grin. He thought I was bluffing.

I looked at the people. "The carriage leaves tomorrow. If you want to go back to what's out there, be my guest. Just don't come back." They didn't know about the 2nd Great Depression or the war.

Only my brother and his husband were on that carriage the next morning. My father cried, but he stayed. There was fury behind Kevin's eyes as he departed. Father said his wife's spirit was here, so he'd remain here. He did, however, beg me to give my brother a second chance. I shook my head. "No one is more important than Noire." My brother shook with fury as he climbed the carriage, and with discretion, I put a loaded gun in the hand of the carriage driver. The driver, Dr. Reeves, raised his eyes to mine and nodded.

My day had come. My hair was regal. My orange threaded tresses were pulled to the top of my head, and my diamond nose ring shone brightly. My fitted shirt stopped an inch below my breasts, and a long full skirt touched the ground. My bare feet walked the earth, and I tried to keep my nerve as I sat amongst the elders.

In my hand was Queenie's kora. I had considered smashing it into tiny pieces. I also thought about tossing my idol into the flames. Hot tears formed in my eyes when I thought of the "resurrection" of my mother. No more crying for that woman. All the pain I carried from wondering why the gods took my mother from me could have been avoided. I didn't have to hurt like that. I saw myself as a little girl in tears and wondered how much of that pain created the woman I was today.

I took a balancing inhalation as I felt the energy of the moon. I knew I was stunning, and for the first time in my life, I walked like it, with my shoulders back and my hips swaying confidently. A few of the boys my age and older kissed my hand and couldn't remove their eyes from me. I blushed each time. They'd never behaved this way toward me, and I told myself not to let the attention go to my head. Only one boy saw my beauty from the beginning. Sahel was in the village. I could feel his presence. It felt familiar.

I imbibed on wine to relieve my nervousness. The wine made me feel light. I wasn't going to let what Queenie and my father did to me affect my first and my last story. I would never be allowed to be griot after what I was about to reveal. I would be killed for sure. No I would be executed. Father Malcolm had exiled his brother, but he'd really had his brother murdered. I knew the Griothood would do the same to me, yet I smirked. Fuck Obsidian.

I had barely spoken to Queenie outside of usual business. My anger would dissipate only to resurge. She was front and center, having the nerve to look like a proud mother, when really, she shoved all of her responsibility onto a blind man.

My mind was a swirl of ideas, emotions, and newness. Then I saw Sahel, in all of his beauty. His eyes penetrated my soul. My stomach tightened, and my heart and yoni yearned for him. He stood in the ranks of his fellow warrior initiates. Each had a look of fury in their eyes like they were headed to war right this second. I thought of how possible that was. Sahel's shoulders were broader, his bare chest more muscular, and his stomach tight and rippled. I yearned to rub my fingers down his tight torso and reach into his kanga wrap. His locs had grown at least an inch. Tonight they were wavy and fell all around his shoulders. I noticed now that he had intricate scarring on both of his breasts. I winced as I thought of a sharp blade slicing through his perfect brown skin.

Queenie walked over to me, stealing my attention. "You okay?"

"Wonderful," I said gruffly. I realized I was gripping my kora so tightly my hands hurt. I loosened up and tried to look relaxed. I knew there would be many eyes on me, seeing how I reacted to seeing the lover I would never marry. I had to be neutral. I had to play this song like only I could. I had to awaken the people with my story.

The new warriors danced to the intoxicating drums, and the girls all had a dreamy look on their faces. I stood like a stone, but those drums called me. Would these new warriors be the ones to murder me for the treason I was about to commit? I swallowed. My eyes didn't follow Sahel, but when he came into my field of vision with his new strength, I couldn't help but remember how he'd handled me when we came close to making love. I thought of Zaire, too.

The last story I had read in the tome came to mind. Father Malcolm had stroked the metal of his pistol that was hidden in the back of his pants. His brother had caused disorder and dissension by inciting the disgruntled people who'd come here. This was after the people decided to erase their history. One night, Father Malcolm's brother stood at the fire and shouted to the people that Father Malcolm had made them part of a cult. He claimed he was risking their lives and they were slowly dying. Their children were dying. They had no modern health care. He claimed that Father Malcolm had bamboozled them, and many of the people openly agreed. Father Malcolm probably agreed, now that his child had died. Before that, his mother had found a lump in her breast. He offered to take her to a modern doctor, but she refused. Za was crumbling before it began. Now I was about to do what his brother had done.

I shook the story from my mind. The chief stopped before each man, pumping him up with gripping words until each one jumped high like a Maasai warrior. In return, the crowd went into hysterics. I exhaled a shuddering breath as the energy buzzed in my veins. The men made loud, guttural sounds from deep in their throats. "Ommmm, Ommmm, Ommmm." One of the boys sung in a high-pitched voice. The girls screamed. Then the seasoned warriors entered the circle and began jumping, too. The drummers were energetic and so was the crowd. Were we phony Africans, or were we like every other society, creating our own reality?

My pulse soared.

Once the commencement was complete, tearful mothers and proud fathers rushed to their sons. Siblings hugged or playfully punched their brothers. Sahel and Zul embraced tightly. Then came the girls who had grown up with these men, but now saw them in a new light. I tried to not look at Sahel, but I saw a few women in his presence, including Abebi, and my stomach girded. The other giggly girls faded in her presence. There were lines on his forehead as he considered something she said. Then guiltily, his eyes met mine. She turned to me and waved halfheartedly. I just sat there with a scowl on my face. One day, she would come to see that I was done with her.

I had a story to tell, a job to do. My people would forever judge me by the story I told tonight. Yalee's drum summoned everyone to gather. I rose from the elders' bench and walked over to the drummers. I sat on a stool to the left of them, positioning my kora between my legs. With my middle finger, ring finger, and pinky, I took hold of the two wooden posts.

Too much of the alcohol had worn off, but I couldn't let my nervousness show. I inhaled through my nostrils. Once the whispering had stopped, I played a complicated rhythm. I felt at ease. The drums entered softly, at first, feeling out my rhythm. We had never practiced together, but within seconds, we were perfectly synced, like two people making love.

I heard a thundering sound and jumped. I could see Father Malcolm so vividly in my mind. He'd shot his brother through the eye. The wound smoked. I drew a deep breath. I was hallucinating.

My mind returned to Obsidian, present day, and standing ten yards in front of me was the shaman. This time, his face was caked in blood. Only, I didn't know if it was him or an apparition. He slowly swiveled his head left to right as if he were shaking his head "no." I widened my eyes. In an instant, he was at arm's length. He stood with his hands clasped in front of his cloak. I clawed at my throat, tearing through my flesh as invisible hands strangled me, the hands of the dead. There was nothing on my neck, but I knew the shaman was the culprit. He watched calmly. Then my fingers spread, flexing involuntarily. The shaman now held up a long needle that curved just so. Suddenly, I could see my face. He took the needle and sutured my lips shut. My screams were muffled. Then I saw Queenie, Zora, and Nok. All three women had guns aimed at my skull.

At the sound of the gunshot, my body jolted to reality. I looked at my fingers that had nearly been broken. They were still strumming the kora. I could breathe, my lips weren't sewn together, and the audience had glee on their faces. The soothsayer had spoken.

CHAPTER 47

Words came to me quickly—words that wouldn't send my people into a frenzy, words that wouldn't get me killed by the Griothood.

I spoke to the melody of my kora:

Keep your soul, Keep your soul, Keep your soul

The jackal

Had a hex that wore him down.

He couldn't eat what the lion had prepared; he couldn't sleep in his grassy bed.

He was heavy.

He saw monstrous birds begging to pluck his eyes away.

Then the owl swooped down and asked, did you place the shroud around you at night?

The shroud that keeps the cold white spirit out.

I only went one night without.

One night is all it takes to make you extinct. One night is all it takes for all to come tumbling down.

The next night you are not wary,

The next night you do not value tradition, your life will perish.

I will take the white ghost from you tonight, but next time your whole clan will disappear like they never existed.

Keep your soul. Keep your soul, keep your soul.

After my story, the drummers went wild. Everyone cheered for me. It was like my story was the best they'd ever heard. I fucking hated it. It was too short and too flat. I laughed, but my eyes roamed the crowd looking for the shaman. He had never been there, not physically, anyway, yet I could feel the residue of his spirit in my soul. I quaked violently, but no one seemed to notice. I thanked the gods that I hadn't done anything stupid, that I hadn't demolished this kingdom with my tongue.

My allegory had been short and overt. Everyone knew I was talking about Thabo and Habtamu. I knew I was talking about keeping the Truth as secret. The people nodded in agreement. The drummers clapped and hugged me. The cheering was loud, and I felt it in my chest. I smiled and bowed my head humbly. Queenie's eyes shimmered in the firelight.

"Now, let's go," I said when I came close to her.

"Speak to your people," Queenie sung, making a sweeping gesture with her arm.

I shook my head. "I've said enough." I just needed to get out of there. My hallucination had drained me.

We walked away, waving to people as we passed. Many placed their palms together and bowed to me. I did the same.

"Zen," a voice called once we neared the gate. I knew who it was. I inhaled deeply before turning back. There was Sahel, his skin shining with perspiration. He ran over to us.

"Excuse me, Griot," he said bowing his head reverentially to Queenie, his locs falling forward. His smile was wide.

"May I speak with Zen for just a moment?"

Queenie gave a pretentious exhalation. "Go ahead." She turned to me. "I'll see you later." She turned and limped away.

He stood there, not knowing what to say. I stood, lips pursed, eyes on his scarification done by steady and masterful hands.

Finally, he said, "You were phenomenal."

I blushed. "Thanks."

Sahel swallowed. "I missed you," he said. His words felt like he had released his soul to me.

I looked into his eyes. "I missed you, too."

"I thought you would forget about me. I've heard about your travels. You've been to the crown jewel of Za and to Ankara." He gave a nervous smile.

I thought about Prince Zaire and felt a flash of guilt.

"I heard what happened." His voice dropped an octave.

"What?" I spat, thinking he'd heard about my breakfast with Zaire.

"The attack at Ankara. I have never been so furious and scared in my life."

I calmed. "I survived. Thank the gods."

"Ase. But the rebels have hell to pay. Trust me. Nothing means more to me than this kingdom...and you."

I felt his words in my gut. I wanted him right now. I shifted uncomfortably, and I pointed to his breasts. I yearned to run my tongue over his scars. "I hate that they did that to you."

He patted the scars like we women patted our braids when they were too tight and they itched. "It's nothing."

"Oh, you're a man now?" I flirted.

"I was a man before," he said seductively.

I sucked my teeth and rolled my eyes.

"What have they done to you?" he asked, eyeing me.

"Me?"

Sahel's slanted eyes lit up. "Yes. You moved into the Harambe circle like you owned Za. I was transfixed." He angled his head. "I think every warrior initiate was yearning for you."

I threw my head back, loving every word. I was about to tell him about Queenie being my mother when I noticed his mood grow dark. I wondered if he'd found out about his grandfather's possession of Thabo.

He shook his head and looked at my feet. "You know I love you more than the world itself."

I said nothing. I simply watched him. I felt a storm brewing in his mind.

Sahel was quiet for a long moment. He started to speak but stopped. He found his words and said, "I found out something that is going to hurt both of us very much." The last of his words left his mouth in a whisper.

I studied him with wide eyes and a parted mouth. "What can hurt more than not being able to marry you and have your children?" I didn't like how, after being so strong, my voice was now shaking.

He balled up his fists and placed them on his forehead. He paced.

"What is it?" I asked impatiently.

"My parents found a bride for me."

The words nearly knocked me on my ass. Tears welled up in my eyes. I knew this day would come, but so soon?

"It may be your first wedding ceremony as griot." His voice cracked.

"That's fucked up."

"I know. I hate my parents for it," Sahel croaked.

My eyes burnt holes in him. "Who?" I growled.

"Zen," he pleaded.

"Who is she?" I was nearly screaming.

He bit his bottom lip. The lips I had wanted to bite just a few moments ago. "Abebi."

He might as well have gutted me right there. I rushed to him and slapped his face so hard it stung the both of us. I wanted him to feel that fire in his cheek forever. His mama should feel it, too. I struck his chest with my fist. He restrained me. "Zen!"

I pushed him away and stormed off. "Fuck you, Sahel!" I hollered, my voice grating against my throat. The words ricocheted against the buildings.

"The dowry was paid while I was away. I would never do this to you intentionally," he cried.

I turned back toward him hastily. "But there are no forced marriages in Za. You could turn her down and marry anyone else, but you've agreed to marry the girl who torments my soul!" I screamed, pointing to my breast. "I hope you die."

"Zen."

Every time I thought my life couldn't be torn into any more shreds, there came another swipe from the lion's claw.

"I'm sorry."

I shouted over my shoulder, "Live your truth, Sahel. Don't you worry about hurting me. I've been through worse."

I was going to kill Abebi.

CHAPTER 48

I sat on the wet ground in front of my new home that had been made by digging into the earth with respect and using her soil—soil that had been cultivated for millions of years. The earth was mixed with the most precious gift from the gods: water. The two were molded into bricks. They weren't baked as they had been in Mesopotamia, but they were stacked into the shape of my home and allowed to settle and harden. From what the gods created, my home could stand for centuries, if there was no flooding or termites.

The outer foundation of my home was complete. Now the men were whitewashing the inner walls, and the plumbers entered yet again. They would bring me clean and hot running water. For this, I gave thanks to Father Malcolm. I had begged for the same glossy flooring Zora had. The people who crafted her floor traveled from Noire and had already completed their work.

I took a bite of a bitter passionfruit and checked my perimeter for snakes. Then, I turned back to my house. It was the only thing that remotely excited me these days. It was the only thing I had control over. Since the earth-shattering revelations from the people I loved and trusted most, I had been in relative solitude. I only spoke to Queenie when necessary, and I hadn't spoken to or laid eyes on my father, Sahel, or Abebi. I kept imagining Sahel and Abebi fucking, and I couldn't help but think that Abebi had this planned since she heard I'd be the griot. I didn't care what my responsibility was; I would never marry them nor would I hold their children. Their children. The thought of it grated my soul.

The atmosphere was shifting. In three days' time, I would be initiated as the griot of Obsidian and the fifteenth griot of Za, and I didn't care.

"What are you doing sitting all alone?"

I cringed. I didn't answer Queenie as she approached.

"Your very own place," she said sitting down next to me. A light drizzle began. The gods were good to us this rainy season.

I grimaced. I wanted her out of my space.

"They've done an astonishing job."

"I suppose," I said.

She ignored my bitter mood. "You have to be careful what spirits you let into your home."

Like you, I thought. "If there's one thing I have learned in the past few weeks, it's to not trust anything or anyone."

She took the blow quietly. "I heard about Abebi and Sahel. I'm truly sorry. But you have to trust that the ancestors know what they are doing, Zen."

"Yeah. I've heard that time and time again."

Defeated, Queenie rose to her feet and dusted off her ass with her hands. All of the good cooking we'd been having was putting pounds on her.

"Your ankle seems better," I conceded. The rain picked

up just a little.

"I'm not limping as much." She took a few steps and said, "I hope you're excited about your initiation. It's right around the corner."

"Oh I am." I added, "Prince Zaire said he'd be here."

Now she cringed. I felt vindicated.

"Do you think he'll come?" I asked, rubbing it in.

"Oh, I'm sure he will." There was something sinister in her voice. "They're going to tell the people about the rebels at tomorrow's Harambe."

I let that sink in as she walked away, leaving the scent of lemongrass in her wake.

A day later, the talking drums sounded loud and strong. I was outside helping Queenie in the garden, and she paused and looked to the sky. "What is it?" I asked with alarm in my voice. Rebels? Death?

"Once you are the griot, I will teach you to understand the talking drum." Her brows furrowed, and she closed her eyes and rubbed her temples until the drums ceased.

Without enthusiasm, she answered, "The prince is on the horizon, and he'll be here shortly."

My stomach fluttered, and I jumped up. He had really shown up.

"We aren't done," she called after me, but she knew it was a lost cause.

I ran into the house to shower away the sweat and dirt from gardening and tending to the chickens. I removed my hair scarf. The day before, Amina had unraveled my hair threads, and now my hair had been stretched to the middle of my back. I tied green fabric around my upper body so that it exposed my midriff. I tied a longer piece of cloth around my waist. It reached almost to my ankles. I put myrrh and lavender oil on my neck and wrists. Whether Zaire hugged me or kissed my palm, he'd be intoxicated.

When Queenie saw me, her eyes stabbed me like a dagger. "Oh, you want to play that game, little girl?"

"What is wrong with looking nice for royalty?" I walked past her, snickering and switching my hips to unnerve her.

Nearly everyone in Obsidian stood outside the gate. They chattered with excitement and surprise. I had to navigate through the people to get a good view. Perhaps many in Noire didn't support Zaire, but he was supported here. That or the people were just excited to see royalty.

With a wide smile, Zaire dismounted his horse. The drummers moved outside the gate and were playing like their lives depended on it. He waved and grinned demurely, but there was nothing shy about him. The people clapped to the beat of the drum. In the horizon, I could see two wagons that were carrying Zaire's belongings.

I held back. I didn't rush to him like the other villagers, although I wanted to. They all wanted to touch his hand or say hello. Then there were the girls. Everyone knew he needed a wife, and the mothers wanted it to be their daughters. Let the next queen be from Obsidian, too.

Zaire gave them his heart-clenching crooked grin, which made girls erupt in squeals. I wasn't jealous. I calmly observed him and his ease in this situation. Then he saw me, and it was as if the others faded away. His beautiful eyes were stuck on me. Zaire motioned to the ladies that he needed to be excused, and their eyes followed him as he moved closer to me. Blood rushed to my cheeks.

Zaire slowly shook his head as he came close to me. "You look divine." His eyes traveled from my hair to my sandals, then he bowed. My eyes looked around in embarrassment. He'd given the people something to gossip about.

"Thank you. It is nice to see you again." I curtsied.

He stepped to me and hugged me. I closed my eyes imagining him on top of me. I savored his masculinity, his seductive scent, and his power. I ran my hands down his bicep. We embraced a moment too long.

"Did you forget that I was coming to your initiation?"

"Of course not."

He pulled away. "Griothood looks amazing on you," he said with a smile.

I blushed. The crowd was transfixed on us, and I did not mind.

He thrust up his hand, and his glaring assistant, Adesewa, hurried over with a box made of a polished, dark wood. "I have something for you."

I looked around again, wishing he could've done this in private. "Prince Zaire, I don't need anything."

"Zaire," he reminded me gently. "Zen, soon you will have gifts from so many people, from every city. Your home will be filled. Allow me to be the first." He opened the box. "Your bangles are quite lovely, however..." With finesse, he unfolded the red silk as he continued, "none are as lovely as this bangle. I do hope you agree."

My jaw dropped. "Oh, my." The bangle was gold with three large diamond settings. "I agree," I responded breathlessly.

One side of his lips curved upward as he lifted the bangle and placed it over my hand and onto my wrist. It fit perfectly. The women gasped. I pushed my long hair behind my ear. I was speechless as the sunlight hit the ornate bangle. I looked around, taking in the stunned faces, my feeling toward the attention ambivalent. Then I saw Sahel. He stood next to Zul. He was taller than everyone, and his jaw set as he observed us. My mouth spread into a wide smile. Good, I thought.

Zaire's chest stuck out as he said, "Right now, I need to

speak to the chief." He licked his bottom lip and bit it. He moved closer so that no one could overhear. He put his hand on the small of my back. "Please come to the royal parish at sunset. I would like to prepare dinner for you."

"You don't have to do that," I said.

"Let me spoil you."

I looked down bashfully. "Okay."

He gave an approving nod and repeated, "Okay." He took long strides to the village walls. Queenie was right. I had to be careful with him. His power was overwhelming.

That night's Harambe would be a ceremony for Zaire. After the ceremony, the people would be told the truth about the rebellion. With her eyes rolling at the mention of the prince, Queenie let me know she wouldn't be attending.

"Shouldn't you be there when the elders tell the people about the rebels?"

"You're pretty much the griot now. You can handle it." She stuck a wedge of sweet potato into her mouth. "You're going to learn. Zaire is a snake, just like his mother."

It pissed me off to hear her talk about him in that way. I was going to ignore her bitterness, but instead, I asked, "What is with you and the queen, anyway?" Was she just jealous and envious of the queen as I was of Abebi? Would I still be jealous of Abebi twenty years from now?

She huffed. "Queen. She's no damn queen. Finda is just biding her time, and her greed will run this kingdom into the ground. She doesn't love Akonos. She just loves the lifestyle."

I shrugged. "What woman wouldn't?" I asked, looking down at the bangle. A bangle that Queenie's eyes landed on the moment I returned to the lair. "That doesn't explain why you hate her."

She crunched on more sweet potato wedges. "You know

she is from Obsidian, of course."

"Yes, I do."

"Well, she was in my set. We were best friends."

I regarded her closely. I found her claim unbelievable. There was depth to everything Queenie did and said, and Queen Finda was shallow. How could they be best friends?

"When your father told me his plan to run away, I told no one except Mansi and…Finda. The griots didn't guess where we had absconded to, they weren't psychic, and, even if tortured, my brother would never betray me. In fact, he was angry when your father and I agreed to return just to save his life." Queenie picked lint from one loc with her fingertips. "It was Finda. The backstabbing sellout told our plans with ease. They came to her, and she sang."

"Perhaps they threatened her."

"Or perhaps she used selling us out to get noticed by Akonos. It wasn't long after that he started courting her."

I thought about what she said. Queenie's claims were thin, based on speculation, but if the claims were true, then the queen was the reason my mother wasn't allowed to raise me.

At Harambe, I watched the women dance harder than they'd ever danced before. They were hoping to catch Zaire's eye. I observed him. He sat straight, one hand on his knee. He was arrogant indeed, but a snake? I didn't believe it. What the hell would he gain out of pretending to like me?

Zaire caught me staring and winked. I averted my eyes. It made me warm whenever he did that, gazed at me like there was no one else in the world.

I waited as the elders and the prince revealed the rebellion to the people. I watched to see if anyone looked guilty, but there were too many emotions—fear, sadness, numbness, hopelessness, and rage. Zaire asked people to let the elders know of any suspicious activities. I could see wheels turning. Again, I looked for guilty people, but I couldn't tell, so I slipped away.

Father hadn't been to Harambe. I saw him at my first storytelling, but I refused to acknowledge him. Guilt crept into my spirit. I lost sleep, as I gradually understood that he and Queenie had done the best they could do. The Griothood had threatened Mansi's life. That spoke volumes. I was mad at the wrong people.

"Father," I called gently into his workroom.

He lifted his head in the direction of my voice and gave me a soft smile. "Hello, Zen."

I walked over to him and placed my hand on his shoulder. I watched him etch out an intricate engraving onto the wood. "It's magnificent. Who's it for?"

"Just trying out a new method." He was lying, and it stung. I knew he was carving a comb for Sahel to propose to Abebi. The pain had coursed through my veins before I cast it aside. I pulled my hand from his shoulder.

"I'm sorry for the way I have been avoiding you." My voice wavered under the weight of my shame.

His hands stopped carving. In a soft tone, he said, "You had to feel out your emotions. I couldn't imagine going through what you did, finding out that the mother you thought had passed away had been alive all this time. I understand the fury and the life alteration that would bring. I want you to know that every time I had to lie to you, every time you asked about her, every time I saw a girl walk down the street holding her mother's hand, I died a little. There were times you needed a mother, and I would go away and cry." He began carving again. "But Queenie, she ached worse. Over the years, it hasn't gotten better for us, either. We have been punished, time and time again for what we withheld from you. I ask you to consider forgiving us and allowing us to love and support you like we have never been

314

able to, especially your mother. You are all she ever yearned for."

I stood still, arms crossed, with my head down. "Okay."

I hugged his neck. "I love you."

"Good. I thought I had lost my sweet girl."

"Never."

I cleaned up the clutter that had accumulated in the workshop since I had last been here. You would think a blind man would be more organized so he could put his hands on his tools, but not my father. I cleaned his knives. "Where's Mali?" He should've been helping father with the cleaning.

"He just doesn't have the heart for carving. Upon returning from warrior training, he told his parents he was through with carving. Now I have to find another apprentice to pass the gift to."

I nodded in agreement. I picked up the knife that I'd purchased in Noire. "How is the knife I bought you?"

"Cuts like no other, such neatness and precision."

"Good. We have to keep it sharp," I said smiling. I had my father back.

CHAPTER 49

I didn't keep to the shadows as I made my way to the royal parish. I didn't give a damn who saw me. The Griothood had no consideration for my well being as a child, and they didn't give a damn about me now. So tonight, I had no consideration for the Griothood's image.

I knocked on Zaire's door, hoping desperately that he'd returned from Harambe. I could smell goat stew through the door. A shirtless Adesewa opened the door. This was my first time not seeing him in his official attire. He kept his mouth tightly shut and refused to make eye contact. There was an ugly tension between us, and I didn't understand his resentment. He had to be at least twenty years older than me, but he was acting like a child. He closed the door behind me and silently retreated down the hall. I noticed a peculiar tattoo on his back. I couldn't make out what it was. A backward seven? Whatever it was if formed an angle and stretched across his shoulder blades and down to his lower back.

Awkwardly, I stood there, eyes darting around the parish kitchen. The grand home was out of place in Obsidian. The royal family rarely visited the large home, yet women were appointed to keep the barely lived-in house immaculate and ready at a moment's notice. The kitchen had a huge hearth and large dark wood cabinets. A round table took up the center of the room.

A minute later, Zaire exited the room Adesewa had gone into. His grin was big and inviting.

"Hello, Zen," he said, and instead of kissing my hand he kissed my cheek, leaving warmth where his lips had been. He's just being friendly, I warned myself.

"Make yourself comfortable. I can't wait for you to taste this meal I prepared for you." He went to the hearth and stirred the large pot. He turned and smiled at me.

I gave him a coy look as I sat at the table.

"What? You don't believe me?" he cried, feigning hurt.

"When did you have time to cook?" I asked suspiciously.

"As soon as I discussed affairs with the chief. I was so excited you would be joining me that I had some villagers bring me some fresh goat meat and beef. It turned out they just had a slaughter for my arrival. They brought me carrots, spices, rice, and everything I needed to prepare my meal. When I was at Harambe with Adesewa, Wajir, my other attendee, watched over the pots to ensure they did not burn."

I still wasn't sure I believed him.

He walked over and held up a wooden spoon toward me. I parted my lips, and the seasoned stew flowed over my tongue. Shocked, I said, "Oh my, this is the best goat stew I ever tasted."

Zaire's smirk was pleased but knowing. "Everyone was so upset I would not be eating the feast they'd prepared. They were even more upset I was cooking for myself."

"I just can't believe you know how to cook."

"Oh, yes. I love the control of creating a dish. When I

was young, I used to go into the kitchen and watch the head chef prepare food. He could not get rid of me, so he began to teach me. Over the years, I began to teach him." He lit up in a way I hadn't seen before. The visual was unbelievable. The prince was cooking for me and preparing my plate.

As we ate, the conversation was easy. There were no awkward pauses.

After we had eaten, Zaire asked, "Can you stay a while longer?"

"I've already broken the griot's rules. What have I got to lose?"

He laughed and called Adesewa. "Do the dishes, please?"

Adesewa scowled, and Zaire gave him a teasing smile. I felt a rush of vindication.

"Your water is still on?" I asked.

He nodded. "Being a prince has its perks."

Zaire poured us tea, and he led me to the common room. The room glowed with candlelight, and potent incense created a sensual mood. He motioned me to take a seat, and I sat on a large overstuffed floor pillow.

I watched Zaire as he used an iron key to open a cast iron lock on a large wooden trunk. He pulled out a small box with polished black wood and sat on the other pillow facing me. His stare was so overpowering, I'd spent most of my time avoiding his eyes and monitoring my breathing. I hoped he didn't register my anxiety.

"This, Zen, is my real gift for you. A gift I could not allow anyone to see."

"Zaire!" I cried. I was still reeling from the bangle.

"What did I say? Let me spoil you." His voice was deep and seductive. I yearned for him to make an indecent move.

He held out the box toward me with two hands.

I nodded in appreciation, inhaling as I lifted the top.

318

Inside the box was a silver pen. I could tell by the way it was tarnished that it was old. "Zaire, I can't take this. It looks valuable and ancient."

"Oh it is, but I feel like it belongs in your possession." He paused and allowed me to peer at it longer. "I am sure I am not supposed to know this, but I have heard people say that as a part of a griot's training, she gets to read Father Malcolm's journal." He gestured to the pen. "This is the pen he used to write that journal."

My mouth parted.

"I want you to have it."

"Where did you get it?"

"It was passed down through my dynasty."

I held it back out to him, shaking my head incessantly. "I'm no ruler, Zaire. You should keep this for your firstborn."

He put his palm on my hand, his energy flowing through me. "You are more powerful than you know," he said with seriousness. "And the pen is mine to give. I will be the fourth to reign over this kingdom, and when I turned seventeen, my father gave me this pen. So please, accept it."

I exhaled. I felt guilty for receiving such an important gift, a gift that should stay in his bloodline. I pushed down the top of the box and placed the box into my bag. "You are so thoughtful. Thank you, Zaire."

"In this time of uncertainty, with the rebellion, I feel one thing is certain." He had a faraway look. "From the moment I saw you, I wanted you." He gave me a bold look, and my breath caught in my throat. "And you are right, I am used to getting what I want. Knowing that this is one of the times that I cannot, bothers me."

I peered at him timidly. I had no idea how to articulate my feelings for him. I wasn't even sure what they were.

319

"I think you're beautiful." I covered my mouth.

He laughed softly. "It is okay. Speak your mind." He moved closer.

"I still wonder why you've shown me so much attention."

"Are you kidding?" he scoffed.

"No, I'm not."

A far off look passed over his face as if he were remembering something. "Your name alone made me want to meet you. I was not supposed to attend the official naming ceremony, but I was intrigued." He laughed. Then he gazed at me. "Thank the gods that I did come to Obsidian. You do not know how beautiful you are, do you?" He paused for a moment.

My pulse surged. Insecurely, I hugged myself.

"I wish you knew your beauty, like I know your beauty, just like I wish you knew how powerful you are. What you have to say is necessary for the survival of Za."

I lowered my eyes. Zaire's mantra replayed in my mind. Every morning I repeated the words he had me say on the palace grounds. Bravely, I looked up at him. Zaire was causing me to behave dangerously.

He stared at me long and hard before he moved closer to me. My heart raced. I shuddered as he reached for my face. I closed my eyes, and he kissed my lips. My nectar flowed between my legs. His hand touched my inner thigh and slid closer to my wetness. I couldn't believe that this was about to happen. Abruptly, a loud knock sounded from another part of the house. He cursed, and I came to my senses. He had only been here one night. What was I doing?

"Zen, you're being summoned," Adesewa called from the other side of the door. His voice dripped with bitterness.

I cursed Queenie in my mind. I rose, straightening my clothes. Zaire got up and silently followed me to the kitchen door. I sighed and opened the door. "Sahel?"

Sahel stood there grimacing, his nostrils flared, and his eyes bulged. "I've been out here, waiting for you to come out." He was breathing like he'd been running as fast as a gazelle.

"What? Why are you waiting for me?" I shrieked.

Sahel rocked in agitation. "What are you do—" He stopped cold. His eyes seared.

I looked back that parish door. Zaire stood behind me, and he wore a ridiculing grin.

Sahel lowered his voice. "I need to speak to you privately." He was addressing me, but his eyes were glued on Zaire. They silently taunted each other.

"You bow before the prince." Adesewa had slipped out of the door too and was glaring at Sahel.

I asked Sahel, "What is it?" I emphasized every word.

Adesewa shouted, "Bow down, boy."

Sahel stood taller. His eyes looked unusual and crazed. I knew that look. He had given the same look to the chief after being shoved.

My eyes widened. I moved closer to Sahel, but he couldn't see me. He glowered at Zaire and Adesewa.

To my consternation, Zaire stepped closer to Sahel. "I don't think you are new here, so why aren't you showing me respect?"

"I'm not here for you. I'm here for her."

Although it was late and Harambe was over, a small crowd formed in front of the parish.

Zaire said, "Zen is doing just fine without you, whoever you are."

That pissed Sahel off, and he snatched my hand and yanked me away from the parish.

321

"Hey!" I hollered.

"I called it off. I refuse to marry Abebi!" he shouted as he pulled my arm.

Zaire sprinted to Sahel. Swiftly, he extracted his knife from his sheath and thrust the knife to the side of Sahel's throat, a second away from tearing through his flesh.

I shrieked.

Sahel froze. His eyes bulged as he realized his life could end at any second. Sahel kept his grip on my hand, however.

"Zaire?" Sahel stammered.

"So informal?" Zaire asked incredulously.

Zaire's knife was on the verge of puncturing Sahel's skin, but Sahel would not let me go.

"That is your name, isn't it?" Sahel tried to hold on to his pride, even with a blade to his jugular.

I cried, "Sahel, shut up."

With an even tone, Zaire said, "I would listen to her. Shut the fuck up, and let her go, please."

More people came running to see the spectacle. Then I saw Zul standing in the crowd and steeling his jaw. There was fire behind his eyes. Sahel stiffened even more, and I knew he too saw Zul. I could see that they were speaking to each other with their eyes. Zul seemed to be saying, "You want me to kill him?" His hand flexed and moved closer to the knife on his hip. Sahel seemed to say, "Not yet." Thank the gods Zaire or Adesewa didn't notice any of this exchange.

My heartbeat soared as I sobbed. Both men refused to back down. They were like two lions fighting for one lioness. Sahel's face was contorted, and Zaire bared his teeth in an evil grin. My tears splashed to the dirt as I pleaded with both men. Neither listened, until finally, Sahel dropped my hand. Zaire waited for a few seconds before he slowly lowered the knife. The crowd and I heaved a sigh of relief.

Sahel faced Zaire and glared at him. His shoulders heaved as he took several deep breaths. Zul watched on, his body still tense, ready to kill for his best friend. Zaire had a nearly imperceptible smirk on his lips. I feared Sahel would strike Zaire, even with Zaire gripping the knife, but then Sahel's eyes flashed to me. Zaire had shamed him. I had shamed him by being alone in the prince's home. With his shoulders lowered and his eyes moist, Sahel averted his eyes and pivoted, trudging away from the parish. Zul glowered at the prince for a while before following.

I felt a strong desire to follow Sahel, but then I heard my name.

I turned toward my father's voice. His walking stick lanced in front of him, and people jumped out of the way. He rushed toward the parish with worry etched on his face.

"Father?" I ran to him and threw my arms around his neck. I sobbed, and my body shuddered.

"You okay? I was in bed when I heard there was an altercation involving you."

"Let's just go." Before I parted, I scowled at the prince.

CHAPTER 50

I awoke when I heard the drums playing my set's presentation song. Tomorrow was the day I would become Obsidian's griot. The Zephyrs were rehearsing their dance to pay honor to me. Falling to my knees, I honored the gods. I thanked them for what they had bestowed upon me. I went outside to hear the drums clearer. I closed my eyes, remembering all the times I danced with my set. The drums had a way of seducing my body and allowing it to do whatever the spirits guided it to do.

I opened my eyes when I realized I would never again dance with the Zephyrs. Even though I was only seventeen, by tomorrow, I would officially be an elder and given the same respect. This was supposed to make me happy, but it saddened me. I had yearned so deeply to get away from the girls in my set, but now that wish would come true, and I felt the void.

I danced. Not my set's dance, but my own. Queenie had probably gone into the village, and I was free. I danced wildly, working up a sweat and breathing hard. My hair would surely shrink from the perspiration, not that it mattered.

Tonight, it would be braided. As the youngest griot, Zora was in charge of braiding my hair in the sacred griot initiate style. I danced for the gods and my ancestors because they watched over me and guided me. When the drums ceased, I was drenched. I moved back and forth to lower my pulse rate and steady my breathing.

"I don't mean to scare you," a deep voice said.

I jumped. There was a shock to my heart. Adesewa walked up to the lair from the direction of the village.

"What are you doing here?" I asked harshly, angling my body away from him.

"I felt I needed to speak to you about Prince Zaire." He came closer. Adesewa would've been handsome if he didn't have a perpetual scowl and pockmarks so severe they could've been seared into his skin during an initiation process. He probably had about twenty years on Zaire, but the prince treated him like a child. I guessed he was supposed to provide guidance, but I doubted Zaire listened.

"What about him?" I stared at him reproachfully.

He took a moment to gather his words. "You know that discomfort you feel when you are with Prince Zaire?" he asked, stepping closer. Adesewa's stare was aggressive, like a stalking lioness.

I folded my arms, knowing I was failing at concealing my fear. Where was he going with this?

"You know how you feel like he is playing some sort of game, and that he shouldn't like a lowly person like yourself?" He played with the pads of his fingers as if there was some sort of residue on them. Had Zaire told him about my insecurities? "Those feelings are real. You should trust your instincts, Zen. He is playing a game, a game that never ceases to thrill him I guess." He clasped his long spidery fingers in front of him. Do you know how many women desire Zaire, how many women want to be the next queen?

325

You're just another one. I must admit you are a bigger thrill for him because you will soon be a griot, one of the most important women in our society. Fucking you will just make him feel even more powerful. Zen, Zaire doesn't give a damn about you. Please don't waste your time or get your feelings hurt, not that I really care about your feelings, but still…" He gave a long sigh.

It was like he grabbed my heart and squeezed it mercilessly. My eyes burned as I scowled at the evil man. My mind raced as I thought of the things Zaire said to me. Don't cry, I told myself. "How dare you come onto my mother's space and speak so nastily to me?" I thought that calling the griot my mother would put power behind my words and cause him to falter.

His lips drew back into a sneer. "So you know?" He paused, thinking. "I guess you plan on going the way of your mother. You plan on having a motherless child, as well? Is that why you're trying to fuck Zaire? What will you gain?" As if everything became clear, Adesewa began laughing hysterically. "You want him to marry you? You think that will get you out of the Griothood? He doesn't want you, Zen. You will never be queen."

My eyes widened. Now the dam crumbled. The tears slid. "Get away from me!" I screamed.

His face tightened. "As Zaire's advisor, I command you to keep your yoni away from him."

My body shook uncontrollably as he glared at me while backing away.

I was still shaking ten minutes later when Queenie and my father appeared from the direction of my new home. They were laughing. Queenie had her arm around my father's arm, as she guided him to me.

I turned around and wiped my tears away, and I put on a look of curiosity.

Queenie said happily, "I hope you enjoyed your sleep."

"I'm sorry. I know there is a lot to do."

She waved my words off. "Your father and I just left your place," she shook her head in bliss. "It is amazing. It is so Zen-like. The artist from Noire captured you completely."

This should've excited me. I should've been begging to have a peek inside, which was forbidden until I officially became griot, but all I could do was give her a fake smile. "Hello, Father," I said as I gave my father a kiss on the cheek.

"Hello, sweet girl. I wanted to come by and make sure you weren't stressed."

I wasn't stressed about becoming the griot, but what Adesewa revealed to me had my soul in turmoil. "Thank you."

He took my hands. "You go out there tomorrow and be your beautiful self."

I hugged him again.

Queenie cleared her throat, attempting to cue Father, but he said nothing. He just moved to her side. She rolled her eyes. "Your father and I have something very important to tell you. We aren't sure how you will take it." Although Father could not see her, Queenie looked at him.

I stiffened. What the hell else would they tell me now? I let out a shaky breath. So did Queenie as she reached into the pocket of her cape and pulled out a wooden comb that was undoubtedly my father's work. "Go ahead, Bach."

He took a deep breath. "Zen," my father said cautiously. "Tomorrow is this woman's last day as griot." He held up her hand and shook it proudly. "For nearly twenty years, I've been waiting on this woman with love in my heart. I've had to hide my affection for her. After tomorrow," he paused. Tears fell down his face and became trapped in his beard. "I'll no longer hide my love for this woman."

Queenie rubbed Father's back. Proudly she said, "Your father gave me this beautiful proposal comb and asked me to be his wife." She broke down in tears, too. They hugged, rocking back and forth.

I laughed and threw my arms around them.

"So you approve?" Father asked.

"I do. I thought the comb you were carving was for Abebi and Sahel."

"I refuse—"

"Bach," Queenie warned him gently, before turning his attention to another matter. "There is one more thing." Her confidence waned. "There is another reason I'm retiring now."

My eyes moved between her and my anxious father and back to her again. Queenie rubbed her round and firm stomach. My legs buckled. She was carrying a child.

Later that day, the aroma of sautéed onions, red peppers, and simmering goat stew wafted through Queenie's house. The griots would be here by nightfall. Queenie wasn't the only one cooking. In the village, a warthog had been smoking since the wee hours of the morning and wouldn't be complete until my ceremony tomorrow. In the morning, the many stews would be simmering for the celebration of the new griot. Yet, all this wasn't enough to take my mind off what Adesewa had revealed to me. I felt ashamed for believing Zaire cared for me. Thank the gods things didn't go further.

I walked to my new home. I saw Mansi gathering bush wood that he would trade with people in the village. I waved, not expecting him to wave in return, but he did. It was hard to picture Mansi as my uncle, but that was who he was. The mute man had risked his life so that my parents could raise me together. It hadn't happened, but he had tried.

The house was beautiful. It felt too large for me to live in alone. I held my ear to the door and listened. The workers were long gone, and no one would enter until tomorrow when they brought in the gifts people gave me. After the feast, I could officially move into my house. My house.

I looked around. Then I put my hand on the cool brass doorknob and turned it. The wood from the door smelled fresh. I stepped in, and my breath was stolen. The curved walls were painted with murals that could've only been my mother's work. She didn't tell me she was going to do this. I went to the mural and ran my fingers along the abstract women carrying baskets on their heads and the children playing. Tears fell. I laughed heartily as I realized my floor was shiny just like Zora's. I bent down and ran my hands over the smooth surface.

In the common room, there were trees in large planters. It was as if someone understood the beauty I saw in Ankara's rainforest. A cozy meditation room had plenty of sunlight shining through. I loved that space.

My bedroom was large, and like Zora's, it had a large tub to soak in. The builders had even given me a second bathroom. I shook my head in amazement. Hah. Even if Abebi would've married Sahel, she wouldn't have gotten all this. I pressed my palms together and praised the gods for the entire space.

I moved to the kitchen sink and turned on the water, just to see if it already worked, and it did. I praised the gods again. The shelves were stacked with plates, bowls, and pots. I had to hug myself. Just as Queenie said, this home embodied my spirit.

As I inhaled the new scent of my home, there was a soft knock. I'd been caught, but I didn't care.

"Come in," I sang.

The door eased open. The peace left the room when I

saw Zaire's smiling face. Searing pain ripped through my chest. I frowned at him as tears built up in my eyes.

"I am sorry. I was told I should come see your home. I did not mean to disturb you." He slowly looked around the room with amazement, but his smile faded when he looked at me.

"I was just leaving," I snapped. "Enjoy."

"Zen. Hold on," he said. His face contorted. He gently touched my arm.

I looked at his hand, and he snatched it away.

"I know I was wrong to pull my knife out. I didn't mean to frighten you," he stammered.

"Stop it," I barked. Zaire's eyes opened wide, and his mouth parted.

"Adesewa told me."

"Told you what?" He tilted his head and squinted.

"That I am just a game for you. You don't give a shit about me."

"What?"

I continued, my voice wavering with shame and anger, "I'm a thrill because it would make you feel more powerful to fuck a griot."

His face was hardened with anger now. "Adesewa said this?"

"Bye, Zaire." I moved to the front door.

"Hold on. Please."

"No."

"Adesewa is a jealous asshole. Excuse my language, Zen."

"I don't want to hear it. I knew something wasn't right about you being interested in me." I swung the door open.

He ran over and put his palm on the door, forcing it closed. I pulled my hand away from the handle.

"Zen, I am sorry he said those things to hurt you, but he has always been jealous of me. Adesewa is a close friend of my mother, so he was given the job of keeping me out of trouble. He is an advisor, so to speak. However, I have always felt like he has tried to sabotage me in every way, but now I know for sure." He looked tormented. "All of those things that I told you yesterday were true. You know it."

Hot tears slid down my face. I was sick of being lied to and played with by everyone.

"What can I do to get you to trust me?" he asked.

"Why do I need to? Nothing can go on here. I'm not available, and I don't have time for friendship."

"Good because I want to be more than just your friend," he said forcefully. Zaire released the door and stepped toward me. He placed his massive hands on the sides of my face, and he kissed me so passionately it hurt a bit. Stunned, I allowed it. I shouldn't have, but I did. I wanted to believe him.

When our kiss ended, Zaire looked as weak as I felt. Now my mind was even more confused. I shouldn't have let him kiss me.

With a pained expression, he said, "I hope you know I am telling you the truth. Adesewa's motives are sick, and he is going to pay for the things he said to you, whether you believe me or not." He looked at me apologetically and walked out.

I went into my meditation room, and although it was bare, I felt the sanctity of the room. The shaman had been here; I could feel it. Perhaps he was in the room right now, guiding me, urging me in the direction of my truth. I thought of his warning to me. Who was not who they said they were? Was it only my mother, Zaire, Sahel, or were there more people lying to me? I closed my eyes and prayed for clarity and confidence, but damaging self-talk took control.

331

Why would a prince like me? Why wouldn't he like someone prettier, more exciting? Why me? What did he truly want? What was his motive? When would he grow tired of me?

Eventually, I lost myself in deep meditation. There was nothing, a hiatus. Nothingness. No thoughts. That's where my clarity dwelled.

CHAPTER 51

That night, I went to Zaire. A galvanizing feeling of worthiness came upon me. I was worthy of his attention, and I believed he cared for me. But I remembered a lesson my father taught me. Detachment. I had to keep myself centered, ensuring that my happiness came from within. Even if everything Zaire said was a lie, I wouldn't fall apart. I needed pleasure right now.

Zaire opened the parish door. Before he saw who I was, he looked dejected. Then delight took over his face.

"Hello," I said softly.

"Come in."

Once I entered, Zaire stood as far away from me as the kitchen would allow. He was nervous. "Can I offer you anything?"

"Wine," I said evenly.

His lips twitched, and he walked over to the counter and poured dark red wine into two glasses.

I sipped the bitter wine then put the glass on the counter by the sink. "I don't know the truth, Zaire."

His eyes pleaded with me. "I've told you—"

I held up my hand, and he silenced himself. "All I know is that I need you tonight."

He eyed me critically. In a deep voice that dripped with seduction, he asked, "What do you mean by that?"

I walked over to him and put my left hand on his chest and reached for his beard with my right palm. He swallowed before he put his glass down and moved his lips to mine. His lips tasted like his wine. He pulled away and looked me in the eye again, then took my hand. He led me to his bedroom. My stomach fluttered.

Zaire's room was decorated in beiges and blacks. A Zaian mask that provided protection hung over his large bed. The decor was tastefully minimal.

Slowly, he led me to the bed, where I sat in angst. He kissed me again, leaning me back until I was lying beneath his trim chest, abdomen, and thighs. There were butterflies in my stomach and a tantalizing dynamism in my yoni.

Heat surged between my legs. My head nodded swiftly, and he undid my wrap with finesse, exposing my breasts. I quivered. No man had ever seen me this way. My skin warmed. I was giving my virginity to the prince, and I was honored. Zaire sucked on my neck for a while. I moaned and ran my hands over his brown skin. His teeth raked over my clavicle and down, down, down, until he took my right nipple into his mouth, and I froze uncomfortably. Breasts were for nurturing babies, not for pleasuring men. He didn't seem to notice my rigidness, and he stood and removed his pants. My mouth gaped open when I saw his dick. It was beautiful, no doubt. The phallus was dark, thick, and erect, with skin pulled tightly over the firm mass and several profuse veins, until it reached a bulbous head. Oh no. There was no way that would fit inside of me. Also I wasn't certain if he'd been circumcised. I didn't know how a penis was supposed to look, and I was too embarrassed to ask. Again, he lowered himself onto me.

"Zaire?"

"Yes."

"I've never done this," I whispered.

He lifted his head and looked at me. "It's alright. I'm going to take care of you."

I relaxed as he slowly pushed his finger into me. I gnashed my teeth and turned my face away.

"I can stop," he offered.

"No," I breathed.

Zaire entered me, and the penetration caused the worst pain of my existence. I groaned and gripped his back, but not because his strokes felt good. It took a while before I felt the slightest hint of pleasure. He was a gentleman, asking me if I was okay frequently. I wasn't, but I lied. Finally, I felt him shudder and moan. He collapsed on top of me for a moment. He rolled over and peered at the ceiling.

After he had caught his breath, he pulled my body over to his. I kissed his chest, all the while thinking that it should've been Sahel.

"Did you do this because you're angry?" he whispered.

"Huh?" He took me out of my mood. I looked at him.

"Did you do this because you're mad at him? I heard he's supposed to marry your friend." There was a sadness in his eyes. I wondered if he'd been asking about me. Zaire continued, "I can erase the pain you feel…temporarily. All I ask is that you give me a real chance to love you."

CHAPTER 52

My mother didn't bother to ask me where I had been, or why I smelled of expensive soap and oils. Thank the gods. She just rushed me inside. There was a loud commotion coming from the common room. Nok and the twins were in deep conversation. I rushed to Nok and hugged her tightly. I had forgiven her for also concealing the truth about my past from me.

She sang, "Congratulations, Zen. You have come so far."

I nodded. I had. It had been less than two months, yet so much had evolved inside of me. My mind drifted to Zaire and the pain between my legs.

"Come eat, then wash your hair. Zora will be here soon."

Zora arrived windswept and exhausted, but still stunning. We hugged like we were long lost sisters. "All right, let's get this hair braided. Man, the ancestors didn't think about a griot having this much hair when they came up with these sacred braids." She teased my freshly washed hair with her fingers.

As she braided my hair in the middle of the common room, the ladies sang wildly. It never struck me as it did now; Queenie was retiring, and this was her last day as the griot. This was her celebration just as it was mine.

A headache and two hours later, the tiny braids were finished. Zora hugged me. "Are you ready for a phenomenal day tomorrow?" Once, she'd been jealous about me taking her place as the baby griot. Now, she was delighted.

I held out my trembling hands to demonstrate how jittery I was.

She nodded her head knowingly. "I knew you would be. That's why I have something for you." Zora looked at the other two griots to see if they were paying attention to us, but they were in their own bliss. Nok was tipsy, and my pregnant mother acted like she was. Zora slipped me a bag with a mixture of dried petals, a powdery substance, and tea leaves.

I sniffed it. The scent was earthy like the rainforest. "What is it?"

"Passion flower. It will help you fall asleep and not let your anxiety wake you."

I stuck the bag in between my breasts. "I need this every night."

She shook her finger. "No, ma'am. Passion flower is quite potent," she warned.

Zora was right. That night, her blend put me right to sleep, and I didn't wake up with the anxiety that the eve of a life-changing day could bring.

The sound of something crashing outside my door startled me awake. My heart thrashed. Once I gained my bearings, I threw back the covers and scurried to the door. I feared that the rebels had broken in. When I opened the door, I screamed and attempted to slam the door.

Three haunting figures with faces caked with ashes stood stark still on the other side of the door. They were here. The rebels. One threw its foot and stopped the door from closing. I screamed again. What a day to die!

CHAPTER 53

"Open the door," the voice boomed. The voice was deep, yet of a woman. I threw my body against the door determined to crush the bones in the foot that blocked the door from closing. Female rebels? I never suspected women.

"Who are you?" There was pushing from the other side of the door, and I couldn't hold them back.

In an eerie chorus they spoke, "We are the three that listen to the gods and deliver the messages of the ancestors. We are the storytellers, the keepers of secrets. You will come with us."

My chest heaved. Storytellers? "Griots?" It had to be them trying to frighten me. It was initiation day. This must be the first rite. I swallowed, wanting to curse them.

"If you don't get the hell off my foot..." Zora threatened, losing her character. I heard snickering. Relieved, I let the door go, and they grabbed me, snatching me into the hall and then to the front door. Their physical strength surprised me.

"Wait. My shoes," I cried.

"No. It's time," the Nok commanded. When we got outside, the old woman lit a torch. They wore white, the unsettling color.

They let me go, and without a word, I followed them far into the dark bush. The earth was cold beneath my feet. My heart's rhythm relaxed. In my cowardly state, my senses were heightened. I listened for the dangers of the bush, not that it mattered. No one had a weapon, not even Nok.

In the middle of nowhere, there was a wooden stool. That alone was haunting. I knew these women, I knew they wouldn't hurt me, but they didn't mind scaring me half to death.

"Sit," my mother commanded.

I walked over to the stool and sat. I attempted to look stoic like I knew what was going on, or like I wasn't jostled from sleep just minutes before and thrust into this mysterious rite.

With Nok's flame, the other two griots lit their torches.

"Who are you?" Zora asked.

"Zen."

"Zen who?" Her voice was acidic. She wasn't the woman I laughed with last night.

"Zen Akke."

"Where do your people come from?" my mother asked.

I took a deep breath. "My people derived from the ancients of this stunning continent. Their sons and daughters were murdered or stolen. They lived as outcasts in a foreign land. One had the intent on bringing his people back home. His name was Father Malcolm. He, Za's founders, and 200 brave souls came to Noire to make a home for us. Now his people, the Zaians, have evolved into a self-reliant, self-sustaining, creative, and strong people. That's where my people come from."

340

My mother fought back a grin. I noticed a tear make a line in her caked on makeup. "Name every woman who has passed into the realm of the Griothood," my mother demanded.

I did so fluidly and with feigned confidence. Then I named the first king and his successors, then random families that Queenie threw at me. At last, they approached the part that I feared. I had to tell a story of my own creation. I wouldn't just be tested on the content of my story, but also the passion in my delivery. My tale was the tale of the Ankaran Massacre. When I ended my story, I was in tears. But the stone-faced women looked at me unamused. I knew I should've made up a fable.

Once I was finished, the women walked off to confer. I felt nauseous as I went over every word that had left my mouth during the telling of my story. I scolded myself for being too flustered and not emphasizing certain words. I should've sung. What if they made me go through an extra month of training?

I straightened my spine when they made their way back.

"Rise," said Nok.

I stood quickly, sending my stool falling to the ground. Nok clucked her teeth in annoyance.

"The Griothood has come to a conclusion about your requested entry into our realm."

Requested? I would've laughed if I hadn't been so damned anxious.

"If we accept you, do you swear to secrecy no matter what may come your way?"

"Yes," I said, my breath unsteady.

"Do you swear to keep your mind sharp and your stories ever-evolving, so that you may teach all who can hear your voice?"

"Yes."

"Do you swear to advise the elders, the chief, and the king with honesty and pure intentions?"

"Yes."

The women glanced at each other. The sun was rising over this portion of the Great Rift Valley. I could tell by the shimmer in my mother's eyes that she was crying again. She stepped forward, pulling her hands from behind her back. She pulled out her key to the Grotto. I put the key around my neck. "Your request is granted. You're now a true member of the Griothood."

With much force, my mother swept me into her arms with a warm embrace. We both sobbed. Nok and Zora wrapped their arms around the both of us. All of us cried.

"I almost forgot." Zora plucked from her breast a folded piece of paper. She held it out to me, and I unfolded it. It was a map without any words.

"What is it?"

"A map to the Grotto."

Thank the gods. "I thought we weren't supposed to write the location down?"

"I lied." Then Zora took my hand and positioned me between her and Nok. We faced my mother. I concealed the map.

In the horizon, the sun was creating a metallic orange display.

Nok said, "Queenie, this is your last moment as griot. For eighteen years, you've served our ancestors, our king, and our people."

I squinted. They released her from the Griothood after eighteen years. Was it because of the baby? It didn't seem fair, but I let the thought go.

"You are loved and will always be loved. Thank you for

passing your blessing onto our organization. Now, at age 38, you may live your life for you. Go be with your beloveds."

Zora reached out and caressed Queenie's belly. Queenie's stoic face melted, and she began to sob. We rushed to her and threw our arms around her. Her eyes smiled. She fell to her knees and cried joyfully to the gods. They'd finally freed her to live the life she'd always desired. My mother could now be with the man she'd loved for nearly twenty years. She could now have her family. When she stopped wailing, I helped her stand. She looked at Nok and embraced her tightly. "I'll miss you, my sister."

"Oh please, this is not goodbye, Queenie," Nok laughed.

Queenie let go of Nok and reached for Zora. "Sister, I know you will help guide my daughter."

"Of course, Queenie. You're making me way too sad, like we'll never see each other."

Queenie laughed. "I don't think I've ever felt like this. I'm glad to be free of the Griothood, but I'm a little sad too. I'm going to miss you ladies."

CHAPTER 54

My initiation day had been a whirlwind, almost too fast for me to enjoy. Once I officially became griot, my face was painted with ashes to match the others. My initiation braids had been hidden under a white wrap.

Queenie blessed me with a beautiful beaded corset like the one worn by the Dinka men. She then left us griots alone and went to my father. Nok and Zora helped me don the beaded corset, Zora wrapped one of her burnt orange skirts around my waist, and my sandals were placed on my feet.

"Zen," Nok called.

I went to the common room. "You have a visitor."

Curiously, I went to the door. It was Zaire. He kissed my cheek openly while the women watched. "I'm not going to keep you. I just wanted to tell you congratulations." I nervously looked back at the other griots, and they left the room with grins on their faces.

I smiled at him. "Thank you." I stepped over to him and kissed his lips long and passionately. "I'll see you soon," I told him.

"Okay. You look stunning, by the way."

"Thank you."

Obsidian was brimming with people. Even Zaians from Noire and Ankara had come to celebrate my passage. My cousin Kwame, his fiancée, and several relatives from Noire had come all this way to see me. Their sacrifice to be here brought me to tears. Nok's friends from Ankara had come all the way to visit the griot that saved Osun. My set, minus Abebi, came over to embrace and congratulate me. It wasn't the perfunctory embrace from before I was griot; they were truly proud of me.

The celebration was exhilarating. Everyone danced up a sweat. We poured libations onto Mother Earth in honor of those gone on, and we feasted. My most important moment was dancing with my father.

My pulse soared as I told my first story as the official Griot of Obsidian. It was the same story I told the griots when they kidnapped me that morning. Zora instructed me on how to add call and response to my stories. I gave the people a cue. Every time they heard the word "rebels" they had to make galloping sounds by patting their laps with the palms of their hands. The dynamic was amazing, and my audience was rapt and engaged. My people cried and winced. When the story was complete, they held themselves as if they could actually see every bloody corpse lying in the mud, hear the rebels being tortured, and smell the homes going up in flames.

I sat at the table with the elders, the griots, and Zaire. It was difficult to stop glancing at him, and we kept catching each other's eye. Anyone watching us probably knew there was something there.

I was stuffed when Abebi walked up to the elders' table. I hadn't laid eyes on her since before I heard that she would be Sahel's bride.

"Excuse me," she said softly. "May I please speak to you?"

Zora screwed up her face. Zora knew who Abebi was and how she was supposed to marry the boy I loved. Zora's glare was severe, and it made me proud.

"Go ahead," I said curtly, my lips in a straight line.

"Alone. Please." Her eyes pleaded with me. Abebi never pleaded for anything.

I threw down my napkin and rose.

I followed her away from the feasting people and to the side of the Elders' Mound where no one could see us unless they walked past.

"What?" I growled, my eyes wide with impatience and anger.

"My father gave back the dowry."

I folded my arms. "Why did you interrupt my dinner to tell me this?"

Embarrassment passed over her face. "I need you to know that it wasn't my idea. I didn't want to marry him."

"But Abebi, of all the men in Za, your parents picked Sahel. You had nothing to do with that?"

She put her hand on her chest and her mouth gaped open. "No. My parents put that all together. They love legacy, and no other family has quite the legacy as Sahel's. He will probably be chief one day."

I walked away.

"Zen, I hope we can return to how we were."

Never that, I thought. I paused. I needed to know. "Did Sahel come to you and call it off?"

"Well...he did, but—" Her words fell away, and I kept moving. I was glad that Sahel had told me the truth, but I was hurt because I knew if he hadn't called it off Abebi would've gladly married him. I knew who was loyal to me.

After my conversation with Abebi, my laughter and glee were a farce. Then I saw Sahel. His sad eyes were unabashedly on me as I danced. Zaire watched me too. I was on edge, afraid the two men would attack each other. I feared that Sahel would be the one who got hurt.

Following the feast, my mother, the griots, my father, and my cousins came to my house with gifts in hand. We waited outside as the shaman gave the home its final smudging. When he left, he had no parting words, just an unsettling glance directed at me.

Everyone hugged me and sang a song of blessings as I went inside alone. I pretended that it had been my first time seeing the place. Then the two griots presented me with a gift—an expensive sky blue dress that I could wear to weddings and name dedications. I cried when my father and mother presented me with a new kora. The one I played now was over twenty years old, and it had been very good to me. Although I loved my old kora dearly, this one was exquisite—the gourd was large, the wood perfectly polished, the strings untouched, and my name had been etched on the back. I strummed the strings, and the sound was flawless. I embraced my parents. Then everyone came in and toured my new home, and we gathered in the common room until it was time for the griots to return to their provinces.

Later that night, there was a knock on my door. Cautiously, I opened it. I smiled, my pulse quickening. Zaire stood there.

I wanted to make love again, but I thought better of it. All day, I'd felt the pain that reminded me of what we'd done the night before. But our hug lasted too long, and his kiss stirred me up.

"Okay. My business is now complete. I just wanted to be the first man in your bed," he joked after he finished making love to me.

I pretended to pout.

He laughed. "I've been thinking about your friend, the goat herder." His words were laced with contempt.

I rolled my eyes.

"He was blatantly disrespectful."

I tensed. Was he going to have Sahel punished?

"He has the fervor of a rebel." He looked into my eyes, searching. Then he lifted a brow. "Has he ever said anything against my father?"

"No," I scoffed.

He looked at me out of the side of his eyes. "Are you sure you're not blinded by love?" he asked playfully, but his tone was laced with suspicion and jealousy.

"I've known him all my life."

"All of us have known these rebels, and yet we don't know them at all."

His words resonated with me. Not Sahel. I knew that in my soul.

His mood became heavy. "I leave tomorrow."

I turned from him. I didn't want to show my sadness.

He kissed my neck and drew his body in close to mine. "Are you brave enough to let me wake up next to you in the morning?"

"Are you brave enough to be seen leaving my place in the morning?" Probably, no one would see him leave. That was a benefit of living outside the village walls, but I didn't care either way.

CHAPTER 55

The first thing I did—after kissing Zaire goodbye—was visit my father. I knocked and knocked, but he didn't answer. I checked the shed, still no answer. I smiled knowingly. He was with my mother and their unborn child. Now, with no reason to hide, they could be together.

I prayed, before I knocked on Zaire's door, that he hadn't left yet. I needed to see him once more before he left. Adesewa opened the door with his usual cold manner. He bowed his head slightly, which was more than he'd ever done before. He moved to the side so that I could enter.

Zaire appeared with a slight smile and his arms opened.

"I am so glad you came to see me off." He wrapped one arm around me and nuzzled my neck.

"Actually, I was hoping you weren't leaving so soon."

He looked into my eyes, seeing if I truly meant it. "You're going to miss me?"

I blushed. "I am."

"If I were king," he said, "I would tell Obsidian they would have to find another griot. I would put you on my horse and whisk you back to Noire. You would be the princess by sunrise."

There was truth behind his eyes. He pulled me to him in another warm embrace and pressed his lips to my forehead, and chill bumps rose all over my skin.

"Excuse me," Wajir, Zaire's quiet and kind attendant, rushed into the room, eyes averted. "We must leave soon if we hope to make it to the feast tonight."

"I'm sorry," Zaire whispered.

We let go of each other.

"Promise me you will come visit the palace soon."

"I promise."

He kissed my lips.

Sadly I said, "I can't watch you leave."

He nodded his understanding.

I forced myself to move to the door. I felt heavy.

"Zen, if you ever need anything, anything, just let me know." Torment crossed his face.

CHAPTER 56

The loneliness was so loud in my new home. My life was empty, and I ached. It had begun to rain, and all I could think to do was sleep. I slept past dinnertime. It was pitch black when I woke to someone knocking on my door. When I opened the door, my mother and father were standing there.

"You okay?" my mother asked with concern in her eyes. Father was behind her, and they were both carrying pots of delicious-smelling food.

"Yes, just unbelievably tired," I lied. I could now smile. The sight of them made me happy as they brought their food into my kitchen.

"How was your first day, sweet girl?" Father asked me as my mother heaped mounds of cabbage, squash, and rice onto his plate.

I feigned a smile and said, "It was—" And suddenly, I burst into tears. Father rose and felt his way around the table. He bent down and placed his arms around me.

"What is it, sweet girl?"

"I don't know. I should be happy, but I've never felt so alone or sad."

My mother handed me a cloth, and I patted my eyes, feeling awful for not acknowledging my blessings. But I couldn't. It was impossible to feel the gratitude.

She said, "I know what you feel. It can be a very lonely life, being the griot." She heaved a giant breath. "However, it doesn't have to be. You can become closer with your friends. When they need to get away from their husbands, let them know they can spend time with you. You can walk the streets and get to know and observe everyone. This'll be the inspiration for your stories. Now you can befriend the other spiritualists. You are one of them. You, too, have a gift. Learn from them, and they'll learn from you. The shaman may be a good place to start."

We laughed at how ludicrous that sounded.

Then, seriously, I imagined drinking tea and laughing with the root twins or even visiting the shaman. It seemed so unnatural.

Father felt his way back to his seat and joined in. "You should befriend the elders. Although you're young, you're one of them now."

"And enjoy your position," Queenie said with a smile. "Travel, sleep plenty, grow your garden, trade with people, pursue any and every creative outlet that jumps into your mind." She stuck cabbage into her mouth.

"But don't forget," Father added, "we're still your parents." He reached for my mother's hand, and they both squeezed.

A chill ran through me.

My mother gave my father a soft smile, and then she looked at me uncomfortably. "You're still welcome to spend your days with me if you like." She looked uneasy. "Anytime. You should never feel lonely."

I noticed she was gripping father's hand tightly. He supported her. I softened. She was trying to be my mother.

We ate, and Father gossiped. He knew every juicy secret in Obsidian. We laughed and hushed him, but he continued, making everyone at the table laugh until we cried tears. Each story was more scandalous than the last.

"Father, where do you get this nonsense?"

"It's not nonsense. People trust me because I'm blind. What does being blind have to do with anything? My mouth is just as big as the next person's," he guffawed.

"You are so silly," my mother cooed. Without thinking, she laid her head on his shoulder. A quick bout of jealousy ripped through me.

"I hope they haven't shut off the water yet," I said, rising abruptly. I turned the faucet, and the water ran.

Queenie and I washed dishes in silence until I asked, "How will I know who the next griot is?" I had two decades to go before I chose someone, but I was curious.

She thought. "From a young age, you can see her spirit take shape. She will embody the ability to keep secrets, she'll more than likely be an enigma to people around her, and she'll be uncomfortable around people her age, but connected to those twice her age.

"Your father didn't agree that it should be you. So much had been taken from you already. In the end, on your fourth birthday I submitted your name to the Griothood."

"Fourth birthday?"

She nodded.

"I knew it when you were two. Amadi confirmed it," she said without wavering. "And boy, were we right." She touched the side of my face with her damp hand. Her face contorted, and she sobbed. She sniffled and then quickly she recovered. "Look at me. This baby has made me so emotional."

353

Once the dishes were dried, anxiety took over me once more. I didn't want them to leave. I almost asked them to stay in the spare room, but I figured I'd better grow up.

Queenie said, "Your father will move into my home once we're married."

"Wow, outside the gates, Father? How will you ever know the latest gossip?" I teased.

He chuckled. "Don't worry. I won't miss a thing."

"I told my brother he could move back into the village. Of course, he's not interested." Queenie grinned proudly. "He wants to stay beyond the walls and, if you want, he wants to help you in the way that he has always helped me. He can guard your home, run errands, help you garden. He'll do anything."

My heart swelled. I nodded. "I would welcome that," I said. I was grateful. The news lifted me even more. I had both of my parents and my uncle. I also had the support of my family in Noire.

As they headed out the door, Queenie said, "Uh...Zen, you have company."

My brows knitted. I looked out the door, and a group of pretty brown faces belonging to the girls in my set stared back at me. They'd come without Abebi. Nervously, I said, "Hello."

Several said hello. The rest silently avoided my eyes.

Queenie waved at me and winked. She and my father walked toward her house. There was an awkward silence in their wake. Each of the girls looked uncomfortably back at me. I became acutely aware of my solar plexus chakra as the pit of my gut tightened.

Jema, with her tall and muscular frame, stepped forward. "We wanted to visit your place and congratulate you...even if we didn't get an invite."

I noted a hint of bitterness in her voice. "Of course," I said feeling ashamed for not even thinking of inviting them. Hell, I didn't think they'd want to visit. "Come in."

I led all of the Zephyr girls into my home. They each hugged and congratulated me while excitedly taking in my place.

"This is lovely, Zen," Los said. She was the oldest of our set, but the tiniest.

"Who painted these walls?" Keeke asked in awe.

"My mother."

Many brows rose.

I took a deep breath before explaining. "I found out, not too long ago, that Queenie is my mother."

"What?!" They all exclaimed. Perhaps their parents didn't know and therefore hadn't gossiped, but I also knew that people were great actors.

I nodded. "Long story. I'll share it another time. Have a seat." I sat down on a plush floor pillow. "Where's Abebi?"

"She didn't feel comfortable," Jema replied.

She'd made the right choice.

Some took a chair, and some sat on the floor.

Jema cut to the chase. "We always felt you didn't want to be in our set."

This was true and false. I'd wanted to be alone, but when I saw them laughing or heard about an adventure I'd missed out on, jealousy burned inside of me. When they joked or broke into a song they'd made up without me, I'd thought they were childish, but I'd yearned to play, too. "I always felt like I didn't belong. It was like the Zephyrs belong to you all, and I was on the outside. You are all so tight. I just never fit in." Being with them felt so unnatural to who I was.

Los said, "I never knew you felt left out. We thought you liked being away from us, in your own space." They were right.

"I guess we have a lifetime to learn each other's spirits." I smiled and made a vow to myself to try harder but not to force it. We talked about my training. They asked about the prince. I blushed and simply said he was a good friend. For the first time, I enjoyed their company. There was something clawing at the back of my mind. "There's something I think you could help me with." I hated asking for assistance, especially because I'd been so standoffish with them.

The girls all looked at each other then gave me their attention.

I leaned forward. My sisters were a resource I had overlooked. "I know you've all heard my story about the attack in Ankara."

They nodded.

"The rebellion is becoming formidable."

Bodies tensed.

"I have to know who the leaders are. But to find that out, I need to know the names of the members. Do any of you think the rebels are amongst us?" I asked. "Has anyone spoken ill of the king or about desiring a more developed Za?"

"We all want certain foreign things," Jema said.

Some nodded.

"I understand that, but would you slaughter people in your own village for those things?" I looked several of my sisters in the eye as if I were telling them a story. "Do you know someone with feelings that strong? Have any tongues slipped?" I asked. They shook their heads.

Keeke cleared her throat. "I don't know for sure… I mean, certainly, he wouldn't kill, but…"

Everyone looked at her. I held my breath.

"Mali has been courting me."

Hearing the name of my father's former apprentice chilled my blood.

"What about him?" Jema asked, shock in her voice.

"He says really harsh things about King Akonos. It makes me uncomfortable."

"Does he slip off at night?" I asked.

"I don't know." She shook her head and said, "I'm going to stop seeing him."

"No!" some of the girls shouted.

"Keep seeing him for right now. See what you can find out," Jema said.

"But be careful," I added. "Don't let him get suspicious of you. They're dangerous men. If he really is a rebel, he'll have no problem killing you to protect his secret."

Keeke's eyes misted. The girl beside her, Modenye, put her hand on her shoulder.

Then there was a knock. Jema bounded up and went to the door.

Sahel entered. His head was wrapped in a blue cotton fabric. His eyes looked around the room at the Zephyrs and landed on me with shock and curiosity.

"We'll be off," Jema said.

I stood and hugged each girl as they exited. Then it was just Sahel and me.

"What?" I asked, standing at the door that was still opened.

"I'm sorry for how I acted."

"You could've gotten yourself killed."

"That's not why I'm sorry. I'm sorry for embarrassing you. I'm sorry for grabbing you and dragging you out of there. But as for how I treated the Zaire, with all due respect to you...fuck him."

"Bye, Sahel."

"I know you have been pulled in by his powers and looks, but he's dangerous."

His words offended me. I wasn't some weak and naïve girl. I saw he wasn't ready to leave, so I closed the door just as a mosquito entered. I was happy Mansi had hung a net over my bed. "Sure he is," I said.

"When I was at training camp, I heard things about him."

I rolled my eyes.

"I heard that one of his maids ended up dead or missing because of him."

"Sounds compelling, coming from you." Each man had accused the other of something unfathomable.

"You think I'm saying this because I'm jealous. Well, I am jealous that he made love to you first."

My cheeks warmed. "What?" I gasped.

"I can tell, Zen. Don't play me for a fool." He closed his eyes in sorrow. "Why, Zen? Because of Abebi. Well, I'm sorry. You got your redemption." His lips tightened, and he cleared his throat. He looked around my house with moist eyes. "Congratulations." With that, he left my space.

CHAPTER 57

I woke up with a smile on my face. It had rained all night, and now the sky over the plains was a gloomy gray. There was a chill in the house, so I lit a flame to steep some tea. Before he left, Zaire had given me one last gift: enough dried herbs and spices to last several months. I made a mint tea, and once it was prepared, I took my cup into the bedroom. I ran a hot bath and soaked my body, more for the warmth than the cleansing.

As soon as I dressed, I started for Queenie's home. I heard something sounding like an ax blade chopping in quick increments. I went around the side of my home and saw Mansi using a hoe to break up the earth.

"What're you going to plant?" I asked. Immediately, I felt silly for forgetting he was mute.

He put his finger in the dirt and spelled out, "Carrots, beets, and yams."

I touched his shoulder, "Thank you."

He went back to his work without any acknowledgment. I was glad to have him watching over me.

As I approached, I could smell pork already cooking inside of my mother's home. I knocked. She opened the door and smiled. "You hungry?"

"Famished."

"Good. Your father will be over soon, too. Before we eat, I want to give you one last gift."

"You've already given me enough." Last night, my home filled with the marvelous sound of my new instrument. Only it could ease the pain I felt for Sahel's sadness.

"Follow me," she said, ignoring me. I followed her around the back of the house. We headed to the chicken coop. "You see those two fat hens and the rooster? They now belong to you."

I melted into tears and hugged her tightly, and she reciprocated. I knew how much she loved her chickens.

"Mansi will be building you a coop soon. The hens are fine egg layers. This doesn't mean you're not welcomed for breakfast, though." We laughed.

We sat down at Queenie's kitchen table but we both soon grew impatient. Where was my father? I was surprised he hadn't beat me to breakfast as much as he loved food. Mother hollered for Mansi.

"I'll go get him," I interjected.

"Okay, hurry," she said, handing me a piping hot piece of fatback. "This baby is hungry now."

I rushed to the village walls, hailing the guards and chewing the fat. I knocked on Father's door.

There was no answer. There was no way I would've missed him unless he went somewhere else first. Father would never begin working before he filled his stomach.

"Father," I called. "We'll eat without you."

No answer. I opened the door.

My heart lurched, and I froze. Steps from the door, my

father lay on the floor. I halted for a second then rushed to his side to see if he had fallen.

"Father," I croaked. I screamed when I saw the blood. Too much blood. His neck had been slit.

The next moments happened in flashes. I saw my hands covered in his blood. I saw the knife I'd bought him in Noire, laying a few inches from his body. People rushed in. I didn't remember screaming, but they were there to pull me away. At some point, Queenie was screaming, too. There was blood splattered on the wall of Father's common room. My father was dead.

CHAPTER 58

My mother and I were taken to the root twins' home. We clung to each other in misery and confusion. Mother was delirious and hadn't ceased crying, although her voice was now painfully hoarse. I cried silently, unable to grasp what had happened.

RoRo gave us a soothing tea that made us sleep without dreaming. It must have been the same as Zora's tea. We slept for a few hours. Then the sobbing commenced. Mansi was there, looking powerlessly at his inconsolable sister. He put his arms around her, and she buried her head into his chest. "I was finally going to be with him. I was finally going to marry him. Who did this? Who did it? Nooooooo."

I thought about the baby.

"We'll find out," Inkar said. "Their fate has already been determined."

I sat in the corner, my throat raw from crying. The sun shone brightly through the root twins' windows, but I was in deep darkness. People moved all around us, anticipating our every need, but I felt alone. My father was gone. Murdered in such a heinous way.

The twins tried to feed me, but I couldn't eat or drink. All I could do was see my loving and joyous father, who had never wronged anyone, lying on the floor with a scarlet puddle around his head. Someone in my village did this, someone he knew. In my whole lifetime, there had never been a murder in Obsidian, and now someone had slaughtered my father. I wanted to die, but not before I killed my father's murderer. Had a woman done this? Maybe she'd been jealous because he was marrying Queenie. No. That didn't feel right. Had I been asking too many questions? Had I caused this? Were the rebels punishing me? It had to be them. They'd slit the throat of others. I started to wail.

"Here," RoRo said. She pushed another cup of tea toward me, but I shook my head. I needed to feel the pain.

RoRo shook her head in disapproval and pushed the cup towards my mother. Her cheeks were slick with tears. Her eyes were red, but she looked at me and told RoRo, "No."

My mother grabbed my hand and said, "Let's go."

I got up from the twins' dinner table. They protested, but my mother, Mansi, and I left without a word.

At my house, the three of us held hands and prayed for a peaceful passing for my father. I thought about his body. The elders were preparing him for interment now. I thought about how his body would be lowered into the ground. Tears sprang forth again. He didn't belong there, under the Earth's surface. I clenched my fist and cursed the ancestors and whoever murdered him. Mother didn't try to stop me as I screamed and jumped. Mansi stood nearby to protect me from hurting myself. Finally, I collapsed to my knees.

Mother wrapped her arms around me, and I felt her trembling and the nape of my neck getting wet. "Tomorrow, I will speak in your place," she told me once I'd calmed.

"No. I'll speak," I said. I was reminded how my first ceremony was supposed to be for Father and Queenie's wedding. I believed he'd tried to save me from having to speak at Abebi and Sahel's wedding by marrying mother hastily. That was my father. He was willing to do everything for me. Now my first ceremony would be his funeral, and Obsidian would feel my wrath.

On the morning of my father's funeral, the earth was thirsty, and the heavens obliged relentlessly. Father's burial was swifter than usual. His family in Noire hadn't even been notified, nor had Nok or Zora. There was no wake for my father. No one needed to watch to see if he woke, not with a slit throat.

I wore a stark white loose-fitting dress and a large straw hat that hid my face and kept the cold rain from my eyes. Mother's eyes were void. The morning was cooler than usual with the rain, but I was too numb to care. When I exited my door, my set stood there with sorrow in their eyes. They gathered around me with love.

When we made it to Father's house, where his body had been prepared for burial and stored, most of the villagers had already congregated. Many refused to look at me. Their lips quivered, and their eyes were full of sadness and pity. But someone was acting. No outsider could get through our gates unnoticed, so the murderer was a villager, someone I'd known all my life. I wanted to grab the people of Obsidian by their arms and dig my fingers in and scream at them. Who was faking their sadness? Who had come into my father's home and slashed a knife across the jugular of a blind man? But I remained mute, my jaw set hard like stone. I was going to find the killer. My eyes fell on the chief and Abebi. After a moment of apprehension, Abebi ran over to me, and we hugged tightly.

The chief came to me and gave me his condolences. "Who are the six men who will carry your father's body?" he asked grimly.

I chose five of Father's closest friends; friends that I knew couldn't have done this to him. I looked at the person who had been my closest friend. "Sahel."

Sahel nodded; the hurt in his eyes was palpable. He walked over to me tentatively and gave me a strong hug. We held each other for a long while. He then joined the others who would carry my father to his resting place.

I moved over to Mother and whispered, "Let me know if anyone is missing." I knew she could calculate this in a matter of seconds.

They brought Father's wrapped, stiff body through the door and all my pain knocked me to the ground. I howled. My mother took my left arm, Mansi took my right, and they forced me to my feet. They tried to talk to me and make me walk. Eventually, my screams calmed, and I moved my feet with Mansi and Mother's guidance. We followed behind my father's body, and the processional crawled to the graveyard. A grim homegoing song had begun behind us. The volume grew as the people of Obsidian snaked behind us in a river of white. The people clapped as they sung, and someone played a shaker made from shells and a gourd.

A young boy pulled away the wood that was placed on the barren grave to protect it from the rain. The white sheet was lowered into the grave, and Father's wrapped body disappeared forever. I didn't watch. I kept my head down. I brooded in disgust as Maki caused a scene, screaming and wailing. When she'd gained control and reined in her antics, the chief was handed a gourd filled with wine. He sipped it and passed it to me. I sipped, as did every elder. My mother couldn't sip because she was not his wife and no longer an elder.

"Excuse me, she's family. You know that." I narrowed my eyes at the chief.

He steeled his jaw and looked to the elders. They nodded reluctantly.

Mother drank.

The chief took back the gourd and poured the remainder into the grave. All the while, the mournful singing continued.

I raised my hands abruptly. All singing ceased, except the singing of a small child. I looked down at Soweto's lovely face. Her mother poked her. The wide-eyed little girl looked back at me frightened and ashamed. Rain splattered on her little face. I stuck out my finger and curled it, motioning Soweto to come to me. She looked to her mother, and her mother grunted, "Go."

The drenched child sauntered to me. Soweto's petite body shook. She stood before me with her beautiful eyes pointed up as they moistened. Had my new title made my little friend fear me? I knelt and hugged her tightly like Zaire hugged the girl who had just had her ears pierced that day in the market. "I love you, Soweto. Go back to your mother," I said, my voice high and sweet. For the first time, I smiled. I remained on one knee. "Go on."

I took a deep breath. "Bachwezi had the joy of a child," I said, my strong voice projecting. I rose and took off my hat. Rain pelted my face. Father's tears. My voice was loud in the vastness of the plains. "Nothing could take his joy. His life force was bright and vibrant. Everyone in this village has laughed because of my father."

The people nodded with pain in their hearts. Some smiled nostalgically. Others sang a reverberating, "Ase."

I closed my eyes and sniffled. "I feel my father right now, and he is wondering why we are singing such a sad song. Why are we bringing our vibrations so low for a man whose vibration only operated on high?"

The brown faces nodded.

"Don't dwell on how my father was found." I squeezed my eyes shut as the splatter of blood across his wall flashed in my mind. I opened my eyes. "In fact, don't dwell at all. Be happy today in your feasting and gathering. Ase?"

"Ase," Obsidian responded in unison.

I lifted my head "I am Zen Akke, daughter of Bachwezi Akke and Queenie Lesotho."

The crowd looked at one another. They wanted to murmur, but they were polite enough to wait until they were behind closed doors. Either they never knew she was my mother, or they were surprised I now knew the secret.

I went on to name all of my ancestors all the way back to the first settlers who came to Noire. As I named them, people took a handful of dirt and tossed it into the grave. Then the people passed the children over the grave.

Once every child, including Thabo, had been passed over the grave, I said, "All of those brilliant people, our ancestors, made it so that I am here today. Your ancestors made it so that you, too, can breathe today. Someone decided that Obsidian was the place for them and therefore you. We eat well. When there is drought, we survive with the help of our neighbors, our family. Our clan is so rich. We own our lives. The descendants of great people have triumphed and multiplied."

I paused, choosing my next words carefully. "Yet, someone wants to end life as we know it. They want to make us slaves to some greedy monsters. We call them rebels, but I call them cowards. They did this to my father. I know you are amongst us, and I will kill any rebel with my own hands." I looked into the eyes of some of the men. Mother grabbed my arm and pulled me away. "I'm not afraid!" Fright passed over the people's faces.

I parted from the people. My mother was on my heels as I stormed home.

"What were you thinking?!" she shouted. She was breathing heavily and trying to maintain my speed.

"I was thinking the truth. I told no lies."

"You threatened people. You also put a target on your back. If there are rebels here, they will come after you for sure."

"So? They already want the griots, anyway. It's time for them to come get us."

"I know you're hurt, Zen, but you can't do that to your people."

"But they can kill my father?" I raised my voice. "Was everyone there?"

"No."

"Who was missing?" I kept walking. I knew the answer.

"Mali is visiting family in Noire."

My heart rammed my chest. Father's murderer.

She called, "We can receive the people at my home if you want."

"I won't be receiving anyone. I'm leaving."

"Leaving to go where?" she cried.

I kept walking. "I'll be in Noire for a few days," I said nonchalantly. I was still in motion, yet I could feel the heat rising from her like she was a kettle of boiling water.

Once we were inside my house, she slammed the door and said, "You have a responsibility to Obsidian. You must be here because you are the griot. Not only that, people want to grieve with you."

I pulled off my soaked white dress and left it in a pile on the floor. I threw on another dress and pulled my orange cape over it. "I prefer to grieve alone," I said dryly. "Right now, I don't give a damn about them. Plus, you told me to travel."

"Zen." Her tone was admonishing. "Please tell me you are not going to be with Prince Zaire. I know you're hurt..." She spoke his name. It was acid on her tongue.

"I go where I please. I spend time with who I want." I

grabbed my bag that was already packed. I ignored her eyes flitting around the room as I gathered my things. She made noises to show her distaste. I filled my gourds with cool mint water. Although I hadn't read the tome since my initiation, I placed it in my bag. I couldn't risk the rebels getting their hands on it.

With folded arms and a frown, she asked, "How do you plan on getting there?"

"Mansi has already prepared the horses," I said, working around her.

Her neck rolled. "Oh, has he?" Her voice was drenched with bitter contempt. Immediately, she turned on her heels and stormed out of my house, slamming the door.

I drew in a slow breath and held it, then released it. I repeated this until my worries faded and until I stopped caring what people would say about me once they found out that I'd thrown away my responsibilities because of grief. One thing I knew for sure, the Griothood wouldn't fire me.

By the time I got to Mansi and the horses, I could feel the heaviness of Mansi's energy. He was brooding as the rain streaked his face. I guessed his sister had never yelled at him the way she was yelling now. She relentlessly hollered, and he ignored her as he brushed the horses. She spoke with her hands, but he kept working. This caused her to move closer to him and shout louder.

I climbed into the back of the covered wagon and placed my bags beside me. I sat with my lips pursed and my cape wrapped around my shoulders.

Now Queenie was crying. "You know, you're not the only person who lost him!" she shouted up at me through the canvas opening.

The carriage slowly moved away from her.

"Fine. Go, but fucking the prince isn't going to bring your father back!" she hollered.

My cheeks blazed as if she'd slapped me. I shot her a seething look. She glared right back at me.

"Let's go," I called to Mansi. He snapped the reigns, and our safari started.

CHAPTER 59

Hours later, I approached the guards in front of the palace. A young man carried the few possessions I'd brought. The sun was setting, and the front of the palace was beautifully lit.

"Hello," I said to the guards. "I'm the Griot of Obsidian. I am here to see the prince about a concern."

"Does he know you're coming?"

"If he knew, he would have told you, now please alert him." I was in no mood to be sweet. The taller man turned and hurried into the palace. Wajir returned. I was glad it was he and not Adesewa.

"Hello, Griot, come in, please." The gates parted with much racket, and I followed Wajir across the bridge and into the palace. "Right this way," he said, taking my bags.

Pema was ascending the stairs when I entered. "Griot!" she exclaimed and gave a curtsy. "Is everything okay?"

"Is Prince Zaire here?" I ignored her question.

"Yes, ma'am. One moment." She scurried down the great hall and disappeared into a room. Wajir stayed at my side.

Just as I began to question myself for coming here, the door opened, and Zaire rushed out. He looked confused. "Zen!" He hurried toward me, drenched in sweat.

My stomach ached when I saw Adesewa coming down the hall from another room. He looked queasy upon seeing me standing there. Just then, something sparked into my mind, but it evaporated before I could form a solid idea around it.

"What's wrong, Zen?" Zaire cried.

I took a shuddering breath. "Someone murdered my father."

Zaire stopped, petrified. There was a look of horror on his face as he looked back at Adesewa. He then rushed to me, pulling me into his arms. "I'm so sorry." He kissed the top of my head.

I broke down in his arms.

"Pema, get my father," he commanded. He picked me up in his strong arms and carried me upstairs. "Wajir, place her bags in my room."

I whimpered. "I'm sorry. I just needed you."

"I am here for you. You know that." He laid me in his bed and quietly rubbed my back as I sobbed into one of his pillows.

"It has to be the rebels. It has to be," I sobbed.

There was a knock on the door.

Zaire got up and answered it.

I listened to him tell his father what happened.

His father stepped into the room.

"Zen."

I sat up. "Sire." I bowed my head out of respect and humiliation. It was indecent for me to be in Zaire's bed, no matter the reason.

"I am so sorry for your loss. I cannot believe a runner did

not let us know."

I bowed my head again.

"My son tells me that you believe the rebels did this."

I nodded. I had no proof, but who else would do such a thing?

"We will find the person who did this. Trust me. I will leave for Obsidian in the morning."

"No, Sire. I'll deal with this as soon as I clear my head," I said.

"No. I have let this go on for long enough." He looked at the ground. "I am truly sorry."

I bowed my head.

"Son," he called, and they walked out to the hall.

Zaire gave me a sympathetic look. I returned my head to the pillow, training my ears to their hushed voices.

"What are you doing?" That was King Akonos speaking.

"What?"

"She's in your bed."

"So."

"Tell me you haven't been with her."

Zaire said nothing. It was an admission of guilt.

"Damn it, son. She is the griot. She has an image to uphold."

"I think she's upholding it," Zaire said with defiance in his voice.

"You know better. Not only are you clouding her judgment, but the griot can't be with a man."

"No, she cannot marry, which is bullshit. Nothing says she can't have a special friend."

My eyes widened. I was glad that he was defending me, but I didn't want him to disrespect his father.

Guilt fell over me as Zaire slid onto the bed. I felt dirty. The king thought I was loose. I wanted to get up and go to Zora's, but then he kissed my temple.

"We have to get you out of these wet clothes before you get sick."

I nodded. I was too weak to undress, so Zaire removed my clothes and gave me a robe.

He walked to the door and called for someone named Ala. "Please draw the griot a bath."

"Yes, sir," the elderly woman said as she curtsied and then shuffled into another room.

"You can relax as long as you want in the bath, and when you return, a hot dinner will be waiting for you."

"I don't want to be a bother. I just—"

He interrupted. "Nonsense. Here you have everything at your fingertips. Anything you want, just ask."

The water was as hot as I could stand it, and the oversized bathroom was covered with steam. Lavender and mint leaves floated in the tub, releasing a relaxing aroma. Candlelight danced against the wall.

The only thing out of place was the maid who stood next to the door. I stared at her, waiting for her to leave so I could disrobe, but she remained, hands folded in front of her with her eyes staring into space. Finally, I decided to remove my robe, figuring everything I had, she'd seen before.

Once I entered the water, after allowing my feet to get used to the heat, she came over to me. She gently pushed my shoulders back, and I obeyed. She went over to the counter where an ornate kettle sat over a tea light and poured me a small cup of tea. The peppermint in the tea was almost too strong, but I felt clear from my nose to my lungs.

She took the cup once I was finished and placed a hot cloth over my eyes. The aroma was divine as I laid there,

374

trying hard not to think about my father, but it was useless. Whenever I felt hatred in my chest, I tried to remember the beauty of our last dinner, but that just made me even more outraged.

After several failed attempts at relaxing, I bathed myself. Again the maid came over to help, but I gave her a curt "no," and she stepped back, emotionless. After that, Ala only intervened to hand me a towel, a silk robe, and an ornate pair of slippers.

"I can twist your hair or tie your wrap," she offered. I nodded. I was in no mood to detangle and twist my thick hair, so I allowed her to put it into big twists and tie a wrap around it.

The bedroom was empty when I left the bathroom, so I sat in the large chair in front of a small table. What I really wanted to do was sprawl out on the gigantic bed before me.

It wasn't long before Zaire returned with Pema, who was carrying a tray of covered plates. The smell elicited a growl from my stomach.

I said, "Thank you, Zaire."

"Not at all. Eat," he said. He sat across from me. The whole time his eyes were distant.

"What's on your mind?" I asked.

"My mind is all twisted. I hate that they hurt you."

I tightened my grip on my fork.

"Father said since Obsidian's beginning, there has never been a murder. I'm just trying to wrap my mind around this." Zaire's eyes shot up to me. "Am I being insensitive?" He gave me a worried glance.

"No." But the subject stabbed my heart. My eyes misted against my wishes.

"I apologize, Zen. You did not come here to rehash this. You came to get away, but please let me assure you his killer will be caught swiftly." His words were firm and angry. "I will deal with that person personally."

I nodded.

Zaire rose and walked over to me. He knelt before me and peered up at me. I fought the urge to reach out and stroke his beard. "Right now, what can I do for you? How can I ease your pain? Zen, tell me what you need." His words were deliberate, like strokes made during fucking. I felt that familiar pang in my lower abdomen.

I placed my hand on his face, and I sucked his lips and tongue. When I pulled back, I watched him open his eyes. "I need you to make love to me."

He searched my eyes. "I don't want to take advantage of you."

"Don't worry. I'm thinking clearly."

"We should wait," he said breathily.

I reached down and stroked him through his trousers. He swallowed as he hardened in my grip. His eyes closed, and he bit his top lip.

"Please don't make me beg," I whispered.

He stood. "Lie down," he said, his voice stern as he tried to gain control.

What Zaire did to me was something I'd never known could be done. I wondered if it was illegal. He parted my legs and put his tongue on my yoni. He made me pull off his sheets, grit my teeth, scratch the back of his head, and pull off my scarf. The sensation reached every nerve and finally concentrated in my womb and shot through my breast tissue and into my nipples. My yoni's release felt so amazing, it was almost painful. My back arched into a dangerous curve as the feeling overpowered. The aftershocks made me quake.

"What did you do?" I panted once he resurfaced.

"Something I never want you to allow any other man to

do to you." He was speaking of Sahel. He entered me, and soon we were both moaning loudly. I didn't care who knew what was being done. I needed this, and Zaire delivered. This was the sex I'd been warned about.

Once we had worn each other out, we slept.

The next morning, I felt Zaire stirring and heard people in the room.

"Breakfast is ready."

"I'm not hungry. I just want to sleep."

Although I felt Zaire in the room, he didn't disturb me all that day. He stayed as I slept. I knew I was keeping him from important affairs, but I enjoyed his presence.

"Zen, it's time for lunch," he called hours later.

I shook my head.

"You have to eat." There was fear in his voice.

"I just want a bath."

He called Ala. When I rose, his concerned eyes were on me.

I stayed in the warm bath until it cooled. I cried again. The maid stood silently by the door and let me have my moment. Zaire entered the bathroom and dismissed Ala.

"Zen, I'm afraid for you."

"What?" I scoffed.

"I have seen the scars on your wrists."

I looked at him. I was petrified. I stammered, "That's not what you think."

"Do not lie."

Shit. "It happened years ago," I confessed.

"What happened?" He asked with pleading eyes.

I wept. "I don't know. Sadness swallowed me whole."

"Like now?"

I groaned, "No."

"Yes, Zen." His eyes glistened. "I need you to promise me you won't hurt yourself again."

"I'm not leaving this earth until my father's killer is found." I'd thought about it, though. Death courted me. It always had, and always would, stalk me. Death would've been so much easier than living with this pain.

When he left the bathroom, I cried out of humiliation.

I returned to fresh sheets. I buried myself in the covers and fell back asleep.

My lethargy continued into the next day. Zaire wanted to call a root doctor, but I refused.

The next thing I knew, Zora was sitting next to me. She pushed my hair back. "What's going on, baby girl?"

"Is it getting dark?" I felt heavy, like I'd slept too much.

"The sun is rising."

Two days gone. Damn.

"Zaire told me he was worried about you. He said you hadn't eaten since the night you came."

"I'm fine."

"You don't seem fine, and I understand. You don't have to be fine, but I can take care of you until you're yourself again."

We hugged.

"You should come stay with me," Zora offered.

"Does he want me to leave?" I would've wanted me to leave. He was used to his own space, and here I was imposing and moping around.

"No. You've just scared him half to death." She stroked my hair. "Should I gather your things?"

I shook my head. "I want to stay with Zaire. He's not the

way you think he is."

She nodded, her smile soft. "I see that. I was wrong. Okay, if you stay, promise me that you will get up right this minute and eat."

I pulled myself up. My legs were weak, and my mouth tasted disgusting. We went out to the veranda. I inhaled. My bones ached from lying down for so long. Zora hugged me again.

There was a knock.

"Come in," she said. Pema brought in a plate of brightly hued fresh fruit.

"Thank you," I told her.

After I had eaten, Zora said, "Now you need to think about going home."

I knew it. Like death, Obsidian was calling me.

"Can I help you, Griot?" Pema asked as I came downstairs after Zora left. She'd been dusting the furniture in the corridor.

"I'm looking for Zaire." Although there was still a heavy shadow over me, I felt some relief. I had bathed, and Zora had braided my hair in thick braids.

"Right this way." She led me down the great hall and to the room where he'd been the night I arrived.

He was in a trance as he wrestled another man. He was shining with perspiration. I got excited watching him and all of his strength. When he won, I clapped. He dried the sweat from his face and smiled as he walked over.

"The griot told me she could wake you," he kissed me. "You had me frightened."

"Thank you for taking care of me."

"Thanks for letting me."

I stayed with Zaire for three more days. I never left the palace grounds, and yet I'd been so content. Zaire had awakened a relentless desire within me. He changed the way I walked. He changed the way I talked, and although we spent nearly every moment that he wasn't conducting official business together, I desired more. I begged him to teach me how to please him and, of course, he obliged. I was addicted to his fingers on my skin and his dick inside of me. My addiction to eroticism frightened me, because I knew it would all come to an end. Then what would I do? When we weren't in the bed, he challenged my mind, thrusting books I never heard of into my hands, and I so desperately yearned to tell him about the books from the Grotto. I tread so close to danger so many times. If Zaire only knew the complication of his history. His musicians played for us, and we swam naked in his pool. When he was away, I read and walked the garden. The cub was gone, but I didn't have the heart to ask what happened to him. The queen was gone, too. Zaire told me she was in Ankara to help boost morale. I couldn't imagine her in the tree homes without plumbing. I guess she wasn't as shallow as I had believed.

I'd been pretending that I didn't have responsibilities back home, but I knew I had to return. I also felt guilty for leaving Mansi outside the gates for so long. I'd begged him to go back. I knew I could find someone to take me back to Obsidian, but he refused to leave me alone.

Zaire and I lay in bed exhausted after one of our erotic sessions.

"Where's Adesewa? I haven't seen him since the night I arrived." I don't know what made me think of the vile man.

My head rested on his chest. I'd felt Zaire's body go rigid. "After what he said to you, things have been tense. I suggested he stay away while you were here."

"Oh." I shook my head. "You didn't have to do that."

"If he has no respect for you, he has no respect for me."

His tone lowered as his finger made a circle around my nipple. "I wish you didn't have to leave."

The idea of leaving him stabbed my heart. "I know. But I have to go back to Obsidian, and I can't keep Mansi waiting."

"I sent Mansi back," Zaire said casually.

I looked up at him, confused. "What? Why?" I felt comfortable because Mansi was here. If anything happened, I knew I'd be okay. I sat up and narrowed my eyes at him.

He held up his palms. "Don't worry, I'm taking you back personally, but only when you're ready. I knew you would feel rushed with him waiting."

I placed my index finger on my temple. That was the first time I'd felt irritation with Zaire. How dare he send Mansi away without consulting me? I closed my eyes, telling myself he meant well. I re-opened my eyes.

"Father should be back soon." He looked at me and ran his fingers from between my breasts to my navel. "If you give permission—if it's in your heart—I want to ask Father to do something that no other king of Za has done." His eyes lowered as if he were afraid.

I looked at him, perplexed. "What?"

"Zen, I love you."

My lips parted. He'd never said that before.

"I want you, not just in my bed but in my life, forever. I want to ask him to give me permission to marry you." He looked into my eyes.

I stopped breathing as he rose from the bed. I watched his naked toned body move across his room and to his dresser. With his back to me, Zaire opened a drawer and pulled something out. I watched him with wide eyes as he walked back over to my side of the bed. I turned toward him as he lowered himself down on one knee. My heart thudded as I tried to ignore his soft penis hanging limp between his thighs. In his massive hands was a beautiful wooden comb. It was a proposal comb. I clasped my chest with my right hand and fought to steady my breath.

"Zen." He closed his eyes for a moment. When he reopened them, he continued. "Please be my wife. Please marry me."

I heaved a breath. It took me a while to speak. "Zaire, your father will never allow it."

"He will, or he will have to find another prince." He was telling the truth. He would give up the throne... for me.

I felt flushed. All I could manage to say was, "but the Griothood."

"They can find another griot." His eyes dug into me and beckoned me to answer. I began to sweat.

My mother was so proud of the moment I'd become griot. She'd known since I was two. Nok and Zora had become my sisters. Our connection was deep, and the secrets we shared bounded us forever. I had come to love the Griothood as well.

I looked at the man who would be king, on his knee before me, his eyes pleading. Did I love him? He made me feel good, real good. He spoiled me. He confided in me. He took care of me in my moment of grief. Being catered to and lusted for gave me a high. But did I love him? I saw myself sitting on the throne, wearing the best fabric, hosting parties, rubbing Zaire's back. This life, nothing could compare. I closed my eyes and gave a shuddering breath. But then I saw Sahel's locs and his joyous smile. Sahel's laugh made me laugh, too, no matter what. He had looked so hurt when he realized that there was something between Zaire and me.

My eyes formed tears. "Zaire, I don't know." I shook my head.

I watched his face transform from hurt to humiliation.

This wasn't what I wanted. Zaire had been the very best friend to me. He rose and nodded. "I understand." He carried the comb out to the veranda and threw it over the railing.

"I need time to think," I cried. "This is sudden."

"It did not feel sudden to me." There was a barely perceptible tremor in his words. "Is it him?"

"Zaire."

"It is." He nodded.

I rose. I sniffled. "Zaire, please give me time."

With his pride crushed, he tied a wrap around his waist, pulled on some sandals, and stormed out. "You can leave in the morning. No rush. I'll go to a guestroom."

I shook as I sobbed. He might as well have slapped me. The last thing I had wanted to do was hurt my friend. I stroked my idol. I looked at the bed. There was no way I could stay there.

Pema walked in with her head bowed in her usual submissiveness. "The prince sent me to help you pack your things for your morning departure."

I nodded. "I'm leaving now." I pulled on a dress.

She nodded and busied herself. I wanted to help, but all I could do is sit there and cry.

She tried to ignore my crying. It was her job to help, not to ask questions. As she put a dress in my bag, she whispered, "Did he hurt you?"

I shook my head and said, "No." I forced myself to go to the bathroom to gather my things.

"Pema," I called.

"Yes."

I looked in the mirror. "Why'd you ask me if he hurt me?" It wasn't that she asked me. It was how she asked me. Had Zaire hurt someone before?

"Just wondering. I'm sorry, I didn't mean to pry," she stuttered.

"Has he ever hurt anyone?" I walked into the room with my belongings.

Something strange registered behind her eyes. Then she shook her head nervously.

My mind went back to what Sahel had said about the girl disappearing or dying because of Zaire. I knew it wasn't true. Let it go. There's nothing there. But I couldn't let it go. "I have a question for you, and I need you to be truthful with me." But I doubted that she would tell me the truth. What I was asking her could get her into a world of trouble, me too for that matter.

"Of course," she lied.

I looked into her brown eyes. "I heard things about Prince Zaire, scary, unforgivable things." What was I doing? I'd just stomped his heart and grounded it into the marble floor. Now I was running his name through the mud. He'd never done anything wrong to me, but I had come too far to stop now. "I need to know if the rumors are true."

"Oh no. There is nothing bad about Prince Zaire." Her smile was wilted. Her eyes weren't smiling, though.

"I know you're supposed to say that, but please... I will never tell what you share with me."

"I have to go." Pema rushed out of the room. I stood there with my heart racing. She was going to tell. Dread enveloped me, and blood drained from my face. I had fucked up...again.

I opened the door, ready to get as far away from this place as I could with my bags, and I almost screamed. I covered my mouth. Pema and Ala were standing in front of the door. They looked as if they, too, could also jump out of their skin.

Pema whispered, "May we come in?"

"Yes," I whispered. My eyes swept the stairs and the foyer of the palace. No one saw them enter, or at least, I didn't think they did. I felt the heaviness of what they wanted to reveal to me.

"Ala is my aunt," Pema said.

"Of course." I regretted being snippy with Ala when she tried to bathe me the other night.

"You said you heard things about the prince. What did you hear?" the older lady asked.

I swallowed, not believing I was going to speak such words. "Well, someone I trust has family here," I lied. "This person told me that people have spoken about a young girl who disappeared." I coaxed, "Perhaps she witnessed something she shouldn't have, or made some sort of mistake. All anyone knows is that she worked here and one night she was no more."

Pema's eyes misted over, and with her four fingers, she covered her mouth as she attempted unsuccessfully to stifle her cries. Ala pulled Pema close.

Ala spoke. "Naiasii was her sister and, of course, my niece."

I stood stark still. My heart thundered. "What happened?"

They looked at each other and had a silent conversation with their eyes. Ala spoke up, but in a soft and paranoid tone. "Naiasii saw something in this room." She looked around like she was looking for an apparition. "She would never reveal to us what it was, but it rattled her."

"What do you think it was?"

Ala lowered her eyes. "I don't know."

But I knew better. They had suspicions. Servants knew everything.

I rubbed my hands down my face. I didn't know much, but something had transpired here. But what did that mean for me?

Pema wrapped her arms around herself. With a far off look, she said, "Just because I didn't see him kill my baby sister, does not mean I don't know he did it." Her voice shook with rage. "She's gone. Just like that. And no one can tell us anything about her disappearance."

I felt detached from my body. I asked, "Do you know anything about the rebellion?"

Ala looked at Pema and said, "We have to go, and you understand why."

Disappointed, I nodded. "Thank you."

The women walked with haste to the door. "Griot," Ala stopped and turned to me. "My father was a shaman. He knew spirits and souls very well. I have that gift also. I can see haints, I can see monsters, and I can see the light in people. The prince is a monster, and I see the light in you. That's why I told my niece it was okay to tell you this." She looked genuinely frightened. "Please, leave this space. Leave this man. Go home and never be alone with him in this way again." She looked over to the bed, still in disarray.

I lowered my head. What had I done?

CHAPTER 60

Even though the sun had set, sweat dripped from beneath my breasts and under my arms. I couldn't remember the way from the palace to Zora's home, so I asked a boy who was a few years younger than me to take me there. He took my bags and eagerly led me to Zora's.

I knocked. Nothing. I knocked again. Damn she wasn't there. Shit. I felt my breath coming too fast. I couldn't panic now.

The boy watched me as I rubbed my hand across my face and into my hair. I clutched my hair and willed myself to calm down.

"Back to the palace?" he asked, eyeing me like I was the weirdest person he'd ever laid eyes on.

"Do you know an old man named Jo Akke?" I spewed. "He needs help to walk. Kwame is his grandson."

The boy nodded enthusiastically and walked. I inhaled and followed, looking behind me every once in a while. The hairs on my neck had been standing on end since I'd left the palace. I felt an unfamiliar energy surrounding me. I begged the gods to watch over me.

I suppressed tears of joy when Kwame answered the door.

"Zen?" He looked bewildered. He hugged me. "Come in."

My uncle sat at the table holding a fan of playing cards. "Zen? What brings you here?" Jo smiled. I didn't.

I told them about my father. Tears fell down the old man's face, and his grandson handed him a cloth. I felt guilty for not coming here sooner. I'd been too busy laying up with Zaire to tell them my father had been murdered.

"The prince and I have become very close friends," I told them. "I've been staying at the palace with him, as I've tried to mentally heal from my pain. I was in a bad way, as you can imagine." I cursed myself for leaving Obsidian and my mother who needed me. "I've heard some crazy things about Prince Zaire. I don't know if they are true, but I want to go home." My eyes welled up. "My driver was sent back home, and I have no way to get back." My voice wavered.

My uncle frowned. "I always hated that boy. Even when he was a child."

"You needn't worry. We will leave first thing in the morning," Kwame said, scolding his grandfather with his eyes.

"Thank you."

"My wife will set up a room for you to sleep in at our house."

My tears spilled over.

The old man and my cousin hugged me at the same time.

My uncle looked into my eyes. "You are a sweet girl. The gods will bring you solace."

The words "sweet girl" were my father's words. The words let me know I was safe, and my father was with me.

I reached into my satchel, and dread cooled my blood.

The tome wasn't there. I started to hyperventilate.

"What, Zen?" Kwame asked, his eyes wide.

"There's a book of secrets. Only griots have laid eyes on it for the past 200 years. I had it this morning, and now it's not in my bag."

"Calm down. I'm sure it's in the palace. I'll fetch it first thing in the morning."

I gasped. "What have I done?" I knew someone had taken it. I never took it out of the bag. I clenched my teeth. Pema and Ala? Did they do it? Pema packed my things. She could've nabbed it when I went into the bathroom. Or was it Zaire? I felt queasy.

"Don't worry yourself, Zen," Kwame said.

"How will you fetch it?"

"I have friends in the palace. Friends that won't say a word about the book."

I allowed myself to relax. I knew in a time when everything seemed hopeless, the gods could fix things.

Kwame grabbed my things, and we stepped out into the oppressive night. I stopped when Kwame placed a protective hand in front of me.

I shrieked, seeing clearly what had flashed in my mind when I'd seen Adesewa a few nights ago. The blood splatter on Father's wall hadn't been blood splatter at all. It was the same as Adesewa's tattoo, a backward seven. Someone had stuck their finger in my father's blood and left a mark on the walls. Was Adesewa connected to the rebels and therefore involved with my father's death?

CHAPTER 61

There, several yards in front of us, was a sneering Adesewa. I hadn't seen him in days. Why was he here, and how had he found me?

A deranged grin curled one side of his lips. Playfully, he tossed a knife up and caught it by the handle repeatedly. He approached Kwame and me. Two tall and muscular men flanked him. My mind hadn't been able to fully work through what was happening, but I knew I was in trouble.

"Hey!" Kwame shouted when the two men grabbed me by the arms and dragged me away.

"Shut the hell up," Adesewa barked and punched my cousin in the gut. The air whooshed from Kwame's mouth, and he doubled over.

"Stop!" I cried out.

Adesewa bent down to get eye level with my cousin, his menacing eyes stabbing into my cousin's worried eyes. "I suggest you not follow us. I would hate for something to happen to your grandfather."

After playfully slapping Kwame on the cheek, Adesewa

stood straight and walked over to me with a fake smile. I glanced at the sharp knife in his right hand as he grabbed my forearm with his left hand and jerked my body to his. "Heard you like to ask questions." His voice was low. "You got your maid friends in some big trouble."

I wept.

"Leave her," Kwame begged. "Please."

Adesewa turned back to my cousin. I feared he was going to strike him again or worse.

"It's okay!" I shouted back to Kwame.

Adesewa sneered at Kwame for an extended and tense moment. Then he mercifully shouted, "Let's go!" The men pulled me away from my uncle's home. They forced me down the road. Adesewa fell in behind us. I felt his sharp blade against my back.

Adesewa asked, "What are you doing here, Zen?"

"This is my uncle's home. I came to say hello."

"Really? At this late hour? I think not. You may have just gotten your sweet uncle murdered. Move," he commanded and shoved me. If the men had not had me by the arms, I would have fallen forward.

The men walked faster.

I started to protest, but I thought better of it. I knew they were going to kill me, but I had to protect Kwame and Jo by obeying Adesewa's orders.

People looked on, prompting Adesewa to sing, "Smile, Griot." No one could see the knife that was cutting into the fabric of my dress.

"You're the one leading the rebels?"

He laughed.

"I thought it was Zaire."

"Prince Zaire, you slut," he corrected me. "Of course, I am the leader. I love the prince, but he is too immature to lead anything, including himself."

Although I was about to die, a sense of relief rippled through me. Zaire was innocent…in this matter.

They took me to a covered wagon with a team of four muscular horses that were a taller breed than Mansi's horses. Royal horses. The only horses allowed in the Noire's gates. Adesewa was using the king's horses for rebel duties.

An obese man with a flat pie face, large sagging man breasts, and a natty beard held the reigns, and he smiled at me like I was something to consume with his gluttonous mouth.

"Get in," Adesewa growled.

I cried, "No." I contemplated screaming. I knew if I got in that wagon, if I were taken away from the city, they would kill me.

"If these men have to wrestle your ass into the back of this wagon, I will personally slit the throat of the other griot slut."

My eyes widened. "Do you have Zora?"

"Get in," he barked, no longer caring if people noticed.

I looked around, my eyes pleading for someone to save me, but they just averted their eyes and shuffled away. Seeing no way out, I did as I was told. The men crawled in behind me. One gagged me with a cloth, and the other roughly tied my hands and feet. I sobbed silently. I was going to be murdered in the bush.

CHAPTER 62

They were moving fast and probably overexerting the horses. I looked at the two men who guarded me with pleading eyes, but like disciplined warriors, they looked straight ahead, as if unaware I was even there.

I thought about Pema's sister who was never heard from again and wondered if Pema and her aunt were dead because of my questions. I could see my corpse lying in the tall savannah grass and the jackals picking my flesh from my bones. I prayed to my ancestors. I'd asked too many questions. I'd been responsible for my father's death. What if my set sister, Keeke, let Mali know I was suspicious about the rebellion, and that was why they killed my father? I'd risked the lives of my set, Queenie, Zora, Nok, Kwame, Jo, Ala, and Pema.

I lost track of time. My head and throat ached from crying. Anxiety and rage dropped a crushing pressure on my chest.

The wagon stopped after what had to be hours, and my pulse raced. The men left my wrists bound but untied my feet and helped me down from the wagon.

I looked out into the night. We were undoubtedly at the mouth of the White Mountains. I shuddered. Why here? In the middle of the vast darkness, I saw a group of men in the distance around a large fire. Some stood, holding torches. Others were seated on the ground waiting in anticipation. There were several covered wagons outside of the group of men.

I screeched and bucked in the arms of my handlers as they moved me toward the curious men. I knew who they were. Rebels. Murderers. My captors hauled me, undeterred by my fighting. Adesewa and the driver of the carriage hastily made their way toward the rebels. Everyone stood. Some excitedly shook Adesewa's hand. I grimaced in disgust. I wondered if tonight was the zenith of the rebel's plan.

Some of the rebels looked at me arrogantly, and others looked at the ground in shame. My face crumbled as I recognized several of the cowards. The fire cast an orange glow over the men's faces. A few had been warriors in the age set ahead of Sahel, our protectors. One man, Amalahali, I'd grown up with. He was in Sahel's set. He might as well have been Sahel's brother. Finally, I laid eyes on Mali's copper skin and severe cheekbones. My soul did a slow burn. My father's murderer.

Adesewa scratched his neck with his index finger and gave me a satisfied grin. He loved the terror in my eyes. He also loved the understanding in my eyes. He whispered something to one of the rebels, and the rebel jogged to the wagon that was in front of the others. A few seconds later, my heart stopped, and I let out a muffled groan.

Zaire stepped down, unrestrained from the wagon, in the same wrap he'd had thrown on after I had rejected him. He carried a red sack in one hand. They'd captured him, too, but I knew he could get us out of this, especially unrestrained. Hope flooded through me. As his father said, Zaire was stronger than ten simbas. Upon seeing the prince, some of the rebels brandished red flags with the backward seven on it.

Zaire gave me a look that told me he was ashamed. He dropped the sack and walked over to Adesewa, and they hugged. I felt a stab to the chest. No. My heart fissured. Zaire was a rebel. That made no sense. The kingdom was as good as his. He embraced Adesewa for a long time, like long lost friends. They whispered to each other when they pulled away. Their exchange was ardent as they looked deeply into each other's eyes. Adesewa gave him a questioning look, and I could see in the fire's light the happiness drain from Zaire's face. Eventually, he nodded.

"Bring him out!" Adesewa yelled with a nod. Two men ran to another covered wagon. The rebels cheered.

Zaire fell to his haunches, looking like he was going to pass out. I caught his gaze, and then his eyes dropped.

The two men brought out a large man whose head was covered and his hands bound in front of him with a rope. I knew immediately that it was King Akonos. No other person in Za walked with his confidence.

CHAPTER 63

Za had fallen. I hunched over, horrified and hopeless. The king had been in Obsidian trying to find out what happened to my father. Zaire said he was supposed to be on his way back to the palace. At what point had they tied him up and thrown the sack over his head? Were they going to kill the king?

Zaire stood and squeezed his eyelids together to force back tears as they lead the king eight feet in front of where I stood. Zaire and Adesewa stood in front of me and faced the king.

Adesewa coaxed him. "Do it. Speak the truth."

Zaire nodded, but he was frightened. He breathed heavily.

The men snatched the sack from the king's head. Startled, he looked around. I was relieved to see that he didn't seem to be hurt. When he beheld his son, tears welled up in his eyes. "Son. They've got you, too. Where is your mother? Adesewa? Zen?" His eyes darted around the dim valley frantically.

Where was Queen Finda? Perhaps she was still safe in Ankara. There was hope. She could raise the warriors too.

Zaire lowered his head in shame. "Father. This is the Rebellion, and I am the leader." Finally, his eyes rose to meet his father's glossy, alarmed eyes.

King Akonos looked horrified. He slowly shook his head. "No. You... No. Why? I do not believe it," he stammered.

Zaire lowered his head again.

The king looked past the men and met my eyes. "Zen, are you hurt?"

I shook my head.

"Why is she here?" He looked even more frightened. "This is who you have become? Mistreating women? Mistreating a griot? That is not the way of a Zaian man, and I thought you cared for her."

Adesewa moved in front of Zaire and put his hands on the prince's shoulders. Zaire's father was wearing him down, causing him to think clearly. Adesewa said calmly, "If you are going to be the king of this new order, you have to be strong. You're showing weakness."

I understood. Zaire was the face of the rebellion, but the true leader was Adesewa. I wondered if Zaire knew that he was being used like a puppet. There was no way Adesewa could've pulled this off without him.

Adesewa returned to Zaire's side. Zaire lifted his chin.

"You bastard!" the king spat, addressing Adesewa. He tried to lunge at him, but the rebels held him back firmly. "I always knew you were no good. You've brainwashed my son," he spat.

Adesewa chuckled.

"Where is your mother? Please tell me you didn't hurt her." A tear fell down the king's face. He'd lost his stoicism.

Adesewa roared with maniacal laughter. "This is why you shouldn't be king. You have no idea what is brewing in your own kingdom. Your loving wife and I are the ones who dreamt up this new Za. She and I have been grooming your son for this takeover for a few years now. And finally, it has come to fruition. Finda's fine, by the way. She's with our friends in Nairobi, making deals like a real leader. Right under your nose," he boasted. The queen had never been in Ankara.

The king fell to his knees, but his captors kept their hands on him. His mouth went slack, and his eyes lost focus. His wife, the one who'd given birth to his child, the queen of the people, had stabbed him in the back. I should've been shocked, too, but I was numb.

Zaire lowered his head as he rocked from side to side. I wondered if he was going to cry. He looked at his father. "We have to stop living in the past. We have made a deal with some Chinese businessmen that will stop us from living like paupers."

"Outsiders." The king said it like the word was sour on his tongue.

"Quit being old-fashioned," Adesewa butt in.

"What do they want? What are you all selling your soul for? Gold, diamonds—" the king asked his son, ignoring Adesewa.

"Are there diamonds?" Adesewa asked with piqued interest.

Zaire addressed his father. "For the past one hundred years, there have been wars fought for fresh water. Lack of fresh water is the cause of many wars. Since the dawn of industrialization, humans have abused the Mother Earth, and now the people of the world need our water. We will give them access to our aquifers in exchange for things that will help us modernize Za—infrastructure, electricity, cars, and modern healthcare."

"You dumbass. What will we drink? Do you not understand why we shut off the water at night? Why we shut off the water of any person who goes over their water allotment? Water is not infinite." King Akonos bellowed.

His words struck Zaire. The muscles in his back tensed. Zaire kept his tone even. "If we do not give it, they will take it."

"That's right, old man," Adesewa said. "We have to stop isolating ourselves from the world. When I approached the men with the deal, they couldn't believe what had fallen into their laps. We give them water, and they fund our rebuilding. Queen Finda said it was time to raise the rebellion. We didn't have time to wait for you to die and for Zaire to become king. The people are fed up with living like this. They just don't know it yet. We knew you were too stuck in tradition to make a bold move, so we made it for you, for Za." He put his hand on Zaire's shoulder. "We'll transform Za into one of the richest kingdoms Africa has ever known."

"You, stop speaking to me!" Akonos glared at Adesewa. "I bet you've been fucking my wife all those years you've been living in my palace."

This made Adesewa double over with laughter. Then Adesewa held out his hand, attempting to take Zaire's hand. Zaire snatched his hand away.

"Oh, you're weak now?" Adesewa frowned at him.

"No," Zaire replied.

"You're afraid. All those days you dreamt out loud about the life you wanted to live with no fear of our repercussions. All those nights you allowed yourself to be who you were born to be. Now, you're scared. You've forgotten why we had to get rid of that bitch. No more hiding."

Heat coursed through my veins. Naiasii. Pema's missing sister. The maids were right. Zaire did have something to do with the girl's disappearance.

Zaire turned to face Adesewa, the profile of his face dark. He turned back toward the king and took a deep breath.

Then he looked back at Adesewa with revived courage. Zaire took Adesewa's hand and quietly repeated, "No more hiding." Again they looked into each other's eyes, but it was different this time. The look was so bizarre. Adesewa gently touched his hand to the side of Zaire's face, and they kissed...passionately.

CHAPTER 64

The king and I watched in horror as the two men kissed with perhaps more passion than Zaire and I ever had. My soul screamed to look away, but I couldn't tear my eyes from the image. Sour bile burned as it rushed up my esophagus. I'd never seen two men kiss. The rebels looked down. They weren't surprised, but didn't want to witness it. My heart broke. He'd said he loved me.

"What the fuck is this?" The king bucked, but the men forced him to stay on the ground. "What have you done to my son?"

"He didn't do anything to me," Zaire yelled when he pulled away. "I love him. I have for years. I had to hide who I was because one man loving another man is not allowed in Za." His voice quavered. "We sold the maid to the outsiders because she caught us together." I heard the torment in his voice because of what he'd done to her, but I didn't feel sorry for him. Although he was a puppet, he was still a monster.

"You do not love men. You don't!" the king bellowed, his whole body shaking with fury.

"Father," he interjected. "I love women, and I love men. I can't explain it. You always knew I desired men. That's why you hate me. I take that back, you always hated me, even when I was a child. Why did you name me Zaire, after a corrupt country that fell apart after a mere twenty years? Is it because you always knew I would disappoint you?"

The king's mouth parted in disbelief. "Zaire means river. Do you know how powerful a river is? It can shape the earth, feed a nation, or flood and cause devastation and death. I always knew you would be a far greater ruler than I would ever be. Do not ruin the prophecy now."

I could feel Zaire's regret. He wanted to end this. Adesewa interjected. "He won't. In fact, he's already proving to be a greater leader than you ever were."

"I'm the King of Za." Zaire shook as he spat out his words. "In the new Za, people can love who they want." He looked back at me with solemnity. "Even griots."

The king ignored his son's words, casting aside his hurt. "You cannot drag this kingdom into the ground for Adesewa. He'll stab you in the back the first chance he gets. Can you not see he has been using you for his own personal gain?"

"See, you are not listening." Zaire shook with frustration. "It is not just about him. It is not about me being with a man. It is about moving this kingdom forward."

My mind wandered off. I wondered if the queen knew that Adesewa and Zaire had been fucking. I thought about Zaire inside of my body, then inside of Adesewa, and my stomach tossed again. What a wonderful actor.

"Gag him," Zaire commanded. He'd become intolerant of his father's words.

The men roughly forced a cloth into the king's mouth. They kept him on his knees.

Zaire looked at me. He took a deep breath and moved

closer to me with his eyes lowered. I watched him with reproach.

"Remove her gag," Zaire said. Behind his beautiful eyes was guilt.

"Why?" Adesewa asked.

"Just do it," Zaire barked. "I never told you to bind her like this."

"You ran to me a few hours ago and told me you were done with her because she chose him. Every time you make a promise to me concerning her, you break it." Adesewa's voice faltered. Surprisingly, it looked as if Adesewa was going to cry.

"I know, Adesewa. Just give me a few minutes. Please." His voice and eyes softened.

Adesewa stared at Zaire for a moment, before nodding to the men who guarded me. They untied the gag. Adesewa trudged away sulking.

I said nothing. I just waited, my eyes searing a hole into Zaire.

He stood in front of me but didn't look me in the eyes. "I was not supposed to fall in love with you, Zen, but I did."

I glared at him. Love. The word girded my stomach.

"Everything was lining up perfectly. Adesewa had just told me about the Chinese businessmen who wanted to work with us, and that there was going to be a new griot. My mother saw an opportunity to find out the griot's secrets."

"You pretended to like me."

"I was supposed to," he admitted.

My heart broke again.

"But that day I saw you," he spoke nostalgically, "I knew we were kindred spirits. I felt something so deep for you, it scared me." Yet here I am, tied up. He inhaled. "We needed to know where the griots go for their secret safari."

I squinted. "Why?"

"There has always been rumors that there is an arsenal in Za, just in case there are threats to the kingdom. Father Malcolm, himself, hid the weapons, people say. If that were true, there would be no better hiding place for the guns than the secret place that the griots journeyed to. It was obvious that the griots journeyed to the White Mountains."

"What makes you think that?" I asked neutrally.

"The White Mountains are protected by monsters... Come on. I always knew the stories were to protect something here. The story has to be a myth to scare the people from ever coming here. So we scoured every inch and nothing. My mother thought I could charm the new griot into telling me where that place was." That bitch, I thought.

He took my virginity for that. With rage in my voice, I said, "Well, you two were wrong on two fronts. Even if I knew the way, which I don't, I would never tell you how to get to the hiding spot, no matter how good your dick makes me feel. And there are no guns." Zaire's rebels could've already stumbled upon the correct cave, but the false wall made it nearly impossible to find the sanctum.

Zaire looked apologetic. "Unfortunately, you made a mistake. When I gave you Father Malcolm's pen, you didn't refute that there was a secret book." He motioned to a rebel who stood behind him. To my horror, the rebel pulled out the leather tome from a red sack.

I whimpered and trembled uncontrollably. Hot tears splashed from my lower eyelid. "You stole from me, Zaire?"

"I'm sorry, Zen, but there are secrets in the book that we need...and there are weapons."

"What?" Why hadn't I finished the book? Was Zaire telling the truth, or was this just another game?

"Even if you don't believe me, I love you." He stepped closer to me and put his lip to my ear. "I was going to end

404

this rebellion all for you, Zen. I truly wanted to marry you. If only you had said yes."

"Don't blame this on me," I whispered forcefully and held up my bound wrists.

"I know." He paused. "I shouldn't have run to him after you turned me down."

Shock gripped me as I processed what he was saying. "You don't want this, do you?"

He said, "I love him."

"Zaire, end this now," I groaned from deep within.

"It's too late. I love you, Zen." He brushed his lips against my cheek and walked toward a brooding Adesewa. It was then that I saw him for the confused child that he was.

His father stared at me, hoping that I'd talked some sense into him. I lowered my eyes in defeat.

"You're going to kill your own father?!" I shouted.

Zaire turned back to me. "Of course not. He will be exiled to Nairobi."

He motioned to a boy about my age who opened a satchel filled with bundled shillings.

"From my friends." Zaire looked to the king. "You will live well if you never try to return. Know that I want the best for my people, Father. My friends should be here shortly to take you away."

The king refused to look at the money or Zaire. His head hung low. His whole world ended because of his wife and son.

I just had to know. "Zaire, did you have my father killed?"

He gave me a look of disbelief.

"I saw that backward seven on my father's wall. The same symbol on your flags. It's the same symbol on Adesewa's back."

"No, Zen. I had nothing to do with that. In fact, I didn't even know until you came to the palace that night." He let his eyes drift to Adesewa. Zaire wanted me to know that Adesewa had him killed.

"Why?" I cried, looking at Adesewa.

"Because as much as I hated it, I knew if I had your father killed, you would come running to Zaire for comfort. I'd begun to lose faith that my lover could coax anything out of you and we were running out of time. I knew I had to force you to tell us the secret. We had to kidnap you. See, taking you from Obsidian would have been too risky. Everyone would've noticed; it would've made things...difficult. In Noire, it was easier to take you. I just had to convince Zaire that he didn't love you. It seems you did that on your own." He scowled at Zaire. "Well, I guess he still loves you, but you're here." He shrugged.

I cursed him. He had my father murdered, took a beautiful life, simply to bait me. "Who killed him?" I screamed. "Which one of you cowards killed a blind man?" I looked to the rebels.

Adesewa smiled. "Mali is a true rebel. He did what he was called to do." He added, "Not that you care, but it's not a backward seven, it's a scythe. Productive and deadly, if necessary. Now," Adesewa clapped, "let's finish this shit. Bring him out."

I held my breath. What else had these fools done?

When I laid eyes on the locs falling over the young man's shoulders, my heart dropped into my stomach. "No." The men who held me gripped me harder as my legs went slack. They made me stay on my feet.

The sack was removed from Sahel's head. His eyes were wide, and his mouth was gagged. He saw me, and he fought hard and nearly broke free, but they overpowered him. He cried silently.

"Why?" I wailed. "Why are you doing this?"

Zaire watched me closely, taking in my reaction to this new development. His lips were pushed together, his brow furrowed. He was jealous.

I screamed, "Answer me, you fucking cowards!"

"Calm down, Zen," Adesewa sang, patronizingly. "We've brought your lover here today because we need your assistance. We knew you wouldn't be inclined to help us, so we have ways of persuading you."

Adesewa took the tome from Zaire's hand.

I shuddered.

"I skimmed your wretched book. So now we know we aren't Africans, at least not in the sense we've been led to believe," he said, shaking the book in the air. His words were laced with bitterness. "We aren't the descendants of a great people who've lived in the Serengeti for centuries. Slaves. Slaves are who we descended from. Slaves who forgot their African ways." He laughed, but he didn't think it was funny. The rebels looked at each other, brows wrinkled, lips murmuring. I thought they already knew since they were so close to the White Mountains and not scared of heathen monsters. Briefly, Adesewa told them about the white men and slavery. The rebels gawked at each other, their mouths slacked and their legacy of greatness snatched away. Several fell to their knees and wept because of the weight of the revelation. They all wanted me dead. I represented the deception. I could tell that the king was digesting the words even though his expression didn't alter. "Slaves. We are the children of slaves. How pathetic. You griot bitches have been lying to us for generations." He pulled his hand back and chucked the book into the night sky. It went flying, and white pages flew out and floated lazily to the grass. "Imagine that. We're fake fucking Africans. But you know what? Our ancestors lived better than this bullshit. Oh yeah. They had cars, electricity, modern medicine, and so on and so forth. We didn't have to live in this primitive way. This was Father Malcolm's decision to make us live in primitive squalor, dying from diseases that man eradicated centuries ago."

He walked over to me, and I took a step back. "Don't shut your fucking mouth now, Zen." He was so close I could smell his putrid sweat and see the craters in his oily face. Zaire fucked him. Suddenly, he reached out and plucked the diamond ring from my nose. I cried out.

"The Grotto, Zen. Tell me where it is."

For the first time since I received it, I thought about the map. "I've only been there once, and it was dark," I said truthfully.

Adesewa chuckled again, but he was attempting to remain calm. He was failing, and I knew I would pay. He pointed at Sahel and his handlers forced him to his knees beside the king.

I cried, "No. Please."

"See, Zen. We know there are weapons in the Grotto, and we need those weapons to overpower Za's warriors. We don't have enough men to fight them with our primitive weapons. We also need guns to overpower those fucking Dembi women. Under the Ur Rainforest lies the largest aquifer. Our friends want access to it."

I shouted, "I've never seen any weapons!"

"Shut up," he spat. "I know there are weapons. It's in the book."

Again, I asked myself why I hadn't finished the book. I thought that by reading it slowly, I was savoring it. Suddenly, the door flashed in my mind, the door with the missing key.

"Please don't hurt him," I sobbed. "I promise you, I don't know the way."

Adesewa's chest heaved. He held out his hand toward a young man to his right. "Machete." Without hesitation, the man removed it from his sheath and handed it to an agitated Adesewa.

"Please, Adesewa. Please. Please." Spit dribbled from my lips as I begged for Sahel's life.

Instead of going over to Sahel, he went to Zaire. Zaire looked at him, confused. Adesewa held out the machete. "Do it."

"No," Zaire said incredulously.

"Do it. You are now the king. You are the backbone of the new Za. They are watching you." He gestured to the men who watched excitedly.

"I won't kill."

"It's too late for that. You sat beside me when I decided to have the elders killed. You were there when we decided to attack Ankara."

My blood boiled. How could I have been so blind? I'd gone to bed with a monster.

Adesewa continued. "You came to me tonight crying because she loves him and not you. She chose this goat herder over a prince. And today, he had the nerve to show up at the palace looking for her." Adesewa's face contorted with the absurdity of such a decision. Sahel came to the palace for me?

Zaire closed his eyes and shifted from one leg to another. I looked Sahel in his stoic eyes. He looked into mine as if he didn't have a care in the world. I closed my eyes and sobbed. I needed to tell them about the map that I buried in my front yard. I opened my eyes. Sahel shook his head at me, almost imperceptibly. He was telling me not to tell them anything.

"You should want to get rid of him." Adesewa was saying. "You love her. Hell, you almost gave me up for her, but she's been using you."

Zaire took the machete. I yelled out.

My eyes bulged. What was Zaire doing? "Zaire. Please. I wasn't using you."

Zaire touched the blade with his fingers.

I screamed, "No! Please don't do this."

"Last chance, Griot," Adesewa said. "See, after we kill him, we'll go after the other griots and then your mother. We'll keep this going until you show us the way."

The men forced Sahel down so that his forehead touched the earth. They were going to behead him.

If I told them about the map, they'd free him.

Adesewa threw up his hands. "If you don't kill him," he shouted, "you know he'll be fucking her before sunrise."

Zaire's eyes went mad. He looked at me, assessed my tears for Sahel, and then he jerked the blade high above his head.

"Zaire," I screamed. "Please."

The king was grunting and shaking his head frantically. He sweated profusely.

I closed my eyes. I had to let Sahel die.

Zaire's arms quaked as Adesewa agitated him. "Show your men why you are the king. They already doubt you because you're in love with a man. Remember how your father looked at you with disgust. Show him that you are, in fact, a man. That blade will slice right through his flesh and bone, just like when you killed the lion cub."

Zaire hollered and swung the blade down. I squealed. I heard the sound of the blade slicing through meat and bone. Then I heard, "Oh. No. Father! Father! What did you do?"

CHAPTER 65

It took so long for me to make sense of what I saw. There was blood, so much blood. Zaire dropped the machete and collapsed in horror. He looked down at the body, but the bloody body wasn't just Sahel's. The king covered Sahel's kneeling body. The machete hadn't killed King Akonos but severed his thick bound arm at the bicep. Three-quarters of his arm hung down, but couldn't fall away because of the rope that attached it to his other arm. I thought of a book in the Grotto, King Leopold's Ghost, and how the Europeans chopped off the arms and legs of the black people in the Congo and stood next to mounds of limbs to pose for pictures. My food rose, my mouth watered, and I vomited. So did some of the rebels. Zaire was on his knees howling.

The men holding me let me go as I retched for a few seconds before regaining control. Wiping away the strings of stomach acid from my lips, I looked at Sahel through watery eyes. He was still kneeling, head to the ground, but I could see him trembling. Thank the gods. King Akonos had jumped in front of the blade and saved his life.

"Help me!" Zaire cried hysterically. One of the rebels tore off his shirt. Zaire tried to use it to stop the bleeding, but the shirt was quickly soaked through.

"Zaire," Adesewa wept sympathetically and placed his hand on Zaire's shoulder.

"Don't touch me," he screamed, causing Adesewa to snatch his hand back. "Father, I'm so sorry." Zaire hugged his father, just as I'd hugged my father's corpse the morning I found him.

I had to do something. The guards had walked away to assist Zaire. I looked around frantically as I implored the ancestors for a solution. I saw it: the machete that sliced through the king's arm glinting in the fire's reflection. Zaire had dropped it just a foot from where Adesewa stood. It was in the grass, forgotten. Everyone rushed around the rebel's camp chaotically. They had forgotten me. Adesewa trembled beside his young lover, ringing his hands and crying out in prayer. Zaire sobbed into his father's chest. At that moment, I thought, Adesewa really loves him, or he knows he's lost Zaire as an ally. In the pandemonium, I crawled forward a few feet and picked up the machete with my bound hands. No one seemed to notice. I prayed to my ancestors who had been stolen away from their homes, those who labored for the White Man, and who suffered through Jim Crow. They had overcome. They were with me, in my veins. They were my strength. With their courage, I charged at Adesewa, the monster who had my father slaughtered. I rose to my feet and pierced Adesewa just above the pelvic bone. He remained standing for a while, as blood bubbled to the wound. I couldn't see his face, but I imagined shock overtaking his features just before he slumped to the ground.

Someone yelled, "Hey!" But it was too late. Adesewa, the true leader of the rebels, was dead.

CHAPTER 66

My body quaked as I waited for the rebels to grab me, punch me, kick me, and/or behead me. Zaire let his father go and stood. He looked down at the dead and bleeding Adesewa. He turned to me, his eyes inundated with pain, and called me, "Lioness." He didn't seem angry. It was more like he was surprised, perhaps even proud. I wanted to say something to him, but something profound and unfamiliar took place. There were loud popping sounds, unlike anything I ever heard.

I looked around, dumbfounded. One rebel fell, then two, and three. They were dead before impact. I threw my body to the ground and slapped my hands over my ears. I was terrified and confused. What was this?

I lay there crying, praying, and trembling. I didn't want to die. I didn't want Sahel to die.

There were more popping noises. Some type of magic by the ancestors? When provoked, they could be livid and merciless. We had turned Za upside down. The gods were going to reset things.

Then the staccato popping stopped. No one screamed,

but there was heavy breathing, groans, and whimpers. I dared not move. I heard footsteps approaching. They were hurried then halting. There were a few more pops.

Suddenly, my wrists were yanked up. I opened my eyes to see my killer, but my tears blinded me. I was being pulled to my feet. Mansi? He had something black in his hand. Something from the arsenal? A gun? Mansi pulled out a knife and cut the rope from my wrists.

I wanted to throw my arms around him, but in an instant, Mansi was off to the king. I winced as he aimed a few more shots into rebels who held up their hands to him. I ran to the king, too. Sahel rose. He was stunned. I hugged him tightly and then removed his gag and untied his arms. He touched the back of his neck and pulled back a hand with blood on it. The blade had nicked him, but thanks to the gods, he would be fine.

I felt a twinge of pain when I saw Zaire's body lying there lifeless. He'd been shot through the breast. I tried to shake off my sympathy and the realization that I still loved him. I tried to shake off the haunting look he'd given me when he called me "Lioness."

King Akonos was writhing in pain. His eyes fluttered open. I whimpered as Mansi assessed the situation.

Mansi cut the ties from the king's wrists, and the severed arm fell away. A wave of sickness washed over me. Mansi jumped up and drew the machete from Adesewa's side and walked over to the fire. He held the machete there for a long time. He never flinched at the flames lapping up at his arm. He returned to the king then looked at Sahel and me, eyes wide. Sahel bent down and held the king's feet. I took the king's hand and held it tightly as Mansi cauterized the wound. The smell of burning flesh and the shrill screams made me gag.

With a scrap ripped from his beige shirt, Mansi tied the remainder of the king's arm tightly. The king no longer screamed, and he slipped into unconsciousness. Don't let him die. Mansi and Sahel lifted the king and carried him to the nearest covered wagon. Ignoring the dead bodies of the men who had betrayed Za, I grabbed the tome and the pages that I could find and, as an afterthought, I grabbed the bag of shillings.

Mansi forced the horses to move as fast as they could. They weren't his horses, but he handled them with ease. We made it to a city I'd never seen or heard of before. It seemed, however, that Mansi knew just where to go. Perhaps it was a place where he frequently bought our supplies. The king's consciousness was touch and go until, finally, he passed out for good.

When we made it to the city, I begged for help in Swahili and English. So many came running. People brown, white, and black. Then came a big car with flashing lights. Just like the story my father told me about my birth. They took the king away.

CHAPTER 67

A week later, my mother stroked my hair as I lay on her lap. "How did Mansi get a gun?" I asked after I told her the whole story of my kidnapping.

I heard her inhale. "Mansi is what you call a keeper." Her voice was soft. "Adesewa was telling the truth. There is a room in the Grotto with guns, enough guns for each of our warriors to have four. Mansi also has access to the Grotto. The griots need three keys. The keepers only need one."

I sat up and faced her with shock on my face. Za was the land of infinite secrets.

She continued. "Long before I became the griot, just before your grandparents died, Mansi was appointed to the position of keeper."

"Because he's mute?"

She shook her head solemnly, and there was a quick flash of resentment in her eyes. "Mansi is mute because he is a keeper."

I gasped, "Someone did this to him?"

"Yes. He went off for warrior training just like every other

416

boy. When he returned, his tongue was gone, and he couldn't speak. I was about 12 when it happened. No one knew why it happened. Of course, he couldn't tell us. It wasn't until I became griot that he wrote me a letter telling me of his secrets."

"You said, keepers... There are more?"

She nodded.

"Who are the others?"

She shrugged.

"No tongue?"

"No tongue."

"They could've killed him."

She nodded. "It is a risk they are willing to take because no one must know about the arsenal unless completely necessary. You mustn't even tell Nok or Zora. See, everything in Za has its place. There are many factions that know things that the other factions don't know, and it was designed that way to protect our way of life. If people know about the keepers, they could easily hold a keeper hostage and force them to take them to the arsenal. The fact that there are guns and their location must only be known if outsiders threaten us and we have to fight. Otherwise, you see what happens when the wrong Zaians know about the arsenal. Father Malcolm always feared a rebellion would take place, especially after his brother betrayed him. That is why he never let the people know." Queenie shook her head. "That's why the masses must never know. It would only take a few to overthrow what our ancestors put in place. Only the keepers know how to shoot the guns, and only they can train warriors."

I nodded and shuddered when I thought how easily Adesewa and Zaire had raised a band of rebels. I could not have imagined the world we'd be in if they had gotten their hands on those weapons and if the outsiders began to take our water.

"But the king knows."

"King Akonos would never reveal the things he heard." A thoughtful look passed over her face. "What about Sahel? Can we trust him?"

"I may have been fooled by Zaire," I said with shame. "But Sahel, he'd never utter a word." The truth was Sahel was even more honorable that I was. The man was as disciplined as the Buddhists monks in the Himalayas I'd read about years ago, never allowing himself to fall to temptation. It wasn't until he almost died that I was pulled into the gravity of who Sahel was. Even if I could not marry him, my respect for him would never again waiver.

I asked her what had been eating away at me from the day of my abduction. "How did Mansi know I was in trouble?"

"They tried to kidnap him, too."

"What?"

"Yes. While he was waiting for you outside of Noire's gates, some of the rebels tried to force him into their carriage, but my brother overpowered his captors. He stole their horses and made his way straight to the arsenal to gather a few rifles. He camped a few miles from Noire and he watched, trailing the rebels, and trying to figure out their next move. Not knowing who to trust in any of the cities, he had no way to enlist the help of the other keepers. He followed them back to the White Mountains, and when he saw they had you he knew he had to act. When he saw the king, he thought all was lost."

I took a deep shuddering breath. "Thank the gods for him."

"Ase."

EPILOGUE

My new and beautiful wooden chair arrived from Ankara. The seat was higher than my other chairs. Now it was easier to stand. I rubbed my stomach as I thought about my father. The baby kicked at the weight of my hand.

"You're something else," I whispered to my unborn child.

I watched Kush, my baby girl, grab her twin brother's shirt and yank him down from where he held onto the wall. He hollered, big tears falling from his pretty brown eyes.

"Kush, leave Kinshasa alone," I sang.

She smiled mischievously, her two teeth jutting from her swollen lower gums.

"Come here," I cooed to Kinshasa. He reminded me so much of his father. He pulled himself up my leg, and I picked him up. I wanted to deny that Zaire had fathered them, but when I held them in my arms for the first time, I saw that there was no way I could lie. I hated Zaire for what he'd done. So many died because of the rebellion, including Ala and Pema, yet even after all that was revealed to me about him, the thought of Zaire inside me still sent shocks to

419

my yoni. It had been two years, and I still loved him. Above all, I thanked him for our children.

There was a knock on my door. "I got it," my mother said from the kitchen. With my baby brother, Accra on her hip, she went to the door.

"How can you cook with him on your hip? Come to sissy," I beckoned him. He reached for me.

My mother said, "I've got him." She never wanted to put him down. He was her second chance at motherhood, Father's parting gift to us.

"Zen, look here," my mother squealed.

I laughed when I saw King Akonos enter my home. He was a walking blessing. The gods had spared him.

Kush screeched and crawled to him. He scooped her up with his one arm.

"Sire, what are you doing here?" I asked, beaming. He sat down on the chair beside me. I placed Kinshasa in his lap and then kissed his cheek.

"Please don't spoil them. Some of my set sisters just got finished spoiling them rotten." I'd been working on getting to know my set sisters individually. Once I'd learned to love myself, the Universe returned that love to me. Abebi got her husband, a young man from a noble family in Noire. The dowry his family paid was unmatched. Yes, a twinge of envy had stabbed me when I heard. Yes, I was glad that she was gone.

The king guffawed as he admired the twins. "I just wanted to see you and these precious babies. You, too, Queenie."

"Mmhmm," she said.

"Is your husband here?" he asked me.

"No. Sahel is out training his younger brother. He should be back soon."

Once the doctors saved the king's life—with their

medicines—the king said he was indebted to Mansi, Sahel, and I for getting him to help before he died. He asked us what he could do for us. I told him that the griots should be allowed to marry and have children. Immediately, he made it so, so long as our husbands were brought into the Griothood, too. When our children came of age, they, too, would be brought into the Griothood.

I hadn't jumped at marriage, though. Yes, I know he would die for me, but could he raise Zaire's seed? Every day, he came by my house pampering me, doing any chore he made up in his mind to do. He brought me gifts and visited my father's grave. Surprisingly, Nok didn't wait at all, marrying a man half her age just days after the edict was composed. Zora remained single, and she finally left Olwethu alone. She said her soul needed to be free of him. When I'd gone looking for her on the night I was kidnapped, she'd been with him, and she'd never forgiven herself. As for Queenie, she hadn't found another love, but she did return to the Griothood.

"Boy, I sure do love seeing them." There was glee in his eyes as he took in his grandchildren. "Are you sure about what I asked?"

I sighed, but there was nothing he could do to annoy me. "I'm sure."

"There has been so much refusal. Mansi still refuses to become my trusted guard, and you refuse to move my grandchildren to Noire," the king complained, but still, he smiled. He made faces at the twins, and they laughed so hard I thought they'd hurt themselves.

"I just want to raise my children and be the best griot I can be. My children can train as prince and princess, but they must be trained here. There will be trips to Noire, but I'm their mother, and the children will remain with me."

The front door opened. Kush shrieked and pitched forward.

421

The king exclaimed, "Whoa!"

Sahel came into the house, and the babies screeched. I was excited, too.

"Sire," Sahel breathed as his splayed hand clutched his chest. He bowed.

"Hello, Sahel."

"The talking drum didn't sound," he said.

"I didn't want to cause a fuss."

Kush clapped her hands, and Sahel picked her up and gave her a ton of kisses. Kinshasa cried out of jealousy.

"Oh, I'm sorry," Sahel cooed picking him up, too. "You know it's ladies first."

The king, Queenie, and I chuckled.

What made me finally say yes to marrying Sahel? When I was pregnant with Zaire's babies, Sahel talked and read to the babies that were not his. I rolled my eyes each time I saw him coming, then I followed that motion with a grin. But the way he took care of them when they were newborns stole my heart. That's when I knew that he would not only die for me, but he could also raise Zaire's children as his own.

"Okay, Zen," King Akonos conceded. "I will stop hounding you about bringing my grandchildren closer to me so that I can see them every day."

I smiled ruefully.

"I know that the prince and princess are in perfect hands."

Sahel kissed Kush, who was fifteen minutes older than her brother. It was so hard to believe that she would be the queen of this nation, this social experiment that Father Malcolm set into motion.

I rubbed my kicking child again, the child that was Sahel's. I beamed at my twisted family. I looked to my mother, now understanding the importance of secrets. There were so many things I hoped my children would never know. My children wouldn't know that their great uncle had murdered their father, or that their father tried to overthrow their grandfather, or that their father was in love with a man, or that their grandmother—who had been exiled with no money—had been a conniving traitor. The people of Za would never know these things, either. They'd been told that Adesewa and the rebels had killed the queen and prince and that they severed the king's arm. Because the heathen monsters had been disturbed and disobeyed, they killed the rebels.

The outsiders still needed water, and with constant dread in my heart, I believed they would return.

The king stood. "I have to speak to the chief, and I will be back to see these beautiful children before I leave." He went over to Sahel, shook his hand, and kissed the babies. "Zen, can you walk me out?"

He knew he didn't have to ask. I was already standing.

When we exited the house, a grim demeanor came over him.

"What is it?"

He reached into the pocket of his linen pants. "I received this the other day." He pulled a small envelope from his pocket and proffered it to me.

I kept my eyes on him for a moment. His energy was so heavy I felt like it was pressing down on my shoulders. I hastily ripped opened the envelope and pulled out a photo that jolted my soul. It was Zaire, hair unkempt, straight-faced, and more striking than ever. Zaire was holding up a sheet of paper. It said, "I am not dead." The blood in my veins crystalized. I dropped the picture. I knew Zaire would return.